THE
Good and Bad
WEATHER

a novel by Edmund Schiddel

SIMON AND SCHUSTER : NEW YORK

In *The Good and Bad Weather,* as in the first two books of *A Bucks County Trilogy,* the village of Cope's Corner and the town of Olympia, Pennsylvania, are wholly fictional and imaginative. None of the characters in this book are based on people living in Bucks County or elsewhere, and all the incidents are imaginary.

The events told in this story occur in the Bucks County village of Cope's Corner during the summer solstice and the five days that follow. The people to whom they happen, as you meet them, are:

FRAN HANTER, waitress at the Corner luncheonette
TAVIO, a wanderer
MAE CADLE, a housewife
EDIE CADLE, her sixteen-year-old daughter
RAFE CADLE, husband of MAE (THE AUTOMOBILE MAN)
TEDDY HUBBARD, semi-retired interior decorator
BO DEWILLIG, friend of TEDDY, and occasional television "spokes-
    man"
BOBBY INGLE, an unhappy juvenile
AL HANTER, husband of FRAN and proprietor of the luncheonette
CORT GLIDDEN (the late), a painter
MIRIAM GLIDDEN, his widow
ROSA WOODHOUSE, her sister

RICHARD INGLE, M.D., F.A.P.A. (Diplomate in Psychiatry), father of BOBBY and Director of Tuliptrees, a clinic for the mentally disturbed

SUSAN INGLE, his wife

FLORA AUGUSTA BOWYER, a spinster

EMMELINE BOWYER, her elder, invalid sister

DON MACFINDEN, a young engineer

NANCY MACFINDEN, his bride of two weeks

ACIE STANES, a Philadelphian

MRS. HUBBARD, octogenarian mother of TEDDY ("MOTHER HUBBARD")

MISS HANKINS, her nurse-companion

HARLOW KIDDER, M.D., physician consulted by DON MACFINDEN

WILLIE BENTRUP, a township policeman

BOOK
ONE

BOOK
ONE

CHAPTER 1

Standing alone, perhaps planted long ago by a caprice of the wind bearing a seed from some vanished arboretum, the apple tree grew above the spring. It was not a noble tree, as the quaking aspens that once surrounded it had been; the gnarled irregularity of its branches started in all directions, like hair wildly stirred by a gale and frozen into a design of the storm. The tree blossomed unusually late in spring, long after other apples in nearby orchards, and the pear and little Mirabelle plum growing in the garden behind it. The apple seemed to hesitate, to withhold, until nights grew short and days lengthened, then thrust forth blossoms, all the more fragrant for being late. In early November, after other trees had borne and frost was imminent, the tree let fall perfect, almost spherical fruit from its upper branches, already russet and dry with autumn. It blossomed seemingly perversely, sometimes in odd years, sometimes in even, as it pleased, a condescension from an earlier time, shadowing the spring, secretly akin to those gray Mediterranean olives which, apparently spent, revive in diminishing but ever radiant flower. The apple's trunk suggested a massive foot, once planted deeply in earth, toes now stubbornly grasping the eroded sand around the spring; and, in the perspectives of its branches, when frozen with winter rime, could be fantasied the faces of children who had played hide and seek beneath it years ago. Tender but inviolate, loved but already mourned, chain saws had ached for it and road crews hungered to cut it down, delaying only

15

because of its age, certain it would, surely, die of itself before another season. But the tree, as though conscious of doom, this year appeared to be making a special effort: it had flowered vigorously, and it could be seen, by the June fall of the tiny fruit, that it would bear richly. Children who had hidden in its branches, some now very old, returned to show it to their grandchildren, each with a different recollection. The tree was called, variously, the Cope's Corner apple, the Misses Bowyers' apple, or, simply, the tree. Whatever people called it, the apple was loved by Cornerites and county folk alike, incredulously gaped at and endlessly photographed by tourists.

Jedediah Cope, a land speculator of the late 1700s and a member of the London Company, still provides Bucks County Pennsylvanians with a confusing set of nomenclatures. At various times since Cope held a franchise to operate a ferry between the place in Amesbury Township that now bears his name and Subberton, the village opposite on the New Jersey side of the Delaware River, it has been known as Cope's Ferry, Copesville, Cope's Hill and Cope's Falls. Nearby landmarks and boundaries appear on old maps as Cope's Creek, Cope's Spring and Cope's Cowpath—now the River Road. This list, however, has narrowed to two: the name of the village itself, and the spring beneath the old apple, which still juts from a length of one-inch pipe into a stone basin with a runoff. Most places named for early Pennsylvania settlers have long since dropped the possessive apostrophe, but Cope's Corner, stubborn as the apple, retains it. Of course, there are other chances for confusion; deliverymen and truck drivers and tourists sometimes get the Corner mixed up with Kulps, Pools, Reiffs, Schammels and Greers Corners, but these are hamlets and villages farther from the river and of another kidney entirely.

Cope's Corner's charms were first recognized after the Second War, when people who wanted a Bucks County sinecure began to buy up the canal-bank houses as they came onto the market, or coaxed, by offering an extra hundred or thousand, old residents to sell. These houses run the gamut from eighteenth-century stone and Greek Revival to imitations of William Snaith modern and Cape Cod cottages.

The Corner, as everyone living in it or nearby now calls it, though only a few miles upriver from the notorious little town of Olympia, lies precisely nowhere in the social scale. Professional people—physicians, well-known writers, artists, actors and New York and Philadelphia executives—live there, as do schoolteachers, house painters and plain, everyday workmen, side by side, in amity or hatred, as the case may be.

With few exceptions, the Corner houses are large by present-day standards; those on the canal side of River Road, which also over-look the river, are now considered desirable, though once were not, and here and there a hill house dominates, if built high enough from road traffic.

The Corner intersection, a fork where Old Hessian Road drops from the hills and meets River Road—a quadrangular plot of grass, on which are planted numerous signs and road markers—has become shamelessly commercial in the last few years. Only ten years ago there were raised wooden walks under the quaking aspens, but these have given way to cement and curbstones, yearly disintegrating from salt put down to melt ice in winter; the aspens (magnificent specimens of *Populus tremuloides* and once the village pride, as is now the lonely apple) are no more. The image striven for in the Corner is "Colonial but casual," "artistic living in a William Penn setting," or so the real estate advertisements have it. But beneath the "heritage indicator" newness can be felt a mercantile guilt and nostalgia for what has been destroyed—clapboards (of aluminum in permanent colors) are screwed onto the skeletal structures of prefabs dotting the hillsides; picket fences and hex signs proclaim, a little aggressively, that charm has not been lost through progress.

The largest of the road signs announces, to those crossing the bridge from Jersey, YOU ARE NOW ENTERING BUCKS COUNTY, AMERICA'S FOREMOST BOHEMIA. WELCOME! There are other, smaller, ones: a Pennsylvania historical marker, giving a short résumé of the Corner's claim to Revolutionary importance; a conspicuous arrow, pointing upriver, directing those househunting to HERITAGE SPLIT-LEVELS OPEN FOR INSPECTION, 1 MI.; yellow-and-black diamond-shaped signs, giving speed limits, mileages and directions for reaching Olympia, Ohmerstown, Harrisburg and a dozen other places; and a school bus warning, cautioning motorists not to pass while children are getting off or on. The eight-storied Cope's Corner Inn, erected only this year by a Philadelphia speculator and as anachronistic in its setting as the Hilton on the banks of the Nile, has its own signs—OPEN EVERY DAY IN THE YEAR EXCEPT THANKS-GIVING and PARKING FOR CUSTOMERS ONLY. Opposite, across the grass quadrangle, is a last, vestigial reminder of the slow-moving days of the Corner of long ago, a rambling, two-story clapboard building that has been there as long as anyone can remember, and has never had to be rezoned for commerce. Across its peeling front is lettered RAFE CADLE, "THE AUTOMOBILE MAN," FOREIGN MAKES OUR SPECIALTY. But the place that really catches the eyes of motorists braking down Old Hessian's steep grade, or approaching from the bridge, is a structure locally dubbed "the luncheonette" or "Al Hanter's eyesore," that might have been designed by Disney as a space stop on the way to the moon in a Disney film about Project Apollo.

The luncheonette is a combination of ingenuity and shoddiness; to have squeezed it onto the oddly shaped scrap of crossroads land, with room for curb-service parking, is a feat any architect might envy; though only a few years old, the gleaming plastics of which its exterior is constructed are already beginning to warp and buckle. It looks like a bit of Luna Park squeezed through Howard Johnson's with jukebox trimmings for good measure. Its sign, staggered orange and orchid neon messages attached to a tall post, outdoes all other Corner markers put together:

AL'S SNAX
HO-MADE DIPS
MALTS   SHAKES
HOMEY-BROASTED CHIX
YARD EGGS 'N KRISPY BACON

A hefty stone's throw from the grass quadrangle's center are clusters of houses, all pleasant properties despite their proximity to the Corner's commercially zoned section. Below the Cadle garage is the Greek Revival house of Dr. Richard Ingle and his wife Susan; Dr. Ingle is the owner and director of Tuliptrees, a clinic for the fashionably disturbed, near Olympia; the Ingles have lived in the Corner since the 1940s. Their house is circled by a yew hedge that has, obviously, only recently been planted; it shields

18

only the first floor from the road forks and the Cadle place, and the fine, Ionic doorway of the house can still be seen where the white gravel drive bisects the hedge.

The one Revolutionary house of any size of which the Corner can boast is directly oppose the Ingles', on the canal side of the road. No efforts have been made to screen it, and its shutters, of the solid variety (without the conventional half moons or stars cut into them, for decoration and light) have been closed since the death of Cort Glidden, whose widow still occupies it. The young Don MacFindens are settling into the property downriver from the Gliddens', a just-completed modern fieldstone-and-glass house, which the elder MacFinden built for them as a wedding present on land held in the family for generations and saved for this very purpose. Don and Nancy MacFinden have only tonight returned from their two-week honeymoon.

Diagonally across the road from the MacFindens' is the Corner's chief showplace, a pretentious, three-story "Spanish" house of the 1920s, said to have been designed by Bottomley, which is palpably a libel. It belongs to Teddy Hubbard, a semi-retired, sixtyish New York decorator, a man of obvious persuasion, as is his incumbent friend of the moment, Bo deWillig; Teddy's eighty-two-year-old surviving parent lives with them—unwillingly—and is known to the village, inevitably, as "Mother Hubbard." The Corner has its quota of *les boys*, as do other Bucks settlements, but Teddy and Bo are the noisiest and most spectacular this side of Hackersville, a nearby hamlet which, by head count, is 67 per cent queer. And, farthest of all from the grass quadrangle, on the canal bank next to the bridge, live the Misses Bowyer, spinster sisters, whose Victorian gingerbread house, like a dirty wedding cake that once was white, is at least as interesting to connoisseurs of county architecture as the Ingles' Greek Revival, the Gliddens' Revolutionary stone, the Hubbard-deWillig horror and the young MacFindens' modern. The smallest of all corner signs, a magnet to cars full of women fond of lunching at the Inn, is attached to the rickety Bowyer porch; reading FLORA AUGUSTA BOWYER, ANTIQUES, GENUINE OR INEXPENSIVE, it makes no mention of Miss Emmeline Bowyer, Miss Flora's elder sister, nor of the legendary (and, perhaps, phantom) one, "not quite right," said to be hidden in the attic.

"But how wonderful!" tourists exclaim. "The entire history of

19

American architecture in one small village!" Such comments are flattering and only partly true; both the Ingle and Glidden houses have been heavily restored; the Hubbard-deWillig place cannot, even politely, be called American; only the MacFindens', the Misses Bowyers' and Rafe Cadle's garage—which no one regards as architecture as yet—are in "original state."

Still, despite the incrustations of commerce, the Corner in the 1960s suggests more leisured days, when its population hovered around 100, tradition insisting that whenever a Cornerite died, another was born, in much the same way as at old-time weddings a mature tree was felled and a sapling planted in its place. Older residents are fond of saying that in the Corner it is always a half hour earlier than across the river, just as in summer it is five to ten degrees cooler. The Corner is trying to have its cake and eat it, to be at once the bucolic, pastoral countryside of Bucks County legend, as well as that legend blown up and folklorized for tourists, summer people and any others who may come. This dichotomy of intention functions well most days, but there are times, like this oppressive, sultry evening, when the insistence of neon and the soft, dark shadows of the past war against each other, generating a permeating melancholy that can be felt by tourists as well as residents. Among the fluorescence lighting the renovations and fabrications, the hex signs gleaming in the dark, the jukebox music oozing from the luncheonette, rises an uneasy suspicion that somewhere along these stretches of hot, intersecting macadam, the very America that was to have been celebrated has been lost.

Along one of the hot, black roads that led from the hills to the river, the long summer twilight was at last beginning to fade. The youngish woman driving the red Oldsmobile convertible could tell almost to the minute when darkness would come. The sweltering day had been in the nineties since morning, and she drove leaning slightly forward in the seat, so her back would not touch the hot leather; but even so, she could feel sweat gather at the back of her neck and run down the ridge of her spine. The skirt of her dress was pulled up around her hips, to take advantage of the air rushing through the ventilators, but the air, too, was scorching, like the day, and gave little relief.

The highway stretched ahead, winding through the hills toward the river. It was a narrow, badly surfaced country road, spongy from the heat, with potholes near the edges, where the shoulders were soft. Two parallel lines followed the road's center—for long, curving stretches solid; in the few straight ones, where passing was permitted, broken into dashes.

To motorists behind her, the woman seemed to be driving erratically, slowing, accelerating in spurts, slowing again. The Olds was making a coughing noise, but she kept going, hoping to make it to a filling station. At last, on a rising grade, the car eased to an even deceleration and almost stopped. The woman tried to use the last momentum to guide the car off the road so others could pass. She was not entirely successful; the car halted half on and half off the soft shoulder and motorists behind blew their horns and swerved past.

She pulled on the hand brake and started to edge across the seat from the wheel to the door away from the road side. Her skirt was damp where she had sat on it and stuck to the leather, hot to her bare flanks. She put out a hand toward the door handle, but before she could reach it the door opened, though she had heard no sound.

Facing her she saw a man in a white T-shirt and dusty white canvas pants. He was tall, with a shock of curly black hair that hung over his forehead almost to his eyes, and his face and arms were deeply tanned. Where the shirt shrank from his biceps there were marks of some bright design, tattooed farther up his arms. He carried a small bundle wrapped in newspaper.

"Hello," he said, staring at the expanse of bare thighs her skirt did not cover, then moved his eyes to her face. "In trouble? Are you alone?"

She gasped, pulled down her skirt and got out and stood beside him on the narrow road shoulder. "I think I must be out of gas— it started sputtering about a half mile back and then just stopped."

"Mind if I have a look?" She nodded and the man pitched his long body forward into the seat, his legs straddling the wheel. He tried the starter. "That's your trouble, all right," he confirmed after a minute. "You passed me back there and I thought from the way your engine sounded that was it." Then he got out.

"I can't understand it," she said. "I was sure my husband filled it only the other day."

21

The man's eyes snapped, once, at *husband*, and he smiled. It was then she really looked at him, seeing that he was beautifully made and young. He wore moccasins, white as his pants from road dust; the pants, tight and short, showed ankles as bare and tanned as his arms. His eyes were jet-black, with a curious, cold light behind them.

"Where are we?" he asked.

She continued to stare up at him, his eyes holding her, then started at his question, repeating it foolishly after him.

"I mean," he said, "how far from a garage or filling station?"

She looked beyond him, to where the road turned. "Not far, I think—half, quarter of a mile, maybe."

"If you've got a can or something, I'll go and get you enough gas to start," he offered.

"Yes." She went to the rear of the car and lifted the trunk lid, taking out a bright red container, handing it to him. "This is very nice of you."

"It's nothing," he answered. He set the can down, far over on the shoulder. "First, let's move you off the road. Get in, release the brake."

She did as he told her. He put his hands against the trunk and strained, and she felt the car move and guided it off the road. "That's it, now put on your brake," he called out to her, and came round to the driver's window, red can in hand. "I'll need money for the gas."

"Oh, of course." She found her purse, giving him a dollar bill.

"That should do it," he said, giving her his flashing smile. "Back in a few minutes." He loped over to the far side of the road and walked toward the oncoming cars.

She drew a deep breath, watching the man as he disappeared around the curve. She had once been pretty in a soft, delicate way, but now she looked heavy and tired and her eyes were red around the edges from weeping. She found a cigarette and lighted it. It had all happened so quickly; she could just remember having passed him before the gas ran out, his thumb raised in the classic, hitchhiking gesture, but she had been too occupied keeping the car going to do more than notice him. His eyes and the way he looked at her when he opened the door had frightened and upset her—

well, he had seen what he had seen, she couldn't help that; and he had asked, she remembered, if she was alone. There was a possibility he might simply toss the can away, keep the dollar and not come back; but whether he did, or whether he returned, she knew she was afraid. Offering him a tip as thanks and driving on would be the wise thing to do—but then she remembered the dollar she had given him was her last; if he wanted a lift, she could hardly refuse. There was nothing to do but wait, short of flagging for help. But help against what? She had her help; besides, it was getting dark; she could have hailed a dozen motorists without finding one who would stop, much less do for her what this man was doing. Her fear was foolish, she reasoned, as much fatigue as anything else, she wouldn't have been afraid at all, if her day hadn't been the kind it had.

She had driven to her mother's house outside Doylestown early in the afternoon, promising to be back in time to help her husband with the rush of business there always was on summer evenings. But her mother's doctor had been late, and even when she started back, she had been hours behind her promise. Her thoughts as she drove had been gloomy—her mother was, little doubt of it this time, dying after many rallyings; she had cried most of the way.

She adjusted the rearview mirror to look at her eyes, knowing there was nothing she could do about them, but she applied fresh lipstick and combed her hair. A second cigarette later, she saw the man returning, his white clothes and the red can bright in the last light, and her fear quickened.

He made a gesture with his free hand as he approached, thumb and forefinger making a circle, to indicate success. Nodding, she stayed where she was, listening as the gas gurgled into the tank.

"Try it now," he said, again opening the far door.

After whirring and a final cough, the engine started.

"Wonderful," she said with relief. "How can I ever thank you? I feel I should give you something for your trouble—"

"It was no trouble," he said, cutting her short. He stood framed in the open door, bronzed and tall in the beginning blue, hands resting lightly on his hips, black eyes watching her. It was as though, when she looked into his eyes, she couldn't speak. "This is the road to the river, isn't it?"

"Yes," she said. "Yes, it is."

"I'd like to get to the river tonight. Could you take me as far as you're going?"

She had expected this. "Get in."

She switched on the parking lights for the first darkness and the dashlights came on with them. The man exuded an emanation, intangible as a gamma ray but explicitly sexual, wholly unrelated to the heat of the day or the dust on his clothes. His size, amplified by the depth of his voice, overwhelmed her; she sat staring until he had settled himself with his newspaper bundle beside her, then started off the road shoulder.

"I don't know why I came away with so little money," she said when they were under way. "If that hadn't been my last dollar, I'd have been glad—"

Again he cut her short. "Forget it."

"My husband and I run a luncheonette down in Cope's Corner," she continued conversationally. "When we get there he can give you something, or maybe you'd like a sandwich?"

"Don't worry about it." He sat, hands hanging between his legs, looking out of the window; then his eyes came back to her. "That's the second time you've mentioned your husband."

"I'm Mrs. Al Hanter, yes," she said, returning his look. "Why shouldn't I mention him?"

Again his black eyes snapped. "No reason. My name's Tavio."

"It sounds Italian."

"My people were Italians. You—you could be Italian," he said, studying her.

"I'm not. I'm Irish—way back, that is."

"But that's all right," he said.

The remark irritated her slightly, but she decided to let it go. She continued to feel him next to her—it would be easier, maybe, if she pretended he was not there. She drove, saying nothing, thinking of the luncheonette where she spent her life; of Al, her husband, carping and sweaty, presiding over the grill; of the grease, the whanging jukebox, the gelid cold of uncooked hamburgers.

"How far is it to the river?" he asked.

"Oh, five or six miles."

"That would be the Delaware."

She nodded.

"I like rivers. Do you?"

"I suppose I must; I live on one."

"There's nothing like rivers. I set my course by them," he said. "I like to make the distance from one to the next between sunup and sundown."

"What happens when you run out of rivers?" She looked at him sideways. "Aren't you going anywhere?"

He raised his massive shoulders in a shrug. "Here, there—I'd like to go everywhere, if I could. I keep thinking there must be something different farther on, beyond the river we're going toward or that hill over there. I'm taking a good, long look at the world and everything in it before it's too late."

"Before it blows up?"

"It's not going to blow up now—didn't you know?"

"Well, you mean before you settle down, then?"

He shrugged again.

"But you have people," she said, as though reasoning with him. "There must be a girl somewhere."

"No girl, only girls." She could feel his eyes appraising her. "I don't like being in a cage, all those square angles—job, wife, mortgage, settling down in front of the idiot box at night, feeding your face. Some guys find out about themselves in time, before some girl locks the door on them forever. If you're not all nailed down and trapped, you can sometimes see something else."

"Like what?" she asked, thinking what he described was like her own life.

"Depends on the kind of eyes you've got. If you're me, you see a big, broad stretch of water beyond the rivers—an ocean, with cities rising out of the curve of the earth on the other side. Golden cities, with sun on them."

A look had come into her eyes as she listened; her fear of him was lessening as he talked. "I've always wondered, does the world curve like that, when you see it from the sea?"

"Yes. I've seen it."

"I've never seen the sea. Oh, I've seen New York from a ferryboat, yes. But I've only heard the sea in a seashell."

"That's not the sound of the sea. Ever try to hear beyond that? There's something else."

"Is there?"

"Silence—real stillness."

"You can't hear that."

"Oh, yes," he said; "there's an inside to silence, and when you get inside it, you can hear what the silent voices say."

"What do they say?" she asked, fascinated.

"They say, 'Don't wait too long. Life waits for nobody.' "

She thought of the luncheonette. "I go along with you on that," she said, an edge of bitterness in her voice. "You can say that again."

" 'Don't wait too long. Life waits for nobody.' "

"This is crazy talk." What he had said *was* crazy, and his saying it again made it crazier. But it had woven a spell.

"You shouldn't drive so fast," he said, breaking it.

"Why not? I'm only going fifty."

"You use more gas going fast."

"Well, the can held two gallons. That's good for more than twenty miles and we're only going two more."

"To tell the truth," he confessed, "I bought only one gallon of gas. I blew myself to a cuppa and a pack of cigarettes with the rest of the buck. I hope you don't mind?"

"No." I'm lucky he came back with one gallon, she thought— or am I? "One should get us there." She slowed without thinking, though nothing about him made her want to do anything but hurry. As if in answer, she felt his hand grip her knee.

"Please don't do that," she said. She could feel the iron warmth of him through the thinness of her skirt, and her flesh tingled. His hand moved upward, to the inside of her thighs. "Please!"

As he had seen at the beginning, she was wearing nothing beneath her dress and he quickly got his fingers to where he could feel her belly and the soft crown of hair below. "Why not?"

"Because!" she cried, slapping his forearm sharply. "If I'd known you were going to try something like this—"

"What would you have done?" he finished for her.

"I'd have let you walk."

"But you did know," he said softly. "You took a pretty good look at me, as I did at you."

She made a sound of exasperation, fighting his hand, tensing and pressing her thighs tightly together. But an extreme lassitude, like

26

a drug, crept through her; she felt the tension in her buttocks slacken as he moved his hand deeper, his middle finger firm and his palm spread against her.

"Ah, that's better," he said. "Of course you knew—let yourself go."

Her legs fell apart. "You've got to stop this," she begged. "I can't drive if you—"

He laughed, thrusting harder.

"I mean it—stop!"

"We could stop the car," he answered. "There's hay in those fields out there. Smell it?"

"No," she said.

The road was now a dull black ribbon, black on the landscape, with the last of the sunset behind them, and the sweet night fragrance of fields and trees swept through the car windows.

"Come on," he urged, "I can tell you'd like it."

"Maybe," she admitted, speaking almost faintly. She tried to forget his hand, concentrate on the twin tail lights of a car ahead. "But no—my husband's waiting."

"Let him wait," he said easily. His finger was driving her crazy. She took her foot from the accelerator for a moment, as if about to do what he wanted, but a spurt of the car ahead seemed to change her mind.

"This is where I turn," she said, cutting left onto a red dirt road and stopping. "You can get out here."

"You don't want me to do that." He leaned toward her and kissed her cheek. "We can go into that field," he continued to argue. "Who'd be the wiser?"

"That isn't why I stopped. Please don't do that any more!"

He withdrew his hand slowly from where it was, but still rested it on her knee. She was trembling. She moved the car forward. The road was rough from where rains had gullied it, and the edges were irregular. The car lurched and swerved from side to side.

"Watch it," he said.

"It's your fault if I'm driving like this. I'll be all right if you'll keep your hands where they belong."

In reply, he took her right hand from the wheel and guided it to his crotch. "That's all for you," he said, pressing her hand against him, "all you want." His hands were sinewy and what she felt between his legs made her gasp, but gave her a piercing pleasure, too. With difficulty, she wrenched away.

"I'm stopping," she cried, "and this time you're going to get out!" And braked so quickly they both were thrown forward.

He made a breathy sound of anticipation. "The sooner the better," he said, misunderstanding her.

"Get out!"

He laughed mockingly. "Are you going to make me?"

She saw he was not going to move and, in exasperation, again raced the car forward, taking the road leading down to the river at increasing speed. "You're making it impossible for me," she told him. "I want you to promise that when we get near my place you'll get out."

She was not through yet, she understood from his silence. "Please promise."

"I don't make promises," he said, after a long minute; "but I remember them. I'll get out when you do. You said your husband would make me a sandwich."

"Or give you something for your trouble, but that was before you started this."

"We could finish it here and now."

She drove resolutely on.

He laughed again. "You're afraid—afraid of yourself."

"I'm not!" They were beginning a steep descent from the hills to the valley. At a sign marked sLOW she changed gears.

"Ah, come on." He made a last pitch. "You admitted you'd like it."

She remembered her *maybe*, but said, "We're almost there now."

"We could keep going."

She glanced quickly down at him, to where his legs, split-rail fashion, were spread in the white pants.

"Don't worry about that—*Serpente* will have cooled by the time we get there," he said.

She frowned, confused. "I thought you said your name was—"

"*Serpente* is what I call him. Get it?" He patted his crotch. "He's a nice one; you'd like him."

Her hands were trembling on the wheel, but she gripped it tightly as she braked for the last steepness of the hill. A blur of

28

varicolored neon rose out of the night, and in a cubicle of white light she could see her husband, working in front of the grill.

" 'Al's Snax,' " he read aloud. "Is this it?"

"Yes."

"So his name's Al."

"My husband—remember that."

"I'm going to hold you to that sandwich."

"All right, but then go. I'll get out and go in first."

He shrugged agreement.

She eased the car into a space lined off from others on a bed of gravel surrounding the luncheonette, turning to look pleadingly at him as she cut off the motor. "Please—I have to live here. You don't. My husband—"

"What're you worried about? Nothing happened."

"You know what I mean—don't do anything to get me into trouble."

"Why would I?"

She quickly got out, slamming the door after her, and walked toward the luncheonette.

CHAPTER 2

There are always frictions and factions in small villages in the path of population increase and industrial expansion, and Cope's Corner was no exception, but until the Bucks fever started, bringing a boom in real estate and consequent zoning distinctions, little had changed, except for the paving of the forked intersection, curb-stones and sidewalks and the building of the Inn.

The first blow had fallen when a group of Corner citizens, headed by Dr. Ingle, tried to force Rafe Cadle to show cause for operating a garage in an area only recently zoned "medium-density residential." The Ingle group had reckoned without the many own-ers of foreign cars, who were dependent on Rafe Cadle's know-how and couldn't get along without him. Rafe could fix any-thing from a new Porsche to old Pierce-Arrows or Rolls Royces. A

29

few Rollses were beginning to appear in the county, usually old limousines come down in the world, with their new owners in the chauffeur's seat—the wrong touch in the right place, as Susan Ingle said, her husband adding that he had yet to meet an old-car enthusiast who hadn't a screw or two loose, and not under the hood, either.

Almost every old-car buff in the township had attended the meeting called to discuss Rafe Cadle's removal. The garage had been in operation long before zoning—this had been the strongest argument—and the elder Cadle had had a smithy on the site until the late 1930s. No matter how unpainted and run-down the garage, no matter that it was a visual obstruction to drivers on Old Hessian wishing to turn south on River Road, the Ingle forces were defeated and sent packing. Rafe Cadle also had come to this meeting, expressing himself as bewildered that anyone should try to close him down. "Why, hell, goddammit—begging your pardon, ladies and gentlemen—I always done my best to help people, like my pappy before me," he had said, and a spontaneous round of applause broke out for him. He added that he saw nothing wrong with his place, but that if Dr. Ingle thought it all that bad, he'd oblige by slapping on a coat or two of paint, damned if he wouldn't. (He never had, of course.) Dr. Ingle had to look at the place every time he drove past on his way to Tuliptrees. Rafe Cadle always hailed him; he held nothing against the Doc, he said, which, Dr. Ingle thought, was as might be.

In any case, as Dr. Ingle had been fond of saying after his defeat, commercialization of the Corner could go no further, for the simple reason it had gone as far as it could. That was before the Misses Bowyer sold the rocky plot to the west of their house for the hated luncheonette. It had been assumed, always, that the Misses Bowyer would "go" eventually—both were in their seventies—but it never occurred to anybody that their old Victorian shambles, and the lots east and west of it, with which their father had protected himself when buying the place as a summer retreat in 1910, could lead to the tricky, underhanded business of the luncheonette. Everyone supposed that the house and lots would pass to a nephew, to whom Miss Flora Bowyer said it had been bequeathed; and, since both ladies were known to be in reduced circumstances, it was further assumed the nephew must be taking care of them, knowing he would inherit. When news of the sale of the west lot to Al Hanter leaked out—a sale oddly not reported in local newspapers under Property Transfers—objections to the purpose for which the ground was to be used were already tardy. But Dr. Ingle, once more rallying to his township duty, backed by the Inn, the Gliddens and Teddy Hubbard, complained and circulated petitions against it. Both the zoning board and planning commission turned deaf ears, declaring it was outside their spheres. There was a fluke (there usually was)—a post office, long vanished, had once stood on the Misses Bowyer's east lot and had been leased from their father; this had established commercial usage before 1953, the year zoning went into effect, and for that reason all or any part of the property was, by precedent, zoned commercial.

Shortly afterward, one bitter March morning, bulldozers arrived and made short work of the aspens that overhung the spring. There had been one pitiful moment, odd in view of her having been the seller of the land, when Miss Flora Bowyer seated herself beneath the old apple tree and declared she would shoot the first man who laid a hand on it. She meant what she said, and after a conference between Al Hanter and the contractor, it was decided the apple tree was half dead anyway and probably could be cut later. Once that was settled, the next thing Cornerites knew, the whole plastic-and-neon disgrace was in full operation. It was only then that Dr. Ingle and his band of protesters learned that the Misses Bowyer's nephew not only sat on the zoning board but was one of the supervisors for the planning commission as well.

The Misses Bowyer, zanily enough, added their plaints to the general distress other Cornerites felt about the garish structure. Miss Flora (who spoke for Miss Emmeline also, since she was in retirement) one day stopped Dr. Ingle and, coming down to the dry wall of red shale that protected her property from the road, gave him a long song and dance.

"If you knew what my sister and I have suffered over this hideous thing!" she said. "For years the big oil companies offered us big prices for the west lot, but of course we didn't for a moment think of selling to them. One garage in the Corner is quite enough." She beamed a look of hatred at the Cadle place. "But when Communists started flying kite lights over our land and threatening to pour hot lead on us—well, what could we do but sell?"

"Communists? Kite lights?" asked Dr. Ingle. In his work at the clinic, he had to listen to almost all varieties of persecution fantasies, but kite lights were new to him and he asked what they were.

"Kites with lights on them, what else?" replied Miss Flora. "The lights are trained on our ferns and flowers. Emmeline and I are not businesswomen—we've always been so sheltered—but we reasoned that if the Communists were going to drop the lead, it might as well be on Mr. Hanter. And that was why we capitulated."

Dr. Ingle looked into Miss Flora's faded, cornflower-blue eyes and then nodded, the way he did when one of his inpatients at Tuliptrees complained that the handsome interne was not an interne but a warlock in disguise, who nightly violated her. "I see," he said.

"Oh, but the Russians aren't the only reason," Miss Flora went on, encouraged by his sober attention. "My sister and I have had many other things to contend with over the years. No one will let us do our own gardening, you know—people come in at night and pick our ferns and flowers to sell in New York."

"Do they indeed?" Dr. Ingle asked, edging away.

"We're almost resigned," said Miss Flora tragically. "The stones in this wall have been disappearing, too; one by one they go, and handfuls of sand are left in their place. Where wind will go, water will go."

"Do you mean you think the wind—?"

She gave Dr. Ingle an oblique look. "Oh, no, we know who is stealing our stones. Why don't you admit to it?"

It was twilight and the dying sun was reflected in Miss Flora's rimless spectacles. She seemed, Dr. Ingle thought, like someone who would turn out to be an escaped patient; people like Miss Flora Bowyer didn't exist outside institutions, or shouldn't. She had not revealed what Al Hanter paid for the corner lot; he had secretly hoped to find out. Rumor had it that a soft ice cream combine was behind it all, and that the price had been $15,000, a lot of money for a rocky oblong measuring sixty-one feet on River Road and eighty on Old Hessian.

"I give up," Dr. Ingle said to his wife afterward. "You can't beat the Commonwealth machine, small ward heelers *and* the paranoias of superannuated old maids. Any further efforts to save the Corner from the Russians will not come from me."

Dr. Ingle had given up trying to keep the Corner pleasant and livable, or so he said; but of course no one twice trounced by zoning boards and planning commissions ever gives up; they may move away, but give up? Never! Dr. Ingle was using his irritations over Rafe Cadle constructively; when his heavy patient roster permitted, he made notes for a paper tentatively titled "Obsessions with the Gasoline Combustion Engine as Related to Social Anxiety in an American Working Class Family." The anxiety he was charting was, basically, that shown by Cadle over the period he had operated the garage; but Dr. Ingle was detached enough to realize that his own anxieties were contributing to the study as well.

It was to be an exhaustive inquiry and had been begun long before local authorities failed to find the garage a nuisance. In the terminology of the planning commission ruling, Cope's Corner was a "medium-density residential community," River Road and Old Hessian arterial streets as well as public highways, the Cope's Corner Inn, Rafe Cadle's garage and the luncheonette community-serving businesses—Dr. Ingle had virtually been told he could put it in his pipe and smoke it. There was no doubt his defeats had given fresh impetus to the Cadle study.

"Medium-density residential"—an almost rural phrase compared with the "high-density" of nearby Olympia—meant simply that houses were not jam-packed side by side but had some protective land, or stands of trees, to give privacy from neighbors. The Glidden house, for example, was separated from the Inn by sumac, locusts and a small stream; the Misses Bowyer's house still had the east lot as buffer; the young Don MacFindens had English hollies and American boxwood trees so tall the Gliddens did not overlook them; the Hubbard place was a maze of wisteria gone wild over the "Spanish" tiles. But the Ingle house, being only thirty feet south of the Cadle place, made both the doctor and Susan aware of each and every car arriving for repairs; they also got a heavy drift of motor exhaust most hours of the day (and sometimes at night, too, if Rafe worked late); worst of all, when there was a downriver wind, their terrace smelled, said Susan, like the New Jersey turnpike at five o'clock of an August afternoon.

Dr. Ingle did, sometimes, have a pipe as he sat beside his study window overlooking the Cadle garage; and, as he made his notes, felt almost the way he did at Tuliptrees, sitting behind an analysand. To him, Rafe Cadle was not unlike a patient, observed at leisure, a kind of pet, really, on whom he could take out antagonisms that clung to him after leaving the clinic. Susan Ingle said Cadle was her husband's hobby and declared that, without him, he wouldn't know what to do with his free time. But then, Susan Ingle didn't mind Cadle; sometimes, when in a hurry, she even bought gas and oil from him, though was careful not to let her husband find out.

No matter what the Misses Bowyer's part in "the luncheonette betrayal," as it was called at Corner parties, the Al Hanters bore the real brunt of dislike and cold-shouldering that followed the place's opening. No Corner people, even those living far out of sight of it and downriver, would patronize the Hanters; the luncheonette was strictly for tourists and people from other villages driving through. The hostility toward Hanter and his wife was lessening a little, though; Miriam Glidden now spoke to them, and guests of Teddy Hubbard had been seen—once—walking up to the luncheonette when their host had run out of soda for drinks. Dr. Ingle couldn't stand the sight of the place, though it bothered him less than Rafe Cadle, who was fast becoming the *bête* of his existence and would (he realized with dispassion) make him as paranoid as the Misses Bowyer, if he didn't "compensate" by finishing the study. Susan Ingle was, perhaps, as well adjusted to Corner inevitabilities as anyone, though her husband considered her to be suffering from acedia, the indifference that overtakes the middle-aged. The Misses Bowyer suffered over what was said about their nephew and nepotism, but they had been suffering for many years anyway, from genteel poverty (now alleviated by the $15,000), the loneliness of spinsterhood, their paranoia and simply being who they were. They had been trained young to see nothing they did not wish to see, and when their eyes strayed in the direction of the luncheonette, they still saw their west lot, the quaking aspens trembling above the spring. And was not their beloved apple tree still there? It certainly was.

"Christ, Rafe! Can't you ever shut them goddam cars off before you come upstairs?" Mae Cadle asked her husband. It was hot as

34

It was an old complaint. The floor between the Cadle living quarters and the garage space was thin; there was hardly an hour when smells of gasoline, acrid whiffs of oil and the fumes to which Mae objected did not drift upstairs.

Rafe perched on the edge of the rust-red Castro Convertible that was the principal article of furniture in their small living room. He was as hot as his wife and sweating, but he was drinking beer to cool off. A row of already drained cans stood on the floor beside him. He had worked all day in the garage, though it was Sunday, repairing a Triumph and a Mercedes, this last the property of Teddy Hubbard, who wanted it ready by next morning. Rafe had finished the Triumph, but its engine could be heard running right along with the Mercedes': he liked to hear engines idle until he got them just right. Motor exhaust didn't seem to bother him in the least; he thrived on it, Mae said. On coming upstairs he had taken off his shirt and pants and sat, legs stretched out, wearing only his briefs.

"You dirty pig!" Mae cried, regarding Rafe's thick, hairy body with distaste. "That girl's got to sleep on that Castro tonight, and there you are, sitting around, sweating into everything, like a nigger on election day!"

Rafe rubbed the damp curlicues of carrot-colored hair that covered his massive chest like a shield. "I wouldn't make cracks about niggers if I was you," he answered her.

"I'll make cracks about anything I please."

"What in hell's eating you tonight, anyway?" Rafe asked a question for a change.

"Plenty." Mae's mouth filled as she took a gulp of Diet Cola and swallowed; then her jaws began to move in a rhythm that never varied; she was never without her Juicy Fruit except when eating, and then she parked it beneath the table. "Goddammit, Rafe, here it is another Sunday, one day in the week you'd think a man'd take his wife and daughter out somewhere. But no! On the lot. Week in, week out. Always on the lot. That's what's eating me and's been eating me for years."

Rafe pronged open a fresh can of beer. "Hell, you know Sunday's my big day in summer." He lifted the can to his lips, draining it.

"For you, maybe, but for me and Edie it's like any other day. I flugens in the close quarters above the garage, where the Cadles lived. Mae Cadle, wearing a cotton "brunch" coat that zipped up the front and her old green wedgies, sat in a wicker rocker, drinking Diet Cola. A fan revolved on the sill of the open window, and a radio, turned low, stood beside it. Mae was a woman who had once been handsome and still had a certain dignity due to her size, but she had aged badly, and tonight her lumpy, blue-veined legs were spread to the coolness of the fan. She was on her sixth Cola of the day; the fake sugar and fruity taste encouraged the inertia that always overcame her on nights as hot as this. From the luncheonette across the way the jukebox blared.

Mae's mind was a mixture of cloying sentimentality and th toughness she had developed as protection against what sh laconically called life, wandering between curses and complaint Her education had been derived from films of the thirties ar radio evangelists; her heroes now were the celebrities of TV—th was one reason she hated summer; she had to revert to rad visual reception in the Corner being poor except in cold weath She repeated her question, more loudly this time.

Rafe Cadle looked at his wife stonily. The lower part of his fa like his hands and arms, was deeply sunburned, but above his e and beyond his elbows, where the line of his cap and the ro sleeves of his work shirt ended, showed white, freckled skin. was a massive, squat, bald man of forty-six; twenty-five years he had been the handsomest young buck in the Corner. But a terness had fallen early on his marriage, and for years now he been channeling his energies into withholding from his wife e thing he could, while working from day to day with a fierce pulsiveness which seemed to have no goal, but which he u stood completely.

"I can't shut the cars off until I get them running perfec I?" he answered, unmoved by her question. Both alluded habit of keeping the motors of cars he was fixing running workshop below.

"That goddam stink!" Mae whined. "*That's* what gives y cancer, what comes out of engines, not cigarettes—I read it where. It's not bad enough we got to live on top of this cro and breathe in all the road exhaust, we got to have it pi from downstairs too."

never heard such Christ-awful noise as today. That traffic down Old Hessian! I'm so hot I'm sticking even to this wicker."

"Why don't you try standing up for a change?" Rafe suggested.

"Don't get me off the subject. Now, why in hell *can't* you close up on Sundays, so we can take a few sandwiches and get in the car and go, like other people?"

"Why the hell should I close up Sundays? We got nowhere to go anyway," Rafe argued back. "Goddammit, you said yourself the roads are jammed."

The Cadles' conversations were peppered with *hells* and *goddammits* and *Christ-awfuls;* they used these and other similar expressions unconsciously, in the same way others use *wells* or *whys.*

"Oh, you! That's not the reason you won't go anyplace. It's money," Mae said, pointing an accusing finger, "that money you've been saving all these years. You ain't never spent a red cent of it on me, or the girls either. A person'd think by now you had enough to quit and take it easy, leastaways Sundays."

"I ain't quitting," Rafe stated, "and I'm going to go on working Sundays." Mae's long way of trying to find out how much he had put away, since old Cadle died and left him the place, was a sore point; she tried it all the time. Rafe had never given her an idea what he had in the bank and had no intention of telling her.

"Hell, *don't* answer, then," Mae said after a silence. "But you sure ought to take off *one* hot day of the summer."

"I had the pumps to look after today, like any day, and flat tires and worse headaches, not to mention Teddy Hubbard's Mercedes to do."

"Yah, that old fairy!"

"Fairies' money's as good as anybody else's," Rafe said simply.

"This is a community for them, all right! What gets me, they all seem to have money." Mae's resentments were many, and Hubbard's affluence one of her major irritations. "Where do they get money for a car like that—that Mer, Mercy—"

"Mercy-dees."

"I hear the damn thing still running, smell it, too. When're you going down and shut it off? You going to let it run all night?"

"Be shutting it off any minute now," Rafe said. His ear was cocked to a wavelength beyond Mae's singsong, the muted radio and the fan—to the motors below; he could separate the sound of a motor from any surrounding distractions and tell to the drop of a tappet how it was doing.

"Well, see you do. And put something back on, before Edie comes out of the bathroom." Edie, the youngest of Mae's three daughters, could be heard showering. She was a constant reminder to Rafe of how he had come to feel about his wife and marriage; the two older daughters were long since married and settled; Edie was still another family sore spot, like the fumes and never getting off the lot. "It's not right for a father to be sweating around with nothing but his underwear on in front of his daughter. Just like a nigger, like I said."

Rafe frowned. "I told you before, don't go talking about niggers." He punched open another can of beer.

"I'm talking about Edie." Mae got up, went to the fridge in the kitchen and got herself a fresh Cola. "You're always griping about what she does, where she goes, who she goes out with. How in hell do you expect her to be different than the way she is, if she sees her father squatting all over her bed, with hardly more on than he was born with?"

"I'm telling you, let up on the niggers," Rafe repeated.

Mae returned to her rocker and stared at him, anger forming behind her eyes. They sat in the sweltering room, largest of four in which the three of them lived, saying nothing. The kitchen and bath counted as rooms, too; besides the narrow place where they were, overlooking the road, there was only a bedroom at the rear; Rafe and Mae slept there, and sixteen-year-old Edie not only had to make do with the Castro but dress wherever she could.

"All right, you son of a bitch," Mae said at last. "You're never going to let up on that, are you? I made one slip, one mistake— *maybe*—and I'll never hear the end of it."

"One?" Rafe laughed. "Don't give me that. After the war, when I was working at Fairless, you were throwing it around. Wasn't a truck driver, white *or* nigger, couldn't have it just by pulling up here. Didn't even buy gas even, most times. And don't give me that *maybe*—I know whose daughter Edie is as well as you. So don't talk about niggers to me."

"He wasn't a nigger—at least I didn't know he was—"

"Must of been mighty dark in the shed, then."

"Yeah?" Mae snarled. "How would you know?"

"Hell, everybody knew, all up and down the river. They knew about the girls, too, before we got them married. Now Edie's going the same way, if you ask me."

"You shut your big trap!"

"Shut yours for a change," Rafe said. "And her pappy ain't faded none since, either. What did you think that was on his skin, Man Tan?" There was the sound of shower taps being turned off in the bath.

"Shh! Not so loud," Mae said, "Edie'll hear you. You know I never was *sure*."

"Maybe it's time she heard who she is."

"You've always been careful about that—the one decent thing there is about you," Mae answered. "Now, put something on! At least get into your pants and cover up those great big fat hairy legs of yours!"

"It's nothing she hasn't seen before."

"And more's the shame!"

"You're no rose yourself," Rafe told her.

"Well, she's *my* daughter." Mae took advantage of the noise made by a large truck coming down Old Hessian, exhaust popping, brakes hissing. "You took her to be yours, too, before she started to develop."

"Ah, shit, woman!" Rafe said to this. "I knew the minute I laid eyes on her she couldn't be mine. Maybe you've got a touch of the brush yourself. All we Cadles were redheads, like me. We never had no pickaninnies until I married you."

"Oh, you're a redhead, all right!" Mae fumed at him. "Pity you don't shave off some of that mat—you got hair everywhere but your head, where your brains should be. Edie may be a deep brunette—"

"Look around the back of her ears," Rafe said, warming to the battle. "Or get a load of her fingernails."

"Edie's got moons on her nails," Mae challenged hotly. "And moons are a sure sign of breeding, *I* always heard."

"And her eyes—"

"Oh, I could kill you sometimes, Rafe Cadle! To think I ever let you lay hands on *me!*"

"You were crazy about it once," Rafe reminded her. "But you got nothing to worry about now. Who'd want to lay a hand on you?"

"I know who you'd like to lay a hand on—"

At that moment the door of the bath opened and Edie Cadle appeared. She wore a white terrycloth robe, and her shining, black hair was damp from where her shower cap had not covered it. Where the robe flared up to her throat, Rafe could see the dark cleft between her breasts, dusky spheres swelling between the folds of white cloth. He often stared at Edie, as if in her delicacy and strange quietness he traced the antithesis of his own embittered life.

Edie paused, looking from one to the other. "At it again. What're you fighting about this time, Papa-Daddy?" She had heard their voices through the splash of the shower, but hadn't been able to make out what they were saying.

"Nothing you'd have any business knowing," her mother answered before Rafe could speak.

A flush came into Rafe's cheeks as he looked at Edie. He could see her lithe, brown legs halfway up her thighs, her taut young body still a little wet through the toweling. His jaw set.

"Who're you going out with tonight?" he asked her.

Edie hesitated. "I've got a blind date."

Mae shifted her position in the wicker rocker. "Blind, huh? Well, who else is going with you? There's got to be another couple on a blind date, to introduce, ain't there?"

"No, there *ain't*," Edie answered, going into the bedroom.

"I'd like to take a strap to that girl," Rafe said. "Not a night in the week but what she's out somewhere." His hand clutched his empty beer can, crushing it.

"Don't you go beating her again," Mae warned. "You beat her enough when she was little. She's too old to beat now."

"I see the way she wiggles her ass at them, the ones who come into the shop. Like a bitch in season, for anybody that's interested."

"Well, those hoods you have hanging around the pumps *would* be interested. You ought to keep an eye on her."

"Keeping an eye's no good. The only thing works with kids like her is a good strapping," Rafe said.

"Don't you strap that girl!" Mae said again. "You've strapped her too much already. *I* say you always got more satisfaction out of it than you should—"

"Let up on that," Rafe warned.

"I won't let up. And I'll say it again. You beat her like you enjoyed it, and it's unnatural. It's immoral. . . ."

There was no letup from Mae. Rafe fell silent, thinking how Edie was nothing like the other children, never had been. She'd always had a wild side to her nature; her moods were like quicksilver, changing unpredictably. She had loved Rafe from the beginning, but Mae had never been able to make her obey; and when she tried to punish her, the girl fought back fiercely, tearing at her clothes and scratching like a cat. Rafe had to do the punishing, and he had belted Edie into submission more times than he could remember. Curiously, she had never fought him back; she had always forced him to lay on hard before she would whimper or utter so much as a cry. The other girls needed whippings from time to time, but they had screamed the house down, even before Rafe laid a hand on them, begging him not to beat them, promising not to repeat whatever they were being punished for. But not Edie—she took it stoically, until Rafe was worn out, then would turn and cling to him as though he was the only refuge she had. Only then did she cry, and quietly, almost as though *he* was the one who should have been punished. As she grew older, Rafe had gotten more and more nervous about strapping her. The turning point had come a year before, when Edie had stolen a five-dollar bill from Mae's purse. Mae had accused Rafe of taking it and, when Edie at last confessed, had demanded Rafe give her the beating she deserved. But that time Edie had fought him back; he'd had to hold her, head under one arm, as he brought the belt down across her plump, round buttocks. Afterward, though, the usual thing had happened—Edie had flung herself against him and cried her eyes out, but made promises not to steal again. "I only did it because nobody ever gives me anything, and never did," she had sobbed. "If you loved me, you'd give me money sometimes. I love you, Papa-Daddy." Rafe hadn't answered, just slipped his belt back on and walked away. The way he'd felt as he lifted Edie's skirt and lashed her bare bottom that time haunted him still.

Mae's strident voice brought him back. "If we didn't have to live here like pigs, maybe Edie'd spend a little more time at home,

41

not always have somebody whistling or tooting for her every night. If only you'd get rid of this place—"

"I'm not selling this place until I get my price," Rafe said, "so don't start that again."

"Your price!" Mae jeered. "Huh!"

"You don't think I'll get forty-five?"

"In a pig's asshole you'll get forty-five."

"You know what Al Hanter paid those old sisters for that pile of rocks—fifteen thousand."

"*Al* didn't pay it. It was some combine paid it."

"Hell, somebody paid it. The Bowyer women got the money now, and it's theirs. This lot's three times the size of the one they sold," Rafe reasoned, "and if they could get fifteen, I'm holding out for forty-five."

"For this shack?" Mae laughed. "You're dreaming! You better sell it before it all falls around our ears." Her admonitory finger rose again. "And let me tell you—don't be surprised if Edie takes off from here suddenly. It's a disgrace, the way you let us live. A young girl like her with no room, no privacy, nothing. Every time somebody goes to the toilet, you can hear the splash all over the house, unless I turn up the radio. No wonder she goes out on blind dates!"

"You want me to stop her now?" Rafe asked.

"No, let her go; poor kid, she's got a right to some fun. But blind dates or dates that can see, they're all the same—men, all after that one, filthy-dirty thing—"

"What's filthy-dirty about it?" Rafe asked. "Once you couldn't get enough of it."

Mae glared. "We're not talking about that. All I'm telling you is, keeping us in a hole like this, don't expect her to go out with nice boys. Now today, for instance, that nice Bobby Ingle was talking with Edie, not that she'd have a chance with him—"

"Who cares about nice boys?" Rafe wanted to know. "I wasn't nice."

"You sure wasn't," Mae agreed. "That thing was on your mind from dawn till dark, and all night, too."

"It's what's on all kids' minds, Bobby Ingle's, too. All I don't want is Edie should get herself knocked up or sick and we can't get whoever it is to marry her. The other girls was knock-up brides, both of them."

"They couldn't wait to get out of here," Mae argued. "They got married, didn't they?" Mae choked on a swallow of her Diet Cola. "I'm losing my health in this place," she said, coughing. "I can't stand it another minute. It's that gas, it's choking me to death. *You hear me?*"

"I hear you," Edie answered from the bedroom. "The whole village can hear you!"

"I guess the cars've run long enough," Rafe conceded. "I'll go down and close up." He reached for his pants, stepped into them, and walked, holding them together with his hands, into the bathroom. Mae at once cut up the radio.

The bathroom was a small cube, wedged between the living room and the bedroom, made of plasterboard and two-by-fours, containing the usual basin, toilet and a Monkey Ward shower unit Rafe had installed himself. The shower didn't always drain right; there was a puddle on the floor and a wet towel where Edie had tried to mop up. He came out zipping up his fly and went to the stairs leading down to the garage. Through a crack in the bedroom doorway, he saw Edie slipping a yellow blouse over her head. Her breasts rose as she lifted her arms, then dropped as the blouse covered them. He stopped. Small wonder you couldn't keep the boys away from her, Rafe thought. Edie was a beauty.

Mae had caught Rafe's pause at the stairway out of the corner of her eye. She could hear him downstairs, giving the engines a last racing before shutting them off, making the fumes worse than ever. Still coughing, she went to the bedroom door.

"Edie?"

"What?"

"You coming out soon?"

"When I'm dressed."

"I've got something to say to you."

"Come in, then, if you have to," Edie said.

Mae pushed the door open. She looked at Edie's blouse. "That's mighty low for a blind date."

"Don't start on me again," Edie said. "I haven't lived in this place without learning to take care of myself."

"And what's that supposed to mean?"

"Oh, Mother, *you* know—you told me always to lock the door of the bathroom, and I do."

"And the bedroom, too, if I'm not here—never forget that."

"Not that it's my door to lock," Edie said.

"Never mind, honey, someday—"

"I'm sick of hearing about *someday!*"

"Don't you talk like that to me! And showing yourself like that in that blouse is only going to lead to trouble. You're going to have to fight him off."

"Can I help it if that's what they all want?" Edie asked.

"You don't have to pitch it in their faces. In my day—"

"I'm going now." Edie cut it short, brushing past her mother. "I'm late as it is." She ran quickly downstairs.

As he closed the garage, Rafe felt a continuing excitement. The memory of Edie's young breasts as she slipped on the blouse flooded through him again, stronger each time he thought of it. If a whipping was needed tonight, Mae or no Mae, he'd force himself to do it for the girl's own good. He was waiting for her as she came downstairs.

"Edie?"

Edie halted, then saw Rafe in the workshop, wiping grease from his hands onto a piece of waste. She waved. "Night-night, Papa-Daddy."

"Come here," Rafe ordered.

Edie made a face but came slowly toward him, picking her way among the cars and greasy junk that littered the garage floor. "I'm all fixed to go out. I don't want to get myself dirty."

"And I don't want you flying around all hours of the night the way you've been doing, with God knows who."

"Oh, Papa-Daddy, don't you nag me too. Mother's been after me—"

"About what?"

"My blouse."

"I can see why."

Edie's dark eyes smiled up at him. "I thought maybe you'd like it, even if Mother doesn't." She rose up on her toes and kissed him lightly on the cheek.

The trouble was, Rafe liked it only too much. "You should do what your mother says," he forced himself to say in a cold voice.

44

He was beginning to shake so hard he was afraid Edie would see it.

"Don't be like Mother," answered Edie. "I've got to run now, Papa-Daddy, or I'll be late for my date." Again she kissed him, her lips brushing the stubble of his cheek, and ran out the door.

Rafe clenched his jaw as he watched her go. The way she had talked and looked at him had paralyzed him, made him forget all about punishing her, even forbidding her to go out. The beers he'd drunk had given him the edge of heightened feeling he'd experienced when he saw Edie in the bedroom, but it would take some of the hard stuff before he could raise his hand against her now. Putting these thoughts from him, he went back upstairs.

Mae had moved her wicker rocker over to the window and was looking out over the crossroads. "Hey, Rafe," she called to him. "Come and look what's calling for Edie!"

Rafe moved to the window. He could see, drawn up by the bridge and clear as day in the light flooding from the luncheonette, what Mae was watching—Edie, opening the door of a pink Cadillac that was almost newer than its paint, an expensive, custom job a good thousand over the list price. The door clicked shut and the car moved away.

"I wonder who he can be?" Mae sighed with envy.

Rafe didn't say anything, but everything about what he saw told him it couldn't be right.

"What were you saying to Edie down there before she went out?" Mae wanted to know.

"Nothing."

"Nothing?"

"That did any good, anyway."

"Well, it was up to you to forbid her, if you was going to," Mae said, getting up. "Christ knows I do what I can, but what more can I do than I do?" There was no answer to this, nor did she expect one. "Come on to bed, now."

"I'm sleeping out here tonight," Rafe said.

Mae turned, staring. "But the Castro belongs to Edie!"

"Edie can bunk in with you when she comes home," answered Rafe. "At least I won't have to."

"Why, you—"

"Skip it," Rafe said. "I'm sick of hearing you talk and what you talk about. I'm beat." He flopped onto the Castro and was asleep before Mae could say more. She had to say it to herself.

"Pig!" she said. "Filthy, dirty pig! *Pig!*" And added to herself, I hope she gets somebody like that. A pink Caddy! At least it would get her out of this hole! Then someone over at the lunch-eonette started the jukebox and it played "It's Hard Not to Be Lonely When You're by Yourself," the summer's favorite, and Mae closed the door of the bedroom.

At the Teddy Hubbard–Bo deWillig ménage, the anticlimax fol-lowing on a successful weekend had already set in. It had all been hectic, to say the least, and the *Bazaar* girls, who had come down with the photographers, had quite lost their heads in admiration of the house, which was to be featured in a fall issue. Not for noth-ing had Teddy Hubbard settled on having everything perfect 1925; it was time for the period to roll round again. He had cheated a tiny bit, though; parts of the furnishings were before the fact, and here and there could be detected a vested interest in Russian ballet of 1913, Bakst and Poiret peeked from behind Robert Chanler screens, and there were *piqûre* landscapes for "charm." There was, even, that Maxfield Parrish chromo of a girl in a swing, or was it a boy? With Parrish it was sometimes hard to tell. But the vivacity of the great dead era was exactly captured in the amusing proliferation of mah-jongg tables, white bearskin rugs, Spanish shawls, zebra upholstery and pernickety tufted and tasseled hassocks—all the fascinating odds and ends of the period no one could seem to forget and couldn't wait to remember. And here and there were touches of the mythography of Eros, so fascinating to journalistic ladies intent on high fashion.

The *Bazaar* girls had donned Lucile gowns, of which the house had a redoubtable collection, and with them went changes in manner; speech reverted to "terribly charming," "madly mahvlz," even the old "too, too divine, my dear." And everyone fell under the spell cast by Noël and Gertie, on tape piped into the speakers with which all rooms were equipped. After photographs of the house appeared, the girls predicted, there would be reproductions of everything it contained; the trend it would spark would be at least as successful as "Clutter Returns" of a few years ago; they expected rashes of cloche hats, tennis dresses, headache bands and a return to shingled hair and flattened bosoms. Teddy had been amassing his recherché furnishings for years, buying up for songs, from auction rooms and thrift shops, the particular kind of tat he fancied and hoped would again become "the rage." Teddy still thought in such terms, being a twenties relic himself, exactly as old as the century. He had lived through it all, so he *knew*.

Getting everything the way the photographers wanted it and *in* had been exhausting and, as hard and calculating about time as he was about money, Teddy was exerting himself toward an early bedtime. He and Bo were driving up to New York in the morning, Teddy to give a consultation on a house being built on Long Island, Bo to do one of his rare television commercials.

Hubbard, a tall, pale-looking man with a stressful way of speaking, as though he could not shape his sentences to his thoughts, was still wearing the plus fours and diamond-clocked socks in which he had been persuaded to be photographed against the décor. Bo had made no such concession and was attired in his usual white shorts and shirt, open in a wide V from the waist, and his feet (one of his better points) clinging to thong sandals, which flapped as he walked. Both men by now would have been in bed but for Bobby Ingle, a visitor from up the road, who had dropped in to return a book.

"Chicken," which was what Bobby was to Teddy and Bo, took precedence over fatigue, especially the fatigue caused by women, and provided both with the lift of a Dexamyl tablet quickly chewed and followed by a gin chaser. Bobby had been led into the den near the library and given a drink. The den was another "conceptual revival" now being plugged by Hubbard.

Bo was doing most of the talking, as he usually did, conducting Bobby on a tour of the many framed photographs of *autrefois,* with which the room was hung. Though he had been in America twenty years, Bo's voice retained an accent, precisely the right number of hissing *s*'s and *d*'s pronounced as *t*'s to lend credence to his claim to being Swedish and "nobly" connected.

"Teddy used to be simply wonderful-looking, don't you think?" Bo asked Bobby, pointing out an enlarged snapshot of Hubbard at Cannes in 1927. The photo showed a well-built, smiling man in a bathing suit of the period, standing next an umbrella on the Carlton beach.

"Well, Old Mother *Carlton* hasn't changed, anyway," Teddy said, in routine response to Bo's spiel. Thanks to the Hubbard income, the pair spent a month on the French Riviera each fall, with the Carlton Hotel as headquarters.

"You must have played basketball, to have looked like that," Bobby Ingle said, wishing to be polite, unaware of the verb's double edge. "Did you?"

"Perish the thought!" Teddy said. "I've never taken a day's exercise in my life."

"My dear," said Bo to Teddy, "you look almost the same as you did then. After all, who *was* the Queen of the Rue de la Paix? And since you've given up eggs and fats to get your cholesterol down and your Relaxacizor and all!"

"Don't call attention to my age and infirmities, Bo, please," Teddy begged, and he laughed in a hard, dry way that showed irritation. He found it tiresome that Bo should go for these young boys quite so obviously. He was coming on strong with Bobby, as they said nowadays, but Bobby was showing no reactions of the kind Bo hoped for. The boy had seemed, at least, to understand what he and Bo were all about when, some weeks before, Teddy had given him a hitch from Olympia; he had even come in to see the house and accepted drinks, a slightly risky thing in view of his youth. He also had found his way to the bookshelves in minutes and borrowed an early Hemingway before he left. Teddy knew it was the library (mostly firsts with dust wrappers, ranging from Fitzgerald to Katharine Brush and even dear old Elinor Glyn) that fascinated—the *milieu* instead of himself—but he had grown accustomed to that.

Bo had passed on to another souvenir, this one of Teddy with a blonde in beach pajamas and signed, with a great flourish, "Gloria, Berlin, 1929." "What is the name of that old actress, Teddy?" he asked. "*I* never even saw Garbo."

Teddy Hubbard did not answer. What a knockout, he was thinking, looking at Bobby Ingle's thick, water-combed blond hair, his lithe boy's body. An ephebe, all the tantalizing fetishes—blue Brooks shirt, jeans, heavy gym socks, dirty tennis shoes. A real catch, if he could be caught. But his parents lived too close up the road. Still, not too young, certainly not too unaware, either. Teddy's experience with "chicken" was that, like soufflés, they either fell at once or didn't fall at all. Bo was spreading his net wide, he saw. He was always chasing either jailbait or trade. Bo was slipping; a few years ago the varieties he liked went for him; he didn't have to knock himself out as he was doing now. Bo was a TV "spokesman," as commercial announcers are now euphemistically called, once successful, but jobs now were few and far between. The Swedish meatball firm, for which his accent had been suitable, had gone out of business; these days he was lucky to fake his accent into plugs for Pennsylvania noodles. His deep tan, capped smile and Does He or Doesn't He hair (Bo did, and was more golden than any Stockholm juvenile) bore witness to the daily struggle to keep forty at bay. Teddy almost laughed when he remembered what ardent ploys he'd had to use to snare Bo; he'd virtually had to promise to set him up for life. He smiled, too, to think of the power over Bo this had given him; he held the financial reins, and had only to tug for Bo to come to heel. Despite this, he was giving him more and more slack of late; the lonely path of queer old age stretched ahead, and, aging though Bo also was, at least he was company.

Bo was pouring Bobby a second drink when a sharp rapping was heard on the ceiling. "Oh-oh," he said, "Madam wants to be put on the pot."

"She's *bean* on the pot," replied Teddy, unable to resist it. "I left her all tucked in for the night."

The rapping from upstairs sounded again. This time Teddy rose. "My mother," he explained to Bobby. "She's going to be eighty-three this week, so if you're a bright boy, you can figure out how old I am without Bo showing you the pictures."

"Don't be vain, Teddy," said Bo. "He doesn't care how old you are, do you, Bobby?"

For the first time, Bobby Ingle showed confusion. He felt no allegiance to either man, and being asked to choose between them embarrassed him. "I think I'll be going now," he said, extending his hand to Hubbard. "Thanks for the book."

"You're very welcome," Hubbard answered. "Help yourself to anything else you'd like."

"You don't mind lending books?"

"Not so long as you bring them back." The rapping was repeated, more vigorously this time, and Teddy raised his eyes upward. "*Really!*" he exclaimed, only he pronounced it "*Rilly!*" in that pseudo-British drawing-room-comedy inflection that betrayed his years more certainly than his appearance or the photographs. "Why *did* I buy her that cane?"

"You'd better go up, don't you think?" Bo urged. "You know Mother Hubbard doesn't like to be kept waiting when she has to pee."

"I'm going," Teddy said, annoyed; he didn't care to have Bo press the details of his mother's incontinence in front of the boy. The incontinence varied, and sometimes he suspected her of using the on-the-pot, off-the-pot routine as a way to punish him. He was saved the distress of Bo's further development by still another summons. "Now, get your beauty sleep, Bo," he said; "you know you've got to be in top form tomorrow for NBC—or is it ABC?"

It happened to be neither. "You take care of your beauty sleep, I'll take care of mine," Bo answered. No one knew better than he what a bitch the camera was, how it found lines even assiduous mirror inspection did not reveal, but being reminded of it only made him angry that Teddy expected him to work at all.

"See that you do, then," Teddy said, and went upstairs.

"I wish that old horror of a mother of his would croak," Bo said, when Teddy was out of earshot. "I don't mean that, really; Mother Hubbard's a perfect marvel, and Teddy's a saint around her. He won't let the nurse touch her when he's home. He carries her to and from the pot as often as she asks to go."

Bobby Ingle said nothing. He was looking at the bookshelves and wondering how he could borrow another book and leave quickly without hurting deWillig's feelings.

"Have another drink," suggested Bo.

"No, thanks."

"For the road."

"All right."

"You don't *read* those things, do you?" Bo, handing Bobby his glass, indicated the shelves of books at which Bobby stared hungrily.

"Of course I do."

"What a waste! I'd have thought a boy like you would be interested in other things."

"I like to read," Bobby said, gulping his drink.

50

"No fun and games?"

"Well, I played soccer at Adamville, before I flunked out."

"I figured you for a squash boy," said Bo, to whom these soccer-squash distinctions evidently were meaningful. He ran a hand along a row of books. He could never quite resist displaying his forearms (another of his good points) and his Piaget wristwatch and rings. On his third finger was a showy brown diamond, on his pinky a seal ring with the deWillig crest cut in malachite; the first had been a gift of an earlier friend, the second Teddy had had made for him at Cartier's.

"No, I played soccer," Bobby repeated, not noticing the display.

Bo then let his body assume a "Phidias" pose (that was what an admirer had told him it was) and smiled at Bobby with wide-stretched eyes—his smashing "pal" look.

Bobby had isolated a Boni *Cities of the Plain* and took it down from the shelf.

"You don't want to read that old camp," Bo said, angry that his charms were not working. "If it's something queer you're looking for, Teddy's got stacks of things that are more fun." Bo knew that part of the library well. "Like this one." He exhibited a silk-bound volume. The plate to which he opened it depicted a laconic, Japanese couple in stiff, elaborate robes, copulating. "This one's called *Geisha Delights.*"

"Well, I don't think I'll borrow that," Bobby said.

Bo hesitated. He had gone too far, but he was drawn on by the need to win, to prove to himself that he could. There was another volume that would do it, if it could be done, a pre-World War I German *numéro* Teddy had used on Bo at the very beginning. He reached for it, flipped to a page considerably more graphic than the Japanese illustration. "*Wärme Brüder*—German for special friends," he explained. This feint, which Bo had used with success more than once, was clearly within Bobby's comprehension, but fell flat. All that happened was that he bolted the rest of his drink.

"I'll be going now," he said.

"As you like," said Bo, returning the warm brothers to the shelves. With the game lost, or this round of it, his interest cooled. "Well, come see us again."

"I will," Bobby responded politely, walking to the door.

"You're forgetting your *Cities*," said Bo, lazing slowly behind, Proust in hand.

"Oh, yes. Thanks. Good night," Bobby said, and he hurried away.

Outside in the warm night, Bo stood on the tiled porch and watched until Bobby Ingle disappeared up the road. "That one doesn't fool me," he said under his breath. "Proust, my ass! I'll bet he's as wise as the next one."

From a balcony above, where Teddy had been watching, came a mocking laugh. "I could have told you. You should have tried *The Sins of Oscar Wilde*, if you were in that much of a hurry."

"Oh, shut up!" Bo flung up at him.

Inside the house the cane rapped imperiously again, this time accompanied by a quavering voice. "Teddy? *Teddy!*"

"Coming, Mother," Teddy said.

C H A P T E R 3

When Fran Hanter entered the luncheonette, Al Hanter had his back to her. Coming into the white light, her face looked flushed and her reddened eyes had a veiled brightness. Al had seen her turn into the parking lot and that there was a man in the car with her; he had watched, from the grill, as she picked her way through the gravel in the four-inch heels she had put on for her visit. He turned, looking at her over his glasses, sweaty and steamed from the grill.

"Where've you been all this time?" he asked.

"You know, I went to Mother's," answered Fran.

"Yeah, but three o'clock you went. You were supposed to come back and help me with the evening rush. You're hours late."

"Not that you worried. You might just ask about Mother, before I tell you why I'm late."

"So how is she?"

Fran's lip trembled. "Can't you see I've been crying?" When she remembered what had happened in the car, and that it had made her forget everything in this day that had gone before, her eyes filled with fresh tears. "Oh, Al, it's all so terrible! Doctor says she's a terminal case now, and that he's done all he can do. She was suffering so!"

"We all got to go sometime," Al said.

"Al, she's my mother!"

"She may bury the both of us yet," he predicted, watching her eyes. "But you weren't all this time at your mother's?"

"Oh, you!" Fran said, anger for his heartlessness flooding through her, but she dried her eyes. "Why didn't you *tell* me the car needed gas? I ran out halfway here. If it hadn't been for this kid helping me, I wouldn't be here yet."

"That who was in the car with you?"

"He'll be in in a minute. I wanted to give him something, but I only had a dollar and that went for gas."

"Maybe you gave him something else," Al said. He took a stack of burgers from the refrigerator, peeled away the wax paper separating them, and put them next to the grill. "I've told you and told you, don't pick people up, it's dangerous."

"I didn't pick him up," Fran protested. "And I didn't give him what you think, either."

"How would I know? You let him pick you up, then. Same thing." Al had his eye on the car and, as Tavio got out, watched him as he came forward and went into the washroom. "That's no kid," he said, getting the black hair, the bright, high coloring and dusty white clothes.

Fran was slipping out of her heels and putting on the flat shoes she kept behind the counter for work. She tied a fresh white apron over her dress.

"*I* don't know if he's a kid or not. He helped me—isn't that what matters? He was there on the road when the gas gave out and he went to get me enough to get started," Fran said.

"Uh-huh," Al answered, still watching her eyes. "Well, he's a kid compared to you."

"You make me sick!" Fran cried out. "Always reading something into people and things that's not there. He told me his people were Italian."

"Looks Polack to me. What else did he say?"

"Oh, just talk."

"All right, he helped you. But why does he have to come in

53

here? I'm up to my ass in work and dirty dishes and've got no time for road studs—that's what he looks like to me, a road stud."

"Give him a sandwich, that's what I promised."

Tavio came in the door, carrying his bundle, the dust washed from his face and hands.

"Al," Fran said, "this is the man who helped me."

"What'll you have?" Al asked, acknowledging the introduction.

Tavio eased himself onto a stool before the counter, lightly and easily, as though it was a horse he'd jumped onto. He studied the menu above the grill. "Hamburger?"

There was a pause long enough for Al to look from Fran to Tavio and back; then he turned to the grill, slapping a hamburger and roll down on it and then taking the orders of a bunch of kids who had driven up to the outside counter in a red jeep. Fran stood a few places from where Tavio sat, his legs in his white pants gripping the stool tightly.

"Is he always like that?" he asked.

"He's been holding down the stand most of the afternoon and he's tired," Fran said.

"But he's not dumb—he got it right away."

She decided to ignore this. One of the kids from the jeep came in and put a coin in the jukebox and it started to blare. Over it she said, "I didn't know your name to tell him."

"Tavio."

"Tavio *what?*"

"Just Tavio."

Al had turned from the grill and come back to the counter, the hamburger on a plate in his hand. "*And* coffee?" he asked, as though granting a favor.

"Why not?" Tavio gave it back. "I like living dangerously."

"I'll bet you do." Al set the plate down. He drew a cup of coffee and placed it carelessly next the hamburger, spilling it. "You," he said sharply to Fran. "Why'nt you lay onto that stack of dirty dishes back there? They won't wash themselves, that's for sure."

"All right, Al." Fran hesitated. "Well, much obliged to you—and good luck." She walked away.

Al had been making a shrewd evaluation of Tavio's physique, and his behavior, if not his mood, adjusted accordingly. A silence

54

fell between them, broken only by the clatter of plates behind the partition where Fran was washing them, deepening as Tavio finished his burger and coffee. He stood up.

"Your wife told me the name of this place, but I forgot. What is it?"

"Cope's Corner. No dangerous living here," Al added.

Tavio fixed his black eyes on Al's tired, sweaty face. "How would you know?"

"Now, watch it," Al said. "This is my luncheonette, my property. You've had your sandwich—"

"And you're trying to rush me out?" Tavio's voice softened and he eased himself back on the stool. "Don't rush me. I like to take my time about what I do, even talking to you."

"I've got nothing to say to you." Al summed it up, backing a little away from the counter. "What've you got to say to me?"

"Is there somewhere I can flop for the night?"

Al looked at Tavio's newspaper bundle, which still lay on the counter. "There's a place under the approach to the bridge, kind of a cement shelf above the towpath," he said. "Fellas like you, vagrants, they sometimes sleep there."

"I don't like that word," Tavio said, even more softly.

"Well, I don't see you got a suitcase or anything."

"No, only what you see." Tavio made a downward gesture. "T-shirt, pants, moccasins. Four pieces. That's it."

"What's the fourth piece?" Al asked, his eyes narrowing.

Tavio laughed. "It could be the other moccasin," he said, "or it could be this." He picked up the bundle. "Take your choice."

"It could be something else, too." Tavio stood looking at him without saying anything so long that Al got nervous. "This may be a little place," he said then, "but we've got township police, state police, too, if we need them."

Tavio got to his feet again, standing tall on the balls of his feet in the white luncheonette light. "Okay," he said. He waited.

"If you'll take my advice, you'll clear out before daylight."

Tavio clutched his bundle and went to the door. Turning, he said, "You gave me advice, so I'll give you a little, too. Why don't you try being a little nicer to her? Your wife."

"Now, listen, you, I'm no wet-behind-the-ears kid to take

cracks like that from you," Al said, "and my wife's no spring chicken, either."

"No, but she deserves better than you," Tavio answered.

"Get out!" Al cried hotly. "Beat it!"

Tavio turned on his heel and left. Al watched him as he dodged through the traffic, loping toward the bridge. Fran was watching, too; she had been standing in front of the sink partition, holding a pile of washed plates.

"Don't think I didn't hear you," she said.

Al's glasses had slipped down on his nose; he pushed them up and stared at her through them. "So what, you heard me. Let that be a lesson to you. You ain't no spring chicken."

"It was you said that."

"And you heard him agree with me. If you could've seen yourself next to him, I wouldn't have to tell you."

"That's right, run me down! When I think what my life might have been if I'd met someone like *him* instead of you, I could cry my eyes out!"

"Go ahead, you been crying all day anyhow," Al said. "You did the best you could, if you ask me."

Fran lifted the pile of plates and dashed them to the floor. "All right, you've asked for it and I'm going to tell you. Tavio liked me! Yes, *Tavio!* He tried to make me—"

"I guessed that."

"—and if I hadn't had to come back here, to this stinking place, he'd have taken me into a field and given me what I've always wanted—a *real* man, not some sweaty old papa like you. And I'd have been crazy about it! He could have had anything he wanted!"

"I told you he was a road stud, remember?" Al answered calmly. "And your heels would have been round enough for him, too."

"You bastard! You know that's not true! You're always accusing me—"

"Finish washing up so I can close," Al interrupted her. "I ought to dock you for those busted plates. I would, too, if I wasn't married to you." He was already swabbing the grill with one hand, with the other reaching for the switch that controlled the neon outside. Top to bottom, the signs went out, leaving only the flood of fluorescence coming from the luncheonette itself.

As the orchid, then orange, halation of the luncheonette signs winked out, followed by the white glow from inside that remained for some few minutes longer, the Corner regained some of its deeper shadows. The Glidden house rose stark and honest from the slight rise on which it stood, its fine, rambling proportions only a little darker than the night sky. Though it was closed on the road side, above the broad, flagged terrace behind, overlooking the canal and river, all shutters were folded back and windows stood open to the hot night. It was cooler inside the house than outdoors, and Miriam Glidden and her sister, Rosa Woodhouse, sat on two facing sofas in the living room, a tray of drinks on the table between them. Rosa was speaking.

"At last they've turned out those hideous lights," she said. "I don't see how you can bear that luncheonette place. It spoils your view, especially from these windows."

"Cort was going to plant hybrid rhododendrons at the foot of the drive so we wouldn't see it," Miriam Glidden replied. "He'd ordered them only the day before he had the episode."

"I don't suppose you'll be planting them, now."

"Oh, yes, I expect to have them planted. Perhaps this week," Miriam said. "After the episode, I thought I'd never plant anything again, but now I know I will."

"I get so tired of that word 'episode,' and the other way of speaking of it, too," said Rosa. "I know 'cerebrovascular accident' covers everything, but to me plain 'stroke' tells the story as well."

Miriam Glidden said nothing to this. She was a strikingly lovely ash blonde with clear, translucent skin; her features were mobile and regular and her nose slightly uptilted, suggesting a certain stubbornness and will of her own. Of medium height, she was delicately boned, and there was a restrained quietness in her manner belied by an intensity that burned behind her widely set blue eyes. Her sister, close in resemblance but of darker coloring, was older, and her brisk, quick movements spoke of a cynical honesty.

"I shouldn't have said that, Mimi dear," Rosa said. "I know you're still suffering terribly."

"Yes, I am suffering," Miriam said.

"But it will pass, you'll see."

"I wonder. I never believed what so many people say about

suffering, that it ennobles or is its own reward, or does anything but make you suffer more."

"I think I'd best cancel my reservation and stay a little longer," Rosa said to this. "I feel I haven't been much help." She had taken charge of the many details consequent on Cort Glidden's death when she arrived, partly because, as older sister, she felt protective of Miriam, partly because she was by nature manipulative. She was evidently in no hurry to return to Canada, to her husband, an Englishman with industrial interests.

"No, you must go now," Miriam said. "You've been wonderful to stay as long as you have. I'm going to be all right. Don't worry."

"But I do worry."

Miriam looked at her watch. "Rosa, we've done nothing but go over this for days."

"Dear, I know it's been hard. How are we for time?" Rosa was dressed for traveling in a dark linen suit, and beside her were her purse and overnight bag; two larger pieces of luggage were already in the white Lincoln Continental parked in the drive outside the windows.

"We've time to burn," Miriam answered. "But we'd better allow forty minutes for Trenton, in this traffic. We don't have to leave for a good half hour."

"In that case, I think I'll have a last drink." Neither had eaten much dinner because of the oppressive heat. Rosa raised the bottle of Beefeater that stood on the tray. "You?"

"No, I have to drive."

Rosa poured herself two fingers, dropped ice cubes into her glass and filled it with tonic water. "Miriam," she said in a more concerned tone, "I simply don't see how you're going to endure it here alone."

"I have no choice but to endure it." Miriam spoke in a toneless voice that clearly conveyed she was tired of talking about it. It had all been said before, was an extension of the long inquest they had conducted about Cort Glidden's death. It was time Rosa left, she thought. It was as if a vacuum existed between them that could absorb any amount of repetition. Cort's cerebral hemorrhage, at forty-seven, had been totally unexpected and massive; one moment he had been applying an impasto to a canvas he was finishing; the next he was sprawled, palette still in hand, on the floor. He had died in a matter of minutes. Miriam felt that staying in the house was natural. She would, if Rosa's advice was any gauge, adjust within the year; endurance was Rosa's word and was, she said, the kernel of it.

"Don't you want me to stay, really?" Rosa asked.

"Don't be silly. You're all packed."

"All you have to do is say the word and I'll phone George and tell him I'm returning next week instead." George was Rosa's husband.

"No," Miriam said with finality, "George has already kept bachelor hall long enough, I should think."

"Oh, you know George, Englishmen. He has his club and poker and racing. He's perfectly happy alone. We're not like you and Cort were. Shall I call him?"

"No, really not." Rosa had already extended her stay twice. "Now I think it's best that I be by myself."

"Of course, you could come with me. George and I'd love to have you, for as long as you'd care to stay."

"No."

"But you've never in your life been alone before," Rosa argued. "You always had Mother or Dad or me with you. And then Cort."

"Rosa, everybody has to be alone sometime."

"I don't see why." Rosa took a sip of her drink. "Well, I do hope you're going to lock yourself in, nights. You can't be too careful living in the country."

"Cort and I never locked a door all the years we lived here."

"Very foolish. But with a man in the house, perhaps it was all right."

"No one ever comes near this house. The only people in the Corner who lock doors are the Bowyer sisters. No, Cort and I—"

" 'Cort and I' what?" asked Rosa, when Miriam didn't finish.

"Oh, nothing."

"Who will you talk to about him, when I'm gone?"

"Maybe I'll talk to myself."

"There! That's what I mean when I say you shouldn't be alone. You'll rattle around in this big house, and before you know it, you *will* be talking to yourself. I know if George died, if I were you—"

"George isn't dead, and you're not me."

"Won't you reconsider?" This time Miriam didn't answer. "Why will you insist on staying here?" Rosa went on. "Keeping up this big house alone—you'll never meet another man. It's no life for someone like you."

"How do you know what I'm like?"

"I know you're young."

Miriam leaned forward and capped the tonic water and secured the lid of the ice bucket. There was a forthrightness in her manner that reminded Rosa of their adolescent days, when it had suggested the shyness that had cut her off from people, as her long devotion to their parents did later on. She said, "Having you here, or being with you and George, would simply be putting it off. I've got to face it sometime. I'm only now coming to believe Cort's gone."

"Oh, you haven't faced it yet," Rosa assured her. "We've always been frank with each other, Miriam, and I can tell you I'm already worried sick about your being alone in this house."

"It's a good house."

"But in such a kooky community. I've often wondered, since I've been here, how you and Cort stood it." Rosa saw the neighbors—the Ingles, the Hubbard-deWillig combination—as vaguely odd or downright pathetic, like the Misses Bowyer, with whose imaginings Miriam had entertained her.

"It's no kookier than other artist colonies. Cort and I lived pretty much out of the world. That was the reason he wanted to buy and settle in Bucks. For Cort, of course, other painters hardly existed; he was absorbed in his work and success and had no doubts about it. He worked so hard, and after success came, he worked even harder."

"I remember. What did he care for most?"

"His own painting. A few people, very few. He liked writers."

"I've always heard that about *writers*," Rosa said; "that they don't like other writers but prefer painters."

"It seems to work both ways," Miriam said. "It was the life I exactly dreamed of and wanted—and now it's over."

A short silence fell between them.

"You needn't worry," Miriam resumed. "There's everything to be done about Cort's estate. Pierre—that's his New York dealer—is coming down soon, to go over the work Cort left. And this house is an occupation in itself. If I get too lonely, I can always play bridge with Susan Ingle."

"That woman!" exclaimed Rosa. "That's what I meant by a kooky community. The times I saw her, she did nothing but describe bridge hands she'd held. As for this house, what you need is a cook-general and a cleaning woman. *And* a gardener."

"This isn't Canada," Miriam reminded her sister. "There are no cook-generals here. Only cleaning ladies, who help you out, to use the local phrase. Cort and I always took care of everything ourselves. You know how he was about not having his things disturbed. Besides, if you keep order, it's not hard. It'll keep me occupied."

"Have you ever thought you might get in someone, a sort of companion, who could help? You can afford it."

"I'm not that old, Rosa." Miriam laughed.

"You're only thirty-three, I know; but age has nothing to do with loneliness. There must be a lot of money now. You could travel."

"I've seen travel widows and what happens to them. No thanks."

"What happens?"

"They lose their heads and jump into the bunk of the first man who asks them. The purser, usually."

"You'd never do that, because you're not made that way, though I am. If I lost George, that's probably what I'd do. But for you, a year of mourning, as Mother said; it's the best way of putting a barrier between you and—and any mistake you might make."

"That was an odd thing, coming from you," Miriam said. "Why would you?"

"I thought you might have guessed about George and me."

"Guessed what?"

"Things aren't the way they were between George and me at first." Rosa drained her glass and set it on the tray. "George is beached, has been for years."

"Impotent?"

"Yes." She paused. "Why I'm telling you this now, after all our weeks together, I'll never know."

"You poor darling!" Miriam said.

"I wasn't prepared for it when it began to happen—it happened slowly—but it didn't surprise me too much when it became fact. George is so much older than I. Funny, we both married older men. Of course, Cort wasn't that much older than you."

"Cort and I were completely happy."

"The years between you made no difference?"

"None. You remember how it was, Rosa—you married George when you were twenty-two, and I had Mother and Dad, and when Dad died, Mother. I'd have married anyone who could take me out of that. I was lucky it was Cort who did."

"Miriam, you didn't—"

"Oh, no. It was a *coup de foudre* between Cort and me. Exactly that. That he was older made it easier, somehow, to love him."

"I was always jealous of you and Cort, did you know that?"

"Why?"

"Because I sensed you gave each other everything there is to give in love. I knew he must have been wonderful in bed."

"He was," Miriam said. "He made love to me to the end, even the morning before he had his—before he died." She suddenly felt exhausted by the talk. Glancing at her watch, she said, "We must start now."

Rosa got up. "I'm glad you told me that, though it doesn't help my worries. Miriam, what are you going to *do*?"

Miriam shrugged, then rose too. "Breathe, eat, sleep. Take each day as it comes. Let's not talk any more. I don't want to think about it." She went through the doors leading to the terrace and toward the car, Rosa following.

"I suppose it's no use asking if you're going to lock the house," she said.

"I told you, we never locked it."

"But you're not *we* now. Cort—"

Miriam slammed the door on her side of the car and gripped the wheel. "Get in," she said. "And *could* we stop talking about Cort, please?"

"Darling, I am sorry," Rosa said, getting in beside her.

Miriam turned the car in the direction of the bridge. Suddenly Rosa cried out, "Miriam! Watch where—"

Instinctively and swiftly, Miriam swerved, narrowly missing a tall man in white, who was walking in the road toward the flight of steps leading down to the canal bank. He turned and stared as they passed.

"My God!" Rosa exclaimed. "Did you see him?"

"Only just," said Miriam, "and luckily in time. No one is supposed to walk in the road; there's a sign saying to use the foot-walk."

"That's not what I meant." Rosa leaned back in the seat and put a hand to her throat. "God!" she said. "*God!* It's years since a man's done *that* to me!"

"Done what?"

"Didn't you see his face?"

"I only saw there was someone in the road, in white; I was too busy missing him to see anything else."

"Perhaps it's just as well," Rosa said.

Dr. Richard Ingle recognized the white Lincoln moving toward the bridge and sounded his horn in greeting. But Miriam Glidden had neither seen nor heard him, evidently, for she did not toot back. Dr. Ingle then heard a squeal of brakes, but looking back, saw the Glidden car continue. Poor woman, he thought, what a plate of bad luck life sometimes serves up! Tuliptrees was full to bursting with "expendables," wrecks who loved the attention he gave them more than life itself, living on, while men in their artistic prime, like Cort Glidden, fell dead. It had been Dr. Ingle Miriam Glidden sought help from when she found her husband. Though the two houses had always been on neighborly terms, the families had little in common. But Ingle, in his kindly way, often looked at the shuttered house opposite his and wondered how Miriam Glidden was taking her loss. He and Susan had called after the funeral, to ask if there was anything they could do. Miriam Glidden had thanked them but said there was nothing. How right she was, he thought; there was nothing he or Susan could do. Anything that could be done would be done by Miriam Glidden herself.

He expertly maneuvered the sharp turn from River Road into his driveway and eased his small Porsche through the porte cochère and into the double garage beyond, beside his wife's Ford. He then locked both garage doors because he knew this was Susan's night to entertain her bridge club and she would not be going out; he would not be leaving the house either, he hoped, but like any doctor, he knew this hope might prove vain before morning. He ran a hand over his face; it was sweaty and hot. He had had a hard day at Tuliptrees, and was looking forward to an icy needle shower, the two martinis he permitted himself on working nights, the quick pickup supper the house had on Sundays, and oblivion.

He entered the house by the kitchen door and went into the dining room, where he saw a single place was laid for him at the long Sheraton table. On the hunt board stood ice, gin and vermouth and the pitcher in which he liked to carry his drinks upstairs. Beyond, in the living room, he could see Susan and her seven bridge regulars; they were changing tables, and Susan was handing out the duplicate boards containing the hands they would replay and later compare.

The tables and cards offered a curious contrast to the sober pedantry of his books, alphabetically arranged in the floor-to-ceiling shelves, the *New Statesmans, Spectators,* and *Encounters* stacked neatly alongside the American magazines his wife read. Often when she complained of having nothing to read, he suggested she might look into something besides *Look, McCall's* and *Holiday,* but he doubted she ever did; those were her dish. These were the caulfat that held Susan together: bridge, flipping the pages of magazines, cigarettes, solitaire—and more bridge. He could hear her voice; she was talking, as usual, with a cigarette in her mouth.

"The noise from the quarry downriver has been unbearable today. Must they work on Sundays? I shall bid two spades."

Ingle listened idly to the talk at the tables as he mixed his martinis:

"Two spades, Susan? I shall pass."

"Four hearts."

"Pass."

"Four no trump." Susan, her voice rising in the excitement of a slam.

"Pass."

"Five hearts." Susan's partner, responding.

"Pass."

"Six hearts." Susan again.

"Double."

"Pass."

"Pass."

"Redouble." Susan triumphant. "Darling, they're your hearts, you play it. I think I heard Dick come in."

Ingle stirred the ice in the pitcher, wondering if Susan would have come to greet him if the hand had been hers to play.

"Dick, darling," she said as she came into the room and put up her cheek to be kissed. "You're terribly late. We held supper as long as we could. What kept you?"

"An Olympia matron who thinks she's Elizabeth Taylor and that Richard Burton's going to marry Ava Gardner. Schizoid, with suicidal overtones," Ingle answered. "A real beaut. I was with her two hours."

"And on Sunday, too. How tiresome!"

"Sundays are the same as any other day to me, Sue. And it wasn't tiresome to me," he added somewhat testily. "It's not only my work but our bread and butter."

"I didn't mean it that way," Susan protested. She took her cigarette from her mouth and stamped it into an ashtray on the table. "Bobby and I went ahead and had our salad and cold cuts; yours are in the box. And, Dick, while I'm speaking of Bobby—"

Ingle raised a hand. "Sue, I'm bushed. I'd like my drinks and shower first, if you don't mind. Can't it wait?"

"It's the same old seven and six—a girl again, of course," Susan went on.

"Why wouldn't it be a girl? Bobby's nineteen."

She lowered her voice. "But, Dick, this time it's Edie Cadle."

Ingle paused in the doorway, pitcher and glass in hand. "What about Edie Cadle?"

"Well, this morning I was spraying the roses on the terrace and I saw Bobby talking to her. When I asked him about it later, he made no bones about it—he'd asked her for a date. Dick, this is serious—you know the Cadle girl's colored."

"How do you know? Cadle's white, and so is his wife."

"They say Edie's not his child. Dick, don't quibble—you know the kind of people they are."

"God knows I should," Ingle said.

"Then, will you speak to Bobby?"

"Where is he?"

"Gone somewhere, down to the Hubbard house, I think."

"You think?"

"Know. To return a book he borrowed."

"Susan," Ingle said, in the voice he used at the clinic when a reprimand was required, "you complain to me about Edie Cadle and in the same breath condone his being at Hubbard's?"

"Well, Hubbard is a gentleman—"

"And about a hundred times more dangerous to Bobby than Edie Cadle could ever be."

"You've said yourself, he's got to learn to get along with all sorts of people—"

"But not homosexuals!" Ingle's voice rose. This was a projection of the concern he felt for his younger son, he knew, but his outburst surprised him. After all, he employed a homosexual psychologist at Tuliptrees, who happened also to be a Negro, and found him invaluable for certain difficult cases; the Edie Cadle and Hubbard concatenation had sparked awareness of how closely sociological problems invaded private life.

"For heaven's sake, don't shout that word!" Susan said.

"I meant, of course, homosexuals of Hubbard's kind," Ingle qualified, speaking less loudly.

"The girls will hear you."

"Yes, I'm sure their being here takes precedence over everything else," Ingle said, not without bitterness.

Susan was anxious to get back to her game. "I'll send Bobby up to you when he comes back, then. And do talk with him, Dick, seriously. I've done all about him *I* can."

You've done too much about him, more than you know, Ingle said to himself as he went upstairs. Susan's possessiveness of Bobby, her resentment of any girl he might be interested in, amounted almost to an illness, but whether the illness would settle in Susan or in Bobby was not yet clear. Her antecedents were Southern on one side of her family, and though she said she had no feelings one way or the other about integration, her hackles rose at the hint of a tarbrush. Ingle disapproved of Bobby's interest in Edie Cadle too, but for reasons different from his wife's. Bobby countered his mother's efforts to envelop him with a *laissez-faire* indifference that probably masked resistance but was, equally probably, part of his boredom with everything. Bobby had always been bored, unlike Houghton Ingle, his older brother, who was following in his father's footsteps and interning at the Institute for Living in Hartford. Bobby had shown no marked aptitude for anything. He liked to read and read everything he could get his hands on, from advertisements on cereals to Dr. Ingle's English magazines, and with this eclecticism had spun a cocoon around himself that was difficult to penetrate. He had not done well at the New England boarding school to which he had been sent at thirteen, nor at the Adamville School, near Olympia, where, as a last resort, he enrolled at seventeen, to fail half his courses and be dropped at eighteen. His reaction to studies was emotional: If he liked the teachers, he worked and got passing marks, but if not, he idled. That he was good in English was no guarantee he would pass a course in it. When his grades came in, he was scolded by his mother and reasoned with by his father; neither had done the least good. Ingle knew that an important change was now taking place in Bobby, but his clinical ability to diagnose in others had failed him in the case of his son. Though he had a fair picture of Bobby's Oedipal structure—that part not obscured by the cocoon and the boredom—he was at a loss to know what Bobby was really like. The information that he was visiting Hubbard disturbed him much more than the interest in the Cadle girl.

After his two drinks and shower, Ingle felt considerably better. He stretched out on his daybed by the window from which, when not as tired as he was tonight, he observed the Cadles and made notes for his paper. Almost at once there was a knock on the door.

"Come in," Ingle said.

Bobby entered, balancing a plate on which was the supper Susan Ingle had kept cold in the refrigerator and a book. "Hi, Dad," he said. "Mother said you'd probably rather eat up here."

"And so I would," answered Ingle, taking his plate. "I'd offer you a drink, but as you see, the pitcher's empty." It had always been understood in the household that anyone over eighteen could have a drink. This frank expedient, Dr. Ingle liked to boast, had resulted in his older son's never taking a drink, not even a social one. The same could not be said for Bobby.

"Thanks," he replied, "but I've already had several." He sat down in the chair opposite the daybed.

"What's the book?" his father asked.

Bobby handed over *Cities of the Plain*. Ingle looked at it, handed it back without comment. "Your mother told me you've been down at Hubbard's," he said, coming straight to the point.

"Yes. To return a book. He lent me this one."

Ingle rolled one of the cold cuts on his plate around his fork. "And how, if I may ask, did you get into Hubbard's clutches?"

Bobby laughed. "They're not clutches, Dad. Hubbard's just an old queer who happens to have books I like to read."

"But how did you meet him?"

"He picked me up one day when I was hitching home from Olympia and asked me in for a drink."

"I see. How do you know he's a queer?"

"Isn't it obvious?"

"Is it?"

"Dad, you're a head man; you've seen him and you should know."

"Yes, I'm afraid I do know," Ingle admitted. His knowledge came from sources Bobby probably knew nothing about. Some years before, he had treated a fifteen-year-old boy at Tuliptrees for trauma that had been induced by an evening spent at the Hubbard house. The boy's parents, prominent Quakers, had taken the advice of the Tuliptrees psychiatrists and had not brought charges against Hubbard, since what had happened could not be undone, and they feared publicity. But Hubbard had been warned that the incident was known and on record.

Ingle wanted to get at this, but wasn't sure how to go about it. Experimentally he said, "You know I don't forbid you to do things and have tried to be frank in explaining to you why I'd prefer that you not do certain things."

"Yes, Dad, you have."

"Well, I'd like you to be open and frank with me about this. Why do you go to this Hubbard's house?"

"I told you, he lends me books."

"Is that the only reason?"

Bobby shrugged. "It's somewhere to go. There are people there, sometimes."

"What kind of people?"

"Just people."

"Were there people there tonight?"

"No. Or only Hubbard's friend. His name is Bo deWillig. Hubbard's mother was there, too; but she's old and doesn't come downstairs."

"How often have you been there?"

"Five, six times. I don't remember exactly. Dad, what is it you're trying to find out? Do you mean, do they try to make me? Well, yes, one of them did tonight."

"Which one?"

"The one called Bo."

"And?"

"And nothing. I borrowed my book and came home."

Ingle set his plate, unfinished, on a table. "This is the truth?" he asked, coming back to it.

"Of course. Dad, don't look so upset. All guys go through this sometime or other."

"By which I take it you mean you've been propositioned by men of this kind before?"

"Sure. But why would you care?"

"Why would I *care*?" Ingle repeated. As Bobby had seen, he was upset; it was one thing to discuss such matters with patients at the clinic, quite another when a son, and a neurotic one, was involved. "Why would I *not* care?"

"Dad, it doesn't mean a thing," Bobby said, backtracking. "You're a doctor, you should know that."

"Yes, I am, but I happen to differ with you that it means nothing. Let me put it this way: When you were at school, you must have learned that when you mention one thing, you exclude another."

Bobby looked confused; he also appeared a little flushed from the drinks he'd had at Hubbard's. But the cocoon had been pierced, if only slightly. He said, "School is where it all begins, if you care."

"I care."

"Nobody talks about it, and I wouldn't if you hadn't asked. There used to be this fag who would crawl under the beds in the dorm and do us one at a time. One night he blew us all."

Ingle winced. He felt tired. If it hadn't been the end of a hard day, he would have been more up to coping with this; but if he did not exert himself now, his tiredness would turn to anger, and then he would lose the patience he tried always to exercise with his son. "But where was the proctor of the dorm?"

"Are you kidding?" Bobby asked. "He knew about it. He was an ex-queer anyway."

Ingle regarded his son steadily. "I'm not sure there is such a thing as an ex-queer, as you call it."

"Well, this one was married."

Ingle said nothing to this.

"You met that proctor," Bobby said. "He was the one who enrolled me, and you were with me."

"Yes, I remember him." Few knew better than Ingle, as the director of Tuliptrees, the various abnormalities that lay lightly buried beneath the most convincing pretenses, but his knowledge of homosexual behavior was entirely empirical. He had been without sex experience of any kind when he married, a fact he had revealed only to his training analyst, who, being Viennese, had regarded it as typical of his class and generation.

"Dad, I wish you wouldn't look like that," Bobby said, genuine distress in his voice. "You asked me."

Ingle did feel, oddly, as though, for once, he was the one being questioned. "Yes, I did," he answered, "and now you've told me this much, I've a right to know—have you ever submitted to advances made by men of Hubbard's type?"

"Advances?" The word sounded old-fashioned the way Bobby said it. "Had my joint copped? It's called that. Once or twice. Lots of guys let them do it to them because it's the only kind of sex they can get."

This time Ingle was truly shocked. Then he transposed what Bobby had said into language more familiar and broke into anger. "There is such a thing as normal sex, you know."

"It's such hell to get. But even girls would rather cop you than get knocked up. It's not the same as getting laid, but it's better than nothing, some guys think."

"Is it what you think?"

"Well, the sensation is special. Dad, don't ask me any more. I told you, it means nothing. I shouldn't have told you anything."

Ingle sighed. What he felt was the heavy disapproval of a Victorian paterfamilias tempered by his concession, as a psychiatrist, that Bobby had all the desires common to a burgeoning libido and was little different, perhaps, from others of his specific generation. "Tell me one thing more," he said. "You don't have reciprocal feelings toward these men, do you?"

"You mean am *I* queer? Christ, no, Dad! I need a piece of real tail worse than anybody ever needed it, but try and get it!" The cocoon had parted. "You were young once, Dad. You must have known what it's like to be hard up. If you and Mother didn't lay the law down to me about girls like you do—"

"You'd like to date Edie Cadle." After what had gone before, Edie Cadle seemed almost desirable.

"Mother told you."

"Yes. She's against it."

"She would be. But I've asked Edie for a date, just the same."

"And then you'll lay Edie, is that the idea?"

"Everybody does."

"Lays her?"

"She's easy."

"Have you—laid her?"

"Not yet, but I'd like to."

"She wouldn't be your first?"

"Of course not. What do you take me for, Dad?"

"I don't know what to take you for," Ingle blurted out, Victorian father shouldering aside psychiatrist. "Have you no consideration for your mother and me?"

"What have you and Mother to do with what we're talking about?"

"Quite aside from everything else, you could catch a disease."

"V.D.? I use Sheiks when I have them, and I know all about what to do afterward, if I don't."

"What if you get the girl pregnant?"

"Dad, you really don't know what goes on," Bobby said to this. "Girls take pills now."

Ingle waited a moment, then said, "Well, I'm making no objection to your going out with Edie Cadle."

"*If* I can get a date—she likes them with a car and money, and you know where that leaves me."

Ingle got up and went to where his wallet lay on his chest of drawers, taking from it two tens. "Here," he said. "I'm going to say something I never thought to say—take Edie Cadle out."

"She's got a date tonight."

"Take someone else out, then. I know what you need. Only, please, take precautions, and if you have any troubles, come to me. Will you promise me that much?"

71

"I've always been frank with you, haven't I? But what about Mother? She thinks Edie's a dinge."

"Is she?"

"I don't know. I wouldn't draw any bead on her for that reason, and you wouldn't want me to, would you?"

"No, not for that reason." Ingle sat down again on the bed.

"You know, Dad," Bobby said, "if you'd let me do what I'd like to do, you'd be rid of me and never have to worry about any of this."

"Don't let's talk about that now," Ingle said. He had had quite enough for one night. What Bobby wanted was to get away from the Corner, anywhere away, any way he could, into some make-believe future that even he had no ideas about. "Has it ever occurred to you that your mother and I don't *want* to be rid of you?"

"She's eating me alive, or trying to," Bobby said. "I don't want to be swallowed by a pack of old bridge widows."

"Your mother is hardly a widow," Ingle reprimanded; but it occurred to him, as it had more than once, that he was a bridge widower.

"Those old fats she plays with are widows, all of them," Bobby said. "Every time I come in, I have to hear, 'Hello, Bobby—Susan, *isn't* he *tall!* I bid one diamond.'" Bobby gave an uncomfortably realistic miming of one of his mother's bridge sessions.

"Your mother's going through a difficult time in life," Ingle said, in a voice unintentionally judicial. "She's overprotective of you, I know; but when she is, try to remember that."

"I can handle her. You know what she worries about? That because I don't bubble it back and forth with her bridge girls, I'm shy."

Bobby did give an impression of shyness until he spoke. "Perhaps it's as well to let her go on thinking that," Ingle said.

"One more thing—can I have the car tonight?"

"Take your mother's. You know I have to be on call."

"She'd never let me have it," Bobby said.

"Take the Ford; I'll fix it with your mother," his father promised, "and make sure you have your driver's license." He almost asked if Bobby had other necessaries, but remembered his earlier words.

Pocketing the two tens, Bobby went out.

"You'll not be needing your car tonight, will you, Sue?" Ingle asked, when he had returned his plate to the kitchen and was on his way to bed.

"No, dear," Susan answered abstractedly. "Why do you ask?"

"Because I've told Bobby he can have it tonight."

"Oh, Dick, do you think you should have?"

"Whether I should or shouldn't, I did," he replied, and said good night before the subject could be further developed. He rarely took anything for sleeping, but tonight found two Placidyls and a Nembutal, fugitive samples from the clinic, and swallowed them. He felt outdated, outmoded and outdone, and wanted to forget that Bobby's generation, with its ambisexual flippancy, frank admissions of rubbers used, prophylactics taken for granted and birth control pills, existed. In twenty minutes he was fast asleep, dreaming an old, type-dream he had had before he married, in which he speculated agonizingly as to whether Susan would be virginal on their wedding night. But this time the dream had a variation, a coda in which all three of the Cadles—Rafe and Mae and Edie— laughed at him until he cried.

CHAPTER 4

The Misses Bowyer's house had been dark for hours. Both Miss Flora and her much older, invalid sister, Miss Emmeline, retired early; it saved on electricity, and there was no reason for them to stay up. Miss Flora was lying wide awake in her big tester bed, her dog Spot curled at her feet. Miss Flora had done her best to get to sleep, but they wouldn't let her. She could hear them outside by the stone wall that separated the house from the road, snipping the tips from her ferns, so that when she went out to garden next day, the ferns would be dead. Or, equally likely, they were pulling up flowers as well as ferns by the roots and carrying them away to sell for the fabulous prices flowers were said to bring in New York. Miss Flora was waiting for some *exact* sound before getting up, and she strained her ears, trying to ignore pedestrian night noises that kept getting in the way of the sounds she was sure she was hearing.

Ah! There was proof—a sharp, dry snapping, obviously scissors at work on the fern tips. "Down, Spot!" she whispered. "Don't bark, they'll hear you." Spot wagged his tail sleepily as Miss Flora slipped out of bed, very quietly, so they would not run before she could see and report them. She moved to the window overlooking the garden and switched on two spotlights that were attached to the gable of the house above and trained to cast their combined 800 watts on the intruders. Their light flooded everything. She was almost positive she could *just* see Dr. Ingle as he slipped around a corner of the wall—a fresh stone concealed beneath his coat, no doubt, and a fresh handful of sand left in the place from which he had removed it. One would think a man of his prominence (a *doctor*, and a specialist in his field, she had heard) would have better things to do than steal stones from old women. But there you were; you couldn't trust anyone. It would go on forever. They would come to torment and frighten her, and nothing whatever could be done. No police would come any more, except some young stripling who would talk about her imagining things and Cope's Corner being the safest of little villages. Next year and next year and the years after that.

Dr. Ingle must have heard her and fled when the beams came on; of course they listened to her every move. Well, the ferns might be killed or the flowers stolen (it did look very thin in the bed where the dianthus and violas grew) but at least she could try to keep them from taking anything else. She flashed the spotlights on and off for several minutes, timing them with a view to trapping the marauders should they be foolish enough to return. But they were clever, had probably already gotten all they could carry away, for this night, anyway.

It would be as well, she decided, to go through the house and check the locks; it was quite possible someone had tried one of the doors and loosened the lock screws. This was always happening. The floorboards along which she walked were dangerous and beginning to warp, because they—those nights they succeeded in getting in—removed the nails that secured them to the beams. It was a wonder they didn't steal the floorboards themselves; nightly, as she made her rounds, she feared this might have happened, and expected to fall into the basement.

"Flora? Flora! Is that you?" came Miss Emmeline's quavering voice from the bedroom at the front of the house.

"Quiet, Emmy!" Miss Flora answered in the special whisper she used at night when speaking with her sister. "They're here, or *have been.*"

"Oh, dear!" Miss Emmeline whispered back in genuine terror. "If only Our Father and Our Mother were here!" References to their late parents, or old nurses, or indeed anything in the past, were hallowed, and at once transposed themselves into upper-case importance.

"Emmeline, please!"

"Flora, I *do* think we might call in the state police—if you're quite sure?"

"I'll be absolutely positive in a minute," Miss Flora said, groping her way down the long, dark staircase. "If they weren't so clever . . ." Her voice trailed off.

It was necessary to move in total darkness, dangerous as this proceeding was, if she was to surprise whoever might be at the locks. She took a step at a time, waited, held her breath, listened, breathed and then continued until she reached the downstairs hallway. The tiniest of noises, hardly a noise at all—like maggots chewing, perhaps—directed her to the door on the river side of the house. The house had many doors—that was another reason it was so difficult to keep them out; they were continually taking the screws out of the locks, and this particular door seemed to be their favorite. This was so that she or Emmeline (or both—they would stop at nothing!) would one day open it, unthinking, and fall into the canal and drown.

Of course the maggoty chewing stopped as soon as she reached the door, but she very carefully slid the huge iron bolt, with which all doors of the house were equipped inside, so as to surprise, then catch *red-handed,* whoever was there. As she'd half expected, they, too, were too quick for her; there was no one outside, no one she could *see.* How could an old woman hope to win against them? They were professionals. She thought, I shall go mad—I can't stand any more of it!

The river door was opened only when Miss Flora had suspicions it was being *specifically* tampered with, as tonight. It overlooked the canal and river and lower escarpment of the bridge. It was moonlight, so she *should* have been able to see anyone fleeing.

Suddenly, on the far bank of the canal, there was a moonlighted flash of nakedness beneath the shadows of the bridge, where the towpath ran beneath it. Miss Flora stood, *rooted to the spot* (she would remember to use this phrase when, later, she gave an account of this to Emmy) and, literally, felt her jaw drop. Staring at the man—for it was a man—she saw at once he was naked *as the day he came into the world* (another telling phrase), and that he had evidently been bathing in the canal.

The man stepped out of the shadows and she saw him plain, rubbing himself with a towel whose whiteness contrasted markedly with the dark skin of his body and coal-black hair. Though she had often observed tramps, whom, despite her many protests, the police continued to let sleep on the cement ledge beneath the bridge—*directly in my line of vision, officer*—this man was not like them. He was, for one thing, young, and, for another, the most beautiful she had ever seen. As he moved, flecked by the moonlight, his body carried in every movement a rippling voluptuousness. He reminded her of statues she had seen as a girl in the galleries of Europe, classic, godlike, and not of this world. But he was not like a statue—she saw the darkness of axillary hair as he raised the towel to his head, and a much thicker, darker clump, just above where his legs began.

Her thoughts then went all foolish and confused as she made an effort to supply him with a fig leaf and a cap with little wings, like a Mercury she had seen in Florence, at the Uffizi. But her censor failed; he wore no fig leaf or cap, and she saw him with extraordinary clarity, even to what seemed a necklace of flowers that hung deeply over his chest but moved as part of his skin. In a flash of ecstasy she almost believed that he *was* one of those Mediterranean gods. I must be going mad, she thought, and felt herself blushing in the darkness. The only other man she had seen *in nature's state* had been Father, when she and Emmeline nursed him in his last illness and, of necessity, *had been unable to ignore certain things.* She had not seen Father *all at once,* only piecemeal, and he had looked nothing like this. *Bare to the waist*—as a con-

76

cept—she was almost but not quite used to; road men, who worked in front of the house summers were often so, rude and *without consideration for women's feelings,* but never to this extent.

Against her will she speculated who this man might be, the while watching every movement he made. He was no Cornerite; of that she was certain. (*And persons, officer, I should hope, are forbidden to bathe on the banks of the canal? Where is the Canal Authority in these matters?*) She closed the door on the unnerving sight, sliding the bolt into place without remembering to be quiet, or notice whether the lock had been tampered with.

At last I have seen it, she thought, the thing that, for most of *the years of my girlhood,* I imagined must be stiff always, like a bone, and which I could never understand *about:* because how could men walk about as they did in their clothes, freely and easily, with a middle or third leg, not showing? (It would show, surely, or did they tie it down or wear some kind of belt holding it against the abdomen?) She knew the *names* for it (Oh, yes, she knew them!) from the nursery's *pee-wee* and the rough references of workmen (which she repressed always) to *parts below, privy parts, thingumbob, love's arrow, dearest member*—that was Burns. And Whitman had called it *thumb of love.* Seeing Father's had seemed to solve the mystery, but now it had unsolved itself. This confusion caused the *oddest sensation;* the experience had both excited and exhausted her; she felt dizzy and light-headed in a way that was not at all unpleasant as she made her way back up the stairs to report.

Her sister's quaver greeted her: "Flora, dear?"

"Yes, Emmy, I'm coming."

"Where have you been all this time?"

"Downstairs." It was possible to have light now; they, without a doubt, had heard the door open, had retreated until another night. Miss Flora switched on the overhead bulb in Miss Emmeline's room.

Her sister lay hunched in a corner of the bed, looking, Miss Flora thought, like a very old child. Her yellowish-white hair, cut short to minimize problems of sickroom grooming, made her sallow, jimber-jawed face seem even homelier than it was.

"Did you see them?" Miss Emmeline asked.

"Not *really,*" Miss Flora answered, lying a little.

"But you must have seen something, Flora—you look so upset!"

"I am upset," Miss Flora had to admit. How much to tell her sister was always a problem. If she told her nothing, Emmeline would later accuse her of keeping things from her; on the other hand, if she related what she had really seen, Emmeline might become hysterical, get into one of her *states,* and be upset for days. She decided on compromise.

"There *had been* someone at the river door, I feel sure," she reported, "but when I opened it, he had gone."

" 'He?' " asked Miss Emmeline hopefully. "How did you know it was a 'he'?"

"I assumed it must have been a man."

"Oh, is that all!" Emmeline showed disappointment; men who *had been* were no novelty; her high-pitched voice with its quaver served only to make her seem more girlish, contrasting oddly with her aged, bent body. "Flora, you *know* that's not all!"

"Well, not quite, no," Miss Flora admitted, still trying to measure how much to reveal, for she could not afford to upset Emmeline, though she no longer gave way to fits of weeping; the lachrymal glands dried up, like everything else in age. "I saw a man on the canal bank, by the bridge."

Miss Emmeline waited for more. "Another tramp?" she prompted.

"I don't think a tramp, this time. He was young."

"Oo! And did he *look* at you, Flora?"

"Oh, no. I am very careful, Emmy, not to be seen."

Miss Emmeline sat up. "Is he still there?"

This presented another problem. Miss Emmeline had not been downstairs in years, *except in her mind,* though she had never admitted to this limitation. Daily she spoke of going down to the garden, to see for herself what was happening to the ferns and the wall, and daily Miss Flora talked her out of it.

"Now, Emmy, don't upset yourself, please," Miss Flora cautioned, trying to head off what she knew was coming. "The man was just passing. A drunk, probably," she added as a frightening fillip.

But something she had said, or not said, had whetted Miss Emmeline's interest. "I'm going down and have a look," she said.

"Dear, you mustn't."

"Flora, you're hiding something from me." Miss Emmeline swung her feet to the floor and reached for her peignoir.

"But I'm not," lied Miss Flora, for propriety's sake.

"I can always tell." Miss Emmeline got shakily to her feet, holding the bedpost for support. "Was the man *bare?*" she asked suddenly.

"*Bare?*" repeated Miss Flora, flushing again. "Why, yes; yes, he was. How did you guess?"

"I didn't guess, Flora, I *knew. Bare to the waist?*"

Miss Flora was silent. This was when her sister could be most difficult; she quickly considered how much effort to permit her. It had been a mistake to tell her anything at all.

" '*One, two, three, four!*' " Miss Emmeline suddenly broke into song. " '*Hang up your Midsummer Men!*' "

"Emmy, don't be foolish!"

"This is St. John's Eve. Don't you recall, Flora, Our Governess—the English one—teaching us that song?" She began to chant in her quavering voice:

> *Hang up your Midsummer Men!*
> *One for Harry and one for Larry,*
> *And two for Bob and Ben!*

"Emmy, really!"

Miss Emmeline swung her hands from side to side as she continued:

> *Sweet Saint John!*
> *Upon your Eve I pray—*
> *Show me the Midsummer Man*
> *Who'll steal my heart away!*

"*Emmeline!*" repeated Miss Flora more sternly.

"Flora, what you saw *must* be a Midsummer Man, don't you understand?" cried Miss Emmeline, becoming hysterical. "Don't you remember Our Nurse in Philadelphia?" Her speech tended to be cylindrical and repetitive.

"Yes, I remember, Emmy, but that was when we were children." She recognized the bad signs—the wild look in the eyes, the exaggerated crookedness of the mouth, the irregular breathing. "But

Our Mother sent that nurse away, because she thought she was a witch."

"Witches know," said Miss Emmeline to this. "She even made us men out of old stockings and stuffing, to hang up at Midsummer."

Miss Flora remembered. "Child's play," she said.

"Oh, *that* never changes, no matter how old you are," Miss Emmeline went on, not to be stopped. "And you're supposed to go out on Midsummer Eve and name over your flowers and touch them as the clock strikes midnight. You'll see him then, the man you're to marry." This was the worst Miss Emmeline had been in some time.

"Please, Emmy," Miss Flora pleaded, "get back into bed."

"Not until I see the Midsummer Man!"

If reason wouldn't succeed, perhaps shock would, Miss Flora thought. "Emmy, I didn't tell you everything about this. You wouldn't want to see him. He was entirely *naked!*"

"Entirely?"

"Yes, I regret to say."

"And you *looked* at him!"

"I couldn't help it."

"Then you must have seen his pencil and tassel!"

"Emmy!"

Miss Emmeline began to pant the way she did when one of her spells was coming on and she needed one of her ampoules. "I knew it, I knew it," she said gaspingly. "When I saw the Midsummer Moonlight, I knew it was the charm!"

"Emmy, remember your condition!"

" '*Name over your flowers, Lady Dear, first the blue and then the red,*'" Miss Emmeline began to sing again. " '*Hark for the bell, look for the Man with the tassel—*'" She broke off and fell onto the bed. The excitement had been too much for her. Her mood changed abruptly. "Oh, if Our Father and Our Mother could only have known, they'd never have left us," she wailed.

"I'll bring your ampoule," Miss Flora said, tucking her sister beneath the sheets.

"*I want to see the Midsummer Man!*"

Miss Flora took from the bedside table the box in which the ampoules were kept and, holding her sister firmly by the shoulder, broke the small, ovoid capsule under her nose.

"Midsummer Men!" Miss Emmeline repeated as she inhaled, and as her breathing became more regular, she began to wail. "It was always the same. I was the older one, you had all the chances."

"Dear, neither of us had any chances," Miss Flora reminded her softly.

Miss Emmeline paid no attention. "You were the pretty one and I was the plain one and *I* never saw a Midsummer Man. All *I* ever saw was Our Father."

"I'm going to give you a sedative now," Miss Flora said. It was a heavy decision, sedative following ampoule, but she made it, and very quickly Miss Emmeline was asleep.

Miss Flora wouldn't have believed herself capable of what she did then. She returned to the door that gave on the river, reopened it, and looked across to the canal bank. But the Midsummer Man—if Midsummer Man he had been—was gone. All she could see was the bridge shadow cast by the moonlight. Disappointment flooded through her and she leaned weakly against the door after she had again closed and bolted it. She hoped the delicious way she felt would at least endure until she was asleep. Odd—she loathed male nudity. Twenty years ago, when Father was alive, she would have borne up better. But now. . . . She took the stairs back to her bedroom as carefully as if they had been still unlighted. Spot still lay on the bed; he was a small dog, white except for the single brown marking that gave him his name, hardly larger than a cat. He wagged his tail, unaware of the battle his mistress had just fought, innocent of the battles to come. It was too many against one. When would it all end? Doomsday?

Long after all other house lights in the Corner were out, those in the young MacFindens' new house still blazed. Even through the big hollies and boxwood trees, which shielded it on three sides, the fourth side being open to the canal and river, its glow could be seen.

Nancy and Don MacFinden had returned from their wedding trip only hours before and their airplane luggage was still unpacked. It had been a magical, whirlwind trip, and like any travelers whose itinerary covered many thousands of miles and much of Mexico in two short weeks, they were not quite "back" yet. Their house had been almost finished when they flew to Yucatán on their wedding day, but they were astonished to see their wedding gifts disposed about the still half-furnished rooms, a week's supply of food in the kitchen and the made-up bedroom, with beds turned down, even soaps and towels in the baths adjoining.

This thoughtfulness had been the work of Nancy's and Don's parents, who came to call even before the luggage could be got out of the front hall. Nancy's mother and father had stayed only a little while, but Don's were still there. The elder MacFinden had brought a case of cold beer, and, since it was he who had supervised the house's completion, was understandably anxious that all should be right and ready. They had all gone over the house from basement to rafters, and indeed it was one of which any young couple starting out in life could be proud. The yellow fieldstone had been specially cut from the MacFinden quarry near Blackstone Locks, and everything had been custom-made. Expense, as Don's father insisted from the day ground was broken, was no object, and everything looked it.

"Yes, I saw this place in my mind long before Don was a mere gleam in my eye," he was saying. "I remember telling Mother, when I planted those hollies and boxwood trees, I said, 'Mother, this is going to be for our first-born, someday.' Didn't I, Mother?"

Don's mother nodded with the patient expression of a wife who has heard a story many times.

"It was 1934, when this land wasn't worth planting anything on," the elder MacFinden recalled. "It was nothing but locusts and bush honeysuckle and bull ivy. Things were so bad in those depression days you couldn't have raised a hundred dollars on it, though the state was always ready to take it for taxes. But Mother and I kept the taxes up, because the land's been in our family for over a hundred years. Last year I turned down five thousand an acre for it."

It was true; the situation was a beautiful one, the last sizable strip of unspoiled river land between Olympia and Ohmerstown. The MacFindens' ground ran through the canal to the river's edge, which could not be said of many Corner properties.

"And now it's all yours and Don's, Nancy," Don's father said. "No mortgage, no financing loans, nothing. All you have to do is live in it and be happy."

"It's lovely, Papa Mac," Nancy said warmly, "and Don and I are simply crazy about it." Even before she married Don, Nancy had so addressed her father-in-law; the families were old Bucks and had long been friends.

"Things weren't so easy for us in those depression days," Don's mother put in. "I sold what few rings and things I had, so we could keep up the taxes on this place and the quarries. We were land-poor. I remember your daddy and I trespassed on the Coates-worths' land to dig these hollies and boxes. They owned the Glid-den place in those days. We planted them together."

"Damned if they didn't just *walk* over," Don's father said, slap-ping his knee. "You'll find one male for every five females, Nancy—that's the way hollies should be set out, so you'll have bloom and color all the year. Without those males, you'd never have any berries."

Nancy smiled. "Yes, Papa Mac, I know about holly trees."

"I hope you know about family trees, too," the elder MacFinden said. "It should be the other way around, though, in families. Five boys would be nice, Nancy, with one girl, the youngest and last, to sweeten things up."

Nancy blushed.

"How's about that, Nancy?" The mortification of the elder Mac-Finden's life had been that Don was an only son; he longed for grandchildren, to make up for the other children he had never had.

"This is no time to talk about that," Don's mother said, reaching for her purse. "Drink up. These kids must be worn out, what with the long plane ride and the drive from the airport."

"I get the hint," Don's father said, but did not get up.

"And Nancy and Don got the other hint the first time you told them the story of the hollies. You'll get your grandchildren, but you won't get them if you sit here all night drinking beer and keep-ing them from their sleep."

"True enough. Well, let's clear out and leave the lovebirds to get down to the serious business of marriage."

Both MacFindens rose. "You're going to have millers all summer and into fall, if you don't get curtains up, Nancy," Don's mother said, commenting on the literally thousands of moths that fluttered at the windows of the house. "Of course, with air conditioning."

"I can't wait to get curtains up," Nancy said, walking with her mother-in-law to the door.

"I've got a bolt of the most wonderful sheer ninon I've been saving that would be just the thing."

"But, Mother Mac, you must leave some of this to me," answered Nancy. "I found some linen in Mexico that I like. You and Papa Mac have done far too much already."

"You know how Don's father is—there's nothing too good for that boy. And for you, now, too."

Don's father had lingered behind for a last word. "So damn many women around," he said jokingly, "I haven't had a chance to ask you—how is everything?"

"Everything's okay, Dad."

"Sure?"

"Why wouldn't I be sure?"

"Fine, fine. Don't mind my asking. We're both married men now. Nancy looks to be a girl in a thousand. I can tell you, though, the first year's the hardest. Soon's you get a few kids around here, the rest will be a breeze."

"You could hardly expect Nancy to present you with a grandson at the end of the honeymoon," Don said.

"All right, I deserved that." MacFinden put an arm around his son's shoulders. "Well, see you tomorrow at Number Three. Bright and early, remember. We're running three shifts." Number Three was only one of the MacFinden quarries, all of which had been working around the clock since the Bucks boom began. At the rate roads were being built and developments were growing up, there was little doubt they'd be working at full capacity for years.

"Okay, Dad."

Still the elder MacFinden hesitated. "Damn," he said. "But I won't say any more about it. You know what I want."

"Yes, Dad, I know."

Nancy and Don stood together on the steps, silhouetted against the lights of the house, waving until his father's car turned into River Road and disappeared. They seemed a couple perfectly matched, neither being tall but almost of a size. Nancy was only an inch shorter than Don, a redhead, with small bones lightly fleshed. Don was compact and muscular and wore his blond, almost tow-colored hair cropped close. Both had the sun of Mexico still on them.

Nancy turned to Don and said, "What a workout! We'd better get to bed, if you're going to get to the quarry at dawn."

"I'm used to getting up early," Don said, as they went back into the house. He took Nancy in his arms and kissed her. "And don't let the old man get you down. He doesn't mean anything by it."

"He means he wants four—no, five—boys and one girl, in that order," said Nancy. "I got the message."

"He wants to be sure he'll have somebody to leave it to," Don said. "He's always worried about that, ever since I was a kid." The elder MacFinden's planfulness had begun early. Don had been sent to the local high school, and then to Rutgers for two years; that was enough, his father figured—no Adamville School and Princeton for a boy who was going to run quarries and work next to the men, breathing stone dust. "How about a drink, doll? There's still that fifth of tequila we brought back."

"I can use a drink," Nancy said. "Shall I get the ice?"

"No, I'll get it."

Nancy went to where the luggage stood, picking up her small bag and carrying it into the bedroom, where she began to unpack. Don went to the kitchen and returned with two glasses and ice, then brought the heavier luggage from the hall. He opened it, found the tequila, and poured them liberal shots.

"Ugh!" Nancy said, as she downed hers. "But it makes me remember everything, especially Uxmal."

Don managed his drink without a grimace. "Why Uxmal more than any other place?"

"Oh, I don't know." Nancy went on unpacking. They had gotten into the habit of drinks before bedtime during the trip because of the heat and the rains, perhaps because of something else, too.

"Wouldn't your father flip if he knew what we've agreed?" Nancy asked. They had decided, after talking it over, against having children the first two years. Both wanted the first fun of marriage and there was no hurry; Nancy was twenty-one, Don only a few months older.

"That'll be our secret," answered Don. "Mind if I shower first? Oh, I forgot." The first part of the question had been a commonplace of their trip, during which they had shared a single bath in the hotels at which they stayed. But the architect Don's father had employed had provided a bath at each end of the large bedroom.

"I'm going to take a nice long tub," Nancy said. "So this is what it's like to be married to money."

Don laughed and poured them another. "No matter how much money there is, I have to be at the quarries six days a week, fifty weeks a year." He undressed and went to take his shower.

Nancy lay for a good half hour in the tub. When she came out, her hair bound in the blue ribbon she always wore at night, Don was sitting up in his bed, smoking a cigarette.

"I thought you'd be asleep," Nancy said.

"You thought wrong. Doll, come here. We'll christen every room, one at a time."

She went to him and let him draw her onto the bed. "Not all in one night, I hope," she teased.

"We could try."

She laughed, but he detected a slight rigidity. "What's the matter? Not in the mood? Tired?"

"I should think you'd be. We've hardly missed a night—only that one at Mérida, when it was so hot."

"I've never felt sexier."

She relaxed against him, and he began what had become ritualistic in their lovemaking in the many hotels of the honeymoon— the long, deep kisses as he pushed back the ribbon from her hair, the lighter brushes of the eyelids as he unhooked her nightgown at the back and slipped it from her, the slow, rousing exploration with his right hand as he held her to him with his left.

She kissed him ardently when it was over. "You were right," she said. "Sexy boy."

"But you," he said.

"I'm all right." This was ritualistic too.

"You didn't come."

"Don't worry about it."

"But I want you to come too."

"I mean, *really* don't worry about it," she said.

Don got up slowly, found a cigarette and lighted it.

"And let's don't talk about it, please," Nancy said, seeing he was about to speak. She reached out a hand to him. "Come back, for the rest of it." She liked, as she said, to unwind, to have him fondle her afterward. He brought an ashtray and lay down again beside her, letting her share the cigarette.

"Mm," she said, closing her eyes and fitting herself against him. "You're like a rock—my nice, soft rock. I love you."

"I love you too," Don said. "But I—"

She put one hand over his mouth. "Not tonight," she said, "not our first night in the house." Her hand caressed him and presently he took a long drag from the cigarette and dropped it into the tray. Wordlessly, he turned to her again, but this time when it was over said nothing. She held him to her until he fell asleep, then went to her own bed.

She lay awake a long time, listening to the rush of the river, the croaking of frogs in the canal, the birds that nested in the hollies.

"I wonder if it's my fault," she said to the darkness. "It can't be his, it simply *can't* be!" And then came the tears that enabled her to sleep, tears that were always the same, whether they fell from her eyes in the hotel at Mérida, or the Mayaland at Chichén-Itzá—where they had begun—or at the Hacienda Uxmal. They were the same tears, wherever she shed them.

BOOK
TWO

CHAPTER 1

The summer morning hummed down the broad sweep of the river, past the trees, heavy with foliage and night damp and dripping in the water's edge. The black-crowned night herons sheltering in the estuary near the bridge, standing in one-footed sleep, woke and raised their wings, craning their long necks toward the sun. No one saw the day come but the wakeful birds, and they made their songs about it even before the light rose from the shallows. Tavio, on his cement ledge beneath the bridge, moved slightly in the first fanning breeze that came with the light, and as the day seeped into the escarpment, sun picked out the design of chained flowers tattooed on his arms. Then, as the breezes stiffened, he stirred into wakefulness.

Tavio lay on his back, dark head turned away from the light, with his newspaper bundle as pillow. Nothing woke him, though he opened his eyes, and it was then he remembered the night before and the woman in the luncheonette, who had given him the lift to this place, and how he had almost been struck by the white car with two women in it as he made his way down to the canal bank. The car had been a Lincoln Continental—no matter how frightened he had been, he had seen that; and he remembered, too, bathing in the canal and rubbing himself clean after the dusty day on the road. He could hear the faraway *zing* of traffic on roads that were already hot, and listened as cars came closer and rumbled across the bridge above him. He smelled the drift of honeysuckle from hedges along the grassy towpath and quickly sat up on the ledge, then dropped lightly to the bank below.

He stretched, stiff from having lain on the hard cement, but that would pass with movement, and clutching his newspaper bundle in one hand, he began to walk away from the sun. The village where he was—Somebody's Corner—looked different in daylight, and as he passed the houses whose gardens came down to the canal, he could smell breakfasts cooking in kitchens and knew he was hungry. At a place where the grass ran down to the river, he stopped and unrolled his bundle, taking from it towel and soap and razor, and shaved at the river's edge.

The row of houses extending downriver ended at a bridge that spanned the canal and led to the road. He followed it, turning back toward the village and walking along the road he knew led to the luncheonette. Everywhere were touchstones of what he liked to sample but avoid entanglement with—men crisply dressed for business in the cities, getting into bright, new cars, speeded on by wives waving from doorways. Early commuters to the places that were death to him and which he hated.

From a house whose tall, glass windows reflected the early sunlight, ran a stocky, blond man in fresh, blue work clothes, who got into a red Dart and drove quickly upriver. A woman—his wife, Tavio knew, from long observation on walks in other places—having seen her husband off for the day, closed a glass door and disappeared. Two men, dressed in colors bright as peacocks', and in the kind of car that brought his hatred even more forward—a big Mercedes, worth some numbers of thousands of dollars he could never have and told himself he did not want—slowed at a driveway. With cold eyes they looked him over from head to foot, with the frank appreciation that, when it came from men, he knew could mean one thing only.

The older of the two spoke: "Going somewhere, fella? Want a lift?"

Tavio shook his head and the Mercedes passed on, but the younger of the two men turned and stared back at him until they were out of sight. HUBBARD-DEWILLIG, he read on the bright, orange mailbox in front of the house from which the Mercedes had come. Then came a stand of trees and a massive house of stone with all shutters closed, reminding him of shoulders turned suddenly away. There was no name on its mailbox, but he saw in the driveway tall rhododendrons that were not planted but balled in burlap and in full bloom; their delicate, varicolored blossoms had centers deeper in color, and the dew of night was still on them. A white house opposite, with a yew hedge and columned doorway, had a mailbox that read simply INGLE, stirring hatred in Tavio—people in houses like that, he knew, were thin-blooded and bare of smiles and deader than all the rest. It was only a few steps to the garage at the intersection, he remembered, with the spring running into a trough and an apple tree above it. A thick, heavy man was at the gas pumps, looked up, then gave a salute from his cap—the freemasonry of the road: no hostility, but a warning implied—keep going.

The luncheonette was across the road, even tawdrier in daylight, where Tavio wanted to stop first. Though a card in the window announced that it opened at seven, he could see there was no one inside. He tried the door to be sure, finding it locked, though the Men's, where the night before he had washed his hands, was open. He went inside and almost at once heard the scrape of car wheels on the gravel and the voices of the woman named Fran and her husband Al.

"Don't gripe about how early you got to get up," Al's voice said in marital, morning discourtesy. "This is your day to open up, so get on in there for the truck trade before it goes somewhere else."

"All *right!*" Fran's voice answered. "But remember, I have to go to Mother's. When will you be back?"

"When I get back. Noon, likely."

A car door slammed and the gravel spattered as Al drove away. Tavio waited until he could hear Fran inside, then came out. He didn't go in right away, but walked around the back of the luncheonette and stood beneath the apple tree by the spring, watching through the windows as she got the two big coffee machines going and the grill warmed up. A small animal rubbed against his pants legs and Tavio looked down, thinking at first it was a cat; but then he saw a small, long-nosed white head with sharp ears, a dog with a single brown marking asking to be petted. Tavio picked up the dog.

"Kindly put Spot down *immediately!*" came a voice from the house nearest the river. "There are laws against stealing dogs in this village!" In another key the voice summoned: "*Come*, Spot-Spot-Spot-Spot!"

Tavio couldn't see who had called out, only saw Spot run away. A window slammed shut. Shrugging, he walked back to the luncheonette.

Two things struck Fran as she saw Tavio approaching: the sickening excitement she had felt the night before, and relief that her husband had gone to Trenton to buy the week's supplies. But this only caused her excitement to mount, because she knew that this time she would not be able to resist; there was plenty of time to finish what had begun last night, if she wanted it that way. But before Tavio reached the door, a truck filled with crushed stone from the quarries drew up, and the driver, one of her regulars, got out and preceded him.

"Hi, Fran," the truckman greeted her.

"Morning, George." At least, Fran thought, George would be some protection. "What'll it be? Coffee and?"

"Adam and Eve on a raft, and break 'em," George ordered, settling on a stool.

Fran brought George's coffee, then turned to the grill, hearing Tavio as he came in, starting toast, breaking eggs into a pan.

"How's Al?" asked George.

"Al's fine." She waited while the eggs cooked, putting off as long as she could facing Tavio.

He was already talking it up with George: "That's a load you got there."

"Yeah," said George. "We travel early, so the bridge cops won't be on and beef about the weight. Where you from?"

"No place in particular."

"On the hoof?"

"Guess you could call it that."

"Looking for work?"

"Depends," Tavio said. His eyes met Fran's as she brought George's order. "How's about some breakfast?"

If I treat him like anyone else, maybe it'll go better, Fran told herself. She said, pointing to the menu board, "It's all up there."

"Make it two, scrambled light, dark toast with plenty of butter."

"Coffee right away?"

"Quick."

94

She repeated the order, remembering he had no money, but if that would get him out, all right. She saw he was freshly shaved.

"There's always work at the quarries," George said to Tavio, who showed no interest. The talk trailed off. "Well, see you, Fran. And say hi to Al." George went out and drove away.

"Why did you come back?" Fran asked.

"You didn't think what your husband said about leaving before daylight would make any difference, did you? I heard him drop you," he added, "and he went on, didn't he?"

Fran brought the eggs and toast he had asked for. "I'm alone here, if you mean that."

"That makes it easy, then."

"This isn't a car on a back road. People come in here all the time."

Tavio ate hungrily. "You can cook."

"I don't suppose you can pay?"

"Trust me." He pushed his plate away, smiling at her.

She wished someone else would come in, but it was Monday, the slowest day of the week; the few cars passing were those of last-minute commuters, intent on split seconds and train schedules.

"I'm an early riser," Tavio said. "That cement was the hardest. But I've been taking a look at this place. I like it."

"There's not much here," she said discouragingly, "only homes and a few little businesses."

"Yeah, I got the falling-down bit over there," he said, indicating the Cadle garage. "That leaves this place and the Inn. So?"

"Please go," she said.

"Still worried, aren't you? About yourself."

She was silent.

"Look," he said, "if you want it now, what could be easier?"

"I told you, this is a business."

"You could lock the doors."

She waited, then sighed.

"Or shall I lock them?" he asked.

"Yes, lock them both. We can go back here."

He joined her in the small kitchen at the counter's end, putting his arms around her before she could speak, kissing her once, on the mouth. Then she felt his hands all over her and she let herself go with him completely, helping him with her dress and watching as he stripped off his T-shirt and dropped his pants to the floor.

"Flowers," she said, seeing the tattooed garland that began at each bicep and ended in a cluster of roses just below his throat.

In reply, he kicked shut the kitchen door. She heard it bang, but after that nothing but the wild words she said to him, and her breathing. It was something she had heard about, terrifying and immediately fulfilling.

"You came like a house afire," he said.

"Oh, how can you use words—!" she cried, still panting, pushing him from her. He had taken her summarily, lifting her onto the metal counter where dishes were washed and stacked. The cold of the metal cut into her. "You were so rough!"

"You liked it. I told you you would."

"Yes. Now it's over, go."

He lifted her lightly to her feet and then dropped his arms, black eyes watching as she bent and picked up her dress and apron and put them on. He seemed in no hurry, sitting on a stool at the sink's end, lighting a cigarette.

"Get dressed," she said. "I've got to open up again."

He laughed at this, but did as she asked, pulling on his pants and T-shirt in two single gestures. "Tell me something," he said then. "You know people around here. Where could I get something to do?"

She opened the door of the kitchen and went into the room with the counter and unlocked the doors. "You heard," she answered. "The quarry is always looking for men."

"Work in a quarry? Not me." He followed her, lazing easily on one of the counter stools.

"Well, there are other places—you could ask over at the garage."

"I know the pitch by heart," he said. "I was a grease monkey when I was a kid, and if I'd played the game, I'd have my own filling station now, owned body and soul by the oil companies. A fine boy, working up, it's called. Well, I wouldn't play. I don't like being owned."

"Things are the way they are. You don't want to work."

"I'll work, but there has to be something at the end of it."

"Like what I let you have?"

"Like what I let *you* have." She could see what had happened meant nothing to him. "No," he went on, coming back to it, "I'd like to know who *are* all these people with the big houses and cars around here."

"They only live in the village itself," she said. "You should see the Fringes."

"The Fringes?"

"That's what they call it around here, the little shacks at the lower end of the road, lean-tos up on the hillsides, dumps that haven't any view of the river, people who don't have cars like the ones you see along River Road. The Fringes."

"America the Ugly," he said. "Don't tell me about that. I want to know about the others."

She moved back of the counter. "Why, they're just people; some do one thing, some another." She wished he would go now, desperately.

He was staying until she told him what he wanted to know.

"That house over there." He pointed to the Victorian pile from which the voice had called the dog. "What do the people there do?"

"They don't do anything. They're two old maids and crazy as bats, waiting for the undertaker. Sisters."

"And that place?" He turned to indicate the big stone house with closed shutters, where the unplanted rhododendrons stood near the drive.

"A widow. Listen—I'm answering no more questions. What are you doing, casing the place?"

"What about the widow?" He held her to it.

"I told you, no more answers."

Tavio reached across the counter and grasped her wrist so hard she cried out. "I asked," he repeated, "about the widow."

"Let me go!" She rubbed her wrist, already aching from where he had held it. "She's a widow, that's all I know."

"Rich?"

"How should I know?"

"Lives alone?"

"I think there's a sister."

"What a burg!" he said. "Sisters!"

"Listen, I only run a luncheonette. *I* don't know the kind of people you're asking about. Why do you want to know all this?"

His hand flexed, ready to seize her wrist again. "Because I like to know things. Does she drive a car?"

"Doesn't everybody?"

"I don't."

"Yes," Fran said, "she does—and she's a lady."

"What kind of car?"

"I don't know. Kind of big. White."

"Ah-hah!" he said, and this seemed to satisfy him. He stood up, picking up his bundle.

Suddenly she saw him afresh, as she had seen him in the last sun of yesterday. The long Monday stretched ahead—coffee, dogs, coffee and hamburger. With. Without. Two Cokes. The jukebox. "Where will you go now? To the next river?"

"Maybe, maybe not. This may be a river where I'll stay a while, until I get tired of it."

It had been a frightening thing to her, letting him have her, no matter how willingly; she craved one word, before he went, that would enable her to face her husband and remember that it had been worth it. "And then what? I remember what you said about the sea. Those golden cities. Are such things all you care about? Is something—something like we did—nothing to you?"

He read her clearly. "You've had it," he said in a hard voice, beginning to go. "Don't worry, your husband'll never find out."

"How do you know he won't?"

"If he does, it'll be your headache. You see," he said, one hand on the door, "it's all that I'm running from, leaving behind. No going back over anything, no strings." He opened the door and went out.

She watched as he walked away down the road, walking in the very middle of the two parallel yellow lines, as though the road and the whole world belonged to him.

"Damn him!" she cried, breaking into tears. "Damn life, damn everything!"

Miriam Glidden lay on her side, beneath blue sheets that seemed almost white in the early light. She had had trouble getting to sleep, but had then slept deeply, at some time during the night shifting position so that now daylight was in her eyes. She opened them experimentally, turned toward the wall, then closed them again.

It had been a night so hot that having windows closed or curtains drawn had been impossible. She had dreamed disturbingly, of what she could, mercifully, not recall, though figures of her dream lingered, like gooseflesh on her skin, forgotten dreams of being touched and loved.

She had driven back from taking Rosa to her train mechanically, almost in a state of trance. No matter how flip she had been about not locking the house and being unafraid, that had been bravado. She supposed her refusal to lock up was a way of telling herself she was not afraid to return to a house in which she had never been alone; at a deeper level, it probably had something to do with her persistent fantasy that Cort could not be dead and would return. She remembered pouring herself a nightcap, then leaving it untasted somewhere on a table, as she went through the house turning off lights and, at last, facing the bed where she and Cort had slept.

She could have slept anywhere else; the house was a rambling one, with several wings that had been added to the main section, in all of which were guest rooms, made up and ready, had she wanted to evade where she was now. There was the conventional Pennsylvania "kitchen" wing, the part of the house that had been built first of all, with a "beggar's room," a kind of loft above it, where once shelter had been given travelers in the days when Old Hessian was part of the stagecoach road to New York. There still were evidences of the occupancy of these "beggars," often not beggars at all but migrant workers, people traveling by horse, even journeyman artists, painters of stiff, mannered portraits, canvassing from village to village in springtime. When commissioned, they had unrolled canvases on which clothes and background for the sitter—even hands—were already executed, and filled in head and face in a day or two, painting the entire family one by one. There were two of these portraits still in the house—forgotten owners, presumably—and it had pleased Cort to have Miriam restore the "beggar's room" to a semblance of what it had been when the journeyman painter had stayed there. Not that anyone slept in the room now.

She thought then of breakfast, marketing, cutting flowers for the rooms, the state of the garden—housewifery. But she was not hungry. It had been one of the strange things since Cort's death, her lack of desire for food. This had worried Rosa, who had found one of her panaceas for it, small sandwiches appearing unobtrusively midmorning, eggnogs brought to the terrace afternoons.

And then the knife struck deeply again, as it had done every morning since Cort had been taken away. All during Rosa's stay she had concealed it from her, often getting up late, when she would have writhed out the pain of absence and dashed water into her eyes before going downstairs. She had escaped from the world of her parents into the life of Cort, or the life she and Cort had made together—but into what could she escape now?

There had been no last illness; there had been no illness at all. That was why Cort's death was so hard to believe. As for "accepting" it—Rosa's insistence—Miriam despaired she ever would. Until now, Death had always had a big "D," part of what happened in life, had happened to others including family, but would not happen to the man she loved. Now it was everyday lower-case, something that had happened, was still happening, would not go away. She knew that being alone now meant staking everything toward the moment of understanding that *it had happened to her,* to find a way of reducing Cort's memory to something she could bear. She had already discovered that whatever new life there would be for her would begin with acceptance of his death—the foreknowledge that he would not be waiting behind a closed door, was gone forever. But so far, all paths led away from this acceptance, and were inextricably tangled.

Mornings when she remembered the sex she had had with Cort were the hardest, and by way of compensation—and entirely against her will, if, indeed, she any longer had one—she had become a connoisseur of that abstract awareness of men about the place, repairing the roads, men framed by the windows of cars passed, even timbres at the end of telephones. Cort had had such a way with him. As she would pass his studio windows he sometimes called out to her (and the vibration in his voice made further suggestion unnecessary), though he might say, as he took down from the easel a canvas on which he had been working and turned it to the wall, "This one's a dud. How about a drink and bed, or bed and a drink? You name the order." And within minutes

100

she would be waiting for him in this very bed and he would come to her fresh from his agony of creation, for love, for solace, but always for the passion that had consumed them from the day they met. And they would lie afterward talking, forgetting lunch or dinner, whichever it was; it was his talk she missed almost more than anything else.

The immediate experience of his death had been shattering. She had been passing the studio window, a spray of flowers in her arms, when a premonition stopped her. She had listened for all those minuscule sounds her ear had grown so accustomed to that, in the course of an ordinary day, she was unaware of them—the risp of brushes on canvas, the click of the mahlstick, the squealing made by casters on the easel as it was moved about. This day all was stillness. She had called his name. No reply. What she had done then had been in shock, she supposed, since afterward Dr. Ingle had given her a sedative so deep it lasted long after Cort had been taken out of the house, and Rosa was imminent. *If only I had seen them carry him out,* she often thought; *perhaps then I could believe he is no longer here!*

What she had done she remembered only as a script for some horror film written for someone else. She had screamed, certainly, screamed again when she turned Cort over and saw his eyes in a broken stare. She had tripped over the mahlstick as she ran through the studio and across the road to the Ingles'—the last people in the world she would have dreamed of asking for help. But they gave it, Dr. Ingle bringing the only order out of the chaos of her incoherence. She had said things, used words she had never known were in her vocabulary, had never imagined using— an entire unblocking of that part of her where Cort had lived in her; her hysteria had flooded over everything. A rescue squad, young men who had left jobs for an emergency that was one no longer, but a routine removal, had been involved at one point; it had been then the sedative took effect, and she had gone out in one last resistive moment, the face of one of the young men branded on her retina. Later she had seen him, spoken to him, but his face was not the face her grief had illumined. That had gone, too.

Much of the horror of what followed came from those bromides Rosa had saved from their childhood and considered it her duty to voice at moments of crisis. "But, Mimi, dearest, to go in that way—

if one has to go—is the merciful way. Cort would have chosen it—you know how he hated sickness."

Miriam knew. She remembered a curious prophecy of his end, lightly given over the driest of martinis at one of the rare parties they gave when they had friends to stay. Their house guests had been Cort's New York dealer and his wife.

"There's nothing wrong about dying, it seems to me," Cort had said, "provided you don't carry loved ones down with you. The *catastrophe*—I use it intentionally in the fuller French sense—the blinding flash—immediate oblivion is the way to go. If death comes to me that way, I hope Miriam won't let me linger, speechless and drooling. She has her orders to kick me hard. In the temple, they say, does it."

All had cringed, protesting, finally accepting it as martini humor; it had been a gay weekend otherwise.

Though Cort had considered himself a happy man, he had known boredom as only painters know it; there had been days when he sat before blank canvas waiting, but what he wanted would not come. The realist in him predominated at such times; if one picture could not be captured, he pursued the next one after, often summoning Miriam to sit to him for what was laughingly called "one last portrait," though he had done a hundred of her, sketches and oils stacked in shelves: herself caught unawares whenever she came across one among the landscapes for which he was best known.

"Don't leave the last thing he did on the easel," Rosa immediately advised. "Anything but that. You'll never reach acceptance if you surround yourself with last things."

Miriam had gone against her sister in this; the last canvas still stood on Cort's easel, disturbingly enough an early nude of herself, which he had sought out from among the rows of pictures lining the studio. Why that one? He had considered it finished, she knew; but then he had told her that painters are never finished.

A loud pounding brought her out of the second sleep into which she had lapsed. It was too early for any visitor; besides, the pounding clearly came from the big door on the road side of the house, which she and Cort never used, preferring any of the other four which the house had acquired in its many renovations. She could hardly go to the windows on that side to see who it was;

they were shuttered. So she drew on a dressing gown and called down to the terrace. Whoever it was had stopped knocking, but she heard a number of blunted sounds, as of heavy, dull weights being dropped on earth—and remembered: the rhododendrons for flanking the drive, to hide the luncheonette. Cort had bought them out of a late winter field, ordering them balled and delivered whenever the farmer who had owned them found it convenient. She went downstairs to the terrace, where she could see the big bushes being placed at one side of the drive.

"You Mrs. Glidden?" asked a voice.

She recognized the farmer. "Yes, I'm Mrs. Glidden."

"Hope I'm not too early?"

"No. I hadn't remembered there were so many, or that they were so large."

"I brought them all," the farmer said. "He wanted them all, he told me."

"Yes. Did he pay you?"

"Yes, he paid. Now all he's got to do is plant them. It'll take a strong back, but I remember he's got it." A pleasantry; the farmer could not be expected to know of Cort's death. He retreated to supervise the unloading of the remaining shrubs.

He, Miriam thought. *Yes, he had it.* Now it will be *he* and *him* again, as it was during the long weeks with Rosa. She watched as the last of the rhododendrons were eased from the truck. At the time Cort bought them, she doubted they would be high enough; the bushes had been hard with frost. But now all were hung heavily with trusses of flowers and stood with their great, cup-shaped blooms moving in the breeze.

She lingered a last minute on the terrace, luxuriating in the fine morning, seeing the full-blown roses in the beds below, roses which, until now, she had avoided looking at, or when she thought of them, saw as closed. They had been Cort's delight, fragrant hybrid teas, in whose colors he detected hues others did not—the light pinks of Radiance, crimsons of Ami Quinard and Étoile de Hollande, the blush-whites of Mme. Jules Bouché. Now, as she drank in the essence of summer that is best tasted before full sun, they seemed to open petal by petal as she watched. They urgently needed attention, as did the entire garden, which appeared bereft without Cort's care. Most sad of all was a neglected cold frame, in

103

which seedlings, overgrown, strained against the glass. She turned away, and her momentary euphoria came to an end as she again saw the rhododendrons: they recalled Cort more clearly than the roses, than any talisman of the house could return him to her. He had even prepared the bed of acid soil that would receive them; there was nothing he had not thought of.

A blurred, white movement beyond the thick, white trusses of the shrubs caught her attention, as the eye is held and arrested by a lighter design in watered silk—merely someone passing on the road. Since Cort's death she had been aware of passersby, but until now had not been aware of any specific one; there was something about this tall, white figure which seemed the apotheosis of all men. She watched, fascinated but guilty, until he disappeared, telling herself it was a mood of her night dreams persisting into daylight, part of the confused interior exile that shrouded her life. A looking glass would tell her more of the day, and she went indoors and found one, searching her face for that part of herself that had died with Cort. As she saw, a different image confronted her; it was the face of a stranger, newly met, with whom she must go on alone. Only the eyes were hers, intensely blue, vulnerable eyes, through which the shadow of suffering showed so transparently. She shuddered at what was to come, made her coffee and afterward had her bath, knowing that, from now on, she could never quite be the Miriam Glidden she had been. Life, she comprehended, was a stencil of days, to be inked in as best one could.

CHAPTER 2

Rafe Cadle in summer did good business not only Sundays, but on most other days as well. Monday mornings, like this one, were almost as heavy as Sunday nights; people returning to the cities after long weekends found his place convenient because it was on Old Hessian, which led to the back-road shortcuts to the Jersey Turnpike and the big traffic circles.

It was shortly after nine on the morning of this Monday when the pink Cadillac, into which Mae and Rafe had seen Edie climb the night before, slowly moved across the bridge from Jersey and furtively drew up in front of the Misses Bowyer's wall. Rafe was in a fighting mood, and Mae was too; since getting up they'd argued whose fault it was that Edie had stayed out all night; though she was a late-late girl, this time was the first time it had happened. Mae blamed Rafe for not forbidding her to go out at all, a change of viewpoint from the one she had held the night before; Rafe had been slow-burning ever since he finished breakfast and opened up the garage.

Rafe was servicing a car when he saw the pink Cad and immediately, without doing more than shutting off the gas pump, ran toward it. Edie was getting out as he got close enough to see the license plate, a Philadelphia one. The man in the Cad showed signs of wanting to hurry on, but Rafe went straight to the driver's window, reached in, and took out the keys before the man at the wheel knew what was happening.

"Papa-Daddy, I—we—" Edie began to explain.

Rafe caught her as she reached the spring, slapping her twice with the back of his hand. "Shut your face and get on over home," he ordered. "I'll take care of you later." Edie burst into tears and hurried across the road. Then Rafe returned to the man sitting behind the wheel.

"Acie Stanes! You!"

"Big as life," the man in the Cad admitted. "How you, man?"

"Don't worry about how I am," Rafe said. "What do you mean, sneaking around here to pick Edie up last night, dragging her back at this hour of morning?"

"Man, I don't sneak," Acie Stanes said. "Edie, she tell me, 'Don't come to the garage, meet me near the bridge.'" He nervously eyed the keys Rafe held in his hand.

"I thought I told you to keep away from this place."

"That was cat's years ago. Gimme my keys," said Acie.

"Not till you tell me how you met Edie."

Acie Stanes smiled, and Rafe could see all over again why Mae had gone for him. Acie was silken-smooth, with the lightest of skins, and had finely cut features; even now, though Rafe figured him to be thirty-seven, he could be taken for ten years younger. He wore a sky-blue shirt, and his black hair was slicked close to his skull, and on his smooth hands, resting idly on the wheel, Rafe saw two diamond rings.

"You can't give me orders," Acie said. "I been hittin' the numbers. Not only I hit them, they hit me. Can't stop them hittin' me. I got magic in the front of my brain. I can't lose. Hand over my keys."

"You're not going anywhere till you tell me where you met Edie."

"Man, I cruise," Acie explained, "like everybody else. I don't have no trouble. I go where I like. Nobody stops me."

"I'm stopping you," Rafe said. "Nigger."

"Don't 'nigger' me. I been passing for years. I'm white as you, now."

"Nigger!"

"I got my pink Caddy and my diamond ring on each hand and, man, if you think that don't do it, you should go to school." Rafe kept watching Acie as he talked, hands clenching the car door tight with anger. Acie was getting more and more nervous the longer Rafe held the keys. "You hotted up because your kid pick me up in Trenton?" he asked. "How was I to know who she was?"

"Where in Trenton?"

"Standing in one of those little alleys off State Street."

"You always was an alley carrier," Rafe said, his eyes narrowing. "A cheap, nigger alley carrier."

"Gimme those keys, or I'll call a cop," threatened Acie.

"I live in this village," Rafe told him. "It'll be me calls any cops around here."

"Well, I picked Edie up in an alley," Acie conceded. "She was on her way to the bus, she *say*."

Rafe threw the Cad keys in Acie's face. "Beat it!" he said.

Once he had his keys back, Acie's courage rose. "Listen, poor white trash," he said, starting up the motor, "you don't talk to *any*body like that, these days—specially not to Acie Stanes!"

"Nigger, I said to beat it!"

"I was good enough for your woman when I was just a kid hauling rocks, don't forget that," Acie said. "Man, I remember how hot she was for it—she could smell me coming! As much as dragged me off the truck I was driving then to get at it. Couldn't get enough, neither."

"Get out of that fuckin' Cad and I'll cut your balls off!"

"Get *out?*" Acie laughed. "Man, you never *did* go to school! I ride, I don't stand on ground, don't lay hand on trash, either—I got white men to do that for me now. You got horns. Anybody always could get pop sex at this corner. When it wasn't your old woman, it was your kids." Acie put the Cad into gear. "You ask me how I know where to find it, I'm telling you."

"All right, you're telling me," said Rafe, suddenly deflated. "But you stay away from Edie, hear?"

"I hear. But I can't stay away from her if she phone me up and beg me to come, can I?" Acie laughed again. "Sharp stuff, that's what I am now." With a flash of his smile he gave the Cad the gas and sped up Old Hessian.

Rafe walked back to the garage and before he went upstairs finished filling the tank of the car that had waited impatiently while he talked to Acie. His face was mottled with fury when he reached the living room; Mae could tell there was going to be real trouble, Rafe was so quiet. He stood staring at her.

"Well, who was you talking to in that Caddy?" she asked at last. Though she had watched from the window, Rafe's thick body had been in the way and she couldn't see who it was.

"I'll give you a hint," Rafe answered. "He wasn't a white man."

"The funniest people got the money now," said Mae, trying it easy; besides, who had the money that shouldn't have it was one of her favorite gripes.

"Funnier than you think," Rafe said, still staring.

"Tell me! I got a right to know who Edie goes out with, same as you," Mae argued. "Who was he? Did you know him?"

"I know him," Rafe said, "and so do you."

"Well, who?"

Rafe was going to make her sweat for it. "Where's Edie?" he asked, ignoring Mae's question.

"Where would she be but in the bedroom? Rafe, I agree you should punish her, but not till she gets her sleep."

Rafe walked to the bedroom door and flung it open. Edie was lying flat on her stomach. "Don't try faking with me," Rafe shouted at her, yanking her to sitting position.

"Please, Papa-Daddy," Edie pleaded. "It wasn't my fault I didn't get home. He had trouble with the car."

107

"You expect me to believe that one?" cried Rafe. "Even if it was true, didn't you ever hear of phoning to say you'd be late?"

"Not that you worried. I didn't want to wake you."

"But you know plenty about phones," Rafe accused, shaking her. "When it comes to calling a bookie number in Philly, that's no trouble!"

"He's *not* a bookie!"

"Did you call him?"

"Why shouldn't I? To get out of this place, I'd call anybody!"

"You let him pick you up in Trenton."

"The bus was late that day." Edie had the answer ready.

"Yeah?" Rafe shook her harder.

"Why not?" She looked up at him defiantly.

"Why *not?*" Rafe was strapping mad now.

"Rafe," put in Mae from the doorway, "don't say—"

"Papa-Daddy, I didn't do anything with him that was wrong, honest I didn't." Edie grabbed Rafe's arm and held it, pressing her face against him. "Don't beat me! All I want is a little fun before—"

"Before what?" prompted Rafe.

"Before I get like Mom and you," Edie said explicitly.

Rafe pulled away. "You swear you didn't do anything wrong?"

"I swear, Papa-Daddy."

"I won't strap you this time," Rafe said, "but if I ever hear of you seeing that man again, I'll beat you half to death." He banged out of the room.

Mae had listened, nodding agreement, shaking her head, thankful Rafe hadn't slipped off his belt and gone to work on Edie, as she'd feared he would. "Maybe that was punishment enough," she said. "You should of forbid her last night."

Rafe's anger was unspent, only searching for an outlet. He felt like taking it out on Mae, she was so stupid. "The man in that Cad was Acie Stanes," he told her.

Mae stared back. "Shuh," she said. "I ain't seen Acie Stanes since he was a kid, and neither have you."

"Oh, yes," said Rafe. "Acie started stopping here when he began making it big, sniffing around for the same old thing, and I warned him to keep away."

"Maybe he wanted to see me," Mae said.

"You? You look like a bladder full of water about to bust!"

Mae shot him a look of hatred. "Is he rich?"

"What do you think buys a Cad like that if not money? He's not like he used to be, when you were jumping him every day on his route!"

"It wasn't every day," Mae protested, as she had a hundred times. Her memory of Acie Stanes was clear in one way, less so in others; it was, after all, sixteen-seventeen years ago, something like that. She added, musingly, "I wouldn't care what color he was, if he was rich. But I don't believe you. It couldn't have been Acie."

"I called his name and he answered."

"Edie wouldn't go out with anybody that old."

"Old enough to be her father, you mean."

"You can't prove anything," said Mae, "you never could." It was an old bone, picked clean. "How old *was* he?"

"You ought to know," Rafe replied cuttingly. "He was hardly more than a potato-water kid when you were taking him on. Figure it out for yourself."

A customer's horn sounded below and Rafe went downstairs, leaving Mae to her window and her rocker. But Mae didn't sit down. As soon as she saw Rafe at the pumps, she broke in on Edie.

"Wake up!" she said.

"*Now* what?" asked Edie sleepily.

"You lied to me. You said you had a blind date."

"I had to say something."

"You knew who you were going out with?"

"Sure, I knew. But—"

"But nothing. Edie—what was his name?"

"His name's Acie Stanes."

Mae turned white. "My God!" she said. "Oh, my God!"

"So what?" demanded Edie. "He's maybe a little older and he's had some trouble. But the trouble's over and he's got money—only the older ones do. I like him. What if he *is* a policy operator?"

Mae was breathing unevenly. "You heard what your Papa-Daddy said—never, *never* see him again!"

"I heard him."

"You promised."

"Oh, no," Edie corrected her mother. "Papa-Daddy said he'd beat me but I didn't make any promises. Mom, please! I'm tired!"

Mae turned and went out, slowly closing the door. Automatically, she went to the refrigerator and got out a Diet Cola, opening it at the sink and carrying it to her rocker by the window.

"It can't be," she kept saying to herself, "it simply can't be! Not Acie Stanes!"

Her thoughts were interrupted by sounds of engines being started below, racing and idling alternately as Rafe worked on them, sending the hated exhaust fumes upstairs. There was one car that was outside, though, and it belched black smoke that floated up over the quadrangle of grass and cooked in the hot sun.

"God, let me die if she's been free with that Acie," Mae prayed. Then she started all over again, trying to remember what she had never been sure of, whether Edie's father could have been Acie Stanes—or somebody else she had forgotten. Maybe if she saw Acie again, she'd be able to make out something, at last be sure. Not that being sure would change anything. It would make it worse. Better to know nothing.

With an almost infallible instinct, Tavio knew how to go toward what he needed and wanted. He had not always known. This knowledge had come at the end of a struggle to find a way of life by which he could be free of the world into which he had been born, a world of precepts, rules and restrictions that had suffocated him and kept him from feeling completely alive. As he thought of himself, since he had walked away from the confining world of which he had spoken to Fran Hanter, he was less a discoverer of the life of no strings than discovered by it, less a chooser of day-to-day freedom than chosen by that freedom itself. He had even learned that freedom is a burden of a kind.

His wandering had grown out of the first dream he could remember. In that dream, which had come to him sometime between his eighth and ninth years (and which he still dreamed, especially on nights he was uncomfortable or cold or wet), he slept enfolded by a giant butterfly, which, on waking, he was sure would have left the bright design of its wings behind on his skin. Always in the dream he was aware that the butterfly and himself were one. The butterfly varied in color and brightness, but when he was in pursuit of a woman (who was to him all women) and was sure he was going to get what he wanted, that was when he could—

almost—describe the last butterfly that had dreamed with him, himself. What the restless boy, playing in back lots, recollected now, fifteen years later, must be, he knew, something that had come down to him in his blood, a ritual hunger that took the place of home and mother and father and work and wife and all the things he was escaping, and that had everything to do with the way he looked to others, and to the way he knew he had been fashioned by that blood. When he saw old statues, he felt this singularity in himself—time stopped in another time—as though he was someone who had been exchanged for himself as a child, who belonged in another world, so long past it had been forgotten along with the time in which it had existed. He had relentlessly used himself to prove this to himself; it was the belief that animated him and made him believe he was more real now than he would have been had he conformed and married an Italian girl named Maria Anna, which, to him, would have been the extinction of individual existence. The life that was like a mortuary once you were in it, like a museum forgotten once you had left it behind.

The wandering life had been, in itself, revelation. He was the son of good, even pious people, and the ways and means of finding the next river (and, after rivers, the sea) had come to him without effort, as if all the resistances and doubts and concessions of his fathers had been visited on him, the ultimate son, there to begin a process of correction, of going back, that would save him from the confines and shackles that had destroyed them. One minute he had been standing at a turret lathe, the work he had been about to finish in his hands; the next he had dropped it and walked out into the day and the night with nothing but the clothes he had on and his newspaper bundle to carry. Faithfulness to himself was the emancipation he wanted; he wished less to change the world than to keep it from changing him. This meant avoiding it, except once over lightly and keeping going.

Tavio's personality in a large degree stemmed from his appearance, and it was possible to deduce his mind's construction from his face. He knew best when he slept that freedom, for him, was identical with what grew between his legs, and what he could do with it and finding out what women were like when he did it. This was a quite primitive and innocent knowledge, and he felt he violated it only at those times when he made some concession, qualified himself, to get what he wanted. Then what he did was not good for the woman or for him. He was unmarked. One passion, however intense, rid him of the one before; all he remembered of the woman was what remained of him as he drew away, and forgetfulness completed the circle. The next woman might be ecstasy or boredom (how could he know which?) and the one following a waste of his spending, or fulfillment by enabling him to play whatever role was required. But he then returned to himself, as a living sponge, though pressed through a sieve, reassembles itself into its original form.

His correction of the life he had been handed had not exclusively to do with his awareness that he was beautiful as few other men were; what he tried to work through for himself often was turned inside out; and if it was a time in which he had money, he would give it and any help needed to the unlikely stragglers of life, less lucky in freedom than himself. He gave freely, in one gesture, afterward forgetting this too.

When the dream, or the dream of an old, long-ago life, erupted in him, he had been unsurprised and guiltless: he had always been prepared for revelation. The trouble with life was that it was always pushing against you or holding you back; but if you floated and refused to let these things do to you what they did, they could be forgotten and then real life happened.

The darkness of his old life, out of which his freedom had come, had been blackness surrounding a long, curving maze, seemingly endless, of days and people and things touched and discarded. But sometimes he saw things now he had touched but not seen then—the days and people were long gone; the things went past him, like the jumble of means-to-ends in the luncheonette that weighted down the drained, bloodless shell named Al and his frightened wife. What had to be recovered on any day like this was a forgetting of those things and the way the woman named Fran had tried to get him to say the last word which would let her believe what had happened had been something it had not been. That was where dreams helped. Tavio's people had never learned how to use dreams to forget; but he had, he was sure— learned forgetting the hour before, living in the hour that was now, guessing at the hours that would come tomorrow, but with indifference. He had learned, too, that most men on any day set out to shed the dreams they have had the night before; but what he wanted was to free his dreams of himself, or any part in them he had had. Because dreams were his desires—the essence of himself—and if on any day he could make his life reveal his dreams, that day, and the sense of calm it brought him, counted as a success. His passionless game with the woman in the car, and later in the luncheonette kitchen, had been the cues of a dream, but cues merely to the woman to follow.

It had been only a year ago that Tavio had finally felt, in what seemed a message intended for his body alone, the decay and ruin of the people he had come from and the places where they lived. He dreamed, in fact, of the golden cities he had spoken of to the woman in the car, now becoming nameless, like her husband. And then the thought of being free, of never being anywhere too long, of having nothing, came to him. After three days and dreams, during which habit had tried to keep him from experiencing what he knew about himself, he at last knew it. It was then, after realizing he knew, that his wandering began. Having been shown without asking (which is revelation) the knowledge of himself as *Tavio*, he had no responsibility to anyone or any place, only to himself. He understood that he was a victim—of himself; that he shuttled back and forth in a world on the lookout for victims of all kinds. And because of this he had learned to be crafty, to be cold, to hide—and, to do this last, to learn quietness and stand still. If purpose there was in him, in being *Tavio*, after having been the restless boy who dreamed, it was now to let the secret life that lay beneath everyone and everything come through to him, to forget there had been right and wrong or true and false in the past and let it come. If it worked for him, it was its own truth; if not, the falsehood took care of itself.

After walking away from the luncheonette, he looked to what remained of the hour and the day. Some new woman in a place new to him must be found; something that happened of itself must be discovered—an open system leading to the next thing, for there was always a path if you followed your footsteps.

With this thought he found himself standing beside the balled rhododendrons near the driveway of the widow's house. He had walked past them earlier and thought, *Hard work!* And there had been at the back of his skull a prickling that told him he was being watched, though he had not turned; self-bound, it was a rule of his never to look back. But it was that sensation that had brought him, circularly, to stand where he was. It would create itself, life happening, if it was going to, as inevitably as the sun rose and set. Now he played to himself a role he liked—waiting in perfect stillness in the midst of movement and noises. Road noise . . . trains heard struggling effortfully somewhere down the valley, whistles transported and magnified by the river . . . the flutter of jets overhead, when all seemed still but was not . . . cries of children . . . the barking of dogs . . . relentless quarry roars, rising, diminishing. He played, too, a second game within the first: looking for symbols, symbols that would play no part for him in anything that might happen. The big, white Lincoln that had almost struck him, which he had traced to this house, was nowhere in sight. He saw only a long stretch of grass beyond the house, running to the river, flower beds overgrown, a ring of garden furniture near the bank of the canal. There was a sister—he looked for her, as if sisters grew in gardens like flowers, to be singled out from weeds surrounding them—but he saw none. But everything would come if he waited.

He waited. None of the things he saw surprised him. He had already guessed most of them; others he was picking up as he waited. He knew there would be nothing difficult about the situation for him, that the only difficulties would come from the widow, and he was prepared to be patient, as only a man who has nothing to lose can be. Slowly he cut the role he would play to her out of the probabilities and the moment. The delicious hunger of pursuit surged through him, like wine throbbing in his veins. The luncheonette drab had been a one-timer, too easy and too glad to get it: what remained of her was the hunger that had been there before. Luckily, her breakfast was sticking with him, for as the new situation formed, he knew he would need his strength. Only two cigarettes remained in the pack in his pocket, and he needed money: the rhododendrons obviously were the wedge.

He speculated on what the woman would be like, picturing her, out of habit, as the kind he could get round easily—older than himself but not middle-aged, with saddened eyes and the virtues

114

of belief and credence he despised. This one was widowed, a plus factor; maybe he would have easy going. If she had children, that would be bad luck, like the sister. But if she was alone, he would spend with her, if he wanted her, the whole of two, perhaps three, leisured days in the security the house exuded: the quality of having long been there and the promise of being there tomorrow. The world of having everything with no strings. Then he would be restless to move on, relieved to get away, and set out for the next river. If she was an old woman, he would simply smile and pass on.

He heard a woman's voice inside the house, obviously speaking on the telephone. If voices told anything, she was no aging widow; her speech floated lightly on the air through the open windows. Though he could not distinguish words, the flow was light and musical, though without laughter.

A screen door opened and closed, and he saw her come out onto the terrace. She wore a light dress, almost like a little girl's, a lady-dress, and from the way she stood and held herself he saw at once that the rhododendrons were not the only hard work there would be to do. The words *and she's a lady* returned to him. Either the woman felt his eyes, or was about to assess the problem of the planting, for she turned and, seeing him, walked slowly to the top of the driveway.

She exceeded his hopes. He recognized at once the double determination of the encounter—the woman's unavailability, and his own necessity to break through that unavailability. It beamed from his smile, radiant as a problem in calculus, challengingly exact.

She spoke first. "Are you from the nursery?" she asked, as if puzzled, then answered her own question. "You can't be, I've only this very moment telephoned."

"No. I saw you had planting to be done and stopped to ask if you'd like me to do it."

She stood against the bright daylight, a white halation where the driveway turned toward the garage, which was cut into the earth beneath the house.

"Why," she answered, hedging, "I don't know. Did anyone send you? Are you from around here?"

"Only passing through and needing work," he said.

115

"Oh." She looked at him with grave blue eyes, seeming to find this wrong. When she spoke then, her voice had a lady-overlay he knew well. "I think not, no," she answered. "As I said, I've called a nursery and arranged for them to do the planting."

"Today?"

Again her eyes watched him, guardedly. "No, I think not," she said again; "but thanks very much." And she turned to go.

"These shouldn't wait," Tavio said, kicking one of the balls of earth around the rhododendrons, and took a step toward her up the drive. "They're fine, big plants, but already drying out in this weather. You should have them put in right away." She watched as he dropped to his haunches and felt the earth in the beds. "Dry," he said, "but I can see someone's already worked the soil."

"Yes, it's prepared," she said. "My husband did that."

Tavio rose, hearing the bad-luck word, automatically nodding, because it was so often part of it.

"My husband is dead." It slipped out before she thought.

"I'm sorry," he said, sobering, seeing the blondness of her hair, her fine white skin, her ample breasts, round and full beneath her dress.

She said nothing to this, and he understood his dismissal had been given; she expected him to go. Her last words seemed involuntary, something of which she was trying to convince herself. Out of the corner of his eye he saw her vulnerability, saw the lady-hauteur and penetrated to the probability that she was alone.

When he did not leave, and as if she read his thoughts, she said, "If you'd come earlier, perhaps." Her words did not matter; their aim, to discourage, carried seeds of opposite intention. "I'm afraid the matter's all arranged," she added.

"But I could do it now," Tavio urged; "you could call the nursery and cancel. See?" He stooped, lifting up one of the plants by the tied burlap, setting it experimentally into the bed. "You could tell me where you want them, and I could have it all done— oh, it's more than a day's work—say by tomorrow night."

Lifting the big plant had been an effort and she heard the hard breath inside his chest. "Isn't it a job for more than one?"

"Oh, I can handle it," he assured her, smiling. Her eyes ran over him, judging. "But if, as you say, you've made other arrangements—"

It worked. She was drawn, then held, by his breath parting his lips. "Well," she said, still considering—but he saw the feint had been successful—and then in her lady-voice, bargaining, "How do you work? By the hour?"

"By the hour if you like."

"How much an hour?"

"Two-fifty, three—it's worth three."

She hesitated a last moment and he returned her hauteur with defiant indifference. Indifference can be a bond, as can hauteur, and he understood he must first be prey and counterbargain.

"I'd like to be paid at the end of each day."

"Very well." Doubt entered her voice; clearly this meant to her the kind of workman who does not come tomorrow. "I wouldn't want you to start and not finish."

"I'll finish." He smiled up at her, standing on her rise, and saw her eyes watching his for belief. Belief formed. She smiled slightly in return. The matter was now clear, the risk between them total, a play of imitation, like the double image of a flame in a mirror.

"You'll begin now?" she asked.

"If you'll show me where the tools are."

"This way." She waited until he had come close beside her, then led the way to a small garden house of stucco, over which a yellow trumpet vine grew. "You'll find the door open. Everything's inside."

He waited a second before opening the door, feeling she was about to add something, and when she did not, sensed that the place upset her. "Someone took good care," he said from inside, examining the rows of spades and rakes hung neatly on the walls, seeing the power mower beneath a tarpaulin, clippers and shears sharpened and oiled.

"Yes, he took good care," she said dully.

Tavio chose a spade and a rake, put them into a barrow and wheeled them outside. "Now, tell me where you want the first one." He walked back to the drive, standing by the rhododendrons.

She indicated the largest plant. "I'd like that one *there*, to close the view. Place the bigger ones where you can see through to the road signs and the luncheonette."

"That's a beginning," he said; "that'll hold me for now." And, flexing his arms, he fell to work. He knew she was watching him, still with her lady-doubts, as he broke into the earth, then began to prepare a deep hole for the first plant. He worked easily, lifting up the spadefuls of earth and tossing them over his shoulder, stopping to rest only after the hole was dug. When he looked up for her approval, she was gone. Though the drive was under tall trees, the day's heat, already intense, was increasing. He stripped off his T-shirt and, when he had moved the big plant into the hole, again looked for her. He saw her then, at a window that overlooked the drive, watching. He made his gesture of thumb and forefinger circled and the other fingers spread as a question.

"Very good," she said, nodding. "Just right."

Miriam stood at the window a little longer, seeing that, like any good workman, he found what he needed as he worked—the garden hose, the nearest spigot for watering, bags of peat moss in the garden house. The window was in the studio, and she remembered then to call the nursery and went into the next room, where the telephone was. The voice in which she spoke, to say she had found someone else for the work, was nervous and high-pitched, reminding her that before she left the garden she had conducted a bit of playacting. The tone she had used with the man had been her mother's, of the *I am prepared to pay* and *That's not at all what I had in mind* tradition, slightly louder than normal, because a workman was being dealt with, and in her mother's world workmen had been stupid and had had to have things made doubly clear.

She knew this was because she had been caught off guard, and all the time she stood at the window she had felt a dizziness she remembered well from Cort, when he would call to her from the studio and make his suggestion about a drink and bed in whichever order—the prelude to her abandonment of herself to him. She had delivered herself into a situation of the explicit kind her sister dreaded for her, a set of circumstances which already had caused her to behave defensively. Since Cort's death each day had been a hallucination, and she tried to tell herself that this was no more unreal or improbable than things which had happened other days. But then she felt her pulse jumping and knew this was not true.

Suddenly she felt trapped, knew she had to be free of the house and the man working outside, had to flee somewhere, anywhere, until the rhododendrons were planted. Let him place them as he liked; she *could* not stand by as, one by one, he waited for directions . . . *and smiled.*

Quick errands are always the best excuse, she remembered, and taking her car keys from the hallway table, went quickly down the inside stairway to the garage. In seconds she was safe behind the wheel and had started the motor, reached for the switch that elevated the garage door. But as the door rose, she saw she was as trapped as before: the rhododendrons danced in the rearview mirror, obstructing the drive completely. The man had laboriously moved them into a graded line, the better to judge and place them in the bed. She let the motor idle, then cut it off, defeated, again turned the door switch, watching the door drop behind her as she got out, climbed the stairs and replaced the keys on the table.

She recognized that this was the moment of horror, of terror of the single day and the days to come. She could not bear to be alone—she could not endure to be not alone; the two balanced like weights on a scale, equally terrifying. It was not true that death brought deadening of the senses: this man, breaking into her carefully guarded world, had brought a telescoping of the last weeks, collisions of intentions, a confusion and breaking of images, the various images she had of herself. Nor was it true that death extinguishes hope: the man was what he was, but she had invented him long before she saw him pass earlier, before she found him standing in the drive. His whole bearing and manner, the expectation she read in his eyes, had dismayed and excited her at the same moment she felt his contempt for her as a woman alone, his pity, which was his sureness of himself. And he had looked at her *as if she existed.*

With an effort, as stern an act of will as she was capable of, she tried to thrust the image of him from her thoughts, but all that happened was that her mind strained toward the brightness of his body, working in the shade, the outrageous roses cascading down his chest, the amorous positions his body could assume with hers.

"Oh, God!" she breathed. "Don't do this to me! Not now!"

She was answered by the sound of a tap being turned on outside and through the window saw him drinking from the nozzle of the garden hose. He held his mouth on the stream of water, lapping like an animal, then turned the water onto his torso,

119

washing the sweat and dirt away, slapping himself dry afterward. Then he returned to the work, continuing methodically and steadily, digging, placing, turning the plants until they were in the best position. She was afraid of everything now, of locking the house and of not locking it, of the morning's end and the afternoon's beginning. No solution stretched itself to her; only next moments came, lingered, were lost. If she could not flee, she could help the day along—for the knowledge of what she felt caused her that intoxication which is not happiness, but despair of the self. Tumbling the contents of cupboards to the floors, she eliminated, rearranged, put them back in new order, working as relentlessly as he; conflict wrested her from the immediate moment to later eventualities, and she saw herself handing his wages through the crack in a door, her other hand held to her throat—again her mother's gestures. The shock came when, the day having risen to its zenith and declined, she saw that the light was beginning to fade. She no longer heard the sounds of his effortful labor and, seized with a fear that he might have entered the house, explored it from attic to basement, finding it hers alone, empty. From the terrace she saw that the door of the garden house was ajar—he had left, no doubt, not waiting to be paid. But this surmise, too, was wrong. He lay stretched out on the floor, sleeping. Her step had awakened him and he turned his eyes to her.

"I expected you'd come to the house to be paid," she said.

"I intended to but fell asleep."

"If you'll come to the door, I'll pay you now."

He smiled, yawning. "I could sleep forever. Would you let me sleep here tonight?"

It took control for her to speak calmly. "I'm sorry, but I can't let you do that."

"Why not?"

"Because—because, don't you see, I can't!"

"Is it because you're alone?"

"Not only that." She looked away. "I'll be in the house when you want your money. You said you wanted it today."

"Yes." He rose to his feet in a single, slow, unwinding movement. It's time for both lunch and dinner."

A pang ran through her, guilt for having munched her own midday sandwich, forgetting—no, not even thinking—that he might

120

have no money to buy food. "You should have told me," she said.

He shrugged. "It doesn't matter, I'm used to it."

He pulled on his T-shirt and followed her to the studio doorway and waited. When she returned with her purse, all fear of him gone, she found him staring through the screen at the portrait of herself on the easel.

"That's you," he said, factually.

She blushed. "Yes. How many hours did you work?"

"Six."

She counted out bills and handed them to him. He took them, stuffing them into the pocket of his pants.

"Did you really mean it—that you won't let me sleep where I was?"

"I . . . It's not fair to ask such a thing. Please go now."

"I'd be very careful and quiet. No one would know."

"But don't you understand, I don't know who you are?"

"My name is Tavio—easy to remember." He saved her another refusal. "If you should find me working early in the morning, you wouldn't know where I'd slept, would you?"

"Good night," she said.

"I'll see you." Making a salute with one hand, he loped away down the drive.

The driveway was now clear enough for her to get out in the car; he had thoughtfully set aside the unplanted bushes. But now she wanted to go nowhere. *I misjudged him* was her thought; then, with honesty, she qualified it: *No, I misjudged myself.* Tavio: though she was not good at names, she knew his was one she would remember. His telling it to her, as if it explained everything, should really have made her think of him indifferently. But the name had lodged itself in her consciousness. She dreaded the perimeter of hours that would lead to morning and his return, and prepared to face the first full night of her life alone.

Offices of clinical psychiatrists often contain unusual objects as decoration, and so do their bedrooms. Since their lives are, virtually, one long busman's holiday in which patients' problems are never far from their thoughts, bedrooms are, in a way, extensions of their places of business. Dr. Ingle's was no exception. It contained, in addition to the sound, comfortable bed and chairs

121

and fine Sheraton chest-on-chest (handed down through Susan Ingle's side of the family), two Egyptian burial masks, a pair of oars crossed on the wall above the bed, the invariable etching of Sigmund Freud, and numerous Aztec and other Mexican artifacts. These contrasted oddly with the photographs on top of the chest —Susan, at the time Ingle courted her, a snapshot of Houghton Ingle in white tunic, standing outside the Institute for Living (when it was still called The Hartford Retreat), and a glossy of Bobby Ingle, wearing his soccer clothes at the Adamville School before he flunked out.

The bedroom had two large windows, one overlooking the garden at the rear of the house, the other facing the Cadle garage, or, rather, the southernmost wall of it—the side Rafe Cadle, at the supervisors' meeting, had promised to slap a coat of paint on and hadn't. On this clapboard wall was painted a six-foot, realistic cigar with a long ash at the tip, a survival from forty years ago, when billboards and painted signs had been put up wherever advertising companies pleased. Beneath the cigar, in letters and a numeral that could be seen at some distance, was the legend, WHITE OWL 5¢. Dr. Ingle, who looked at modern paintings now and then, often thought the 5 might well have been painted by Robert Indiana or Jasper Johns; in fact, it was so well painted he considered it put both those artists well in the shade.

Ingle had awakened refreshed after his night and was glad it was a Monday, because on Mondays—always barring some unforeseen patient crisis—he did not go to his Tuliptrees office until after lunch. He had had his usual hearty breakfast of fresh pears, two coddled eggs, Danish pastry and coffee, brought to him in bed by Mrs. Schaaf, the Ingle housekeeper and cook. Daily, or at least on days when Mrs. Schaaf was there, he gave thanks for her, because Susan Ingle was a poor cook, indeed not a cook at all; often, when Mrs. Schaaf was sick or away, Ingle found himself munching marshmallows on his way to and from Tuliptrees, or—greatest of cholesterol sins—having a cheeseburger somewhere along the way. Mrs. Schaaf liked to spoil him, not only because she considered Susan Ingle a dilatory wife, but also because she liked him and was impressed by his being a doctor.

Now the first cigarette, smoked in a holder with a filter in it, and Ingle was ready for that time of the week he relished most, three entire hours in which he would be undisturbed. The photographs on the chest symbolized nearest concerns—Susan, becoming daily more obsessed with numbers in any form, bridge, canasta and Russian bank when only one widow was available, even solitaire when she was alone; Houghton, no longer a concern, the son perfect who, following his internship at Hartford, would join his father at Tuliptrees, to take some of the burden from him; and Bobby. But Ingle didn't dwell on his younger son; the talk with him had been disturbing, and, like the good father-psychiatrist he was, Ingle had delivered the memory of it to his unconscious, in the hope that a solution for Bobby would rise to the surface of itself.

He reached for his writing board and pen and took from the bedside table one of several black notebooks. It had been much handled and consulted, judging by its foxed edges, and on the front was written, in Ingle's rather scrawly hand, "Cadle Notes and Observations," the sum of the study he had been conducting for over ten years.

To drive from his mind the many distracting noises of any Corner morning, he opened the notebook and methodically turned pages, spot-reading, as was his habit, the many entries before entering notes for this week. His eyes traveled quickly down the pages as he occasionally lighted a fresh cigarette, or let his gaze stray for a moment to the White Owl cigar and the 5.

In the early pages the material was somewhat generalized, the kind of notations any sharp observer might make from a distance, in this case the thirty feet separating the Ingle and Cadle houses, and the hundred-odd feet beyond, where the gas pumps were, and where space for parking could be seen obliquely from the north window. These early entries had been limited by the wall on which the cigar was painted, though there was a small window in the lower part, where, looking down, Ingle had been able to hear and observe activities in the garage; the second floor, windowless, had made information about what went on in the Cadle living quarters less easy to garner.

One early entry, made almost ten years ago, began:

Cadle is a white male in his thirties, of stocky and muscular build, with remarkably thick red, almost carrot-colored hair;

the body hair also is red, androgenically distributed. Subject probably is of mixed Celtic and English stock, though it is possible, judging from long monologues delivered to assistants during the repair of automobiles, that another strain may be present, probably Polish.

Farther on was an entry about the birth of the Cadles' third daughter, which had occurred six or seven years earlier, transcribed directly from Rafe Cadle's speech heard through the window:

"Goddammit, I hoped that when Mae pupped Edie, she'd give me a boy. I always wanted a boy. Three girls are one too many."

The family, it was clear from the entries of this period, were then hard-working and relatively contented; but that the wife had "pupped" a girl rather than the boy Cadle hoped for had been the beginning of the trouble. Ingle had commented here:

This child was not christened, apparently. The family seems to have no religious affiliations, the father invariably working from dawn to dark on Sundays as on weekdays, the wife rarely leaving the house.

On the following pages were other isolated details of the Cadles' daily lives. At some point, shortly after the third daughter was six years old, Cadle had begun to show signs of personality change, Ingle had noted:

Where once he was jolly and good-natured, he now is often surly toward his wife and daughters—though never his customers—showing classic symptoms of removal and long periods when he exhibits no emotional responses whatever. Typical schizoid detachment.

From here on, entries were dated and more detailed:

July 4, 1955. Subject and wife engaged in violent quarrel over "getting off the lot" (actual phrase, repeatedly used). When wife complains that she never gets to go out anywhere, subject counters with the now standard accusation that he was well on his way to becoming "somebody" in his world, but that on learning that the third daughter was not his, "all I ever believed about house and home"—his phrase—"fell to pieces." He added, "All I got now is work, it helps me forget that nigger bastard you pupped on me." This quarrel was followed by violence—use of strap or whip on the wife, and, afterward, on all three daughters.

Here on a fresh page, Ingle had written:

After this, Cadle began to confine himself almost entirely to working in the garage, indeed, sometimes sleeping there also, when quarreling upstairs has been protracted. Subject has aged markedly—fronto-occipital baldness, florid complexion, weight gain, marked lordosis while standing at pumps. Severe beating of two older daughters continues. Both are known locally as "five-dollar girls" (is this why he beats them?) but also give themselves gratis as, according to Cadle's increasingly frequent tirades, their mother did, when he was in the navy, and later, before opening garage business, when he worked in a factory near Trenton. Subject obviously from time to time drinking heavily.

This background grew ever more detailed as the years passed and Dr. Ingle's notes thickened. It was in 1958 that Cadle, suddenly, had detached himself emotionally from his family, becoming obsessed with new foreign cars that were beginning to flood the American market. At this time he painted, himself, the secondary sign on the garage front: THE AUTOMOBILE MAN. FOREIGN MAKES A SPECIALTY.

Ingle discussed the motives for this:

Cadle has gathered around him not only many drivers of the cars he repairs (evidently skillfully) but also young boys of this and other villages, who seem to have nothing better to do than idle about the place. Cadle seems impelled by motives entirely escapist and often works past midnight. One motive clearly has become established: an effort to detach himself from his wife while retaining control of the daughters sadistically. Effort not entirely successful. Subject's drinking still spasmodic but heavy, and increasing in frequency. After imbibing, his speech becomes loud and his breathing stertorous.

The older daughters absent themselves from the premises whenever possible, but are foully abused and punished when they return.

Here the sections of the study became enriched with transcriptions of actual dialogues, and as Ingle read through these, he felt a twinge of guilt at the method by which he had "broken through" the barrier of the upper Cadle walls.

This had happened quite by accident. Susan Ingle, being a gardener, though an indifferent one, received many catalogues from nurseries and, to judge from what almost daily appeared in the mailbox, was on countless mailing lists. One day Ingle had brought in the day's letters, and among them was a catalogue from an Oregon firm specializing in tricky bathroom shelves, plastic shower appurtenances and the like. As he leafed through it, his eye was caught by an advertisement for a gadget with the tantalizing name of Big Ear. The diagram illustrating it showed what appeared to be half radio speaker and half miniature radar. The copy alongside the illustration invited, "Listen in on your friends up to ½ mile away! Evenings of innocent fun! *You hear everything without being detected!* 'Ear' transportable anywhere, operates for pennies on regulation flashlight batteries. Only $49.95 plus shipping charges." After a brief conflict about the moral issues involved, Ingle ordered Big Ear for use in collecting more specific Cadle material, and had it sent to his office, from which he smuggled it into his bedroom; when not in use, it was kept locked in a closet.

Big Ear, whatever its intrusive immoralities, had been a shot in the arm to the Cadle study, and a tape recorder followed in due course. The investigation had been flagging; the older daughters had married and left home, and without the tensions they created the household had been, for a time, relatively quiet. It was when Ingle put Big Ear and the playback of tapes into which it had "spoken" to use that he was able to make his detailed entries. After all, he reasoned, Big Ear and the tape were serving a legitimate purpose; all names would be altered when the final paper appeared in *The Psychiatric Quarterly;* and it was no more dishonest than Pentothal or, for that matter, the telephone tappings and tapings of conversations allegedly conducted by the FBI. Ingle turned to one of the "Big Ear" pages:

November 4, 1959. First ego-dissembling factors observed. From overheard conversations it is clear subject has questioned his being the father of Edie from the beginning. Accused wife today of being a whore and having had relations with many men during his absences in the war years and afterward—the *leitmotiv* of most quarrels. Edie, he insists, shows signs of colored blood and is the daughter of Acie Stanes, one of wife's younger paramours. This the wife denies, but when cowed by subject's violence, concedes Edie may not be his daughter. "But Acie wasn't a real nigger," she insists; "he wasn't much darker than you or me. 'Beginner brown' was what he was—*if* it was him." She, herself, seems unsure of who the father actually is. Edie is not present during these violent episodes and as yet apparently knows nothing of Cadle's accusation, though she senses something is very wrong. Subject now "punishes" his wife and the "daughter" by running the cars in the garage and those in the lot outside for long periods and at all hours. Often he can be seen manipulating the accelerator pedals in rhythms suggestive of infantile or adolescent masturbation, slowly at first, then increasingly rapidly until "orgasm" (*i.e.*, the maximum use of engine power) is reached. He then proceeds to the next car, repeating the action. Elation accompanies these performances, and there is, even, an expression on his face after shutting off the motors which suggests the moment of disgust following sexual satiation. Subject seems to be endeavoring to confirm the image he once had of himself as sexually athletic.

Another page flipped:

August, 1961. It was at this time that investigator filed complaint with Planning Board and Supervisors, questioning Cadle's right to operate a garage in this area. Though investigator has had many confrontations with the subject, most were casual, daily greetings. Meeting to discuss Cadle's removal was upsetting to all parties except, curiously enough, Cadle himself. Subject's concealed aggression was evident in his offer to paint out cigar advertisement. But he is consciously proud of his refusal to meet community standards of cleanliness and conduct, and being condoned by Planning Board in his behavior. . . .

September, 1962. The subject earns considerable money from his business, but except for necessities of food and warmth, spends nothing, according to his wife, who accuses him of hoarding. He repeatedly ruminates on the day when he will be able to get a price of $45,000 for the corner on which the garage is located. Edie is beginning to manifest ambivalence to the beatings Cadle administers, though these are decreasing in frequency if not in severity. She addresses him, both when affectionate and when pleading, as "Papa-Daddy," perhaps an insistence of her unconscious that the role he plays with her is less paternally double than ambivalently "father-lover." Subject obviously derives sadistic satisfaction from these punishments, and is usually intoxicated, but experiences guilt afterward, when he reverts to the compulsive racing of the engines. Since drunkenness is not, as yet, habitual, it is probable that his bouts are brought on by the abrasive factor of sexual desire for his "daughter," of which feeling he is becoming more and more conscious. Thus, his manipulation of the motors is an outlet for his fear that he may lose control of himself and yield to his libidinous wishes, which the punishments conceal. Whenever circumstances intensify this interest, he threatens to "strap" Edie in the pattern of transferring his guilt to her. Edie protects herself as best she can by absenting herself during subject's depressed days, but is obviously over-fond of him in masochistic ways. . . .

February, 1963. Subject is evidencing physical decline due to increased drinking. Beer is consumed in massive quantities, as many as 75 to 100 cans being put out weekly for the garbage collector, a crony, who jestingly congratulates him on the number. But whiskey is also used, usually in pint bottles kept near the cars under repair. Subject's tolerance for alcohol is very high. Conditions limiting the study rule out more than cursory observations, but subject suffers from vascular distension, dyspnea, ataxia, and is extremely florid and edematose;

his face and torso are covered with blotches caused by extrava-
sation of blood below the skin. . . .

May, 1964. Relations between subject and wife have
reached breaking point. She nags him incessantly, any subject
or incident bringing on long harangues. Cadle, when matters
upstairs become unbearable, takes refuge at rear of garage,
where he burns greasy rags and debris in a rusty oil drum.
These fires appear to ease his tensions somewhat, and have an
almost ceremonial quality. Frequently, too, he drives cars up
and down the road, to make sure they "work." Neither wife
nor "daughter" show inclinations to flee the situation, though
former is overly permissive of Edie's many dates, in the hope
that she may, like the other daughters, marry and "escape."
Motor exhaust from manipulation of motors increasing, fumes
intensified by unseasonably hot weather. Subject now gives
marked evidence of psychomotor degeneration. Edie, intuiting
his active sadistic need, and unconsciously acknowledging the
passive masochism in herself, responds with reciprocal aggres-
siveness. Some eruption of the extremely strained relations
between the three may be expected.

After reading this entry, Ingle closed the notebook. Somehow
today he could not bring himself to get out Big Ear and listen
and transcribe, even set the tape to do it for him. He had taken
great pains with the study; it was nearing completion, but now
he felt an onrush of that very acedia of which he accused his
wife. Replacing the notebook, he got up, showered again because
of the rising heat, shaved and was downstairs half an hour before
lunch.

Susan was in the garden, paying off the yardboy, who had
spent the morning weeding the periwinkle beds and digging up
tufts of grass that had grown between the terrace flagstones.
Lunch was laid beneath the trees. It was a beautiful garden, if a
small one, entirely planted with white flowers, which Susan preferred; the beds of roses and peonies perfectly complemented the
white Greek Revival dentil blocks and cornices of the house.

"Sleep well?" Susan greeted him.

"Very well." Ingle returned her kiss.

"You were snoring when I came up last night," said Susan; "the

129

girls stayed late, so I didn't look in to say good night." Though the Ingles still sometimes had sex relations, they long since had settled for separate bedrooms, partly because Ingle preferred the north room and Susan the larger of the two second-floor bedrooms at the front of the house. "And how goes Operation Exhaust?"

This was shorthand for the Cadle study. "Didn't go. I didn't feel like working on it this morning. My contributing anxieties were too much."

"Speaking of contributing anxieties, Dick—this smell of gasoline and exhaust!" Susan sniffed and made a face. "Though I suppose it has been worse."

"Yes, I smell it," Ingle said. A light, gauzy exhalation could be detected drifting through the thick yew hedge. "But this is America."

"Not only America. Do you remember Rome two years ago? And Paris? We almost suffocated. Your mail's on the table. Your new *Encounter* came."

Ingle placed the magazine to the left of his plate, along with letters he would open at Tuliptrees. "How much do you pay that boy who weeds?" he asked.

"Dollar and a half an hour and transportation."

"Transportation? He has a car, hasn't he?"

"Well, his gas to and from Chalfont, where he lives. If you knew how hard it is to get anyone to come and work. To show you, Miriam Glidden telephoned to ask if just possibly the boy I had knew of someone to plant her new rhododendrons. Have you seen them?"

Ingle shook his head.

"They're simply gorgeous. It seems Cort Glidden bought them before he died. They're to hide her view of the luncheonette."

"Well, why doesn't she get the nursery where he got them to plant?"

"They didn't come from a nursery." Susan went on to elaborate and Ingle detached himself from her detail, as he had learned to do with a garrulous analysand. Where he picked her up again was "But imagine her calling me!"

"Why shouldn't she?"

"She only called because she wanted something, and her sister

130

left last night. Maybe she's finding out what being alone is like. If she'd learn to play bridge—"

"She won't."

"Such a pity. Her sister wouldn't either." Here Ingle again closed his ears.

"About Bobby, Susan," Ingle broke in when he could. "It seems to me that with a strapping boy like him around, you shouldn't have to go to Chalfont for help."

"Bobby's still sleeping," Susan said, her inflection making clear this was not her fault. "He came in, oh, I don't know—after I got up to take an aspirin before my last sleep."

Mrs. Schaaf had come out from the kitchen with the Thermos tureen from which Susan served cold soups in summer. Susan waited until Mrs. Schaaf had gone indoors again. Then she said, "Dick, you did speak to Bobby?"

"We had quite a talk."

"Well?"

"It was nothing you'd care to hear about."

"By which I take it you got nowhere with the Edie Cadle thing."

"I got nowhere with it, but Bobby did."

"Dick, what do you mean?"

"I told him he could go out with her if he likes. He likes."

"Dick, really!"

"She seems very popular," Ingle said. "So popular that she had a date last night, anyway, with someone else."

"Then where did Bobby go in my car?"

"I don't know."

"He took it."

"And brought it back all right?"

"Yes," Susan said, "I checked when I got up."

Ingle was not going to go into his reasons for letting Bobby do as he wanted. "I daresay, if he's still asleep at this hour, he found something to do."

"Dick, is this all you care about this Edie Cadle thing? You know the kind of people they are!"

"Yes, Sue, I know." He sighed. "Dear, I have three analytic hours this afternoon and a control conference afterward."

"But you haven't time to talk about your own son."

131

"I have time, sometimes; but when I do, you're playing cards."

Susan never argued this. She said, "I suppose it's all a part of what's gone so wrong with us."

That was one Ingle never argued.

"Surely, we can talk now, Dick," Susan pursued. "What *are* we going to do about Bobby?"

"I wish I knew."

"But, Dick, you of all people should know what's the matter with him. You help other people."

"I *try* to help others," Ingle qualified. "Evidently I can't help Bobby."

"What *is* the matter with him?"

"If you want it straight—Bobby's struggling to find a personal myth by which he can live independently of the social myth, which has failed to work for him."

"That's gibberish to me. Tell me in plain words."

"In plain words? After last night, I've about come to the conclusion we should let him entirely alone."

"Let him go on wasting his summer, his life?"

"Let him waste the summer. About his life, he'll have to work that out for himself."

"But he doesn't want to *do* anything."

"Except eat the best food and sleep and go out with girls and be given twenty dollars to have fun with. I know," Ingle said.

"And sleep the clock around," Susan added. "Dick, why is he like this? He seems so bored."

"I daresay he is."

"But why?" Susan's expression was almost tortured in its intensity. "Houghton wasn't like that—he used to do all my weeding without my ever having to ask, anything else I wanted, too. Haven't we done everything for Bobby we did for Houghton?"

"Houghton's another organism."

"He takes after *my* side of the family," Susan said.

Ingle did not dispute this. He waited. "Bobby simply wants not to work and to take no responsibility."

"And read. He reads all day. I worry about his eyes."

"Don't worry about his eyes."

Susan came back to Edie Cadle. "I simply won't have him paying attention to some horrible girl like the Cadles' daughter."

132

"She's pretty," Ingle said.

"But everyone knows what she is."

"Do you?"

This was when Susan wished she weren't married to a psychiatrist. "I have eyes and ears, and so do you, Dick."

"Yes," Ingle said, remembering he had the biggest ear of all; he had never told Susan about the method that had brought his Cadle study forward into focus. "She's a girl living in sordid circumstances, yes, but who are we to say Bobby can't go out with her if he pleases?"

"But her morals! She's very free with herself, everyone says."

"Well, that's Bobby's problem. What would you say if I told you Bobby's as free with himself as Edie Cadle, when he has the chance to be?"

"I wouldn't believe you. Bobby's my son, and I know he's not that kind of boy."

"He's my son, too, and it's true. He told me. I asked him."

"But who is it *with?*"

"That I didn't ask. Sue, the sooner we both realize that teenagers have sex—casual sex, they call it—the sooner I think we'll come to grips with what's wrong with Bobby. If there is anything wrong with him. He may simply need more time in which to grow up."

Susan was upset. She lighted a fresh cigarette, her second since the discussion began. Her smoking routine, like her recourse to numbers, was compulsive; in his youth Ingle had seen some actress who had used the cigarette the same way—the extraction from the pack, the tapping of the end, the bobbing between lips as, through speech, a match was held to it. "But we weren't like this, Dick."

"That's got nothing to do with it," Ingle tried to explain. "Stop trying to strangle Bobby with those apron strings. Not that I think you could."

"Do you mean you ask me to condone this—this casual sex you speak of? To not object to his wanting to date the Cadle girl?"

"I mean that exactly. There are worse things—those two men down the road, for one."

"Hubbard's a gentleman, and they say deWillig's from a noble Swedish family. *I* don't know, Dick; the country's full of unmarried men like them. Everybody knows them, they go everywhere."

Susan coughed on her cigarette. "Have you any reason to think they might seduce Bobby?"

"They've already tried."

"But why didn't you warn me of this before? I'd have forbidden—"

"Stop forbidding. I didn't know until last night. Don't worry, Bobby can take care of himself. That's not the kind of sex that interests him, though he's probably had a number of homosexual experiences, as have most boys of his age." Ingle added the "probably" because he wanted to get no deeper into the discussion.

Mrs. Schaaf came back at this moment, bringing the rest of the lunch in a dome-covered silver dish. After they were alone again and Susan was ladling out the vichyssoise, she said, "You used that word last night in front of the girls, and I don't like it. *I* never had any such experiences." She stood or fell by what was germane to her own experience.

"Nor did I. We're exceptions, I can tell you. After my years at Tulip, I could tell you things about your bridge girls you wouldn't believe."

"Please don't." Susan tired easily during discussions, and she cared little for her husband's shop talk. "That reminds me," she said. "You had a Tulip call about an hour ago. You're to call back."

Ingle put down his spoon.

"Dick, do finish your lunch. It can't be too urgent—maybe your girl who thinks she's Liz Taylor."

Ingle got up. "She's no girl, and she's the most urgent case I have at the moment. I'll call now." He went into the house. When he returned, his car keys were in his hand.

"Dick, you haven't eaten a thing."

"I know, dear, I'm sorry. But I have to go."

"I'd arranged your favorite—tongue in aspic, with horseradish sauce. Try to remember to eat a sandwich or something during the afternoon."

"I will," Ingle promised.

As he backed out of his drive and turned in the direction of Tuliptrees, he saw that Miriam Glidden had been successful in finding someone to plant the rhododendrons. Through his trifocals he looked at the man straining to lift the heavy shrubs, sweat pouring from his shoulders with the effort. The man straightened as Ingle went by and he saw the chain of roses tattooed on his chest. He waved a friendly hand—a greeting not returned—and an intuition struck him. The symbols of psychological analysis are compelling, and Ingle always found it difficult not to be analytic when confronted with the stuff of life. The best he could do, as he brought his eyes back to the road, was to repress the intuition and try to be a good across-the-road neighbor and mind his own business.

CHAPTER 3

"Yes, your penis is somewhat small for a man of your size and build." Dr. Kidder's dispassionate admission, as he turned away and went to the basin to wash his hands, caused Don MacFinden to redden. Not that what the doctor said was news to Don; he'd lived with his small penis all his life, when adolescent hoping against hope that it would grow and become as large as those of other boys; but it hadn't, it had remained small, and, though normally developed, had been the major humiliation of his life. After his confirmation, he had gotten up courage enough to consult his pastor about it, but the only suggestion he had made was that Don should pray and hope that God would hear him and do something about it. Don and the pastor had prayed together, kneeling side by side in the rectory; but if God had heard, He had not interceded to aid nature.

As Don put on his clothes, he was glad Dr. Kidder wasn't looking at him. The examination had embarrassed him, as physical exams always did. This one hadn't been as bad as some, his army one, for example, when the sawbones had lined up thirty boys for short arm inspection and yelled, "Hold out your dicks, pull back your foreskin if you've got one and when I come to you, squeeze!" After which he proceeded down the line, making jokes as he went. When he reached Don, he had wisecracked, "You shoulda been thrown back and fucked over, boy—*that's* not going to make any girl happy!" Don had had to live with this and endless jokes that followed all during his army hitch.

Dr. Kidder hadn't been like that at all. When his nurse beckoned Don to come in, the doc had advanced and shaken hands warmly, as though greeting an old friend. Dr. Kidder was only a little older than Don and showed the pinpointed attention and immediate personal interest of a young doctor starting practice, not yet calloused by years of listening to patients' troubles; like the beginner he was, he was not only earnest but said a little too much, Don thought. Don had chosen to come to Dr. Kidder rather than one of the Olympia or Trenton physicians, and had driven up to Dutch Falls after his lunch hour at the quarry.

"And how did you find your way up here?" Dr. Kidder asked, after he had motioned Don to a chair opposite his desk.

"Why, I picked you out of the phone book," Don confessed. "You see, I live down in Cope's Corner and what I have to ask about is rather personal, so I figured coming to you would be, well, more private."

"I see. Well, ask away," Dr. Kidder said.

Don blurted it out. "I came to consult you because I'm having one hell of a time with my sex life."

"Are you married?"

"Yes. I've just returned from my honeymoon."

"Then you haven't been married long."

"A little over two weeks."

"Have you any reason to think there might be an organic cause for your 'hell of a time,' as you call it?"

"I'm built very small."

Dr. Kidder nodded, with no more expression than if Don had been reporting a hangnail. "But your sex drives are normal?"

"As normal as anybody else's, I guess." Don had been through this with the army psychiatrist, and he answered straight from the shoulder.

"When did you first have intercourse?"

"Sex? When I was thirteen."

Dr. Kidder detected the slight distinction in Don's voice. "Was your first experience with girls?" The question came rapidly and Don replied equally quickly.

"Of course, girls, but if you're asking about the other, I went to Olympia High and I was no different from other guys."

"You mean, you conducted experiments with each other?"

136

"You could call them that, yes."

"What kind of experiments were they?"

"Oh, you know. Horsing around in the showers."

"And were you the active or passive one in these experiments?"

"I guess the active. They weren't experiments, actually; all any of us needed was to pop our nuts, and that's what we did. If you want to know did I like boys, hell no! How did we get onto this? I didn't come here to jaw over kid stuff. I like girls, period."

"Of course. But it's not at all unusual for boys of that age to indulge in such activities," Dr. Kidder said, dismissing it. "Now, tell me, if you can, why you think you're having trouble in relations with your wife. It is your wife?"

"Yes. Well, I think it's because Nancy has a very large vagina. I'm small, as I said—and I guess that's it. I can't seem to satisfy her the way I'd like to."

"You mean, bring her to climax."

"Yes, I mean that."

"Have you ever succeeded?"

"No, not once."

The doctor nodded. "I'd like you to undress completely. We may as well do a thorough physical while we're at it."

Don was used to being told how well coordinated he was and how good his reflexes were, and Dr. Kidder guessed right away he'd been a boxer. He got through all the doc's proddings and pokings and tappings like a breeze, until it came to the prostatic examination.

"If you should have an erection or slight emission, don't pay any attention," Dr. Kidder said, as he inserted his finger and explored Don's rectum. Don winced and bore it. Later, when the doctor pushed back his foreskin and fingered the meatus, Don's penis rose to its full size. "Very good," the doctor said; "you're experiencing psychophysical erethrism." He added that tumescence is the automatic consequence of manipulation in most persons; Don's triggerlike response was not unusual and indicated normal, healthy reflexes. It was then he agreed with Don about how small he was. Seeing his embarrassment, he added, as he dried his hands and went to his desk, "Well, we can't all be built like stallions, you know."

Don had come prepared for some jokes and couldn't help wondering if Dr. Kidder was built like a stallion himself; the doctor was only a little taller than he, and through the white tunic buttoned up the side Don could guess he couldn't boast the muscular development *he* could; thanks to his boxing and work at the quarries, he knew he had a fine physique. With his tow hair and fresh, healthy looks, Don had never had trouble getting dates. But this other thing, that had brought him to Dr. Kidder, was something you couldn't tell about; he'd learned that in his twenty-one years. In the showers you found out that the runt of the football team was, as the phrase went, really hung, while six-foot Adonises were apt to be as small as himself.

Was there anything that could be done? He watched the doctor as he made notes on the card, on which he had printed Don's name in block letters, taking his time about it, penning a few words, then pausing to think. Don guessed he might be doing this to give him time to get over his embarrassment and compose himself for the talk he supposed would follow. A telephone rang in the next room and there was a knock.

"Come," said Dr. Kidder, looking up, and the door was opened by the nurse. The doctor excused himself and went out.

Don was glad for the break, because no matter how he tried to conceal it, he was nervous. He felt cold and his hands were sweating. He almost wished he hadn't come. Clearly his "endowment"— that was what his pastor had so long ago called it—was not enough for Nancy. On their wedding night in the hotel at Mérida, all had seemed to go well at first, until, during sexual foreplay, Nancy had performed the ritual, feminine caress of his scrotum. All at once her mood had subtly changed; and though Don had been deeply roused, her feeling transmitted itself to him and he felt deflated. Or simply tired, perhaps, which could have been the case, their wedding having been the exhausting display it was. Nancy's parents had insisted on an outmoded formality—morning dress, six bridesmaids, flower girls, a wedding breakfast with a band. Neither Nancy nor Don had really wanted this, and they had been grateful to get on the jet for Miami, where they changed to another for Yucatán.

"What's the matter, honey?" Don had asked.

"Nothing, dearest. Why?"

"Is it because I'm small? Is that why you drew away?"

"I didn't!"

"But something happened," Don insisted.

"No, no; you're imagining things," Nancy protested, and, as if to reassure him, had locked herself around him, kissing him passionately. "What difference could it possibly make, about that?"

Don had reflected at the time that his private parts were not unknown to Nancy, nor were hers to him; they'd had relations a number of times during the period between their engagement and marriage, not always consummated and, invariably, furtive ones, but relations nevertheless. There had been no drawing back on Nancy's part then, as there had not been with other girls he'd had before her; but the marriage bed and a wife were another story, evidently.

Perhaps it was merely nuptial tension; marriage manuals said that many couples did not experience orgasm the first night. Or maybe it had something to do with a book Don's best man had jokingly sent as a wedding present, which bore the unpromising title *The Perfumed Garden of the Shaykh Nefzawi,* but was a real humdinger of sexual information and fantasy, listing the eleven classic positions for intercourse, and another twenty-five, presumably unclassic, practiced in India. Nancy had abstracted it from the other gifts and they had read parts of it aloud together; it had relaxed some of the nervousness they both felt about all the visiting of relatives and rehearsals Nancy's mother had made them go through. Part of the book seemed to have nothing to do with sex and contained such suggestions as having the woman don and let fall a pair of long drawers, and, after bending over, placing her neck in the opening and turning a somersault. They had been disappointed, actually, to find Nefzawi, with his prescriptions of techniques, his superstitious concerns about potency, more puritan than hedonist.

At the bachelor dinner much of the discussion had been about the book. Don hadn't enjoyed the ribald talk too much, since what it all came down to, according to one of his ushers, a medical student at the University Hospital in Philadelphia, was that what women liked was the largest possible penis inserted as deeply as possible; he'd added that it worked both ways, that what men essentially desired in a woman was a deep, prehensile vagina; "The Big Fit," he said, was "in" and always had been. Don hadn't

139

paid much attention to the rest of the talk—recipes for distilling jackal gall, said to insure potency, records for long-standing erections, and how many virgins could be deflowered by one man in one night. None of it had been aphrodisiac to Don, only funny; he had agreed with Nancy, while they read the book, that they had no need to kitchen-test the old Shaykh's recipes and could knock spots off him.

Whether something had "happened" or not, Don found himself detumescent on his wedding night.

"Do you hate me?" he asked, as they lay in the tropical darkness.

"Of course not, you silly. You're probably tired from everything. I am," Nancy answered, being nice about it, making it easy. Whatever it had been, Don had not been able to get to sleep. Next morning, after breakfast, they'd both felt better and had gotten up early, to go on to Chichén Itzá. Nancy had been wonderful then, too, as though things hadn't petered out and they hadn't had that long, clinical talk.

As he waited for Dr. Kidder to return, Don went over that time after their first breakfast, as he had gone over it daily since his marriage. Neither he nor Nancy had been tired then, and he had been very ardent, spending himself a little fully for a man who had to climb over jungle ruins. He had been wildly gratified, so gratified that he'd been able to conceal from himself that Nancy's pleasure had been somewhat less than his until it was too late.

"Christ!" he had muttered as the guide knocked on their door, reminding them it was time to be ready. "I've come. I couldn't help it."

"You were divine, darling," Nancy said. "We'd better get up now."

But as the honeymoon lengthened, it became increasingly apparent that Nancy was not experiencing orgasm. Don had tried to tell himself the fault was not his, or not entirely, no matter how small he was "built." Nancy had even complimented him on his hardness, his ability to sustain.

"Darling, you were marvelous, don't worry about it," she said, as she always did.

"But you came for me when we made love before we were married," Don insisted. "I know you did."

140

"I *kind* of did," Nancy qualified; "but that was different."

Those snatched times of lovemaking had taken place in the rear seats of automobiles and mostly involved manual manipulation of Nancy's clitoris and, once, Don had jabbed his penis vigorously against her labia until he ejaculated, the dimensions of the car limiting them to this method, since they could not stretch out. During the honeymoon Don began to wonder if the pessary Nancy's gynecologist had fitted her with could be blamed for their troubles; it smelled of rubber and talcum, and perhaps was enough in itself to discourage that *sostenuto* he supposed was required. At his request, she had put aside the pessary and was on contraceptive pills for the moment—no matter how much the elder MacFinden longed for his first grandchild. But this made little difference, and the plain truth was that he was screwing himself piebald. Luckily, he consoled himself, he was capable of several orgasms in one night; and, since each was more slowly achieved, he hoped their very protraction would serve to bring Nancy to the climax that was mandatory. Some nights, as he struggled, he thought of the wild joke about the whore who was so deep one of her clients, fingering her, had found himself in up to his shoulder and then crawled inside. There, in the distance, he saw a team of horses approaching, driven by an old man with a long, white beard. "How in hell do I find my way back?" the client asked, as the old man approached and reined up. "Danged if I know," was the reply; "I been lost in here for twenty years and ain't never been able to find my way out." It was all a little too much, even for Nancy, and Don blushed as he remembered last night and her plaintive "No, stop! I'm all right—I felt *some*thing, really I did." But Don knew better.

For a small woman, Nancy did seem to be "built deep" as Don was "built small." How he hated thinking of it in those terms; but there it was. Even when they were having premarital sex, the size of Nancy's labia had surprised him, though he had called it excitement then; later, when he discovered how deeply embedded her cervix seemed to be, he had been even more astonished. As Nancy said, "automobile" sex was bound to be different, casual and usually hurried, involving anything short of the real thing—*coitus interruptus,* mutual masturbation, manustupration, the whole frustrating gamut. Nothing at all like the paced, graded excitement of the marriage bed, where there was ample room and time for leisurely approaches. But in a way, their "automobile" sex had had its points, had been less like those Do-It-Yourself instructions in *The Perfumed Garden*. Despite anxieties and guilt about his smallness, the wonderful luxuriance of Nancy's "equipment" (there was that way of thinking again) thrilled him whenever he thought about it—during coffee breaks at the quarries, driving home, showering. Hell! He was getting excited about her now; a little more of this thinking and he'd get another erection, and not one brought on by the doctor.

Don started slightly as Dr. Kidder came back to the consulting room. "Now, Don," he said, bringing his attention back, fingering the card on which his medical history was written, "we have what amounts to a perfect bill of health; except for childhood diseases and a tonsillectomy, you've never been sick, not even an appendectomy."

Don nodded, waiting.

"There is nothing wrong with you whatever, organically; I am forced to conclude that your trouble is psychological."

"Are you suggesting I should see a headshrinker?" Don at once disagreed. "But why? I'm hot as a fox, when it comes to sex—I've never been hotter for anybody than I am for my wife. It's just that I'm too small for her." He quoted what one of the ushers at his wedding, the medical student, had said.

"But the sensation you so wish to give your wife may be less important to her than her sharing in your pleasure," Dr. Kidder said. "This thing about large penises is a hangover from primitive potency worship, as is the importance men attach to having their penis up inside a woman's vagina."

"Then you agree a large penis is considered desirable?"

"Yes, yes. You have no trouble satisfying yourself, Don?"

"No, or at least I have trouble only when I'm afraid I'm not ever going to be able to satisfy my wife."

"Ah, 'afraid'—there's your key word." Dr. Kidder almost pounced on it. "In almost all cases it should be possible for a woman with a large vagina, which you say your wife has, to lead a perfectly satisfactory sex life with a man whose penis is small. In point of fact, the clitoris is the source of all sexual pleasure in women." He shook his head. "Your friend, the medical student, should have told you that, instead of what he did tell you. It seems to me a question of loss of confidence, this feeling of yours that you must deeply penetrate. The danger about this is that, though you have no real inadequacy now, you easily could develop one, and that could lead to marital troubles."

"It's already led to them," Don said miserably.

From the way Dr. Kidder pushed back his chair and stood up, Don could tell the moment of prescription had arrived. "The crux of this is your smallness," he said. "If you could drink a magic potion that would make you bigger, you'd drink it, wouldn't you?"

"And how!" Don said.

"There are no magic potions in this world, but there are other things. Though you have no organic difficulties, this is an inadequacy based on fear. It may be relieved by your wife's experiencing complete satisfaction. Have you ever thought that you might try a prosthetic device?" asked the doctor.

" 'Prosthetic'?" Don looked blank. "I don't know what it means."

"In medical usage, 'supplying a deficiency'; an artificial limb is a prosthetic device, for instance."

"You mean a dildo?" Don asked. "I thought only lesbians used them."

Dr. Kidder showed his distaste for the word. "We prefer another terminology." He saw by Don's expression he had both shocked and offended him.

"No gizmos for me," Don said, using the old army term for any contrived gadget.

"Don't reject the suggestion entirely," Dr. Kidder said, raising a hand. "Whether you know it or not, medicine since ancient times has always recognized your problem, and there are available, through prescription, a number of devices from which you might choose." He opened a desk drawer and brought out a small pamphlet, turning it around so that Don could read it. "This is a reliable one, in my opinion the best. It's called the C.T.A.—merely a trade name for 'Coital Training Aid.' "

Don stared at the pamphlet, on the cover of which was a somewhat abstract representation of an erect penis with a flange at the base, to which was attached elastic for holding it firmly in place. The first word his eye fell on was "impotence."

"But I am not impotent," he said angrily.

"Of course you're not," Dr. Kidder agreed. "Impotence is only one of many conditions which have led to the wide and successful use of the C.T.A. There are other indications for its use. Yours, for one."

Don felt worse than at any time since he'd come to the office, but his hesitation and confusion were, evidently, nothing new to the doctor.

Dr. Kidder waited a moment, then said, "It comes in a number of sizes and circumferences, and I suggest it would be a solution for you. Since you're here, we could decide which size would be best for you—and for your wife—and order it now. It's simply a matter of my telephoning; you'll have it day after tomorrow. I'll get in touch with you then for the fitting and give you the necessary instructions."

Don still hesitated, shaking his head.

"What's your objection?"

"Simply that I have a cock of my own and want to use it," Don answered without hesitation.

"I like your frankness. There's no use beating about the bush in matters as serious as this. Don't worry about that part of it. The C.T.A., when fitted, will conform to your penis in its erectile state and can be attached or removed quickly. If you prefer, it can be put on after intercourse has begun, unobtrusively. Your wife needn't know about it, at first, anyway, though most men find it easy to be frank with their wives about it. It will permit you both the freedom from anxiety you need, and to achieve mutual satisfaction. You will ejaculate normally, and yet remain firm afterward, should your wife's climax be delayed. It has the virtue, you see, of making you independent of the need to 'keep going.' "

Don considered another moment. "It sounds like a real bill of goods," he said, laughing. "What can I lose?"

"I think you'll not regret your decision," Dr. Kidder said.

It took only a moment to decide on the medium-to-large size, which came in two lengths, of which Dr. Kidder suggested the longer. "I may add," he said, "that a small orifice may be made in the tip end, for religious reasons." He handed Don the C.T.A. prospectus. "Why not take this with you, read it at your leisure? I'm not of the school that believes in withholding details of what I prescribe from my patients."

Don was surprised at how quickly he had accepted the idea; the visit to Dr. Kidder ended in a very relaxed way. When he got back to his office at the quarry, he read the prospectus until he knew it practically by heart. It made riotous reading and was much more direct than the old Shaykh's *Perfumed Garden;* he was almost sorry he couldn't show it to Nancy, who would have gotten a charge from its explicitness and lax grammar.

> The C.T.A. [he read] is designed to relieve the problems of patients suffering from psychological and/or organic impotency . . . *ejaculatio praecox,* epispadias . . . marriage counseling. . . . It is a faithful reproduction, with all visual characteristics accurate to the last detail. The plastic used is indestructible and non-toxic . . . magical resemblance to skin texture. . . . It is even tender to the touch!

Don didn't know what some of the words meant and had no dictionary in his office, but was sure that, whatever they were, they had nothing to do with him. He tore the prospectus into small pieces and threw them into his wastebasket. Reading the thing had gotten him excited, and though he knew he would get hell from his father for leaving Number Three before quitting time, went home early. Nancy couldn't understand what the hurry was, but said she was ready for bed any time he was. He had himself a knockout time with her, but was not sorry he had let Dr. Kidder order the C.T.A., because Nancy was as unsatisfied as ever.

Mae Cadle belched. The frozen fish sticks with tartar sauce she had fixed for midday dinner were already giving her digestion trouble, though dessert was still to come.

"'Scuse *me!*" she said, daintily raising her pink paper napkin to her lips. "Something's repeating."

"What in Christ's name was that mess?" Rafe asked, pushing his plate from him. It was the only thing he had said to her since sitting down at table; he had glowered and wolfed his food and Mae hadn't been able to get a word out of him.

"You used to like fish sticks," she reminded him. No matter how calloused from their constant quarreling and bickering, Mae always felt hurt if Rafe didn't like what she put on the table. "But you finished it, and there's cake to come."

145

"I'll skip the cake." Rafe got up. "If you'd stir your stumps and get on over across the river and buy some honest-to-God substantial food, instead of this canned and frozen shit, maybe you wouldn't sound like a sewer pipe."

"Don't use words like that at the table!" Mae protested. "If you'd drive me across the bridge to shop, or let Edie drive me over—"

"You can still walk," Rafe stated, "and Edie's not driving any car of mine." The Cadle Buick was almost never used, though almost daily Rafe ran it up and down the village, like the others, to make sure it was kept limber.

"I'm not walking any bridge, not in this heat, not with a perfectly good car down there." Mae fanned herself with her napkin. "Well, same old story, shoemakers' children never have any shoes."

This was yet another bone with little left on it to pick. Truth to tell, Mae didn't like cooking anyway, and fixing anything like fresh vegetables was not her idea of fun. She liked much less having to go out of the house at all and seldom did; she felt she looked so terrible. Besides, her feet killed her most days, and her legs weren't what they had been. She had long since settled the food problem by phoning her orders to the grocery in Subberton, ordering by the dozen frozen things she could get on in a hurry and staggering them throughout the week. Rafe serviced the grocery's two trucks, so the bills worked out almost even. The household diet consisted of crab this and shrimp that, of wafer-thin sweating steaks and sauces and unlikely soufflés and breaded chops, with liberal desserts of ice creams, thawed cakes and cookies, for Mae's sweet tooth, as she said, never gave her a minute's rest.

She belched again as Rafe went downstairs. It was no wonder her stomach was nervous; her nerves were on edge, too, what with Rafe's blowup at Edie and the news of Acie Stanes. It was a miracle she'd been able to eat anything at all.

The cause of her uneasiness—she had to face it—was the ever-unresolved doubt as to whether Acie Stanes was Edie's real father. Mae was anything but guilt-ridden about her past and didn't fall for all that horse manure about lies having short legs or chickens always coming home to roost. She'd had the call once, even felt the spirit years ago when, nightly, she made a point of listening to

146

radio evangelists; but somehow her faith hadn't stuck. Life had proved too much for it, and now she got more out of watching TV when it was working, or tuning in on the disc jockeys. Yet she still sometimes had her moral days, and this was one of them.

After all, she figured, Rafe had left her to go into the navy, and afterward, too, when he worked down in Trenton; she knew he'd had his jig-jig and plenty of it, as she'd had hers. When you thought of it, many were the girls today who'd married one man to conceal being pregnant by another—her two eldest daughters had. No, she hadn't been like that; she had come to Rafe if not white as snow, at least not already in the family way; their first daughter had been born a safe nine and a half months after they were married. What she'd done while Rafe was away was no different from what other wives did, only most had been smarter than her and hadn't gotten caught. Acie Stanes had been bad luck —could she help it if she'd still had her looks then? If when she was running the pumps and saw Acie driving up she went all queer and funny inside and *had* to have him? Women had feelings like that, just as men did, not that she'd ever been able to get Rafe to admit it, he was so thick-headed. From the time Edie was born there'd been no living with him, and he was getting worse all the time. Most days she couldn't figure out anything about him, what he thought or why he did the terrible things he did, like beating the girls and her until they were almost ready to go on the streets to get away from him. He went from quiet to moody to wild rages over nothing she could see was wrong. When he was still doing his duty by her as a husband, she had stood things better; but ever since he started telling her how awful she looked and what a mess she was, she had hated him. It wasn't only Acie Stanes who bugged him, it was everything and everybody else too. Nights she'd lie next to Rafe, kept awake by the awful sounds he made in his sleep, not the kind of snoring other people did, but a grunting, raging breath in his throat that sounded for all the world like the cars he raced downstairs and couldn't get off his mind, even in his sleep. No other woman would have stood it this long. If only—

If only— That was the story of life. No matter how she thought around it, the doubt was there, would never go away, would stay to torment her and bring her down with gray hairs into her grave. Acie Stanes, though sixteen-seventeen years gone and potato water, as Rafe jeered, still had the power to push away all fears of hellfire and make her remember long-ago joys.

She wiped a tear. The whole fault was life's—and Edie's; and of the two, Edie was the more to blame, for she had brought Acie Stanes back. The way she had been building up hatred for Edie all day almost scared her. Even if Acie wasn't Edie's father—but she wouldn't go back into all that counting and remembering now. She'd think of Edie and her own good. Edie wouldn't understand why she must never see Acie again, but she'd have to take that on credit. A promise was what was wanted now. Maybe it was a blessing in disguise; it was high time Edie got up; she was getting to be too much of an afternoon girl, staying out late, sleeping later. But Mae understood that part of her motive for hauling Edie onto the carpet was curiosity, the wish to know what Acie was like now. She was a little ashamed of this, but she had a right to know, and it was necessary. Rafe wouldn't tell her a thing, it would have to be Edie who did; the two of them worked hand in glove against her anyway. What else could she do? Once she'd made her mind up, she didn't wait, but charged right into the bedroom. To her surprise, Edie was wide-awake, sitting up in bed.

"Well!" Mae began, hands on hips, arms akimbo. "We're going to lay around here all day, are we? You must be slept out by now."

Edie stared straight ahead.

"What are you doing?" Mae demanded. "Daydreaming?"

"Oh, Mom, don't you start on me too!"

"It's time somebody told you what's what," said Mae.

Edie turned her head and looked at her mother calmly. "If anybody's going to tell me anything, it won't be you," she said quietly.

It was irritating, how Edie could be so like Rafe, sometimes imitating what he said, even the way he said it—one more proof of their working against her. Mae decided to take a different tack. "Edie girl, don't say things like that to me. I—"

"Yes, I know"—Edie beat her to it—"you're my mother."

Mae sat down on the bed's edge. "We've got to have a talk."

"I don't want to talk."

"Whether you do or not, you've got to."

"What is there to talk about?"

148

"Honey," Mae said, "I know you told Papa-Daddy you didn't do anything wrong with Acie Stanes, but did you?"

"Why would you care? You never care with anybody else."

"You can tell me the truth," Mae said earnestly. "I have to know. What's he like?"

Edie said nothing to this.

"Tell me if you did anything wrong with Acie Stanes!"

"Why?" Edie asked again. Then, suspiciously, "How did you remember his name?"

"I guess I remembered because it's such an odd one," Mae answered, trying to brush it aside.

Edie wouldn't let it be brushed. "Yes, it's odd—but I only told it to you once. What is this? I saw the way you looked when I told you, too."

"Your Papa-Daddy says he's a bookie."

"What if he is? That's not the reason you're upset. Who is he, somebody you know?"

"Your Papa-Daddy knows him," Mae temporized.

"But you do, too. Don't you?"

Mae hadn't looked ahead. Now she tried to go only halfway. "Well, yes," she admitted, "but it was years ago."

"I don't understand." Edie held her to it. "Acie didn't say anything to me about knowing you."

"He was just a boy when Papa-Daddy and I knew him." This was truth. "How long have you been seeing him?"

"I'm not going to tell you."

"Edie," said Mae, "there are lots of things you don't understand—"

"There sure are!" Edie agreed, interrupting. "This house is *crazy!*"

"You must tell me," Mae persisted, though Edie's temper was rapidly shortening. "Did you let him touch you?"

" 'Touch me,' Mom? Of course I let him touch me! That's what it's all about—you should know!"

"I don't know anything of the kind," said Mae with severity. "I know you've been free with yourself with boys—"

Edie laughed. "Oh, Mom, let up!"

"I just know you have."

"Well, if I have been, I'm not going to tell *you* about it!"

"You are! If you don't, I'll have Papa-Daddy ask you, and you know what that'll lead to."

Edie laughed again, but this time there was an odd catch in her voice.

Mae tried a last time: "Edie—"

But Edie wouldn't let her get anywhere. " 'I'm your mother and you owe it to me.' " She once more took the words from Mae's mouth. "I don't owe you anything. And I'm not as dumb as you think—*I've* heard about what used to go on here when Papa-Daddy was away. Is that who Acie is, somebody who used to come by here then? Is he?"

The tables had been turned. Mae was silent a moment, then said, "What I want for you is some nice boy, like that Bobby Ingle. He's crazy about you."

Edie could be hateful, spiteful, too. "We weren't talking about Bobby Ingle, Mom. We were talking about was Acie one of those who used to come here. How about that, Mom? That's one you owe it to me to answer. But you don't want to, do you?" Her mouth trembled. "It's a crazy day when a girl has to be careful who she goes out with because he might be somebody her mother—"

"Stop! Don't you say it, don't you say *that!*" Mae cried out. "No, nothing like that," she lied firmly.

"Then—*what?*"

Slowly Mae got up from the bed. This was where morality, religion, failed you. She should never have tried to find out anything from Edie; she had only made things worse.

It was clear Edie thought this too. She jumped out of bed and began to pull on her clothes hurriedly.

"And where do you think you're going?" Mae demanded, relieved to be back on mundane questioning.

"Out."

"Don't go off like this," Mae pleaded. "Edie, honey—"

"Shut up!" Edie was dressed now, and without picking up her purse from the bureau or even putting on her bracelets, made for the stairway.

"You better not go down there and get your Papa-Daddy all riled up again," Mae cautioned.

Edie paid no attention. Mae heard her slam the downstairs screen and could hear her walking hastily toward the road.

150

Mae went to the refrigerator, to get a Diet Cola. It was too hot to live, much less do dishes. She found her way to her rocker by the window and sank heavily into it. And then it struck her like a chill. She knew right away what it was. She had fought it too long not to know when it was coming out true and clear. She gave a little sigh, almost of relief. There were only two choices—either Edie was Rafe's child, or she was Acie Stanes's. Through the confused pattern she was trying to straighten out, old years and forgotten dates came back to her and began to fall into place—September, no, *October* it was! And then she *knew:* Acie Stanes and that long, hot August, yes, August had been the very last time she had let Acie have her. It had been Acie!

It had seemed, at first, that this might be one of the rare days when persecution subsided a little, or so Miss Flora Bowyer had at first hoped. But she soon realized that this Monday was to be no different from others, what with the weekend depredations on privacy and property, which could be counted on to reveal themselves one by one as she made her morning rounds. For one thing, there was distinct evidence that all doors had been tampered with; for another, ferns and still more stones from the front wall were missing, as she had known they would be. The flower beds, too, betrayed the marauders, being unusually full of ground glass and —a new cruelty—sharp pieces of broken crockery, cunningly hidden to sever an artery in the unwary. And it was only a little later that an obviously dangerous man (a Colored, if she was any judge, and bent on the mischief inborn in his race) drew up in front of the wall in a large car. At first she thought the sun must be overly bright, because she distinctly saw the car, a very large one of the kind she considered "puffy," as pink against the red shale of the wall stones, those that remained. But pink it was. *Pink!* Well, Coloreds!

Miss Emmeline had noticed the car at almost the same moment, and was equally on guard at her upstairs window. Who knew what terrible plots were being hatched, with all this disintegration between the races? No doubt there was a connection between this disturbance, the Communists and the kite lights, not to mention men who had been at the doors the night before; everyone knew

151

the Russians loved Coloreds—who was that singer who had defected to them and then returned? Somebody.

Neither sister was surprised to see that the horrible Cadles had something to do with it; Cadle had stood, covered with grease (and no doubt *smelling*, thought Miss Emmeline, though from her upstairs vantage she was spared actually knowing), conducting a loud conversation with complete disregard for female sensibilities. Both she and Miss Flora had seen Cadle slap his daughter (if his daughter she was) and had heard some of the phrases he had used. Simply frightful! Not that they hadn't always known the Cadles to be trash, and not too white, at that. Miss Flora had been about to phone the state police and Miss Emmeline to shout her usual "Cadle! *Do* you mind conducting your conversations else-where?" when the Colored in his vulgar conveyance moved on. And only minutes after this, both sisters had heard a series of great thumps, nothing serious, really, only what appeared to be large trees being unloaded at the Glidden house.

But it was always something. Miss Flora went upstairs to confer with her sister. It required more than one to get the story straight; Miss Flora couldn't be everywhere at once, neither could Miss Emmeline. Their policy was to compare notes and try to decide what it all could possibly portend. Miss Emmeline was of the opinion that the Colored had intended abducting Spot, and had been frustrated by the fortunate circumstance that the dog was drying in his basket after his morning bath under the garden pump. Miss Flora said nothing to this; she decided to withhold news of an earlier and much more upsetting intruder, who also had tried to lure Spot away. Spot had not been dressed and decent, but since the abductor, or thief or whatever he could be called, was male, she supposed too much harm had not been done by Spot's nakedness. Emmeline, however, would have been most upset to learn that Spot had been seen without his "frilly"; except when being bathed or walked privately in the rear garden by Miss Flora, he wore a small pair of boxer shorts, to shield the eyes of villagers from the sight of his privates; she, of course, never looked.

Miss Flora prided herself on her restraint: She had recognized the first intruder as the man cavorting on the canal bank—and *that* she was determined to keep from her sister, lest her unfortunate nonsense about Midsummer Men be repeated. But Miss Emmeline, alas, was not to be fooled; long before Miss Flora knew she was awake, she had been watching from her window, alternately observing her sister as she examined the flower beds, employing for this their mother's opera glasses, or, as there began to be signs of life in the luncheonette, their father's binoculars, both kept *instant to hand* on the windowsill. It was at such times that an extra visual dimension helped, for through the glasses Miss Emmeline had been able to see the earlier visitor, *big as life* beneath the apple branches, suspecting who he was. She continued to watch as he went into the luncheonette—changing glasses—and had breakfast, with that Hanter woman, common as barn paint, coiffed and made up as though for some workmen's frolic, hurrying to serve him, wasting no time whatever. Mercifully, Miss Emmeline had been saved from what followed—the Hanter woman, almost as dreadful a monster as her husband *and a hussy to boot,* conducted the man into the luncheonette kitchen and closed the door, confirming what she had always suspected, that it was a front for prostitution, as the Cadle place had been in the past. Not that matters were too much changed there, either; the daughter now *openly* solicited by day, and had been picked up the night before by—*superb putting together!*—the very Colored who had returned her this morning. Who *were* they all? What did they all want in the once peaceful little Corner?

Miss Flora saw her sister was a little too excited for the early hour. "Emmy, put down Our Father's binoculars and get back into bed."

Miss Emmy returned the binoculars to the windowsill; things were for the moment quiet anyway, and Miss Flora then filled her in on the night's thefts and destructions, and they discussed for some time what the pink car and the Colored had meant. Miss Flora held to her theory of the abduction of Spot, Miss Emmeline to hers, that it was all a part of racial disintegration.

"Integration, dear," Miss Flora corrected.

"Thank you, Flora, I prefer *dis*integration," Miss Emmeline said. "That woman, Flora, is soliciting again."

"Which woman?"

"The Hanter woman."

"Really? And whom?"

Miss Emmeline waited a dramatic moment. "Why, the man who stood beneath the apple tree this morning."

"Was there another man, Emmy?"

"Flora, you know there was."

"So many men pass by."

"This was a *special* man," Miss Emmeline insisted, enjoying her sister's discomfiture. "*I* think he and the Midsummer Man you saw on the towpath last night are one and the same!"

"Don't be foolish, Emmy." Safer to return to the luncheonette as a topic, good always for a quarter hour of mutual complaining; for, though Miss Emmeline had jointly signed the deed of conveyance to Al Hanter and knew the ground had been sold, it made more contention if she pretended she did not know this and the Hanters were squatters.

"Was the Hanter woman alone?" Miss Flora asked.

"Quite alone. She took the Midsummer Man into the kitchen and closed the door."

"How shocking!"

"Yes, and when he left, I saw him walking down the road in the direction of the Glidden house. He may well have *ideas in his head.* I think, Flora, you might just check to see if he is there."

Miss Flora was quick to take up the binoculars, training them on the Glidden place, then focusing to the driveway. "Bushes," she said. "Not trees, as we thought."

"Let me see!" Miss Emmy literally wrested the glasses from her sister. She had excellent vision and knew Miss Flora didn't see too well at the best of times. "Rhododendrons. Very large and in bloom. But, Flora, if Mrs. Glidden plants them there, it will cut off our view!"

"She shouldn't be having plantings put in so soon after her husband's death. Why, when Our Father and Our Mother left us, I waited *two whole years* before I even seeded a bed!"

"Flora!" cried Miss Emmeline. "He's there! The Midsummer Man's talking to Mrs. Glidden!"

"I don't believe it."

"See for yourself." She handed over the binoculars.

Again Miss Flora focused, but all she could make out was a blurred impression of movement. "I can't confirm, Emmy, I really can't."

154

"You're withholding from me," Miss Emmy accused. "*I* saw him clearly, *bare to the waist,* with strange, red markings on his upper body."

"Tattoos. Roses." Miss Flora gave it away without thinking.

"A fancy man, of course!" cried Miss Emmeline in triumph. "Why will you prevaricate, Flora? You knew all the time who he was. You saw him under the apple tree, too, didn't you?"

Miss Flora was not going to be called a liar. She handed her sister the binoculars. "You watch as long as you like," she said, "but, dear, *don't* overexcite yourself. I've got to open the shop now."

It was one thing after another all day. Though the Misses Bowyer kept close tabs on that part of the Corner they could watch—the Cadle shambles, the hated Hanters and their luncheonette, the Glidden house, the Ingles'—other activities, like those of Teddy Hubbard and Bo deWillig, generally eluded them. Still, they knew Miss Hankins, Hubbard's mother's nurse-companion, from whom they extracted fascinating details. They wished they could see past the big hollies that shielded the new home of the young MacFindens; but they didn't mind too much, the MacFindens hadn't yet had time to become interesting to them. Today they didn't care about anything but Mrs. Glidden and her fancy man; indeed, they almost forgot themselves. Miss Flora, in fact, so forgot herself that she actually *quoted a price* on her great-grandmother's Sheraton writing desk, which she had no intention of selling ever, any more than she expected to part with the many other fine family pieces with which the house was crowded. The genuine antiques mentioned on her sign were not for sale, the heirlooms merely come-ons; only the inexpensive—commonplace ironstone tureens, majolica vases, Currier and Ives prints—had price tags, and few cared to buy at her prices. She didn't really want to sell anything anyway; she *had* her stock and wanted to keep it, because nowadays stock was almost impossible to come by. But the sign brought in the lunch ladies from the Inn across the way, and she could then tell her stories of persecution. And today Miss Flora had had a ball, though she never would have admitted it; she was too busy getting ready for the night and what was to come.

CHAPTER 4

Beneath Bobby Ingle's laconic surface lay a despair that was more individually realized than his father, for all his love and intuition, suspected. Now, the trial and error of the night slept off, came afternoon with its guilt over having slept late and having been permitted to do so by his mother—confirmation of another day. To Bobby, any day was a betrayal, merely a repeat, differing slightly in temperature and mood, but not, predictably, more promising than the one before.

Though it was afternoon, the panic of the lost morning had yet to be dispelled by reassurance of the self in self-love. He got up, went to the bath, and returned, on the way back to bed catching the image of himself in the wardrobe mirror. He paused, staring into the glass, face speculative and intent, then breathed in deeply, puffed out his chest and watched the muscles of his abdomen contract. He turned from side to side, following himself with his eyes, inspecting his body with pure, unashamed admiration. Then he thought of Edie Cadle and got back into bed. This meant *selfsex*, for despite his search the night before for the *realsex* his father had condoned, he had not found it. His night had proved one in which nothing worked for him, and he had spent it driving aimlessly around, stopping for beers, until at last he gave up and came home. He had slowed going past the Hubbard house, which was dark, then accelerated, wondering whether, *if* lights had been on, he would have stopped for what Bo deWillig so obviously had offered him. *Othersex*, if not *realsex*, not the same, nothing like the same, makeshift merely, but sex, was to be had there; but the talk with his father, as he had thought it over, bothered him; he had told much too much.

What he felt as he lay in bed was an extreme of the experience common to healthy young men of nineteen: indecision as to whether to fling back the sheet and get it over, or to keep the sheet pulled up to the chin and take a chance that the night would bring the *realsex* he needed. Handicaps in this department of his life being what they were, he decided (as, to his shame, he did most mornings) not to take the chance. He performed the ritual joy-

156

lessly, fantasying Edie Cadle as partner, fears and panics for the moment abstractly at bay.

But beneath the momentary pleasure of orgasm, the futility, which only *realsex* could assuage, remained. He lingered a last few minutes, putting the hour together from sounds within the house and outside the window. The same old Corner, which he loathed, documented by sounds of chain saws buzzing, quarries roaring in the distance, cars racing past, birds and cicadas carping of summer in the trees—less a real village than a stage set floating in limbo; so all days spent in the Corner seemed to him now. Every day he told himself he should do something, "anything," as his mother said; but the moment he tried to will himself to do something, he felt absolutely incapable of doing it and would do anything else to keep himself from doing what he knew he should do.

Fantasies helped; they kept the day at arm's length. These were explicit and uninhibited. He took a flyer in imagining what Edie would be like once he got past the brassière, if she wore one, and the panties below, if she wore those. And on the probability that she would be available tonight; though he had not taken the chance, he knew that by then he would be eager and ready.

The day communicated itself to him through habit—shower, a plea to Mrs. Schaaf for coffee from the top of the stairs, first cigarettes. The day was, so far, shapeless, no worse than yesterday, but acceptable because he still had seventeen of the twenty dollars his father had parted with last night. He had his *Cities of the Plain* to go on with—the first volume only, he had discovered when he read himself to sleep; the second was still on the Hubbard shelves. If deWillig had not come on so strong, he would have been less hurried, would have seen the second volume and reached for it before leaving. And he had youth, but this catalyst he took for granted. With this cluster of imponderables, he faced the tedium of the daily, inescapable interview with his mother.

When he came downstairs, he found her seated at a card table with her back to the windows to take advantage of the breeze, playing patience. A cigarette burned in the ashtray beside her.

"I almost woke you. I was afraid you'd sleep the clock around," she said, with hints of disapprovals to follow. "You almost did."

157

Her mood could be guessed from the nervous, quick way she riffled the cards.

Bobby met this with silence.

"You might say something pleasant."

"Good afternoon." Bobby returned her irony.

"How can you sleep all that time? And in this heat! I'm ashamed to have Mrs. Schaaf know."

"I was out late."

"Yes, I heard you come in." Disapproval mounted. "You know, you needn't think just because you talked your father into letting you take my car last night that it's going to be a regular thing."

Another silence.

"Because if you've got any such notions in your head, get them out at once."

A frown was all that Bobby managed to produce. This almost certainly ruled out Edie Cadle this evening.

"I noticed this morning that the gas gauge was way down," his mother continued. "You must have driven around a lot."

"I did."

"But I thought you had a date."

"I didn't."

"Then why did your father let you have my car?"

"It's too complicated," Bobby answered.

"Complicated? I think I can understand if you tell me."

Bobby sauntered to the coffee table near the bookshelves, picking up at random a copy of *Punch* and several of his father's *Spectators* and *New Statesmans* and flopped with them into a chair.

"I think you owe me the courtesy of answering when I say something to you," said his mother.

"What else do you want me to say? You've said it all for me," Bobby, already between *Punch's* pages, replied. "I know this is Dad's night to stay at Tulip, and I know it's one of yours to play bridge with the girls. So no car for Bobby."

"Don't call them girls. They're older women and your friends as well as mine, and you should speak of them properly, by their names."

"If I could remember them—there're so many of them, and they all look alike to me." This was true; Bobby found it difficult to

158

distinguish between one middle-aged mask and another, particularly if they were women and wore glasses.

"Don't be rude."

Silence.

"Are you going to spend this day the way you spent yesterday? Doing nothing?"

"I don't know."

"I had to have a boy come all the way from Chalfont, to do the weeding on the terrace. While you slept."

Bobby shrugged.

"I want you to know your father and I talked about you. He wonders why, with you in the house, I have to hire help for the garden. Houghton always used to do things like that for me without my having to ask."

"Don't give me old Hoot's virtues," Bobby answered testily. "Not today, please. I'm sick of hearing about Hoot anyway."

"And your father and I are sick of your attitude." His mother picked it up. "As well as tired to death of your refusal to do anything."

"I know that, don't tell me again."

"Why don't you have ambition like other boys? Don't you ever want to grow up and *do* something, amount to something, be somebody?"

Bobby turned a *Spectator* page, noting there was an article on Mods and Rockers—youth discontented like himself, but more glamorous because English—and made a mental note to come back to it. Sometimes, as he listened to his mother, he felt she was not really speaking but miming to a record.

"Answer me!" she demanded.

"I don't know what to say."

"You could tell me what you said to your father that made him change his mind about Edie Cadle. You must have said *something*."

"Nothing in particular. We talked. I answered his questions."

"Such as?"

"Oh, how long had I known Teddy Hubbard and how did I meet him."

"How did you meet him, by the way?"

"I was hitching from Olympia and he offered me a ride."

"Long ago?"

"This spring, after I flunked out of Adamville." He laughed. "When I became the county's oldest dropout."

His mother sighed. "And now you borrow books from him, though at school you couldn't be bothered with books."

"Hubbard's books are different from school books."

"Your father doesn't approve of your going down there," she said sharply.

"I know, he told me."

"Do you know why?"

"Sure."

"I hope you'll do as he asks."

"I hadn't thought," Bobby answered with lack of interest, remembering the second volume of *Cities*.

His mother lighted a fresh cigarette and, holding her cards tightly, asked, "Tell me, is what your father told me true? That those men have—I don't know how to put it—"

" 'Made advances?' " Bobby cued her. "That's Dad's phrase."

"Well, is it true?" She gave him a quick, searching look, then shuffled her cards.

"They're kooks, both of them," Bobby said to this. "But it's someplace to go, and Hubbard has a real library. Everything."

"Such men are pathetic. I'm glad you're my son. I know I need never worry about you and things like that."

"You worry about Edie Cadle."

"Your father said, too, that I'd have to get used to something else about you I can't believe—that you have intimate relations with girls. Casual sex, he called it."

Bobby was getting bored. "Better not ask that. I might tell you."

"Bobby, I am your mother. But anything like that I'd rather not know about."

"Then why ask?"

His mother flung down her deck. "Is that why you're suddenly so interested in Edie Cadle?"

From his father Bobby had learned the value of pauses as short-cuts to the end of arguments. He waited.

"I wish I understood," his mother said. "What did you tell Daddy?"

160

"I don't know what it was I said that changed his mind, but he told me to do as I pleased," said Bobby.

"Don't you understand the way *I* feel about it? A son of mine, with a—" She broke off, seeing Bobby's expression. "You're just hanging around until I go out, so you can call her up, isn't that true?"

"All right, I admit it." Bobby piled *Spectators* and *New Statesmans* on *Punch* and tossed the lot back onto the coffee table. He sat staring out of the windows, expression now fixed in the steady frown that invariably settled on his face during these discussions. His mother went on with her game—red queen on black king, seven, six and five in red and black sequence. Suddenly Bobby's frown vanished. Past the yew hedge outside he could see Edie Cadle's dark head as she walked by; she looked to be in a hurry and was headed downriver.

"I think I'll take a walk," he said, getting up.

"To avoid answering my questions."

"Yes."

"I only wish I knew what it is you want out of life."

"I want to get away from the questions," Bobby answered from the door.

"Go, then!" his mother said, angry. "I'll have gone by the time you get back, but Mrs. Schaaf will give you your dinner."

"*If* I come back for dinner."

"Bobby—"

But by then he was outside and past the hedge.

"Edie!" Bobby called out. She was already several houses down the road, nearing the Hubbards', walking rapidly against the traffic, heavy at this hour with workmen and commuters returning. "*Edie!*"

She turned quickly around, and as he caught up with her, Bobby saw she had been crying.

"Are you alone?" he asked.

"What does it look like?"

"I mean, are you going somewhere?"

"I'm going nowhere, or I'd like to," she answered in a sobbing voice. "I wish there *were* a nowhere!"

She turned and started walking again and Bobby fell into step beside her. "I was going to call you. What's the matter?"

"Oh, you wouldn't know—you'd never have heard of what I'd have to tell you." She was angry as well as crying, and the way she said it made it sound like his fault.

"Maybe I would," he said. "Try."

"No. You'd have to be who I am and live where I live and have people like I do to know anything about it." Her small, brown feet in sandals made a tap-click on the black macadam of the road; even her walk was angry.

"But where are you going in such a rush?"

"I guess it must be anywhere, since there's not a nowhere to go to," she said. "Just trying to get out of this horrible place!"

"I don't like it either. Tell me what's wrong." Bobby wished there were somewhere to walk besides the road, but the only way to get away from traffic was to go down to the towpath. "Let's cross over to the canal at the bridge below the Fringes," he suggested. He was not sure he should have used these words speaking to Edie, since they connoted the small, poor houses at the village's end, distinguishing them from houses like the one he lived in and other big, restored properties near the Corner intersection; Edie was, technically a Fringe dweller, though her father's garage was where it was.

"All right," she agreed, sighing. "Maybe if I can be away from them for just a little while I can stand it better when I have to go back."

"Who's *them?*"

"My mother and father. The horrible place I live, too."

Once they had crossed the small, red bridge and had climbed down to the towpath, she stopped crying. "You feel better already," he said.

"A little."

"I wish you'd tell me what it is."

"I'd rather not talk about it. Or I mean I *can't.*" She smiled. "I do feel better, just being away this long."

They strolled along the soft, spongy turf of the path running alongside the canal, with its tufts of daisies and wild roses and yellow iris growing at the water's edge. The grass was worn where the mule teams that pulled the excursion barges from

162

Olympia to Ohmerstown had made a path, but on the slope extending gently down from the canal bank the carpet of green was thick and untrodden.

"I was going to ask you for a date tonight," Bobby said, walking close beside her. "Unless you already have one."

"Tonight I don't."

"You did last night. I wish I could have seen you then, because then I had a car."

She stopped. "No car? Where could we go without a car?"

It was the same old story; there was no way to escape from the Corner except with a car or on foot, as they were. The towpath was pleasant, but in the direction they were walking it would lead them back to the intersection. Bobby thought of his seventeen dollars—not quite enough for a drive-yourself deposit and dinner or a movie and the hourly rates charged for rented cars.

It was Edie who saw his quandary. She said, as she resumed walking, more slowly, "Oh well, some other time, then. It doesn't matter." But he could see it did matter.

She was wearing clothes that looked slightly rumpled, a yellow blouse, a bright red skirt that brought out her high coloring. He was grateful to her for pretending she didn't mind and moved closer to her, feeling her warmth, wishing it was any time of day but what it was, the slow, lingering sunset of a hot summer's day. Still, if he had not run out to catch up with her, he might have lost her and the night too. She walked with her eyes straight ahead, as if she would be late getting back.

Bobby touched her arm. "Don't let's hurry," he said; she was so completely what he needed that he was already trying to see ahead, think of ways to slow the walk, take her out of her mood into his.

Half to herself she said, "There's nothing I can do. I am who I am, and that's the way it is. So since you know all that, too, perhaps we'd better go back."

"I don't want to. I want to be with you."

She turned and looked in his eyes. "Listen, I know why you ran after me, why you've been phoning me, what it is you want. You've heard all the stories about the Cadles and you think you can get what you want from me just like that!" She snapped her fingers. "It's not true, no matter what you've heard."

163

"I haven't heard anything," Bobby lied, "but if I had it wouldn't have made any difference." What she said about his wanting her was so true he felt ashamed. "I like you," he said for want of anything better.

"I like you, too, Bobby. But so what?" The hopelessness with which she had spoken at first seemed now to be replaced by indifference. "I start walking down the road to get away from the Corner and you follow me—and we're going back to the place I want to get away from."

"But I thought you got away all the time," Bobby said. "You were away last night, weren't you?"

"What do *you* know about last night?" she demanded.

"Why, nothing," he answered, confused. "What do you mean?"

"I'm sorry, it had nothing to do with you. Yes, I get away whenever I can, no matter who it is. Whoever'll take me."

"But I asked you for a date yesterday."

"I know. But I'd already called somebody else." She paused. "Oh, I've got to tell somebody or die!" she said in her earlier voice. "You know where I live, my father and mother. Mom and Papa-Daddy. How we live all cramped up over the garage. All my life my Papa-Daddy has beaten me, but no more than my sisters— they got out and away. Leaving me. There's nowhere I can ever go to be alone. There's no privacy. Mom's the worst—Papa-Daddy's beaten her into nothing. She's so worn down she hardly ever fights back now. If it weren't for Papa-Daddy, I'd have walked out and as far away as anyone can walk."

"But he beats you!"

"He can't help it. And not so much now. But I love him, somewhere in him there's a little something left my mother didn't take away. He looks terrible and dirty and old now, but you should see him in old pictures—he was wonderful. I— Oh, I don't know!"

Bobby waited. Edie said no more for the moment, standing in the light that came from behind the hills, the sunset no one who lived in the Corner ever saw because of them. "Maybe a job would get you away," he said. "That's what my mother and father are always telling me."

"I know. Stand on your own two feet. Hold your head up. Do something. I've had a couple of jobs, but I hated them. My sisters were waitresses before they married, and that was what I did or tried to do. I was lousy at it because I hated being pinched all the time and the way men look when you lean over to take their orders or clear the table."

She was walking so slowly now she was hardly moving, her feet in their sandals deftly avoiding the stones in the path.

Bobby stopped, touching her arm. "Let's go down there," he said, indicating the slope on the canal's far side, where the grass grew soft and thick.

"If you like." She let him take her hand and lead her to a shady spot beneath a tree. They sank down together on the grass, Bobby a little above her, leaning on one elbow. Where her blouse fell away from her sunburned shoulders, he could see the rise of her breasts and the slightly darker cleft between them. There was a film of moisture at the nape of her neck where she had quickly pinned up her hair.

"But you," she said, continuing what she had been saying, "your people are somebody. You've got it all made and ready for you."

"Maybe that's the way it looks to you," answered Bobby, "but what they've got ready for me isn't what I want. I'm a mess, I guess; my family keeps at me night and day about it."

"You went away to school—a school somewhere far away."

"Yes. That was a big sell. It's all a big sell, don't you know that? Who wants to study to be something ten years from now? Not me. There's nothing but *now*, that's all that matters. To me," he added.

"No," she said to this, "there's more than that, though I don't know what. The way I live, I don't have much time to think about it. Never alone, never by myself. It's *now*—and now *what?*"

"I'd like to kiss you."

She raised her shoulders in a shrug. "They all start this way."

"Who?"

"Others."

"I don't care about them." He moved down on the bank beside her and took her face between his hands, pressing his lips lightly against hers. To his surprise she offered no resistance; her body grew limp and she let herself fall back on the bank.

"I liked that," she said. "Not hard and rough, not trying to do everything at once."

"I'd like to do everything."

"Yes, I know. But why right away?"

165

He laughed, kissing her again. "You mean, a little at a time?"

"Maybe I mean that. Others— Oh, why pretend? Some others I've known kiss like animals, all that tongue business. Girls aren't dumb, you know. They know what all that means."

"I'm glad you liked me," he said, sobering. It was a longer kiss this time and she raised her hands to his shoulders, holding him.

"I liked that one even better," she said. For the first time since they had been together she laughed. "Bobby," she said. "Bobby Ingle. What my mom calls a nice boy."

"If she knew what I'm really like, she'd faint," Bobby said. "My mother still believes all that about saving yourself for the woman you're going to marry. She doesn't say it but talks all around it. I wonder what they think we *do* about it all, that sex they talk all around, too, but never want to bring out into the open."

She found this funny.

"Why do you laugh?" he asked. "What did I say?"

"Oh, nothing; only that in my house there never was any talking around anything. I always knew what my Papa-Daddy looked like and what everybody did. It was never a surprise to me."

"But you like it?"

"Sometimes, not always."

"I like it when it's *real.*"

"Isn't it always real?"

"No, often it's fake—like you know when."

"Oh, that," she said. "I don't think girls do that as much as boys. At least I didn't."

"And don't now?"

"Of course not!"

"Never?"

"Why should I?" She raised her arms and clasped her hands behind her head, looking up at the sky. "It's crazy, this," she said, "to have somebody to talk with like this. Is it crazy for you too?"

"A little," he admitted. "My dad's a big head man; he knows part of what it's all about. Sometimes I've been able to talk to him, but my mother never."

"At my house," she said, "it's taken for granted, but not in nice ways. My mother knows I go with boys, men too, sometimes, but my Papa-Daddy is always threatening to beat me if I do anything wrong, as he calls it."

166

"Meaning something that's fun and you like to do."

"Of course. 'Anything wrong' always means that."

"Do you do what you like?"

"Yes. I always did."

"And does your father still punish you?"

"I'm scared to death of him, though I love him, too. Mom keeps calling me an afternoon girl, as though she means something else."

"Well, I'm an afternoon boy," Bobby confessed. "I hate mornings, don't you?"

"Not especially."

"This," he said, spreading his hand toward the sweep of the river below, "this is for me. And night."

She nodded. "I sometimes wonder what they think is going to happen to me. I suppose they think I'll come home someday with third finger left hand all taken care of and a deed to a big house and a new big car and the husband who's at the end of all that."

"Will you?"

"In the end, I think that's what will *happen*. Something will take place I can't guess about, and there it'll be, all wrapped up and ready to open and out will jump somebody like Papa-Daddy was once and my mom as *she* was—Edie Cadle's got a man at last. And then, in a few years, we'll be like Papa-Daddy and Mom are now."

"What could happen? You mean you might get pregnant?"

"Not me," she said. " 'Getting caught'—not for me. No, I'll never get pregnant until I really want to; I learned all that from my older sisters who weren't so lucky."

"You take the pills?"

"If I want to have sex I have sex, if you mean that."

"God, how I mean it!" He drew in his breath and held it, his lips in a straight line. Then he relaxed and his breath came out in a laugh. "I wish you'd relax a little."

"I will, if you like."

"Just like that?" He snapped his fingers as she had done earlier. "No holding off? No 'I can't, I don't want to' or 'Stop, you're hurting me'?"

"No, none of that. Only—"

"Ah, I knew there'd be the stall."

"Not really. Only that today—tonight—I'd rather not."

"But why? You've no worries and I've got the—"

"Yes, you've got them—I felt the box in your pocket, I could hear it rattle as you walked. No, it isn't that. It's that I don't like to the very first time. Maybe that's a hangover from good women or something."

"Have you ever—the first time?"

"Yes, and that's why I decided I didn't like it. It's better to wait and first think about how it's going to be."

Bobby's breath again betrayed him, but this time he did not laugh. "Well, I'll be thinking about it," he said tensely, "but don't stall me any more than that if we're going to have it together—if you meant what you said."

"I meant it."

"Do you want to go back now?"

"Do you?"

"No. I'd like to see your breasts, *really* see them."

"All right," she said, and raised herself slightly from the grass as he lowered her blouse.

"They're wonderful!" he whispered, cupping them in his hands. Then he kissed them, taking the taut brown nipples in his mouth. "God, Edie!" he said. "You're as ready as I am, and you want us to wait?"

"You can wait," she teased, playing with his hair. "You see, I have to find out about you, too. I love blond, curly hair, I suppose because mine is so black and straight. Are you blond all over?"

"Shall I show you?"

"No, not yet." She lowered her arms about his neck, hanging from him playfully, then drew him down on top of her, her hands moving downward, exploring without shame. Then she said, "No more now. We'd better get up and go."

"I can't get up for a minute," he said. "But you're right. If it's not to be now, I'll have to stop or go crazy!"

"Don't do that," she said. She pressed her hands against him, pushing him from her. They lay, both breathing deeply, for some minutes. "Now," she said, getting to her feet, brushing her skirt and adjusting her blouse. "Now I think I'd like to go back."

Bobby slowly rose. "What will you do—about *them?*"

"Oh, stick it out another day, as I've stuck it out so far. What will you do?"

"Go home. Save it for tomorrow. Read. I can get the car tomorrow night. What shall we do? What time?"

She looked at the sky, growing gunmetal dark with the summer heat. "Like now," she said, "this time of day. We can have sandwiches somewhere and then finish what we started today."

"Really finish!"

"Of course."

"Is that a promise?"

"Yes, a promise."

They climbed back to the towpath and he kissed her a last time, then they started walking toward the Corner intersection.

When they had reached it, she said, "Do you see it as I do?"

"I don't know, but it's ugly and I hate it."

"And do I hate it!"

"But it looks better to me now than it did."

"Why?"

"Because of you. Because of what we're going to do tomorrow."

She looked at him levelly. "So what they say about Edie Cadle is right, you see. It doesn't bother you?"

"If you knew what they'd say about Bobby Ingle if *they* knew— why, then you'd know my answer," he said.

"I've never heard anything about you, except that you're a nice boy."

"Wait and see."

He helped her up the low escarpment near the bridge that led to a flight of steps and, at their top, the intersection of black roads. It was entirely dark now, and the luncheonette was jumping.

"Are you hungry?" he asked. "Shall we go in?"

"I'm starved."

"So am I."

Al Hanter, when he saw them, took a long look over his steamy spectacles, then, catching his wife's eye, jerked his head. Fran Hanter was washing plates. She came out of the kitchen.

"Hi, you kids," she said, her eyes traveling from one to the other, her expression conveying surprise at seeing them together, seeing them at all at the luncheonette. "What'll it be?"

They ordered, as they waited listening to the jukebox play "It's Hard Not to Be Lonely When You're by Yourself."

Then Edie said, "Do something for me, will you?"

"*Almost* anything. What?"

"Walk with me to my door."

"Why wouldn't I?"

"You'd be surprised," she said, "what a surprise it would be for me, and for *them*."

"Why?"

"Oh, it just would," she said.

When they had finished eating and Bobby had paid the check, leaving a sizable tip beneath the plate—for luck—he wondered how his miseries of the afternoon and the dull boredom that followed the talk with his mother could be only hours in the past. He left Edie at the garage door, catching a glimpse of her father inside, his head buried beneath the hood of a car he was repairing. There was no good-night kiss, and he wove his way through the cars parked near the road, letting himself into his dark house with the latchkey kept always beneath the doormat and went upstairs to read. He opened *Cities of the Plain* again, turning to the page where he had put it down last night. But M. de Charlus and the conversation between Swann and the Prince de Guermantes palled and he leafed ahead, skipping, to "The Heart's Intermissions," a section of the book as yet uncut by any reader. This told him something about Teddy Hubbard he had suspected—that his books were merely props, as were all the tassels and hassocks. He read on into the night, slitting pages, hearing his father, then his mother, come in. Balbec seemed far away from their voices, low and wordless, but nevertheless strained—talking about him, he supposed. And then sleep came, tunneling him down into dreams as deep as China and not at all akin to those of the phantoms in *Cities*. His were of Edie's breasts, which tormented him deliciously until morning.

Teddy Hubbard's mother, at his suggestion, had kept most of her old tea gowns, all of which were distantly related to the kind worn by the late Marie Dressler in films of high society, bias-cut, sacklike and with gussets, gores and insertions designed to conceal the sagging flesh to which women as old as Mrs. Hubbard are heir. Most were of panne velvets or laces, but she had a few lighter leftovers, too, for weather as hot as this, *broderie anglaise* or tulle.

She cherished these garments, so little of the past remained to her except memory; Teddy knew a little seamstress to let them out or take them in from time to time, whichever was necessary. Besides, these sumptuous clothes went with the house, added to the "high camp" image of Mother Hubbard which was relished by the house's visitors.

This night, with the heat showing no sign of letting up, Mrs. Hubbard was propped up on her cane chaise longue, an old Elsie de Wolfe piece Teddy had bought at auction, wearing her lavender *broderie*. She was being read to by Miss Hankins, her nurse-companion of many years.

"Hasn't anybody *nice* died?" Mrs. Hubbard inquired peevishly. Miss Hankins always began with the *Times* obituaries, first reading the one- or two-column coverages of notables, working through the two-inch unimportances to the really nobodies of the paid "Deaths" insertions and In Memoriams.

"Nobody we know, I'm sure, dear," answered Miss Hankins; "not in the *Times*, anyway. I'll try the *Trib*."

"Now, let's see," Mrs. Hubbard said. "Are you sure you read me everything about What's-her-name, that actress, or was it opera singer?" Though devoted to the obits, Mrs. Hubbard usually forgot the names as soon as she heard them.

"Yes, dear. Opera singer." Miss Hankins was rejecting names they had been over already. "Siegel, Silver, Simmons, beloved father of Anna, esteemed colleague . . . I'm afraid that's it for today. There's nobody else, nobody at all. Don't you want me to do the theatrical sections? Sometimes they have people you like to hear about."

"No, not tonight," Mrs. Hubbard said. If only any of them *knew*, she thought, how bored I am! She hated the way she was kept, like a fusty antique, in her upstairs rooms, hated everything including, some days, even Miss Hankins. *And was bored!* She sighed. In one's eighty-third year, how bored can one be? "It was always that," she said aloud. "Food, sin and death."

"What was that, dear?" Miss Hankins asked, though she had heard perfectly well; her patient's often startling comments—pushed, as Miss Hankins thought of it, under the very doorsill of death—were best disregarded. It was time for her tranquilizer anyway, and of course the heat was bothering her. On any day what Mrs. Hubbard referred to as "my body duties" were onerous, but today they had been more than that.

Mrs. Hubbard did not repeat what she had said. She took the tranquilizer tranquilly.

"Now, we're feeling fair, aren't we, dear?" Miss Hankins asked.

"I feel the same." Mrs. Hubbard invariably said this, no matter who asked how she was. "I've been the same for years."

Miss Hankins patted and rearranged the chaise cushions of lace and down, to make her charge more comfortable. "Never mind, dear," she said soothingly, "Mr. Teddy and Mr. Bo are going to give you a great big party for your birthday, and that's something lovely to look forward to."

"Don't want any party," Mrs. Hubbard said. "I only like parties where there are gentlemen *and* ladies."

"Of course." Miss Hankins sought for some subject that would get Mrs. Hubbard off that one. "They'll soon be back, I expect."

"Where did they go?"

"Mr. Teddy had some business on Long Island, remember? I told you earlier. And Mr. Bo has a job doing a new TV commercial."

"Hm." Mrs. Hubbard's *hm*'s always indicated reservations. She had no more use for Bo deWillig on television than she had for him in the house.

"And I daresay they'll be picking up lovely things for your party," Miss Hankins added.

Mrs. Hubbard took refuge in silence. She disliked her son's parties, and though (as the exclusively male guests always said) she was "wise" to what went on, she had never really accepted *les boys* or anything she supposed they did after she was carted back upstairs. The monstrous fusses they made over her when, transported downstairs on the Inclinator, freshly waved and made up, were only one more boredom, though she did her best to be polite. She once dearly loved gentlemen, but Teddy's and Bo's friends seemed to her like children who had somehow not made it successfully in Maeterlinck's *Blue Bird*. Something wrong with the genes, she'd once heard, or perhaps their nurses had left them out in the snow or dropped them as children. Who knew?

172

One explanation was as good as another, or were all the same, now. She remembered George V's "I thought men like that shot themselves," and even some of the "special" novels with which the house was well supplied, and which she had once read in an effort to understand. In these books the protagonists were depicted as confused and guilty, or helpless and weak, or unaware or drifting. Usually they jumped or almost jumped, or simply walked, into the sea. . . . Teddy had never had any guilt that she could see, nor had he been any of the other things; he was tough as shoe leather in his dealings and had made a mint, she knew. When she had been younger, she had minded very much both finding out what they did with each other and the way they talked about it; as it was now, revulsion and resignation were fused.

Miss Hankins detected an odd expression on her patient's face, and divined the ruminative mood. Seeking to head off trouble, she said, "You know you'll love the party, dear. Think of it! Eighty-three years young! And you do look so much younger than that."

But this was not what was wanted. "I think," Mrs. Hubbard said, "that my bladder pill's not working again."

"Oh, dear!" Miss Hankins at once went to help Mrs. Hubbard to the *chaise percée* that stood alongside the other. "Don't you worry," she said encouragingly. "We'll pop another into our mouth and that'll do it."

"None of them work, really," Mrs. Hubbard said. "How I wish I were dead, in the next world, where I *hope* bladder troubles are unknown!"

"You're going to be fine, dear, fine," Miss Hankins assured her.

Teddy and Bo had made several stops for drinks during their drive home, and when they got to the house were windblown and tired. Teddy's business had gone well; it always did. But Bo's day had been a horror. The sponsor had complained that he looked fat, and had objected to a slight nervousness he said he detected as the commercial was spoken. The film, which would occupy forty seconds of air time, had been made over and over in a series of ten- and fifteen-second shots, to be crosscut with images of noodles being poured steamily onto a plate. Luckily, the noodles were already taken and done; all Bo had had to do was smile and smile, ever more dazzlingly, and do it again and again.

Bo had quite forgotten about Bobby Ingle from the moment he saw Tavio on the road as they left that morning; he couldn't stop talking about what a beauty he was.

"Now, in Sweden," he said to Teddy, "it would have only been a matter of making the open proposition, and no doubt he would have been glad to oblige. But then, being queer in Sweden is a more civilized matter."

"Yes, I know, everybody's queer there, according to you," Teddy, sick to death of this thesis, replied. "If that were true, where would all the little Swedes come from?"

"Everybody's *everything*, don't you understand?" Bo asked.

"Only in the Middle East," Teddy disagreed, "and there you remember how it was, all the warnings we had about subtle mouth diseases. Look what happened to poor old Gide and Oscar Wilde. I'll be upstairs putting Mother to bed," he added, leaving the Arab world for more immediate duties. "Pop a couple of frozen somethings into the oven. I'll make the salad when I come down."

"I will, as soon as I take in these molds," said Bo. There had been one wonderful thing about the day, a real windfall; in a thrift shop they passed they had found a graded series of tall, oddly shaped copper molds, of a kind once used in kitchens of great mansions for shaping desserts. A great bargain, Bo considered them. "And all phallic as they can be," he said happily, as he unloaded them from the rear of the Mercedes. "I'm going to make a kind of pink blancmange we used to have in Sweden—for Mother Hubbard's birthday. With a cherry on top."

"Go play with your toys, if you must, Bo," replied Teddy, who had driven and was the more tired. "But first get on to our dinner."

Mrs. Hubbard's evening meal had been prepared by Miss Hankins and had long since been consumed. "And what kind of day have we had?" asked Teddy, as he came upstairs.

"On the bright side, mostly, I'd say," Miss Hankins reported. "We've had three of our bladder pills. We're not the least bit tired."

"Not the least bit," Mrs. Hubbard confirmed. Her smile for Teddy was one of gentle rebuke, but her hands as she lifted them to his shoulders during the ritual cheek brushing betrayed fondness. "I'm used to being awake," she said. "Don't worry. Did you have dinner on the road?"

174

"No, Bo's fixing something."

"Hm." At the mention of Bo the smile faded, but the rebuke remained.

"You must take something so you'll sleep in this heat," Teddy said, beginning the nightly ritual of coaxing, "so you'll be fresh for your birthday later this week. Remember?"

"How could I forget? *I'm* the one who'll be eighty-three."

"I think one of the little *red* pills," suggested Miss Hankins.

"I am sick of pills. I want to die!" Mrs. Hubbard said suddenly, looking balefully at both of them. Such fallings away of the veil were not uncommon.

"Now, dear," said Miss Hankins.

"I am not happy here. *Do you understand that?*" Mrs. Hubbard cried out. "I would be pleased to die!"

"Mother, try to realize—"

"Oh, I realize, I realize everything," Mrs. Hubbard said, still in a loud voice. "My bladder may not, but *I* do." Her old, spotted hands began to tremble. "Oh, if only you could have seen the error of your ways!" she went on. "Thank God, your father died before he could see what you are!"

This was nothing new, to either Teddy or Miss Hankins; the veil was falling aside more and more lately.

"I think two of the little red pills," said Teddy.

"I think two," Miss Hankins agreed. "And later on, when she wakes—"

"Body duties! I loathe them! I'm nothing but old bones and skin! Why can't you hand me the bottle? I'd know how many to take!"

"Nonsense, Mother," Teddy said. "Nobody knows how many exactly. If you take *too* many, you simply wake up again."

"I know how many," said Mrs. Hubbard. "Seven of them for every forty pounds of body weight. Twenty-one, and I'd be out of the way forever."

When she got like this, there was nothing to do but give her four of the little red pills, which Teddy and Miss Hankins, between them, contrived to do.

Downstairs in the kitchen, things were not going so efficiently. Teddy found Bo polishing the molds at the sink, surrounded by messy dabs and puddles of Copperbrite, having forgotten entirely to get something from the freezer to begin dinner.

"Bo, really! Can't you do one single thing to help?" Teddy complained. "Why didn't you start something?"

"I forgot," said Bo.

"There's forgetting and forgetting," Teddy commented, going wearily to the refrigerator, taking from the freezing compartment two macaronis-and-cheese, which he put into the oven at top heat, to hurry them up. Then he began to wash and dry lettuce for the salad.

"I could really cook, if you'd let me," Bo said.

"You couldn't boil water."

"Well, it's true, I wouldn't go through all *that* camp of drying each lettuce leaf on a towel."

"You always make such a mess," Teddy said. "If you'd clear as you go, as I do."

"I am *not* a domestic," said Bo. "Go ahead, dry your old lettuce! I'm going to have me a drink."

"Why don't you?" Teddy agreed. "It might improve that nasty disposition of yours."

"Well, *who* has to wait while *who* puts Mother Hubbard to bed?" Bo wanted to know. "It's no wonder I polish copper!"

"If you will please shut up and get out, I'll have dinner on in half an hour," Teddy said, with patience.

"I'll be only too glad," replied Bo, leaving the kitchen.

Teddy could hear him in the den, banging the ice bucket about and making as much noise as possible with the cocktail shaker. Bo evidently had a number of drinks, and then the hi-fi system came on, playing his favorite record, fortissimo: *Prélude à l'après-midi d'un faune;* he identified with the faun, Teddy supposed. The *Prélude* was such a Ford, but the choice ones seemed always to prefer such low camp; worse, Teddy knew Bo would be stinking by the time he brought in dinner, crying in his drink about his lost youth and career. But he was not prepared for the sullen rage and hostility that greeted him as he carried the plates to the den and placed them on the table.

"The whole thing's your fault," Bo began at once. "What happened to me at the studio today could never have happened if I hadn't got mixed up with *you!*"

Teddy's guess had been correct: the lost career was to be the lesson for the night. "You'd better eat, get some of that macaroni in you, to sop up the gin," he suggested.

"But I wish to stay drunk!" Bo imperiously announced. "It is only by being drunk I can endure you!"

Teddy began to eat his salad, being of the opinion that people lived longer if they ate greens before starches. "You're slipping," he said to Bo. "Getting old, like everybody else. Just as you couldn't get Bobby Ingle last night, so today you were a mess at the studio."

"Who said I was a mess?"

"What you told me in the car left little doubt."

"They gave me my check before I left—they'd never have done that if I hadn't been all right, would they?"

"But you said something happened," Teddy reminded him. "What happened?"

"Bitch!" cried Bo. "You're trying to confuse me!" He looked very sorry for himself. "A deWillig advertising noodles! It's too much!"

"Stop crying in your drink, dear; try crying into the macaroni. Same thing as noodles."

"Oh, you're so insensitive! Can't you understand what I'm worried about is my future, my security?"

"I've always understood that. But it's your looks, too. You should give up those shorts and baring yourself to the midriff," Teddy advised. "Get into the middle-aged slipcover, like your mother." Teddy's camp often involved his so alluding to himself.

Bo had put the *Prélude* on the automatic, and it was beginning a third time. Teddy went to the turntable and cut the music off.

Silence fell like a flatiron; Bo could only argue and quarrel with music in the background; without a sound track he was lost.

"I'm clearing the fucking hell out of here," he announced, getting to his feet.

"Why don't you?"

"You always say that—you don't care what becomes of me!"

"Well, it is my house. Go or stay as you please."

"Yes, your house, and I hate it!" Bo shouted. "I hate you and your horrible old mother and everything in it!"

"I thought you were clearing the fucking hell out."

"I am!" Bo shouted even louder, and made for the doorway. He

177

turned, remembering bitterly that Teddy always kept the keys to the cars in his pockets, only one of the many "controls" against which Bo fumed.

"I can read you like a book," said Teddy. "Here." He flung a leather key case across the room, where it landed at Bo's feet—the keys to the Ghia, which Bo much preferred to the Mercedes, considering it more dashing and youthful. "I know what's got your balls in an uproar—that *numéro* we saw this morning on the road."

"Well, what if he has?" Bo answered, his lower lip pouting.

"I couldn't care less. Only, it's a little late—it's past eleven. Get wise, Bo—you're an old man to someone like that. You saw how he gave us the brushoff. He's trade, if anything, and uninterested trade, at that."

"Maybe that was because he saw me with *you*." Bo underlined it. "Who's an old man? Not me!" Now he had the keys to the Ghia, he felt better. "That number looked local to me, and I'm going up to the garage to ask Rafe Cadle who he is. He'll know if anybody does."

"Yes, Rafe will know," Teddy agreed indifferently. He added, "But if you drag him or anything else back here, be quiet about it. I got Mother off to a good night's sleep and I don't want her wakened."

The rope, with all its slack, had been tossed to him, but Bo had sudden misgivings. Seeing these, Teddy urged, "Go on, go; get yourself laid—if you can. At least I won't have to hear any more about your career." He gave it the Ed Sullivan pronunciation, *kreer*, as a joke.

"You've never wanted to hear about my career!"

"Maybe because you never had one."

"I did! I *do* have one!"

Teddy laughed. "Then what are you doing here—with me?"

"Oh, *you!*" Bo screamed at him. "I hate you! *I hate you!*"

"All the more reason for getting out," Teddy answered, with the complacence he had developed for these scenes. "And don't forget your house keys. I'm about to lock up."

Bo slammed out of the house. Teddy heard him roll back the garage doors and the furious way he started up the Ghia, backing with a squeal of brakes into the road. He headed upriver, good as his word, toward Rafe Cadle's. It was too bad he hadn't eaten something, Teddy thought, but then tried to forget about it; if he had permitted himself to fret over Bo's almost daily tantrums, he'd have been dead long ago. He had learned little in his sixty-five years, but one thing he had come to accept was that when a day was over, it was over and time to forget it. And after neatly washing dishes and locking up, he went to bed.

BOOK

THREE

CHAPTER 1

Amid the bedlam of background noises heard around the clock by Cope's Corner residents—motor traffic, quarries, passenger planes zooming overhead in the New York-to-Harrisburg lane, jets, motorboats, freight trains laboring up the Jersey shore—one sound could be heard above all the others. This was the "siren" of the firehouse in Olympia, seven miles down the river, which blasted off weekday mornings at seven, at noon, and at five o'clock. It also announced fires that had broken out in the area, summoning by arranged long and short signals members of volunteer hose companies from surrounding villages when needed. This noise, which caused Olympians to stop dead in their tracks and shudder, was like a gigantic breaking of wind, and when it was heard by people in outlying areas (it sounded more obscene some distance away) they set their clocks or, if members of fire squads, listened for the exact, repeated blasts that meant a two- or three-alarm call. Then they either laughed or giggled, depending on which sex they were (and a few screamed), because no one could disguise, no matter how often they had heard it or how accustomed to it they had become, what the sound reminded them of. It resounded up the valley, echoing through the hills, and, laughter or giggles (or screams) over, day could proceed to its next phase.

Those who heard this impolite noise may have needed to be reminded of the time, or to be told that there was a fire somewhere in the vicinity, but they did not have to think twice to know that it came from Olympia. It seemed symbolic of that aggressive little town: self-advertising, boastful of historic charms, blatting of the attractions at its Playhouse (from a sound truck cruising the countryside), insisting on its espousal of Art for All. Olympia was, in many ways, the hub of Bucks County life, at least that which clustered on the river within sound of its "siren," which owed its shattering volume to the bomb-scare days of the fifties. Olympia needed no sound to make itself heard. By day it was crowded with natives and tourists, dodging the stone trucks roaring through the streets, and at night its bars were filled with people who had heard disparaging things said of it and had come to find out if they were true. Not only was Olympia heard, it was felt as a vibration, by people from communities surrounding it as well as by sightseers come from far away.

To most of these Olympia *was* Bucks County, and the lovely, lush landscape extending westward from the river was hinterland, beneath notice. The town was supposed to have been the setting for two best-selling novels soon to be made into films, bitterly resented but ardently aped and reread. One crotchety novelist (not the one who had written the best sellers presumably laid in Olympia) complained that the town was peopled by outsiders, and that the real countians were just everyday folks; Olympia, he pointed out, was not the whole of the county and should not be taken to be representative of it. "Bucks," opined one local newspaper editor, "is a state of mind"; he hoped, perhaps, to attribute subtle attitudes of mind to its residents, or perhaps he had read this about another place and hoped to make a wide shoe fit, but it didn't. Whatever its good and bad points, Olympia seemed one more American community trying to keep up with Westport and Woodstock and Carmel; it had been dubbed, with some accuracy, a rich man's Provincetown without the sea.

Olympia and the Corner were little different from other small places being devoured by suburbia, but there was no altering the image tourists had made of "the county" for themselves: it was Bohemia-on-the-Cheap, accessible, capable of being absorbed over a cocktail, easily left behind. Visitors came in all seasons, hungry to "see the canal," the "quaint streets" (*quaint* was an operative word in Olympia), to eat in its generally drab restaurants and to hesitate over parting with small sums for souvenirs. There was big money spent in Olympia, but not by tourists, most of whom were blue-haired moms on all-expenses-paid bus tours that wound up with a Playhouse matinee; they saved their spending-money dollar for a bag of 69-cent gumdrops and an ice cream soda at The Palace of Versailles, a Victorian lean-to on the river with wicker chairs painted pink and gas chandeliers, before reboarding the bus to return to wherever they had come from. The heavy sums were dropped by the well-heeled professional people living beyond the town's perimeter, in "simple" $100,000 houses, old or new—the successful writers and television executives, Madison Avenue boys who used the county as a dormitory, medicos and their wives, "hidden rich" or "in" groups, who kept to their own pyramids and abhorred the 69-cent moms and their "Blue Hair" Playhouse, as it had come to be called. Olympia stood to its surrounding hamlets and villages in somewhat the same relation as does Cannes to the Riviera and Grasse to French hill towns of the Department of the Var. But Olympia was no Grasse, and its airs were far from perfumed, its chief odor, in fact, often being a stench of cesspools so foul as to send tourists and natives come to shop scuttling back to their cars, expensively parked in nearby lots, or left cheaply at the town's edges; on a warm June day, Olympia's canal was as fetid as those of Venice in September, with about as much hope of anything being done about it. But, man, was it ever *quaint!*

Residents of outlying villages like Cope's Corner went into Olympia, if not daily, several times a week, to drink or eat, have prescriptions filled at the Olympia Pharmacy (the clearing house for valley gossip), buy a hammer at the hardware store or pick up the new James Bond at the library. Then they hurried home before the commuter traffic began; for traffic—how to get where you were going without taking hours doing it—and parking—or trying to find a place to park once you got there—were the two biggest headaches in Olympia as everywhere else.

One of the more conspicuous signs planted in the Cope's Corner grass quadrangle announced speed limits of fifty miles per hour, except where otherwise indicated. LIMITS STRICTLY ENFORCED, the sign added in red afterthought italics, as if to convince itself, if not motorists. Not only were limits unenforced (it was questionable whether they could be, local police being few and cars being as they are) but the qualifying markers along the roads (SLOW,

185

CHILDREN PLAYING, SPEED 35) went generally unnoticed. Speeds of seventy and eighty were not uncommon in the Corner itself, once the intersection stops had been complied with; after that, on the stretch of curving road leading to Olympia, anything went, and it was every man for himself or every car for itself; often they seemed one and the same as they streaked by, a unit welded together by speed and hurry, beyond any cop's jurisdiction, out of sight before he could blow his whistle.

The countryside where trees had not been cut to make way for the demands of traffic was dense with buttonwoods, great oaks, towering rhododendrons, even blight-surviving elms, but at seventy miles an hour few were aware of these unless, coming a cropper at one of the tortuous turnings, some teen-age driver found himself spattered halfway up a trunk, his companion, likely as not, hurled face down into the canal. Then the tree appeared and was realized, unlovely, jaded and tired at the end of summer's road, all birds flown in terror from its branches; the canal was seen to be what it was, a sluggish, murky unpleasantness full of slime and frogs, deep enough for drowning.

The county, like the rest of America, had lived so long in the age of the automobile that the high accident rates were taken for granted. Cars were everywhere: cars bought and paid for, cars traded in as down payment with two years of payments to come on the next, but cars, in either case causing their owners—or owners in part—anxieties of depreciation, fenders bent or door locks sprung, tires worn smooth. Heavy, freight-carrying (but usually underpowered and overloaded) vehicles jammed the narrow roads, straining the bridges and struggling up the steep hills, with processions of honking, travel-depressed travelers behind. The road building program that would eliminate these hazards had long been on the state's agenda—but nobody wanted anything changed. Bucks roads had been cleared for horsemen and carriages; even the traffic of the thirties had been too much for them. But soon would come the gigantic cloverleaf intersections, one above and one below Olympia: for cars, not people, as the valley protective associations, which had fought Harrisburg for years, complained to no avail, not unlike the birds, chorusing their protests above the ear-splitting dins. Migration patterns of valley birds were changing; they seemed to know, as did the people, that soon the exhaust from

Rafe Cadle's garage, that cooked over the Corner, would be fused with the smogs of Olympia and Gasoline would be king.

The procession of cars between the Corner and Olympia on any day was not limited to tourist buses and out-of-state cars. The Al Hanters drove to Olympia at least once daily, invariably separately, Al in his Chevy station wagon to pick up the Philadelphia papers, Fran in her red Olds, on some last-minute luncheonette errand. Both kept their cars parked on the lot, which had been constructed to accommodate thirty customer cars. Rafe Cadle was not only on the road at all hours in cars he was repairing, but often drove to Olympia simply to get the hell away from the Corner and Mae, who hated him for leaving her behind; Rafe rarely used the Buick, pampering it for the antique it would one day become. The trips of Dr. Ingle to and from Tuliptrees were paced and necessary, but Susan Ingle was as compulsive about driving as she was about bridge and cigarettes, often running up mileage of a hundred miles a day going nowhere but returning for lunch and dinner and then going out again for bridge afterward, picking up the girls and delivering them. When using one of the two Ingle cars Bobby traveled an unpredictable maze designed to get him as far from the Corner as possible—Corner to Princeton, Corner to Trenton, Corner to Anywhere, returning by back roads leading through Subberton or Olympia. Bo deWillig, especially when Teddy was in New York, used the Ghia to do errands, go out to lunch with some crony appearing at the Playhouse, or cruise the Olympia streets for "chicken." In addition to the Mercedes, Teddy kept a perfectly reconditioned 1922 Pierce-Arrow (a monument to Rafe Cadle's skills and Teddy's indifference to costs) which was used for "prestige" meetings of guests arriving by train in Trenton, Yardley or Hackersville. Miriam Glidden, though owning only the Continental, used it whenever she went out and had never been seen on foot in the village. The young MacFindens already gave evidence of restlessness, their triple garage—waiting for one other —being empty most of the day. Ironically, the Misses Bowyer, responsible for the hundreds of cars that rolled into the luncheonette lot every day and parked and rolled on, had no car and wanted none; those rare times Miss Flora had to go into Olympia she used the taxi ($6 round trip and a dollar tip). Less affluent, Fringe people exhibited similar patterns. Many families, though well below the $5,000 minimum yearly income bracket the county boasted, owned two or three cars, usually secondhand, one sometimes parked in the road to rust in all weathers, until a son or daughter could scrape together money for a license to drive it. One old soak, at the Corner's lower end, used his car to drive the thirty feet from his house to the mailbox and back. And there was one childless Fringe wife whose husband worked in West Trenton, so afraid of rape that she spent the better part of his working hours driving from one end of the Corner to the other, drinking progressions of coffees at the luncheonette, breakfasting and lunching there as well, visiting the Misses Bowyer and, at last, exhausted, parking outside her house to await her husband's return, all car doors locked from inside. A sad case, of course; the woman drove Susan Ingle almost wild, the way she shuttled up and down the road, stopping at the signs and then accelerating and changing gears in front of the hedge. The doctor, who had to hear all about it at least once a week, admitted it was an odd neurosis, but dismissed it with a shrug, as he did cases not his own. Only Mae Cadle was housebound, living in squalid, self-imposed purdah, a Hindi word she almost certainly had never heard.

It was, as Teddy Hubbard said, very late. Bo drew up in front of the Cadle garage in the Ghia a few minutes after midnight, as Rafe was closing. But Rafe was always obliging to good customers, whatever the hour, and when Bo questioned him about the man seen that morning in the road, had quite a lot of information to pass on.

"He's a wop with kind of a funny name. Hit the village last night. Fran Hanter over there gave him a lift and he's been here ever since, or was, most of the day, anyway."

"When did you see him last?" asked Bo.

Rafe pushed back his billed cap and scratched his head. It had been a long, hot day; he had to think a minute. "Around sunset. The guy got himself a job planting trees over at the Glidden place. But he left there and went down to the towpath. Maybe to sleep; I know he slept down there last night, on the ledge."

"Thanks, Rafe." Bo winked and turned the Ghia toward the bridge, stopping and getting out at the stairs leading down to the canal. The place was in darkness, except for the dim glow cast by

188

the bridge lights, but Bo saw at once there was no one there, and went back to the Ghia. He considered for a minute what to do, then swung the car sharply into the luncheonette lot and, with a spatter of gravel, set out for Olympia. Teddy had been right, it was too late, but at least he could have a few more drinks and something to eat before returning to the Corner. He was doing almost seventy by the time he reached the Fringes, the Ghia taking the curves and uneven road grades lightly as an insect hovering, and, in case there was activity on the towpath, Bo beamed the car's spotlight onto the canal banks, where the road ran parallel, as he drove. All he saw were night-bird watchers in a canoe, paddling slowly upstream. Luck was not with him; the quarry he sought had, no doubt, taken to the road and gone on. But he would make sure his absence from Teddy would be long enough to give him doubts and regret for what he had said, leading to apologies in the morning.

Olympia wore its characteristic Monday night look, that of a small town recovering from a tourist weekend, dark except for the big street lamp hanging above the Busy Corner, only a few cars parked beside meters hooded for the night. Bo knew his way around and tried two places where the man might have gone: Ben's, a beer joint on Monkeywrench Alley, and the White Hare, where the bar was square; but both were half empty, doing only light hangover business from the weekend. This left, since it was beginning to be Tuesday, only The Wharf, a lavender night spot patronized mostly by queers and queens' molls and lesbians, not a likely place to find the quarry he was pursuing.

Bo had, years ago, purchased the bartender, whom he could count on to fill him in on the dirt and who greeted him with effusion. "Mr. deWillig! Handsome as ever!"

Bo gave his routine eyelash response; he was accustomed to being the bird with brightest plumage and took this as his due. "Where is everybody?" he asked the bartender.

"There's a guy in the back room running a blackjack game and stripping them all bare" was the answer. "I speak figuratively," he added, seeing Bo's expression, "meaning he's taken everybody's mind off drinks and is cleaning up."

"Anybody we know?"

"Nobody *I* know, but he's been breaking up the whole place ever since he came in about an hour ago."

The clamor in the next room bore out what the bartender said. Bo ordered a drink and sauntered to the doorway. The room was heavy with smoke and crowded, but seated on the floor beneath the dart boards, legs crossed under him, was the man he had seen in the road. He was prime quarry—not only were the men and boys surrounding him going to pieces over him, but the women, too, were conducting every diversion they could think of to get him onto their side and away. The woman who was working hardest, one of the local lady artists, known as Evil Days because of the bad times on which she had fallen, saw Bo enter and greeted him.

"Hi, Bo. Buy me a drink."

Bo called the order to the bartender. "Who is he?" he asked.

"A god," said Evil Days. "A god in blue jeans. *God!*"

"He wasn't in blue jeans this morning," Bo said.

"You *know* this god?"

"No, only have seen him."

"He's had the deal for almost an hour." Evil Days took the drink the bartender brought her. "His name's Tavio."

As cards were dealt onto the floor and antes upped, Bo saw that what the bartender said was true. There was a pile of ones and fives in front of Tavio which grew with each hand played. He seemed oblivious to the *double entendres* being hurled at him.

"I'll stand on *that!*"

"Hit me, Tavio!"

"Me too, Tavio. Hard!"

One player, though, was trying to break the winning streak. "I'll go down for double. One on each."

"Are one-eyed jacks wild?"

"Call them knaves, dear."

"No, only deuces are wild."

Bo and Evil Days wedged their way to where Tavio squatted.

"Get those tattoos!" Evil Days said. "I wish I were rich."

Bo was silent, trying to decide on a strategy.

"Hang up those nets, Bo, it's no use."

"*Blackjack!*" cried the man who had gone doubles. "Now we'll show you!"

Tavio relinquished the pack. Then he gathered up the bills in front of him and rose to his feet.

"Come on, Tavio, you can't quit now!" the players who had lost cried. "Give us a chance to win it back!"

Tavio did not answer, simply moved toward the door, the bills held lightly between his hands in a ball, ignoring the quips flung after him.

"Well, you god with the roses, are you always so lucky?" Evil Days asked, putting a hand on Tavio's arm.

"Sometimes," he said.

"I wish I had a little of your luck."

"You can have all of it," Tavio said, pressing the bills into her hands, moving swiftly away, past the bar and out into the street.

"Wait!" shouted Bo, running after him. "Didn't I see you this morning, up in the Corner?"

Tavio turned. "Did you? Oh, yes."

"You remember? We—I offered you a ride."

"I remember. I didn't want it."

"How about a drink?"

"Don't drink."

"Well, then, a Coke or sandwich?"

"I've had both."

Bo knew the ropes; this kind of resistance was genuine, and the only thing that could break it was money. But money clearly meant not a thing to this man, which fascinated Bo almost more than anything else about him.

"You won," he said, "and then gave it all away. Why?"

Tavio shrugged.

"Don't you like money?"

"It likes me too well."

Bo was, for once, stymied. "Then what do you like? Tell me."

"Not interested," Tavio said, beginning to move away.

"Don't go!" cried Bo. "If you're going somewhere, let me give you a lift."

"Maybe we're not going the same way."

"I'll take you wherever you want to go," Bo offered. "My car's here."

Tavio looked at the Ghia. "Okay," he said, "you can drop me where you tried to pick me up this morning."

Bo took this for a deal, sealed by the symbol of the Ghia. "But that's where I *live!*" he exclaimed, amazed he was making it.

"That's where you can let me out," Tavio repeated.

Once inside the Ghia, riding slowly toward the Corner, Bo reached into his bag for other tricks. "I'd have sworn this morning you were wearing white, not blue," he said, giving Tavio an admiring glance.

"Maybe I was," Tavio answered, as though he couldn't remember.

"But blue jeans are for you!"

Tavio was silent.

"So you live somewhere around here?" Bo pursued.

"No."

"Then where did you change your clothes?"

"In the store where I bought these. When I'm through with one set, I leave the old ones behind."

"You left your other clothes in the *store?*" Bo's fetishes were odd; he sounded as if he wanted to add Tavio's old trousers to his collection. "Which store?"

"Don't remember," said Tavio, bored with it.

"So you're just making it from one place to the next?"

"If you want to look at it that way."

"But where did you expect to sleep tonight?" Bo caught himself in time and did not reveal what Cadle had told him; he knew this was pushing his luck, but it was now or never. And his triumph over Teddy, if he netted this quarry, even if only by the expedient of a bed unshared, drove him on.

"I sleep where I please."

"Look," said Bo, "the house where I live is full of beds."

"No, thanks," Tavio said to this, "I'll get out where I said."

"You mean, 'Thanks, but no, thanks'?"

"Just—no."

Though Bo had driven slowly, they were now more than halfway to the Corner. He stalled for time. "I heard you've been working at the Corner, planting trees."

"Who told you that?"

"Someone I asked."

"I work sometimes."

"I saw those rhododendrons. Hard work—but that wouldn't bother you." Bo tried it on again, giving Tavio a long look.

Silence.

"You know, you wouldn't *have* to do work as hard as that." But Bo saw Tavio wasn't listening; he was watching the road as it unwound, his eyes straight ahead. He employed the symbol that had seemed to work. "Do you like my Ghia?"

"It's all right."

"What cars do you like?"

Despite the lusciousness of the quarry, Bo was becoming exasperated. When there was no reply to this, he said, "You seem glad enough to ride in them."

"Sure."

"Is there anything you do like?"

Tavio turned his eyes toward Bo, looking him over as if for the first time. "What I like you wouldn't know about," he said.

"Don't be so sure of that. After all, you were in that bar."

"So what?"

"It's that kind of bar."

"Is it?"

"And you were listening to what they all said."

"I wasn't listening, I was winning."

They were getting close to the Fringes of the Corner, the rows of small houses where the road narrowed sharply before fanning out at the intersection. Tavio already had his hand on the door handle, ready to get out. Bo had saved his trump card for the end. Money, cars, innuendos—all had failed. He flashed his smile, bringing the Ghia to a halt in front of the Hubbard driveway. "Come on," he said, "I'll find out what you like—I'm versatile," and let his hand rest on Tavio's thigh. He felt the thigh stiffen. "If it's—"

He never finished. The next thing he felt was a hot flash of light beneath his left eye, where Tavio's knuckles struck him. A trickle of blood ran from his nose onto his shirt. It was lucky he had drawn up at the side of the road because by the time he could see to turn the Ghia into the drive, his head was spinning. Tavio had left the door open as he got out, and as Bo maneuvered the car into the garage, between the Mercedes and the Pierce, he could hear the door scraping the brightly polished lacquer of the Pierce's rear fender—there would be hell to pay tomorrow. Before letting himself into the dark house, he took stock: he was starving hungry, and his hangover was already beginning, but worse, he had committed *lèse-twenties*—damaged the Pierce, which, of all his ghastly camp, Teddy loved most. The hunger would be swallowed up by sleep and the hangover would take care of itself; the rapidly swelling eye could be explained, even boasted of and turned to advantage; but the Pierce's scraped fender would mean playing Little Boy Blue for days, until Teddy finally forgave.

CHAPTER 2

June's lunar crescent, rising thin as a nail paring twelve days earlier, had seemed to bring the summer news everyone waited for. The signs were promising for the month's remaining weather: the sky had been clear, there had been rain in the moon's lap, and the rain had come in ways farmers and gardeners hope for, at night, steady and gentle, or as showers during afternoons, with red skies clearing at sunset. People had already complained, as the moon waxed to full quarter, of the damping off of plantlings, predicting the cool, wet summer supposed to follow an open, almost snowless winter and a tardy spring. But the day of portent, midway between equinoxes, had given the cue for what was to come. No one living in the valley now needed weather reports to tell them that the solstice had brought summer with a vengeance. Almanacs, ever cautious, predicted a week of Clearing, Fair, Pleasant, Sunny, Sunny and Warm weather, with only a single Unsettled for Saturday. No one believed this; Sunday's 96 degrees and Monday's only slightly less humid 94 augured poorly, and the slight fluctuations of the mercury portended calms rather than storms that would break the heat.

Most birds presaged the days more accurately than either almanacs or forecasters, waking at first light and early retreating into the motionless foliage of the trees, where they took refuge, only low nest builders, like hummingbirds, sometimes stirring lower branches, larger ones—song sparrows, mourning doves, purple martins, grackles, scarlet tanagers—preferring the deeper shade, perched still as porcelain near the trunks. In the upper air sparrow hawks moved swiftly in predatory arcs as usual, but below, on the canal banks, where the heat gathered in the shallows, ducks hid their heads beneath their wings until the sun should drop and bring coolness. Flowers, too, told the story, peonies drooping, only daisies standing erect and unvanquished in their beds.

It was too hot to be anywhere but outdoors. Miriam Glidden lay asleep in the glider at the far end of the terrace. The day had taught her a frightening lesson. For the first time since Cort's death, she had realized the rancor that was at the root of her suffering, anger against him for having died. And she was still playing a role, even in her sleep, a role inside the many she had played to herself all day and to Tavio. The syllables of his name rose and dropped with each breath she drew: *Ta*—vio, *Ta*—vio, *Ta*—vio.

It had been easier to see herself as someone else, a woman who, alone (and *deserted*—why did that word incessantly penetrate, as though Cort's death had been an act of aggression?), had no choice but to play out lines remembered from other situations, other lives. Her playing of these other Miriams represented consciousness turning in upon itself and wishing to see herself as she appeared *to him*. It was these other selves that had visualized his touching her, that had heard his voice speaking of her portrait, that had warned him to come no nearer. Her real self—but the things she had done since his leaving at sundown, before she fell asleep, told more than anything.

She had pondered whether or not he would return, and had gone at once to inspect the rhododendrons he had planted, seeing the care with which he had placed them, the expertise of the sharp, black edges of earth enclosing the mulch beneath each. The tools he had used, too, had been cleaned and replaced on the racks where he had found them. Nothing remained of his presence except a rolled bundle of newspaper, which he had left behind on the potting shelf of the garden house. This held her eye, and, curious as to what it contained, she picked it up, gingerly and carefully, as a snooper steams open a letter. She unwrapped it, observing the exact newsprint that was uppermost. The contents had requickened the feeling she experienced when he told her he had not had lunch—a half-squeezed tube of shaving cream, a brush, clean and dry, a safety razor and packet of blades, a comb, a small Turkish towel bearing the name of some hotel almost worn away by use. These, then, were the bare necessities of the man she had first feared: no gun, no— What had she thought (or hoped) to find? Ashamed, she rewrapped the things in the newspaper and returned it to the shelf so it would seem untouched and undisturbed.

He would come back, this had told her, if ever she had doubted it. And there were ways in which she could evade him. The house locks, no matter how little used, were more than adequate. The car stood, ready to go, in the garage. She could, even, telephone Rosa, to say she had had second thoughts about her invitation to visit, and set out forthwith, leaving a locked house and an envelope containing a day's wages.

Her day of invented activity had tired her, and she had gravitated easily to the pattern of her life with Cort and the variation of it she had continued with Rosa. The makings of Cort's ceremonial martinis stood in the pantry on a silver tray—gin, vermouth, shaker, paring knife for the zest of lemon he had liked. Rosa was a long-drink girl and had insisted on tonic water; that, too, was there. And, as the sun dropped behind the hills, Miriam poured herself a relaxing two inches, filled the glass with tonic, and carried it to the glider. Memory at once furnished the featureless oval that had become Cort's face. How impossible to remember with exactness the faces of those we love, she thought; even Rosa's familiar mask of caution and laughter now eluded her. But she recalled Tavio's features with a clearness that was almost distortion. As from behind a glass pane, she saw him watching her, and the more she tried to avoid his eyes, the closer and more intense they became. Death and life, she thought, were different sides of a mirror. And finally she closed her eyes and stared at the image on her retina, the swatch of black hair triangulating down the forehead into a point above the eyebrows, the eyes, black, with only glints of lesser black, the asymmetrical smile, the lips both cruel and sensual. She tried for an imposition of features that would make Tavio's disappear and Cort's come forward—Good

196

triumphing over Evil, prompted a voice that was not hers. But the trick would not work: she was obsessed, and her compact with herself had been sealed, without volition, the moment Tavio had come up the drive. Besides, Cort no longer *was*.

At last decision came to her: Being what she was, she would fight this obsession, beginning with herself. She felt exhausted; the drink was not what she wanted and she set it on a table beside her, and before she knew it she had stretched out in the glider and fallen asleep.

When she next opened her eyes the almost full moon was dropping in the sky at the end of the garden. The air hung heavy and motionless in the trees and all was quiet, as though the usually noisy Corner had raced back in time; quarries were still, there was no traffic, and she could hear the river flowing. The cicadas began their shrill, chirping cadences and the moon disappeared behind the buttonwoods near the canal. It was still oppressively hot; the heat seemed to rise from the river mists like white, airless down left behind by the moonlight.

Suddenly a sheet of lightning lit up the sky and she saw Tavio standing a few feet away. She started up, rationally listening for the thunder that should follow, but there was none, it was heat lightning merely. Another flash winked on and off. Her eyes had not deceived her: he was there and had not moved. She tried to remember how long she had slept, but had no way of knowing if it had been hours or minutes.

He spoke. "Don't be afraid."

She stared at him through the darkness, hoping for another flash that would enable her to get up and run into the house. "How long—when did you come back?"

"Just now," he answered. "You were sleeping."

"Yes, sleeping," she repeated, slowly realizing she had known this would happen, happen in this way. "I must go in."

"Why must you?" he asked, his voice soft in the warm dark. "Please don't. Please stay."

"But why should I?"

He said nothing to this, leaving the question for her to answer for herself. The lightning continued to flash in the sky beyond the trees.

"I asked you not to come back," she said.

"But you knew I would. Didn't you?"

"Yes, I knew."

"How?"

All at once it seemed the easiest thing to talk to him; she realized how long it had been since she had spoken with anyone but women. "Because you left your bundle in the garden house."

"You found it?"

"I saw it when I went to close the door." The thought struck her that somehow he already knew this, was testing her to see what she would say.

"You looked at what is in it?"

"Yes."

"Why?"

"Because—because I—well, I think I was still afraid of you."

"But you're not now." His voice had moved closer in the darkness.

"I don't know," she said. "Nothing like this has ever happened to me—and it mustn't happen!" She conjured up her decision to fight him, beginning with herself, and rose from the glider. There was a sound of glass shattering—the glass she had set down earlier, falling to the terrace stones. A bright flash—the brightest of all—gave him to her fully and she saw that he was moving toward her. She stared at the stiff new blue clothes he wore, bluer than daylight in the lightning, knowing that it would always be like this that she would remember him, as she remembered Cort, not as he was the first time she saw him, but as the composite he came slowly to be, standing with a fistful of brushes in one hand, his mahlstick in the other. The mahlstick and its clatter as she fell across it that day shattered the silence, like the breaking glass.

She said, her voice only a little louder than a whisper, "Please don't come nearer. I—you see, when you've lost a husband, as I have—what I mean is, I want to be alone."

"Oh," he said, and waited a long minute. "Are you sure?"

"I . . . oh, why are you doing this?" she asked miserably. "I've told you how it is. Please go."

"Maybe you should forget."

"I can't!" Her breath caught in her throat. "Have *you* ever lost anyone?"

"I've lost everyone."

198

"Then you should know."

"I do know." He moved toward her, standing so close she could hear his breathing. A memory of his body with the roses cascading down his shoulders struck her and she closed her eyes tightly against him, finding, not to her surprise, that the image remained.

"Please," she said a last time, "leave me now—sleep in the garden house if you must, but leave!"

She heard his breath closer. "I knew you'd change your mind," he said. "That's why I came back."

"And you thought it would be this easy," she lashed out at him, defending her memory of Cort as well as herself. "I was in love with my husband. I'm still in love with him."

"Of course," he said soothingly, as if she were a child. "I saw that about you."

"But you!" she exclaimed, trembling. "Is this what you do? Prey on women like me, who are suffering, who can't fight you back?"

He replied in the same, soothing tone. "You're not fighting, not fighting at all."

"Then what do you think this is?"

"Not fear," he answered; "you're not afraid of me, you admitted that."

The lightning had stopped but a faint afterglow remained, staining the sky over the river. She saw him more clearly now, enabling her to guess the hour and how long she must have slept.

"Yes," she said helplessly, "I admitted that, but whether I'm afraid of you or not doesn't matter." She broke into tears, covering her face with her hands, and sank down onto the glider.

"It matters," he said easily, sitting down beside her, as if waiting for her tears to stop. Then she felt his arms around her and with a single, last sob let herself fall against him. "You see, you're not afraid." His breath quickened as he felt her breasts, firm and bare beneath her dress. "You," he said. "Your name—what is it?"

She told him.

"Miriam. And you must say mine. You remember it."

"I remember but I can't say it."

"Tavio?" He said it for her. "Why not?"

"I don't know why, but I can't."

He lifted her face to his, kissing her softly on the lips. "I'll teach you to say it," he said, kissing her again.

"No," she answered him, shaking her head, "no." She had let him hold her, passive and soft, but now she dug her palms into his chest and pushed him away. "This mustn't be!"

"Why do you say that?" He took her hands and held them in his. "I saw the first minute how it would be between us, and so did you. Why do you deny it?"

"In my world there are denials. I told you, I loved my husband." She sighed. "That's all—I can't say any more."

The white down of river mist was drifting up toward them from the garden, and the trees overhead exuded a last fragrance of night.

"Miriam," he said, "speak my name."

She sat very still. He will go now, she made a last prayer to herself. It is the key to something in him, this insistence of his that I say his name. If I don't say it he will leave, no longer exist, and this will never have happened.

But he did not go. "I was right," he said, "you knew from the beginning too."

The struggle was over. "Yes, you were right, I knew." She took his face between her hands and kissed him passionately.

"Miriam, Miriam!" The pale, golden smell of her maddened him; his hands, rough on her skin, moved to the buttons of her dress.

"No," she said, "not here."

"Where, then?"

She indicated that he should release her, then got up from the glider, taking him by one hand and leading him toward the house. "There are steps here," she warned, guiding him inside.

"Can't we make a light?"

"No. It will be easier for me in darkness." She walked a little ahead, still leading him, until at the top of a steep staircase they came to a low room. There was glow enough coming through the windows for him to see a low, old-fashioned bed with a quilt on it. He waited for her to speak. She said, "This is a bed I've never slept in. It has to be this bed."

He took her in his arms again. "Which bed doesn't matter. Let me undress you. Quickly!"

"Yes," she answered, returning his kisses. "Oh, yes, yes!" And she felt him roughly rip the buttons from her dress and tear her slip from her body. She stood naked before him as he kissed her breasts, her belly, the soft down below. He knelt before her, clutching her to him, hands cupping her buttocks.

"Lie down," he commanded.

She let herself fall back onto the bed and waited, hearing him as he stripped off his clothes, then felt and heard, in a single instant, the slap of his body as he flung himself on her. As he entered her, gently, she made a low sound, like a moan, because he was big, as she had known he would be.

"Wait," she said.

"Waiting is good."

"Yes." She already felt consumed by him, possessed utterly, at once satisfied and tormented by his bigness, the hardness of his breath, the roses unseen in the dark but bright as she remembered them. She let him know he could do anything, and it came to her in a surge of gratitude that this was unlike any time she had had with Cort. This was guilt and fire, violence and penitence—fulfillment of grief by betrayal of what Cort had been to her and she to him. From the beginning she was with him . . . slow . . . quick . . . quick . . . slow, her rhythm the same as his, but in reverse, as if they were old lovers and she had known him always. The fountain of dreamlike ecstasy surged through her and slowly fell away into a silence of breathing. This had been no dream; he was both harsh and tender above her. They lay quiet in the last night stillness, listening to the calls of night birds in the trees. Then, passion returning, they clasped each other again in a flood of fresh pleasure, complete and exhausting. At last, when the first, spidery daylight crept through the night mists into the low room, they slept.

It was the clatter of tools being moved in the garden house that brought her halfway out of sleep, a sleep deep and without memory, like that she had known under drugs given her by Dr. Ingle after Cort's death. Then she heard the thrust of the shovel into the ground by the driveway and came fully awake. The sound had been there for some time, like the beating of her heart, and she saw by the light over the river that day was well along. The night lay like a luminous transparency on her memory, remembered sensation complete to the very edges. She stretched, searching her mind for guilt, but found none; her mind, like her body, was empty but for simple hunger and the knowledge that nothing had ever been like last night and would never be again. It had been a mutation, a flower of no color known in the spectrum, as quickly opened as it was quickly folded.

The telephone was clamoring—rooms away—and then she remembered where she was, in the beggar's room above the old stone kitchen, to which she had brought him—refusing to speak his name—because she had shied away from her own bedroom and Cort's, or from any of the guest rooms. The ringing persisted, and at last she roused herself, going naked down the stairway and across the house and up to her own bedroom.

"Hello!" she answered, almost angrily.

"Miriam! It's Rosa! I've been calling and calling and getting no answer. Are you all right?"

"Yes, of course," Miriam answered. "I was in the garden." The lie, a beginning, small one, brought guilt at last.

"I simply had to call you. I had the strangest premonition that something's wrong. Is it?"

"Of course not, dear; I'm perfectly fine."

Miriam listened, providing the assurances her sister seemed to need. She was well, it was a lovely day but very hot, the premonition had been foolish. As she hung up she knew that the first, pristine freshness of the day would not return: guilt had now sprouted its fast-growing vine—already she could feel its tendrils. The shovel, cutting into the earth, reminded her that this was a day to be faced like any other, a day of mending and making do with what life offered, a day that *had to be.*

By now many things were known in the Corner about Tavio, and opinions about him had been formed by those who had seen or talked with him. All, save Don MacFinden and Teddy Hubbard's mother, had seen him; Don had just missed him as he drove off to the quarry that morning, and Mrs. Hubbard, who didn't get up until after eleven, was unaware of his existence. But Miss Hankins had seen him. It chanced to be the hour of day she liked most, before her patient stirred and the long hours of reassuring, cosseting, denying and simple enduring began. From her room in the absurd "Seville" tower she had spied him as she was doing her hair. She paused, brush in hand, and said aloud, "There, Hankins, my girl, is what God might have sent you. But He didn't. Your fate will be always to minister to the lame, the halt and the blind—until you are lame and halt and blind yourself." Miss Hankins often talked this way to herself, when there was no one to hear; it was almost like having a companion of her own. Later she would tell her only village cronies, the Misses Bowyer, about the man now almost out of her sight—or maybe she'd be selfish and keep him for herself. To remember. "Forever," she said, "forever and forever and forever." Was that the line? No. " 'Tomorrow and tomorrow and tomorrow.' One too many tomorrows for you, Hankins, old girl."

It was known, for example, that though Tavio had slept on the cement ledge beneath the bridge the night before, he had found another place, and a more comfortable one, for spending Monday night. Al Hanter, who didn't at all like Fran's attitude and the way she was behaving toward him, had put Willie Bentrup, the township cop, onto the problem, briefing him on Tavio's undesirability when Bentrup came in for his regular coffee and Danish. Bentrup, when afterward he had his tires and oil checked at Rafe Cadle's, picked up a few more details—that Tavio had evidently found himself at least a temporary berth at the Glidden place and so was no longer, strictly speaking, a vagrant. The Olympia police had passed on to Bentrup the story of the blackjack game and the information that it had been Bo deWillig who drove Tavio back to the Corner during the small hours of the morning. Nancy MacFinden had remarked to Don, after he came home early from Number Three, that she had seen an odd-looking man in the road the previous morning, and that he had stared at her.

Don had shown the instant alarm of a husband of two weeks. " 'Odd looking'? How was he odd?"

"Perhaps strange would have been a better word," Nancy qualified. "I only saw him from the porch, and only for a minute. It was after you left for work. He was kind of wild-looking, too."

"What else? What did he look like? Why didn't you tell me this before?" Don demanded to know all at once.

"He was tall. Dark. *Very* sunburned. Don't worry about it, darling; I only mentioned it for something to say."

"I worry about anything where you're concerned," Don gallantly said, thinking of the pleasure the C.T.A. was going to bring her. "Maybe you shouldn't be here by yourself days. Did you lock the door?"

"Yes, I locked it."

"Well, see you keep it locked when I'm away," said Don.

Both Teddy Hubbard and Bo deWillig had been unable to forget Tavio after they spotted him. His contemptuous refusal of a lift had irritated both; most men on foot, when they saw the Mercedes, hopped to it and got right in. Tavio had occupied a good deal of their conversation going to and from New York. Teddy, who slept poorly and was an early riser, made a point of dressing quickly and taking an early morning walk through the village. Not that he expected anything new; Bo was quite alone and dead to the world when he looked in on him, his black sleep bandage over his eyes and, no doubt, Flents in his ears; he wouldn't be functioning for hours. But Rafe Cadle was up and doing, and when Teddy made his rounds of the place, noticing first thing how carelessly the Ghia had been parked and the denting and scraping of the Pierce-Arrow's fender, that was what he talked to Rafe about.

"God damn!" Rafe sympathized with Teddy's description of the damage. "That breaks my heart! I worked my fingers to the bone getting that car to look like it does—gave it five coats and had a Simoniz glaze on it not even damp could get through!"

"It's got to be fixed," Teddy said. "If I bring it up later this morning, can you go to work on it?"

Rafe scratched his head. "Christ, Mr. Hubbard, I've got the place full up." He thought. "Let's see—that Olds goes out this morning, but I like to have lotsa space around the Pierce, so nothing'll scratch it more than it's scratched now." After further figuring, he said, "Tell you what—you bring the Pierce up about noon, and I'll have room for it by then. I can't duplicate a high finish in—when did you say you're going to be wanting it?"

Teddy hesitated. Rafe knew this was because letting the Pierce go overnight, even for necessary repairs, always made Hubbard anxious about its safety. "Well, I won't really be needing it until Friday," he answered, "but I never know. If you finish it before then—"

"I'll get to work on it soon as you drive her up," said Rafe. "I'll get onto that dent first, get enough matching paint on her so nobody'll notice it. Going to drive in the parade? There's an old-car show down in Olympia Sunday."

"No!" Teddy's voice conveyed how distasteful such an exhibition would be to him. He had often been invited to take part in the Olympia antique auto shows, but always refused. The Pierce, white with scarlet-tufted leather upholstery, was much more impressive when used privately, he considered, preferably at dusk, when its spread of headlights caused other cars to slow down and their occupants to whistle with envy. "We're having a little celebration for my mother's eighty-third birthday Saturday," he explained, "and I'll need the Pierce to pick up guests at the station. They get a bang out of it and it holds nine with the jump seats."

"Oh, I'll have her ready long before then, don't you worry," Rafe promised. "I know she's the apple of your eye."

"Well, she damn near is," Teddy confessed.

And the village gets a bigger bang seeing the stack of fairies you always bring back in it, Rafe thought to himself. But he said, in tones more respectful than those he used with Bo deWillig (after all, Teddy had the money), "The nickel plate holding up okay?"

"Everything else is fine but the fender. And you might check the carburetor and crankcase and dust her out while you're at it."

"I'll hand her back to you sparkling bright. Mr. deWillig was here last night—no, it was after midnight, I was closing—asking me about some man he'd seen on the road." Rafe played it safe, lest the man turn out to be some friend of Hubbard's—the oddest were.

"Oh?" replied Teddy innocently, hoping to learn more.

"He did. That good-looking Eye-tye that's in the village was the man he had in mind, I expect. Couldn't recall his name last night, but it's Tavio. Doesn't seem to have a last name, if you get me. He's over at the Glidden place."

"The Glidden place?"

Rafe lowered an eyelid. He saw this was no one Hubbard knew, and made the kind of joke his customers relished. "It's those quiet ones like Mrs. Glidden are hottest for that stuff, I always say."

"Are you sure?" Teddy asked. "How do you know this?" Though the Hubbard-deWillig ménage was on road-speaking terms with Miriam Glidden, the two houses did not visit; but no information of this kind was beneath Hubbard's attention. It would cool Bo off to know that the object of his chase the night before had found a woman—or would hot him up more, perhaps; equally as punishing.

"Well, tell you," Rafe said, warming up, "I get up and open here usually, oh, at six, six-thirty, and when I opened the door this morning, I saw this Tavio coming out of the Glidden house like he owned it."

"Maybe he slept in the barn."

"No, sir—came right out of the terrace doors, big as life. Practically zipping up his fly. Went up to the luncheonette, to get himself a big plate of eggs."

Teddy laughed. "What makes you sure it was eggs?"

Rafe joined in the laughter. "A guess, was all. Nope, eggs, oysters, black olives taken with milk—none of that really fills a man up again. Only rest. Well, whatever it was he ate, back to the Glidden house he went."

This seemed all Teddy could get, and, after again promising to bring up the Pierce, he walked away toward his house, slowing up at the Glidden driveway to note the showy stand of rhododendrons. He slowed enough to see Tavio as he moved out the wheelbarrow from the garden house.

"Morning," Teddy greeted, village fashion. "See you've been doing some planting."

"Yep," answered Tavio, not looking to see who it was.

"I think we've met before," said Teddy. "Yesterday."

Tavio turned. "Yeah. I recognize you now. You and your fairy friend."

"I beg your pardon!"

"I saw your friend last night. Full of funny ideas."

Teddy never wasted a minute. He had found out far more than he needed to know already. If an account was going, he pushed it; if not, he put it in the inactive file. Without a word more he walked away.

Tavio's encounter with the Hanters at the luncheonette had been equally unpleasant.

"You still hanging around?" Al Hanter asked as Tavio came in, though he knew about his getting work at the Glidden place.

"I'd like some breakfast," Tavio replied, telling Al what he wanted.

"You got money to pay for all that?"

Tavio flashed a sheaf of bills. "Well, I guess I've got no choice but to serve you," Al said. "If it wasn't the law, I wouldn't." He started Tavio's order.

"How's your wife?" Tavio asked as he waited.

"Don't worry about her. Eat and get out."

"I'm not worried about her or anything else," Tavio said easily. If the guy had been decent, he wouldn't have turned the knife like this. "It's only that your wife trusted me for what I ate here yesterday, and I wanted to pay her."

"So she trusted you, did she?" Al pointed to a row of signs above the grill. NO TRUST. NO CHECKS CASHED. WE SHOT THE LAST SALESMAN AN HOUR AGO. He raised his voice. "Hey, Fran! Come in here!"

Fran Hanter emerged from the kitchen. She looked first at Tavio and then at Al.

"Did you give this guy trust?" Al asked her.

Fran turned her eyes from her husband to Tavio. "Thanks," she said, "thanks for giving me away."

"I only wanted to pay what I owe," Tavio said.

"Take his money," Al told her. "I'm not in business for my health."

Fran punched the cash register and put the money inside, then, without looking at Tavio again, walked past him to the kitchen.

Tavio made quick work of the food Al set before him. He got up.

"All right, stud boy, you've had your breakfast," Al said. "This time don't come back."

"As long as you're in business you can't keep me out."

"I hear you got a better place to eat anyway. Cushy rich widow."

"You want to say that again?"

Al didn't want to. He turned back to his grill. When he heard the door close after Tavio, he called to Fran. "Come out here!"

Fran came.

"So that's what you did when I was in Trenton yesterday?"

"How do you know I did anything?"

"Last night," Al said. "You were still hotter than this griddle. I might of known somebody warmed it for me."

Fran laughed at him. "Oh, no, I was all cooled off by then, Daddycakes. Only you're more daddy than cakes. Sure I let him have me. I only wish you were going to be away today, too, so I could let him have me again." She took off her apron. "He did something for me—last night I didn't even feel you, or care. I'm not afraid of you any more, Al." Going to the cash register, she took out a ten-dollar bill and pocketed it, then slipped into the heeled shoes she kept below. "I'll be at Mother's the rest of the day and tomorrow, too, if she's still as bad as she was."

"Maybe she'll kick the bucket today," Al said vengefully.

Fran didn't answer. She went out to the lot, got into her red Olds, and drove away up Old Hessian.

The Misses Bowyer had wasted no time. Early in the day Miss Flora had telephoned both the state police and Willie Bentrup, to report that not only was a prostitute soliciting at the luncheonette ("someone you will recognize when you arrest her") but that a man ("dangerous and, I would not mention this detail were it not my duty, *tattooed*—possibly a seaman of some kind") had tried to abduct Spot. All this Willie Bentrup's wife, who took the calls, dismissed as Bowyer foolishness and didn't bother her husband with. But there had been another man, Miss Flora said ("a flashy Colored"), who had spent much of the morning before obstructing the road ("no doubt searching for the prostitute, *among other things*"). "What other things, Miss Bowyer?" Bentrup's wife asked. "Well, he was driving a *pink* car, very large," elaborated Miss Flora. "Between you and me, I think he was a high yellow." This part sounded more interesting, a new variation in the Misses Bowyer's cast of oppressors, and Mrs. Bentrup did relay this to her husband. The state police, dozens of times burned and twice as many times shy, ignored Miss Flora's calls entirely.

Willie Bentrup asked Rafe Cadle if he knew anything about a high yellow in a pink car.

"That goddam son of a bitch!" cried Rafe. "I almost called you about him myself. He's been dating Edie."

"A high yalla? Dating Edie?"

Rafe flushed. "He's real light, lighter than that. Passing. A numbers man from Philly. I read him the riot act, but I wish you'd keep an eye out."

"Sure thing, I'll do that, Rafe," Bentrup promised and drove off.

The few words about Acie Stanes had rekindled Rafe's anger

and put him in a bad mood, and when he went upstairs to get his breakfast, Mae Cadle remarked it.

"Got out on the wrong side of the bed again, I see."

"Shut your face!"

"I heard you down there, talking to that morphadite," Mae said. "What did he want?"

"How would you know if he's a morphadite or not?"

"Well, a morphadite's a man that's half woman, ain't it? Except that Teddy Hubbard, maybe he's too old to tell. Maybe he's a woman that's half man."

"Let up on Teddy Hubbard."

"I asked you what he wanted." Mae's hatred of the garage did not preclude an insatiable interest in its clients.

"His Pierce's got a dent in the fender, and he wants me to clean her up and check the carburetor and the oil."

"Oh, it's got a dent in it, has it?" Mae repeated, mincingly. "When I think of the people who are starving and people spending their good money on old crates like that!"

"That Pierce is worth real money," Rafe said.

"Yeah, like our Buick I never get to ride in—that'll be a real antique too, someday. When we're dead and gone."

"Hubbard told me he's turned down ten thousand for that Pierce."

"I wouldn't give him five cents for it," said Mae, dishing up Rafe's fried eggs and shoving the plate before him. "That old Pierce smells worse than all the other cars put together when you run it. A real stinker."

Rafe began to eat.

"But you're not telling me what Willie Bentrup wanted," she nagged.

Rafe wasn't going to talk about Acie Stanes. "It was about that Eye-tye hit here yesterday. Tavio. Willie wanted to know where he was."

"Well, I could have told him that. Soon's he got what he wanted off Fran Hanter, he made for that Mrs. Glidden's and's been there ever since. Just ask me what goes on in this village."

"You got eyes in the back of your head."

"Only in the front," Mae said, with the complacence of one who is telling less than she knows. "I saw him go in there yesterday and Fran Hanter couldn't wait to get it. They did it in the kitchen."

"With Al watching, I suppose."

"Al goes to Trenton Monday mornings. You know that."

"No kidding!" said Rafe.

"And that Mrs. Glidden's not above letting him have it, either, if you ask me, or why is the Eye-tye over there?"

"Nobody's asking you. The Eye-tye looked okay to me. Needing work, maybe. Well, he got it, putting in those bushes."

"Lots goes on behind bushes."

"You should know."

"I've heard it called everything but putting in bushes," Mae said. "I've seen him going up and down since he came. He's choice, I'll give him that."

"And that's all you'll give him," Rafe said insultingly. "What did you say his name was?"

"He's a wop, isn't that enough? If you know so much about him, why don't you and Fran Hanter get together on it?"

"Because I never get out of this Christ-awful dump, that's why!"

"You got feet."

"They're killing me already. Whew! This heat!"

"Too early to start on that," Rafe said. "Where the hell's Edie?"

"In the bedroom. Now, you leave that girl be, Rafe Cadle. You know she was in the house all night, didn't go out. Bobby Ingle brought her right to the door, real nice, before dark."

"I saw."

"And she's got a date with him tonight."

"Yeah?"

"Why shouldn't she? *He's* what I'd like her to marry."

"His old man's the one put the finger on me, tried to close me up, remember?" Rafe reminded.

"That was long ago. Ingles've got money, you know that. I hear the doc gets fifty dollars an hour, just for listening to rich people tell him their troubles."

Rafe picked his teeth. "Well, there's different kinds of money. Few times Mrs. Ingle stops here for gas, she pays me out in exact change, to the cent. That's not money to me."

"Rich people are like that," Mae argued. "They're careful with their money, that's why they've got it. It's why you've got yours, too, not that *I've* ever seen a red cent of it."

210

"Well, I told you, you got feet. What's keeping you?"

"Rafe, you are the shit of the world!"

"Could be. I asked you about Edie. Get her in here."

Mae went to the bedroom and brought a sullen Edie to the table, her hair in curlers.

"Hi, Papa-Daddy," Edie said.

"I hear you've been going out with the tone," Rafe said, watching her strangely. "Just be sure you don't wake up and find yourself out on a limb."

"You don't like anybody I go out with."

"Well, I guess Bobby Ingle's some improvement over yesterday," Rafe conceded. "But don't go getting your head full of ideas—nobody like those Ingles're going to let no Cadle inside their door with all those columns and carvings."

"Bobby's nice. I like him."

Rafe kept watching her. "And don't you go using the phone today, either of you, get me?"

Edie's mouth opened in surprise. "Uh-huh!" said Rafe. "I thought as much—it's not Bobby Ingle, it's that dinge you were out with all Sunday night. That's who you're seeing, isn't it?"

"It is *not!*" both Edie and Mae protested in one voice. "You *ask* Bobby Ingle, if you don't believe it!"

"You're both hungry for that dinge's ready money," Rafe said. He got up to begin the day's work. "Just don't make any calls," he repeated as he pointed at Edie. "You, too," he said to Mae. "I'll be listening to see you don't go out, either. You do and I'll beat you both into the middle of next week!"

"What does he mean?" Mae asked, when Rafe had gone downstairs.

Edie was silent, but Mae could see there was something.

"Tell me."

Edie blurted it out. "All right! I *did* have a date with Acie tonight. I was going to call him to tell him I can't go."

"Don't you dare call up that man!" Mae said.

"But what if he comes and Papa-Daddy sees him? I'm going to call him anyway."

"You want him to beat you? He will—I could see it in his eye—and this time I won't stop him."

"If he doesn't beat you first."

211

"Oh, he's not going to beat *me*," Mae said, in an odd voice. "Them days are over. If he does, I'm going to report him—that man's crazy as a bull bat today, and not with the heat."

Edie was torn. She didn't want to be beaten and knew Rafe meant what he said. She settled the morning by having a sunbath in the back yard. All the time she felt Rafe keeping an eye on her. Afternoon went better, because Bobby Ingle had said he'd come for her early, at five. Her date with Acie, made before Rafe had seen her drive up, was for eight, at the luncheonette. Well, let them figure it out, what to do if Acie came to the door. They were the ones who wouldn't let her make a phone call.

CHAPTER 3

Bobby Ingle had been wrong the night before when, drowsing over his Proust and thinking of Edie, he supposed his parents were talking about him. They had been discussing something that concerned him not at all, not that Dr. Ingle had wanted to discuss it. His three fifty-minute hours, followed by a long control conference, had tired him. Though not more tired than usual physically, he was in no mood to talk. Susan Ingle had started it when she came in, shortly after he did.

"Oh, hello, dear. When did you get in?"

"Just now," Ingle answered. "Have a good game? Did you win?"

"I lost. Again. Tonight I had a Yarborough. I haven't had one in years. Not since I was a girl—when you could call up the Coca-Cola people and they'd send over a case as consolation."

Ingle had to search back in memory for what a Yarborough was —a bridge hand with no card above a nine. Fantastic odds existed against such a hand's being dealt, and he recalled that the Coca-Cola consolation story had been one of the first he had ever heard her tell, before she lost her Southern accent. A warning he had not heeded because he was so in love with her. "Too bad," he said; "I'm sorry."

"A Yarborough's always bad luck," Susan said. She still looked angry and worried about it. "Dick, you remember Miriam Glidden

212

asked me for the name of someone to plant her rhododendrons? Well, she found someone. I don't like the look of him."

"Oh? Why not?" Ingle privately suspected his wife had had a normal reaction to the man's good looks but was unaware of it.

"There's something *wrong* about him."

"Well, he's no concern of ours. He's not working for us."

"But I don't like the look of things over there."

"Susan, it's late. And remember—other people's lives."

"You haven't seen this man."

"Yes, I have. I saw him as I left for Tulip. He looked up to the job, I must say."

"Well, certainly *you* know about men like that."

"Now, wait, Sue—what would I know?"

"He's a tough. Anyone could see that."

"He's probably got the rhododendrons in by now and is long gone."

"Oh, no; he only planted half of them," said Susan. "He may very well come back tomorrow."

"It's already tomorrow," Ingle said, looking at his watch, "and I've other things to think about than Mrs. Glidden's workman."

"If that's what he is. I've never understood why perfectly good-looking men should have themselves tattooed. Ugh! Why, everyone's heard about his being there. Tonight the girls talked of nothing else."

Ingle could not repress a smile. "So he's good-looking now."

"You know what I mean. Cort Glidden's hardly cold in his grave."

"And you suspect Mrs. Glidden of being as attracted to this workman as you are."

Ingle understood his wife's alienation and isolation from herself and the conflicts resulting from it, though was often, as now, impatient with her; he had so often followed her doggedly to the unknown destinations of her confusions.

"Dick," she said, "I've taken a lot from you, but I don't have to take that. I suppose the man's handsome in a way."

"He's one of the most handsome I ever saw," said Ingle; "and remember, I was in the war and have examined a few."

"Oh, why do we have to go into this so much?" Susan demanded.

Ingle looked at his wife. The unexplainable had always to be allowed for when judging conduct. He said, "I think you're upset because you lost tonight."

"That has nothing to do with what we're talking about." The stakes Susan played for were high—one or, sometimes, two cents a point—higher than she could afford when not winning. "Besides, I'll recoup next week. It evens out in the end."

"Does it really, Sue? I've often wondered."

"Most always it does."

"But not always."

"Dick, cards are my only pleasure. Pleasure costs money."

"And when you lose, you go into a snit about the first thing near to hand. Tonight it's Mrs. Glidden's workman."

Susan's temper could become very short, and her tongue, which had an edge to it, viperish. "Don't try to turn me into one of your cases. I started playing cards because you were never home at night like other husbands. And the war."

"You started playing cards because of a lack of interest in people —and a lazy mind."

Susan's eyes opened wide in anger. "Lack of interest in *people?* But playing cards, I see people all the time. As for my mind—do you think it doesn't take *mind* to keep track of cards outstanding and remember the order in which they've been played?"

"Calculators can keep track of millions of digits."

"I'm not a calculator!"

"You sometimes behave like one."

"How did we get into this? *I* said a few things about the man Mrs. Glidden hired—"

"—and who bothers you."

"He does *not* bother me!"

"I suggest you try to forget about him and mind your own business. I intend to," said Ingle.

"By which you mean you approve what may happen over there —what may already have happened?"

"Sue," Ingle said, with final patience, "what is it you think may have happened?"

"Isn't it obvious?"

"Not to me. If you mean that Mrs. Glidden may be sexually attracted to this man, suppose she is? Very little is known about

214

what widows feel and do—it's one of the great unexplored questions."

"You'd condone her sleeping with this man?"

"If she likes. It's none of my business, and I suggest you not make it yours." Ingle walked to the stairway, pausing with his hand on the newel post. "And remember, tomorrow—no, tonight it is now—we take the Braithwaites to the Ferry Slip for dinner and the Playhouse afterward." Braithwaite was one of Ingle's associates at Tuliptrees.

"I remembered and canceled my game," Susan said. The Braithwaites were one of the few duties Ingle required of his wife. Once a year they had the other doctors and their wives over for dinner and the play, and the wives and doctors punctiliously had the Ingles in return. "But I can tell you, the play's terrible—some television comedian in an old twenties play that was probably no good to begin with."

"It'll have to do."

"No one goes to the Playhouse any more, except those awful blue-haired mothers. They're calling it the Blue Hair Playhouse, you know."

"Well, would you rather have Mrs. Schaaf do dinner here and sit around talking afterward?"

"Dear God, no, Dick! You'd only talk shop. Anything but that!"

"Well, then."

"You know how I've always felt about that," Susan said. "Dinner and bridge, yes; dinner and conversation, no."

"I know. But you didn't always feel that way. There was a time—"

"*Don't!*" She interrupted him, one hand raised. "I can't stand to talk about it."

"Someday you're going to have to talk about it."

Ingle looked at his wife, and tenderness suffused him. Once she had been part of him; part of her still belonged to him. For a moment he saw her as she had been, dark hair parted symmetrically in the middle, ivory skin, vivid coloring. Her hands had been like flowers, soft and fluid in movement and ivory-colored, like her face; now, in their rings and surrounded by bracelets, they moved nervously, like small rakes with no work to do.

"Oh, Dick," she said, "Dick. What happened to it? The way we once were? Once we were happy—I liked living where we are, doing what we do."

"You mean what we did."

"Yes. Where is it gone?"

" 'To flat Coromandel.' "

"*What?*"

"Only something I remembered from a poem. When you asked, 'Where is it gone?' it came to mind." She did not follow him. He sighed: a deep intake of breath and a complete exhalation of it— one of the surest signs of *Angst* in his patients, purest anxiety imposed on fatigue. "I wish I knew."

"I sometimes think it's living here, in this place that was so lovely and that's being ruined. The *noise!* Those quarries! Don't you hear them?"

"Now?"

"Yes, now." Susan slightly inclined her head, listening. "They're there. Beneath the other noises, beneath everything. Don't *you* hear them?"

Ingle strained his ears, but could hear only the light overlay of the night sounds of any summer night.

"And that constant stench from the road!" Susan went on. "Perhaps we should have done what you wanted to do, when Tulip was remodeled—live there, so you could be in residence."

"It's a little late for that." At one time, whether to live at the clinic or not had been a daily topic, settled by Susan, who had decided against it. "The Braithwaites are installed and like it."

"Ah, yes; the Braithwaites."

There would now be tears and she would tell him of the voices she heard speaking beneath the quarry sounds, or the conversation would be turned—by Ingle, who, from long experience, knew precisely when to say "Let's call it a day."

"Yes," she agreed, and started turning out lights. "Is Bobby in?"

"I'll look and see." Ingle mounted the stairs. A crack of light showed beneath Bobby's door and he knocked lightly. There was no answer. He opened the door and saw Bobby asleep, one thumb in a book lying beside him. Gently he lifted the book and placed it, face down, on the bedside table and turned out the light. Susan was coming up the stairs as he closed Bobby's door and they met on the landing. "He went to sleep with his light on."

"He so often does."

"Sue."

She came toward him, putting her head against his chest. "Oh, Dick, I can't think why I got so upset."

"Tension. Forget it."

Usually they parted here, to go to their separate bedrooms, but tonight Susan said, "Shall I come to you?"

"Please do!"

"You're not too tired?"

"Sue, there's tiredness and tiredness—I'm not tired in that way at all."

"I'll be only a few minutes then."

Those now rare times when Ingle and his wife slept together were unlike any other part of their life. Ingle had long since played a role that had in it something of a father, overly considerate, anxious not to tire her. Tonight he was surprised by Susan's ardent warmth, her evident wish to recapture what they had once felt for each other. For the first time in years, Ingle felt young. When it was over and she had gone back to her own room, he could not put from his mind the suspicion that the man who worked at the Glidden place had something to do with the way Susan had felt and had made him feel.

Bobby Ingle knew his father's Tuliptrees schedule as well as Dr. Ingle himself. Just as he had known yesterday that it was his father's morning at home, so today he recognized the early stirrings across the hall as the prelude to Tuesday, when his father relieved Dr. Gough, his partner at the clinic, in Tulip One. Tulip One was the ward for very disturbed or violent patients. After lunch, Dr. Ingle would spend two hours in Tulip Two (clinic code for the building where less serious cases were treated) so that Dr. Braithwaite could have the afternoon off. And tomorrow would be the day on which shock treatments were given. Luckily, this was not Wednesday, for there was a rule in the Ingle house that on that morning no one spoke to Dr. Ingle, not even Mrs. Schaaf, when she brought his coffee. But this morning father-approach was permitted as well as questions and answers, if they were kept simple. Bobby got out of bed and, hastily putting on a robe, knocked at his father's door.

"Come in." Ingle looked up, one sock and garter on, his other foot raised as he drew on the black silk, smoothed it, and clasped the garter to it. "You? At this hour?"

"I hope you don't mind."

"No." Whenever Bobby tried to think of his father as he must once have been, such details as the garters and particular kind of socks he wore got in the way. This morning, with black shoes laced and with his fresh, white shirt and dark blue rep tie already on, he seemed a hundred. "You must want something," Ingle said.

"I do, Dad."

"Well, speak up."

"Can I have your car tonight?"

"Your mother and I are dining with the Braithwaites and going to the Playhouse afterward."

"Oh," said Bobby. "But I thought, since this is Tuesday, and you usually come home around four, that I might have the car at five."

"Don't be too sure I'll be home at four." Ingle slid his belt through the loops of his trousers and buckled it. On any morning he was inclined to be preoccupied with the day ahead. This morning he had been thinking of Tulip One and what faced him there, the bedlam for which the original Bedlam had been named, and, more particularly, a new case, the son of a psychotic couple who was on a hunger strike.

"But, Dad, you just *have* to let me have it tonight."

"What if I say no?"

"I—I don't know what I'd do."

"Who is it, Edie Cadle?"

"Yes."

"Then it'll have to be your mother's car."

"She'd never let me have it. Will you ask her for me?"

"I think you should ask her yourself," Ingle said, putting on his coat.

"She's down on me this week."

Often when Ingle looked at Bobby he regretted the permissiveness under which he had been brought up. A few good clops at the right time might have sidetracked some of Bobby's passive re-

218

bellion. "Since you're up, why don't you do a little work around the place? Trim the hedge—it needs it. And you could rake the gravel in the drive and give your mother's car a wash."

"But it's so hot!" Bobby protested. "It's eighty already."

"I intend working through it."

"You make it sound like a deal."

"It is. Try doing it and then ask your mother for her car. Now, if that's all?"

"That's all." Bobby started to go.

"One minute," said Ingle. "When you're doing the hedge, don't cut it on the Cadle side, either on the terrace or out front."

"Okay. Less work for Bobby."

Ingle went to the window of his bedroom and closed it. The Cadle motors were already beginning to run. "And I hope you'll remember what I said last night. Please be careful."

"I will be," Bobby answered as his father left.

He returned to his room, where he put on old clothes in preparation for doing the work his father suggested. After Mrs. Schaaf's breakfast, accompanied by astonished questions about his being up so early, he got out the clippers and started on the front hedge.

Almost the first thing he saw was one of the rhododendrons, that had been standing in the Glidden drive, being moved. The man doing the work was unknown to him, and as he turned at the sound of the clippers, Bobby saw his sweating torso and the tattoos of roses.

"Hi," Bobby said.

Tavio paused to wipe his face with a towel. The white house with the Greek columns and bowknot carving over the doorway was of a kind he disliked, and he saw that the kid cutting the hedge went with it—tall, blond, big-boned and, probably, muscle-bound with privilege. "You look as if you don't like what you're doing," he said, by way of returning Bobby's greeting.

"I don't. Do you?"

"Sometimes I have to work to eat," Tavio said, leaning on his shovel. "Not you."

"That's what you think." Bobby waited while a truck passed between them. When he could be heard once more, he said, "If you knew how I hate this village!"

"Why don't you leave it?"

219

"Fat chance." Bobby was already bored and a little winded from the effort involved in manipulating the clippers.

"Why don't you cut that hedge the right way?" asked Tavio.

Bobby stopped. "What do you mean?"

Tavio rested his shovel and walked across the road to the Ingle hedge. "Hand me the clippers." He took them from Bobby and, holding them high, vigorously shaved off a section of yew. "Put your back into it," he said, "like this."

Bobby took the clippers again and imitated the movement Tavio had shown him. "I'd rather chop the whole hedge down than do it this way," he said. "It's breaking my back."

Susan Ingle appeared on the front porch. "Bobby!"

"What, Mother?"

"Come in a moment, please."

"But I've just started this."

"Come round to the back." Susan Ingle turned and went indoors. Her tone conveyed unmistakable disapproval of the man who had crossed the road. Tavio, catching the intonation, returned to the Glidden drive.

Bobby skirted the side of the house, finding his mother finishing her coffee on the terrace. She looked tired around the eyes.

"I appreciate what you're doing," she said, "but I prefer you not to talk to that man."

"Why not?"

"I simply prefer it."

"He was working at the Gliddens' and came over to show me how to hold the clippers." Bobby felt his biceps. "He was right, too. It's work."

"I know, but please don't talk to him."

"How can I help it, if I'm cutting the hedge?"

"You can work back here and cut the front later, when that man has gone."

Bobby looked confused; he sat down in the chair opposite.

"What ever got you started on the hedge in the first place?" his mother asked.

"Dad said it needed trimming."

"It does, but usually I have the boy from Chalfont do it."

Bobby sat, moving the hedge clippers in the way Tavio had shown him. "It was a deal I made with Dad," he confessed. "I

220

asked for his car tonight, and when he said you were going out with the Braithwaites I asked if I could have yours instead. He said if I did some work around the place you might let me have it."

"Stop playing with those shears!" his mother said nervously. "It seems not to be up to me to say whether you can use my car or not. I suppose you're going out with Edie Cadle. And I have nothing to say about that, either, evidently."

"Oh, Mother! I thought that was settled!"

"Not by me." Suddenly his mother spoke in a harsh voice he had never before heard her use. "Have you never thought that I'm a Southerner? So are you, too, on my side, even if you were born and brought up in the North. You had a great-grandfather who fought at Antietam. Does that mean nothing to you?"

"It means he fought at Antietam."

"Do you know what Antietam was?"

"A Civil War battle fought in 1862."

"I'm amazed you know that much, with your school record. But you don't at all understand what I'm trying to tell you."

"Yes, I do. You're trying to tell me Edie's colored."

"Isn't she?"

"How would I know? Why would I care?"

"Bobby, really!"

"I guess this means I can't have your car."

His mother's face seemed to freeze. She closed her eyes. "If that quarry doesn't stop crushing stones, I'm going to scream!"

Bobby stood up in alarm. "Mother, are you all right?"

She sat for a moment with a strained expression, her face tired and drawn. Then she opened her eyes. "Go on with your work," she said.

"You mean go on cutting the hedge?"

"Yes, why not? Go on, *talk* to that man over at the Gliddens'! *Go* out with your Edie Cadle!"

"Well, *he's* not colored, anyway," said Bobby, trying to make sense of what she was saying.

"He's a tough. Your great-grandmother, whom you wouldn't care anything about, once said that in fifty years all America would turn gray. I'm glad she's dead, so she can't see how true her prediction was."

"Gosh, Mother, I kind of liked the man across the road—he only tried to be helpful."

Susan Ingle got up and went into the house, and Bobby returned to the front hedge. But though he tried several times to resume the talk with Tavio, he got only silence and a cold shoulder. He reverted to cutting the yew his own way; it was less tiring. He didn't finish, because when he went to the kitchen to get a Coke, he found Mrs. Schaaf at the pantry phone. She hung up as he came in.

"I think you'd better go in to your mother," she said to Bobby, a frightened expression in her eyes. "She doesn't seem very well. I've been trying to reach your father, but they say he's in Tulip One and can't be disturbed."

Bobby went to the living room, where his mother sat at her card table. "What nonsense!" she said, when he asked her how she was. "That Schaaf woman is an idiot! Calling your father, when I'm perfectly all right!"

"But, Mother," Bobby said, concerned, "you don't look all right. Are you sure you don't want me to try to get through to Dad?"

"We never disturb your father when he's in Tulip One," she said. She stretched out her hands before her, as if examining her nails. She said, "It's a gray world at best, Bobby. I've tried to keep you from finding that out, but now you seem intent on knowing, there's nothing more I can do." She picked up her fresh deck of cards, shuffled them, and then began laying them out, red on black, black on red.

CHAPTER 4

Don MacFinden, even before he and Nancy were married, had almost never gone home from the quarries for lunch. Like his father, he left shortly after daylight for whichever quarry he was supervising, carrying a lunch pail. Even after the elder MacFinden had worked up into a yearly gross of six figures, his wife continued to pack both his lunch and Don's as she cooked their breakfast. The MacFindens were heavy eaters, and neither Don nor his father would have thought of setting out for work without substantial breakfasts under their belts. And Don's mother had always taken pride in the lunches she put up for them, seeing to it that there was too much rather than too little—two or three ham sandwiches apiece, fruit in season, almost always a thick wedge of pie or cake and a Thermos of hot coffee.

Nancy, when Don had asked for his lunch pail the first morning he set out for Number Three, had looked blank; cooking early breakfast she had been prepared for, but not having come from lunch-pail people, she had not thought ahead.

"Don't worry about it, doll," Don had said, making light of it as he ruffled her red hair and kissed her goodby. "I'll get a sandwich off the old man." That had been out of the question, since his father invariably was at Blackstone Locks on Mondays, and Don had had to make do with a lunch at Dutch Falls, on his way to Dr. Kidder's office. It had been a drugstore sandwich, skimpy and not of the kind he was used to; it was just possible that his leaving Number Three early, after his reading of the Coital Training Aid prospectus, had had something to do with his feeling hungry as well as having a case of afternoon hots.

This morning Nancy had tried to put up a lunch that would stick with him, had even gone over to her mother-in-law's to get Don's pail, one of his few bachelor belongings that had not been transferred to the new house during the honeymoon. She had taken in stride a lengthy set of rules about what MacFinden men would and would not eat.

"Now, ham Don'll eat always," her mother-in-law said. "He'll eat it seven days a week if you give it to him. Same with beef. But don't waste your time trying to get him interested in chicken or turkey or lamb or the insides of animals, anything like that. No liver or kidneys. Don's just like his father—roast beef or ham or nothing. Even on Thanksgiving and Christmas I have to have a ham as well as a bird, because neither one will touch fowl."

"But why, Mother Mac?" Nancy asked.

"Don't ask me why. They simply never ate fowl or lamb. Or fish. That was one of the very first things I learned about Papa Mac— his peculiarities about his food. No this, no that. No greens, just meat and potatoes. Yellow vegetables, yes, but nothing like snaps or peas. And Don's always been the same way. Meat and potatoes, ham, pie, cake. I *think* they eat the fruit I always put in the pails, but it wouldn't surprise me if they didn't."

The food Nancy and Don had eaten in Mexico hadn't been a sample of his preferences, evidently; after trying the so-called Continental cuisine, which had been offered them at the better hotels and restaurants, they had found it safer to stick to eggs, beans and enchiladas because they seemed to mix better with the Enterovioforma they had taken daily throughout their trip.

"And always put in plenty of salt, Nancy," Don's mother said. "I get these little miniature Morton shakers by the dozen at the Acme. They're both big salt eaters."

Nancy tried to get all this straight as she listened.

"You'll find it worth it to baby them about their lunch pails. Give them plenty, then you can be sure they won't find some excuse to come back midmorning and hang around the kitchen. That's why I got into the habit of doing my baking middle of the week. If I baked weekends, I had them both underfoot all the time. Course, I'll be baking less, now Don's yours. Anyway, get them out of the house with their pails and you can call that part of the day your own. I never could stand having a man come home for lunch."

Nancy had only partly absorbed her mother-in-law's suggestions: "No cake mixes; you couldn't fool either of them. And they both like their bread homemade and sandwiches without the edges trimmed." She had been a little surprised, this morning, at the interest Don showed in every item she had put into his lunch pail.

"What's that, doll?"

"Cheese sandwiches. I didn't trim the edges, like your mother said."

"But that's store-bought bread."

"I know. I guess I should have taken the loaf of her own bread she offered me—she knew I wouldn't have mastered all this equipment yet." Nancy indicated the rather formidable array of ovens and dials with which their kitchen was equipped.

"Tell you what," Don said. "I have to pick up our transparencies in Olympia anyway, so forget the pail for today and I'll come home for lunch." Throughout their trip, Don had airmailed his color films to the Olympia photographer who had supplied his Zeiss-Ikon and viewing equipment, and souvenirs of the first days of their honeymoon were ready. "I'll be back at noon."

As it turned out, Don was back at the house at eleven-thirty, with several dozen boxes of finished slides.

"How did they turn out?" Nancy asked, as she prepared lunch.

"They're beauties," Don answered, holding the slides up to the light. "Oh, these of Uxmal are wonderful! Here's one of us together that those people from Toledo took." Nancy and Don had had the problem of all ardent photographer couples, finding someone to snap them together, instead of endlessly posing each other. "Boy! Will Dad and Mom get a charge out of these!"

Don was so excited by the pictures, Nancy could hardly get him to sit down and eat his lunch. "I thought we'd ask them over for supper tomorrow—it's going to take more than one evening to show them all, though. Why don't you call your folks, too?"

Nancy privately thought that a space of a few days between in-law visits would give them a chance to settle in better, and give her the hang of the kitchen; after all, both their parents had been there Sunday, and she had had the long visit with Don's mother yesterday. But she said, "I'll call them right after lunch."

Don seemed to be liking the plate of cold ham and roast beef which, mindful of his mother's hints, she had provided. Before she could sit down herself, the phone rang.

"Our first incoming call," she said.

"Take it, will you, darling?" Don asked.

Nancy lifted the receiver. "Hello? Yes, this is the MacFindens'. Who? Dr. Kidder? One moment, I'll call my husband."

Don took the phone and Nancy sat down at the table. "Yes," she heard him say. "Yes. Well, I appreciate that. Thanks for going to the trouble. Okay." And he hung up.

"Who's Dr. Kidder?" Nancy asked, when Don returned.

"Oh, it was something about one of the men at Number Three," Don answered; it was his first marital lie, and he didn't do it at all well.

"But I thought the quarry doctor was Dr. Bensberg. Is Kidder somebody new?"

"Yes. One of the boys who drives for us hurt his hand," Don embroidered; "the doc was calling about his compensation." Even innocent lies have short legs, and Don flushed when he realized what he had said.

"Oh" was all Nancy said.

Don wished Dr. Kidder had called him at the quarry instead, but remembered he had given his home number along with other information. He hadn't expected to hear from the doctor so soon, but Dr. Kidder said he had been in Philadelphia on a consultation and he had seen no reason not to pick up the C.T.A. for Don while there.

Nancy thought Don look abstracted when he kissed her before going back to work. "Darling—that call," she couldn't help asking him. "Are you sure there's nothing wrong?"

"It was what I told you."

"It wasn't something about you? You're not sick or anything?"

"Of course not," Don assured her. "Look, doll, I may be a little late getting home."

Nancy was sure then that Don was keeping something from her. After telephoning her mother and Don's, she looked up Dr. Kidder. He wasn't in the Pennsylvania book, and she had to search the New Jersey directories before she found him. *Kidder, Harlow, M.D.,* she read, noting that he had a Dutch Falls number. Then she tried to put it from her mind, feeling guilty that she'd pried, because it meant she had not quite believed Don's explanation. It wasn't the same as telling a lie, merely the other side of the coin. Still—it was unlikely the MacFinden Quarries would use a Jersey physician. Or was it?

Dr. Kidder had suggested that Don should come in after regular office hours for the fitting of the C.T.A., around five-thirty. All afternoon, as he supervised the loading of trucks and checked waybills and lading, the thing for which the letters stood—Coital Training Aid—kept running through his mind; the C.T.A. and its growing mystique were exerting a curious influence on him. He felt, he told himself, like a primitive adolescent about to be initiated into the phallic rites. But he recognized that this was only a way of trying to be humorous about the situation and conceal his real feelings, which were more than serious. He showered before setting out for Dutch Falls, prepared for any further examination that might be involved, trying to pinpoint what it was he felt exactly. Like a bad little boy about to be punished for masturbating in church? A little. But as he waited for Dr. Kidder to finish with a late patient, it came to him: he felt as he had that day so long ago, when his pastor had prayed with him in the rectory.

Dr. Kidder greeted him seriously and at once reached into his desk and brought out an oblong, white cardboard box, at one end of which was stamped 1 C.T.A. *Medium-Large.* "Here it is," he said, lifting the lid of the box and exhibiting it to Don. The prospectus had not misrepresented it; it was, in fact, so accurate a reproduction as to be startling. What Don saw appeared to be an actual penis in full erection, somewhat over six inches long, with indeed all the lifelike characteristics and minute detail promised. Except that it was, perhaps, a little too pink and had two flesh-colored, elastic loops at its base, it was everything he had once prayed for. "As you see," said Dr. Kidder, holding it up, "it's as much like the real thing as it could possibly be."

"Except that—"

Dr. Kidder waited for him to finish, and when Don did not, went on. "There's a booklet of instructions, but using it isn't strictly a Do-It-Yourself matter. There is one technical point I want to make absolutely sure is clear to you. Suppose you undress from the waist down."

Don did as the doctor suggested while he located a tube of K-Y. "The first procedure is to lubricate your penis well," Dr. Kidder said, handing Don the tube of jelly. "This or any other good vaginal lubricant will do." He watched intently as Don rubbed the K-Y on himself, cautioning, "But not on the scrotum—we want that to be perfectly dry. I'll tell you why." Again he held up the C.T.A. "You see these two elastic bands? Loop them together on the underside—like this—before you put it on." He demonstrated, then handed Don the C.T.A.

Don, blushing furiously, wriggled his limp penis into the hollow tube; unlike the time before, it was not cooperating. "Like this?" he asked, unnerved by the doctor's seriousness.

"No doubt you will have an erection when inserting it at home," Dr. Kidder said encouragingly. "That's it, you're getting the idea. Now, rotate it back and forth, until your penis is entirely inside. There." At last the doctor smiled. "Sometimes the easiest things are the most difficult to do," he said, understanding Don's nervousness. "This is the part, now, that I want you to be especially careful about." While holding the plastic form firmly against Don's crotch, he took first one and then the other of the two elastic bands between his fingers and looped them around his scrotum. "This secures it."

Don stood, looking down at himself; now it was on, it did look like a part of him; his pubic hair helped to hide the rather blunted edge where the tube joined the body.

"Not too tight?" asked the doctor anxiously. "It's most important that the spermatic cord, which is very delicate, not be constricted."

"I think not tight enough," Don said. He felt the elastics move and suddenly the entire thing snapped loose and dropped to the floor.

The doctor picked it up and, after wiping it on a Kleenex, handed it back to Don. "Try again. Take *both* the bands between the fingers of both your hands and pull them back, so that you can insert your balls through both elastic bands at one time." *Balls* had been a slip. "Pull both the bands up as far as you can behind your testicles," he corrected himself. "It should now be on and stay on."

"It seems to be this time," Don said.

"Walk around. Try to walk normally."

Don walked up and down the office several times.

"The bands are not too tight?"

"No, they're fine."

"Okay, then," Dr. Kidder said. "You see, it's simply a matter of becoming accustomed to it." He reached for Don's scrotum, making sure the adjustment was correct. Don felt his penis stiffen at last.

That was everything, except Dr. Kidder's adding that the C.T.A. should be washed thoroughly with soap and lukewarm water after each use, dried, and replaced in its box. "It'll take you a while to get used to it," he said to Don sympathetically. "You may not wish to use it every time you have intercourse, only when you feel it necessary."

"You mean, for special effects?" Don asked, laughing in his relief that it was over.

Dr. Kidder's face remained impassive.

Don remembered the instructions when he unlooped the elastics from his scrotum and took the C.T.A. off. He had been so absorbed and embarrassed that he had quite forgotten his erection.

"You're doing fine, boy," Dr. Kidder congratulated him. "My

money is on you." He washed the C.T.A. while Don dressed and handed it to him in its box, with the lid secured by a rubber band. "Let me know how you make out."

"I will," Don promised.

"You're on your own now. Good luck!"

Don knew he was going to need luck. He didn't want to think now of how he would contrive to put on the C.T.A. when with Nancy. What if she saw him doing it? What if she saw the box and asked what was in it? What if—? Breathing hard, he put the box into the glove compartment and drove as quickly as he could back to the Corner.

The heat lay like a gray pall over the river, and on the canal banks the rushes that grew at the water's edge drooped; the trees, with leaves turned in supplication or promise of rain, stirred only slightly in the wind from the south. Even the cicadas had stopped their yellow drone; only Tavio's shovel, relentlessly cutting, could be heard, and, after a brief silence, as the last of the rhododendrons was lifted into place and the earth tamped down, the Corner became as still as it ever was in summer.

In the nightmarish morning that followed her hanging up the phone, Miriam Glidden felt guilt close in upon her, relentless as the wind that brought only a stirring of the hot air. The first thing she became conscious of, after Rosa's voice, was that she had run through the house naked. Quickly she found a robe, only to cast it immediately aside as she bathed, combed her hair and dressed among her familiar surroundings, none of which made her forget the beggar's room. She tried to think clearly. What made it painful was the hours she had slept on alone, that time after Tavio had left her. What had he done during that time? What any man does in the morning, she supposed, remembering the one other man she had known intimately, Cort, whose name was now like a pain at the bottom of her breath—guilt.

She retraced her steps to the wing where the beggar's room was —anything to try to put the sound of the shoveling outside from her mind, and the moment she must again confront him. There was a small bath at the foot of the stairs to the room, long unused, even by guests, and here she found evidences of his morning—a bath mat with footprints still wet, a damp towel, a blue denim jacket hung behind the door. On the basin were his razor, a comb and the squeezed tube of shaving cream, which she had seen yesterday when she unwrapped the newspaper bundle in the garden house.

Automatically she hung up the mat and towel to dry, wondering wildly what she should do if he came again into the house. She had not eaten since yesterday; her head swam with hunger. She made her way back to the central section of the house, where he had not been—or had he? The kitchen was undisturbed and as she had left it; he had not eaten his breakfast here. She hurried to heat yesterday's coffee. If only, she thought, Rosa would appear and rescue me. I would pay him off and try to believe nothing happened. But this hope failed her: She had spoken with Rosa on the phone less than an hour before; that had been the moment to cry help, but she had lied as smoothly as if she had been lying all her life. If this day was to be a prolongation of the one before, she could not endure it. The vision of last night's ecstasy flashed through her senses, then drained away with the inevitability of vivid sensations remembered.

The first words she would say to him would be the key, the whole battle. In her mind she rehearsed his dismissal, learning it by rote: ". . . so here is your money, and if you will *please* go," the voice of all imperious women—her mother's intonation again, that had settled so many situations with finality.

There he stood in the shade of the terrace, a blue form against the gunmetal sky, the shirt he had taken off while working hung about his shoulders, sleeves tied in a knot in front.

"It is finished," he said. "The plants are all in—and so am I." With a single, sinuous movement, he dropped to the stones of the terrace, rolling onto his stomach, pillowing his head on one out-stretched arm.

The first words were prepared, but she could not speak them, and at once she saw that he would not have heard them; he was asleep. Already a pattern of familiarity was established—she recognized the pace of his breath, even and deep, as it had been when she lay beside him in the beggar's room.

At first she was angry that he could so control and dismiss her; she had been prepared to fight him, if necessary, with the battle inside herself. But slowly her helplessness became clear to her, and

230

she found herself again accepting it. There was a terrifying quality in the ease with which he held her, a violence no less valid for being momentarily subdued in sleep, a gentleness accentuated by his breath. The meridian of the day had passed, but she was unaware of it. She felt alone in a familiar world that had become sensuously without time, in which his sleeping presence was the only reality. After a time she realized that he had moved, turned onto his back; that she was waiting for him to wake, with a mixture of anxious affection and irritation of the wakeful for those who conduct their lives in dreaming, removed from all necessity to reckon hours. Countless times she followed the rise and fall of his chest, from the deep hollow where his neck ended to the flat plate of muscles where his jeans began.

At last his breath changed and he sat up, fully awake, staring at her. Then he got to his feet and walked to the beggar's wing, as though he had known the way always. She heard the sound of water. He is gathering up his things and will go now, she thought; but when he returned, carrying nothing, she tried to remember her first words.

They came out differently. "You will go now. I must pay you."

"There is nothing to pay."

"You finished."

"Yes."

"Well, then."

He looked at her a long time before he spoke again—incredulity. "It was the way to you. We made it together. You know that."

She was silent.

He came forward, his hand reaching to touch her cheek. It was a brusque caress, almost uncouth, and angry. "You tell me to go because you think you are doing a duty, mourning your husband. But you want me to stay, as I want you to ask me to stay. You must ask me."

"My husband had nothing to do with last night."

"You learned that? It was as if we had been together a long time."

"Yes."

"You were alive, as he is dead. You were close to yourself again. New."

She heard his words, remembering how her body had moved away from the trap of grief of the last weeks, toward some mystery in him, the life and force and energy of him that held her.

"I don't know," she said, confused.

"What is it you don't know?"

"There are—things."

"What people will think and say?"

"Not that."

"Then what?"

"Day—*days*," she said. "The time of day and what to do about it. Meals. Staying in or going out."

"That's easy."

"Not for a woman. You're a man—hungry."

"Yes, I'm hungry," he admitted. "But no going out for us—I want to stay here."

"I suppose that's best." The daylight shone full on his features, sober and questioning, as yesterday they had been smiling. The day was slipping away. "Then come in," she said. "I'll make us something—is it lunch?"

He shrugged.

She led him through the house into the kitchen, conscious that again it was she who was showing the way. She went through the motions of cooking, watching him as he sat straddled on a chair, looking about him like a man taking directions with a sextant.

"Why did you want all those rhododendrons planted?" he asked.

"To cut out the view of that luncheonette. It's ugly."

"So's what's inside it. I had breakfast there."

"Did you? I've never been inside it."

"Well, I can tell you, it's ugly. The woman, the man."

She turned. "The woman!"

"You want to know, don't you?"

"You had her, as you had me."

"It was she who had *me*," he said. "It wasn't like us, the way we had each other. It was hatred. Hatred's part of it."

She felt a pang of jealousy. "But *why?*"

"That's how I find out what I am."

"I don't understand," she said.

He watched her, quietly, for a long time as she moved about the

232

kitchen. Then he said, "It's all part of a search. Not like the search for love, but the search to come with someone, as we came last night."

She had turned away from him again. "I think, after all, I'm afraid of you."

"But it's so simple," he answered her. "When it's good, like it was with us, it's freedom. When it's not like that, it makes a prison."

The word frightened her. "Were you ever in prison?"

"No. Only imprisoned by life. You know about that."

"In a way, perhaps." She had brought the plates to the table and set his before him. She saw his hands, of an extraordinary beauty, like those in old paintings, the nails flushed and round, showing not at all the hard work he had finished. It seemed easy to talk to him now. "But what we had last night I had with my husband, too. Most times."

"It's not always like that, Miriam, it can't be," he said, beginning to eat.

The use of her name deterred her from saying more. She watched him.

"You see," he went on, "if you live in a world where freedom is for everybody else but yourself, it's different. You have to run away, as I did, to stay alive. To not hate yourself. Do you understand that?"

"No."

"You wouldn't; you've always had the freedom of your kind of world. Still, your life must have been a search, too?"

It was a question she couldn't answer.

"But you could move inside your world as you pleased. With me, it's a question of always moving, leaving, going on. I have to go on. I can't stop. Something—like you—will happen, though I can't ever guess it." He pushed his plate away, evidently satisfied. "In moving on, you see, there's a chance, and when there's someone like you, and I make it with them, I can go again."

She in part understood him, understood that his newspaper bundle symbolized the pilgrim's sack; but his words dismayed her, and she remained silent.

"It took courage for you to let me stay last night," he said.

233

"If I had said no, would you have gone?"

"I wouldn't have touched you." He saw she did not believe this. "I'm two people, maybe more," he said, as if warning her.

"Are you? What are the others like?"

"Not like I am with you."

"Cruel?"

"Sometimes. And sometimes I don't know who or what I am."

"Then what are you like?"

"I can't predict. But sometimes, when I'm one of my other selves, that's when I feel closest to what I want, what I search for."

"And what is that?" she asked, held by his eyes, the gravity with which he spoke.

"Life. *Real* life, the feeling of being alive in your body, not dead and trapped, like the ones I call others. It's like a wave, when it comes, and beyond it there's another—like it was last night with us."

"Yes," she said, remembering.

"We'll be together again like that."

She nodded, again feeling the numbing pleasure that was like tiredness but was not tiredness, only a dreaming toward ecstasy, toward him. She could do nothing that was not prompted by his eyes—he had engulfed her, was all around her, everywhere. She felt isolated on an immense plain, all silence, punctuated only by his voice.

"There's no hurry," she heard him say.

She wondered briefly what Rosa would have thought, had she seen the compliant way she had behaved, leading him to bed. But now, aside from a necessity to be with this man, it was difficult for her to know what her feelings were. There was no hurry, he had said, and there was not; this she felt and believed, already accustomed to the hours that would have no number, the things she found herself already doing.

Later, after a tumult of words and movement through darkness, beyond suffering, beyond guilt, even feeling, there was only nothing. The hysteric squalor of the hot dark, the intimacy so deep and tortuous it was unbearable without pushing him from her and taking refuge in sleep, enabled her to remember where she was—in her own bed, with the deep, rhythmic breathing, which had become the only measurement of time there was, beside her. She

234

heard the rain as it came, drilling on the roofs, pouring through the windows, and once more she plunged into a telescoping void that was sleep.

CHAPTER 5

The Ingle telephone rang. Bobby, getting out of a shower, listened, towel in hand, waiting for someone to answer. The phone kept on ringing. Then he remembered that Mrs. Schaaf had gone home early and his parents had left to meet the Braithwaites for dinner at the Ferry Slip, in Olympia. Quickly he ran to the upstairs extension. "Hello?"

"Bobby," Edie's voice said without preamble, "there's a complication. Listen—"

"I'm listening. I hope we still have our date?"

"Yes. I only have a minute to talk. I called to ask you to meet me at the luncheonette instead of here. You have your car?"

"Sure, but I don't understand. Last night you wanted me to walk with you to your door—"

"Please—the luncheonette. Later I'll tell you why."

"Okay. In about half an hour?"

"Sooner if you can. And, Bobby—don't wait in the car. Go in the back door, so my Dad won't see you."

"Whatever you say." Bobby hung up, confused, especially about her not wanting to have him wait outside.

He went back to his room to dress. He wasn't sure what to wear, but since he had cadged another ten dollars from his mother, he could afford to splurge a little and decided to dress up rather than down.

He was always excited by clothes and tonight paid special attention to everything, both for practical and esthetic reasons. Drawers were a nuisance when you were going to have sex, one more thing to take off, but wearing none even more of one after you had had it. He compromised with jockey shorts and stuffed a half dozen folded Kleenexes into the hip pocket of his slacks. Then he put on an Alexander Shields shirt, a legacy from his brother Houghton, a red silk one-of-a-kind job he knew would impress Edie. He made sure he had his box of Sheiks and a tube of mints, in case he had hali after eating.

Luckily, getting his mother to agree to let him take her car had been easy, once she got over her crazy mad about being a Southerner and Antietam and the quarry noise and America turning gray. That must have been what his father meant when he asked him to be patient about his mother's difficult time. But once in the car, he had other things to worry about—whether to buy a pint now, or wait to see what Edie wanted to do, making sure the robe was in the back seat, because they were going to need that. Not to mention that he was so excited by what Edie was going to let him have he was having trouble concealing it.

He backed out, turned toward the Corner quadrangle and pulled into the rear of the luncheonette parking lot and went quickly inside, as Edie had asked him to do, so the Cadles would be less likely to notice.

Among the things remaining from the former Hubbard house in Briarcliff Manor, which Mrs. Hubbard had sold at Teddy's insistence, was a 1911 gold-leafed *bombé* "Louis XV" Victrola; her husband had presented it to her as a birthday gift in the days when they kept a box at the Metropolitan alternate Monday nights. Mrs. Hubbard had refused to be parted from the Victrola and its records, which now stood in her sitting room, its broken-spined albums crammed with memories of what she alluded to, banally enough, as opera's Golden Age. Quite often, when she was feeling sentimental, she asked Miss Hankins to abstract some old favorite and wind up the machine and play it for her. Miss Hankins, being tone-deaf, hated all the records, whether favorites or not; but she was more familiar with them, really, than Mrs. Hubbard, because she could remember their titles, in which albums they were, and how often they had been played. Mrs. Hubbard couldn't remember, except spottily, and to her they always seemed a new experience.

"Let's have Gerry doing that pretty thing about summer and roses," she said tonight to Miss Hankins, after she had had her supper. Gerry was, of course, Geraldine Farrar. Though Mrs. Hubbard had been a bit old to be a real Gerryflapper, she had been one in spirit, and had worn her pearls from ear to ear, under her chin, as the Gerryflappers had done.

"That will be 'Love's Like a Summer Rose,' " said Miss Hankins, going to the Victrola. The song was one of her particular unfavorites, being about love, to begin with, and full of Omar Khayyám bits: *Fallen its petals lie, Quickly to fade and die; Thus do love's pleasures fly, Lost in the tasting. . . .* The song did end on a good line (probably lifted from a better, she suspected): *Forget memory's entreating.* She found the record, placed it on the turntable and lowered the needle into the grooves. After a moment of acoustic scratching, the Farrar voice emerged, faraway, diminished, but even the old horn recording could not entirely dim its brilliance.

Mrs. Hubbard listened, nodding, forming the words with her lips, until the record ran through. "Ah, yes," she said, as she did always, " 'Forget memory's entreating.' " She sighed. "Lovely line, isn't it?"

"Lovely, lovely," Miss Hankins ritually repeated.

"Gerry had fire. Naught like her today!" Mrs. Hubbard said. "Let's have another Gerry."

Miss Hankins looked resigned. "One of the duets with Clement?"

"Who?" asked Mrs. Hubbard; she had forgotten Clement.

"Or one with Martinelli?"

This name she did recall. "Him!" she said. "Always strained. I stopped listening to Martinelli that day he couldn't get through *La Juive.*"

Miss Hankins knew the Martinelli story well (it was indeed famous) and it gave her pleasure to correct Mrs. Hubbard. "It was the *'Celeste'* from *Aida* that he couldn't get through, dear; I doubt *La Juive* ever was sung in the afternoons anyway."

"Whatever it was, he didn't get through it. That's what one may expect from attending matinees, I suppose." Interest had already shifted for Mrs. Hubbard. "How about a nice Tosti instead?"

"Which one? There are so many!"

"Not the *'Dopo,'* " decided Mrs. Hubbard, who sometimes remembered very well. "I think the *'Serenata.'* "

Miss Hankins could not bear Tosti. For some reason she couldn't understand, she never heard the words right; maybe it was the fault of the soprano and the fact the record had been made long

ago. She knew perfectly well the opening phrases, *Vola, O serenata: la mia diletta è sola;* but what she always heard was, *Mitt
me, my pompous loved one, my fairest Gwynplaine sleepeth.*
Absurd! Just as, when Sembrich began the *Bel raggio lusinghier*
from *Semiramide,* she heard *Buddy Roger-er-ers loo-oosing his
hair.* Too foolish!

"Now, I think, a Caruso," Mrs. Hubbard suggested, Tosti over.
He was, to Miss Hankins, the worst; as she often told the Misses
Bowyer, his voice affected her like a cat. They had the '*Vesti*' from
Pagliacci and then '*Hantise d'amour,*' by which time Miss Hankins
was a wreck. Luckily, just then Mrs. Hubbard heard the call of
nature; this heeded, she forgot the Victrola and turned her attention to her birthday party.

"I'll wear my rose tomorrow, if it's not too warm," she said.

"The party's not tomorrow, it's not until Saturday."

"Grace Coolidge had the very same dress," Mrs. Hubbard continued, paying no attention. "Hers is in the Smithsonian. I wonder
if mine will ever be?"

Miss Hankins discouraged development of such questions.

"Mary Pickford's curls are there," said Mrs. Hubbard.

"Dear, they're not! Don't you remember, the last time we were
in Washington, we went to the Smithsonian and asked especially
to see the Pickford curls, and they weren't there?"

"Well, where are they, then?" Mrs. Hubbard demanded to
know. "They are of historic importance, they should be somewhere!"

"Dear, don't you think your little lie-down, now? With the fan?"

"Don't turn that contraption on! I hate electric fans! But you
could fan me, if you liked."

Often Miss Hankins felt like a human punkah as she stood ply-
ing one of the many "church" fans that Mrs. Hubbard kept in her
bedside table for warm moments. This one, which Miss Hankins
herself chose, showed a group of jolly geishas serving an obviously
Pinkerton kind of man with sake.

"Ah, nothing like *real* air moving," said Mrs. Hubbard appreci-
atively. "That will do, now." But the geishas reminded her of
Madama Butterfly, and nothing would do but Miss Hankins should
play Gerry's "*Ieri son salita.*"

"Now, that's music enough," Miss Hankins said firmly, as she

238

closed the phonograph. "Mustn't get tired. Shall I read to you?"

"Yes!"

"What shall it be today?"

"*The Man from*—I never can remember."

"*Brodney's,*" Miss Hankins filled in, thinking it might as well have been *Lloyd's;* this turn-of-the-century novel was one of which Mrs. Hubbard never tired. She knew it by heart, almost, as she sometimes said, but still always found it interesting.

"Read the part where Lady Edward denies herself cigarettes, so she can save them for the Brodney man."

Miss Hankins found the part and read it out, but did not bother to say there was no Lady Edward in the book.

Mrs. Hubbard found it as delightful as ever. "Now, if Mrs. Harding had been *that* kind of woman, poor Warren would never have had that coffeepot scandal on his hands."

"Teapot Dome."

"I used to wear Harding blue, and Grace Coolidge liked rose. Grace Moore had a nice blue named for her, too."

Miss Hankins feared mention of the late diva would lead to more Victrola souvenirs, so she said, "It's time for my walk now. You'll be all right until I get back. Or Mr. Ted will come, if you need him."

"And where will you go?"

"Only to the Misses Bowyer, at the Corner."

"Those fools!" Mrs. Hubbard had never met the Misses Bowyer, had only heard of them from Miss Hankins. "Are men still stealing their ferns and flowers at night?"

"I think they *think* they are," Miss Hankins said diplomatically.

"Idiots, the both of them! Well, run along, and try to bring back something new for a change."

Miss Hankins probably wouldn't pass on anything she might learn from either Miss Flora or Miss Emmeline, because Mrs. Hubbard tended to get things mixed up and toss them back the wrong way. Not that I'd tell *any*thing, after that gramophone siege, she thought, as she set out up the road. It was oppressively hot. She wore her "sensibles," white, therapeutic nursing shoes, the one concession she made to summer; the rest of her clothes were the same year round—olive gabardine suit, ecru blouse, a bandeau around her head.

She found the Misses Bowyer in quite a state. Since Miss Hankins' visits were unannounced, they took place, as today, in Miss Emmeline's bedroom, with Spot in his little boxer shorts comfortably ensconced on the bed; this saved Miss Flora having to repeat so much afterward. Miss Hankins got it from both of them, both barrels.

"Miss Hankins, *have* you seen the extraordinary man who's come to the Corner?" Miss Emmeline at once asked.

"Why, I don't think I have," replied Miss Hankins, having decided to keep the man she had seen for herself.

"And he's an evil person, I fear," put in Miss Flora. "Pursuing women. Widows."

"Widows?"

"Yes, Mrs. Glidden."

"Oh, I am astonished!" said Miss Hankins. "But who *is* safe, these days? I take it you've seen him?"

"Many times," both sisters chanted as one. "All day yesterday. And today. He's everywhere."

"And you, Flora, saw him Sunday night, on the canal bank," added Miss Emmeline.

"Hush, Emmy," said Miss Flora. "Not that."

"And what is he like?" Miss Hankins pursued.

Neither Miss Flora nor Miss Emmeline could wait to describe him.

"Ah—I think, perhaps, I did see him, then," conceded Miss Hankins, "but from a safe distance."

"It's so very close this evening," said Miss Emmeline. "Poor Spot, he pants so. Flora, do bring up some of that orangeade you made. It's a secret recipe," she confided, when Miss Flora had gone downstairs. "Oranges, port, maraschino and Vichy water."

"Port?" asked Miss Hankins. "In this weather?"

"The port is Our Father's—very mild. Flora puts in only a few teaspoonfuls. You needn't worry, the orange cuts it."

Miss Emmeline used the time Miss Flora was out of the room to inquire about the Hubbards, as unknown to her, except by hearsay, as she was to them.

"She's quite potty, especially with this low barometer. Of course, she'll be eighty-three come Saturday."

"Eighty-three! Think of it!" Miss Emmeline was almost eighty herself.

"Yes, her son's having quite a do for her." Miss Hankins managed to put *son* and *do* in quotes of disapproval.

"And the son's friend?" Miss Emmeline added her own quotes.

"The same. He's what we called a spiv in England."

"T-t-t!"

Miss Flora returned with three glasses and a large pitcher of orangeade on a tray.

"I say, this is a bit of all right! Delicious!" Miss Hankins inclined to be more British when with the Bowyers than when at the Hubbards'. She drained her glass in almost one swallow. "May I ask for more?"

Miss Flora replenished her glass. "It always seems to be something," she said, and told Miss Hankins of the attempted abduction of Spot, of the shocking behavior of the luncheonette woman, of Cadle's inconsiderate shouting at the Colored in the pink car.

"Not pink, surely," said Miss Hankins.

"Pink. And what with the flowers and ferns all going, and the wall stones, and the nails disappearing from the floors, we simply don't know where to turn," Miss Flora said.

"Not a board but isn't loose," confirmed Miss Emmeline.

Miss Hankins thought it more prudent not to comment.

"But Flora's not telling you what she saw on the towpath Sunday night," said Miss Emmeline.

"I told her, Emmy," Miss Flora said.

"But not that he was *entirely nude!*"

"Oh, was he, really?" asked Miss Hankins. "How shocking!"

"Yes, I'm afraid he was," Miss Flora had to admit.

"He's a Midsummer Man," said Miss Emmeline.

Miss Hankins finished another glass of the orangeade. She appeared a little flushed. "Why, this *is* Midsummer Eve! Or, at least, it is in England. And tomorrow's Midsummer Day."

"I've never really understood how it could be midsummer in June," Miss Flora said, trying to keep off difficult subjects. "It's always seemed to me it should be in August—that's really midsummer."

"No, Midsummer Day's tomorrow," Miss Hankins said.

"Our Governess, who was English, taught us that when we were children," said Miss Emmeline reproachfully to Flora. "Of course he's a Midsummer Man. There's still hope for us all." She looked slyly at Miss Hankins. "Especially you, my dear; you're by way of being almost a junior miss, compared with us."

"I'm afraid I no longer have hopes," Miss Hankins confided. "I seem destined to care for old mothers of old men, men of a certain peculiarity, I might add." She set down her glass. "I've been too long on this case . . . and I must be going."

Perhaps it was because of the port in the orangeade she had drunk that, as Miss Hankins started walking toward the Hubbard place, she saw the Cadillac drawing up in front of the luncheonette as distinctly pink. Hankins, Hankins, my girl, she said to herself under her breath, you're getting as potty as everyone else in this village. Another of those orangeades and you'd be seeing purple cows! She looked back. "Damme!" she exclaimed aloud. "It *is* pink!"

The luncheonette door opened and Fran Hanter came in. Al looked up from the newspaper he was reading. It was a slow hour. He saw that his wife's face was very white and could see the blue veins in her temples.

"I thought you weren't coming back till tomorrow," he said.

Outside it was still light, but the lamps were already lighted on the bridge. "Mother's much worse," Fran answered; "they've taken her to the hospital." She took off her high-heeled shoes and stepped into the ones she wore for work.

"You don't look like you'll be much use around here," Al said. "Why don't you go on home?"

"I can't bear to be alone."

"Go to the hospital, then."

"They told us not to. They said to wait and they'd let us know." Fran looked up at the clock. The hands pointed to five minutes of the hour. Then it was five minutes after. "Funny," Fran said, talking to the wall, "we never had a good picture of Mother, only snapshots. I'm going to get a blowup of one we took on that picnic two years ago, before she fell sick."

"Yeah," Al answered, "but don't talk about it now. Customer."

Bobby Ingle came in. "Hi," he said.

"Hello," Fran returned his greeting. Al said nothing.

242

"Do you mind if I wait here a minute?" Bobby asked. "I'm meeting somebody."

"Edie Cadle," Fran guessed.

"How did you know?"

"I've got eyes." She was glad to have someone in the place tonight as a buffer against Al, anyone. "See you've got a car tonight."

Bobby nodded. He moved to one of the stools behind the cash register, where he could watch the Cadle place.

"Why aren't you picking her up over there?" Fran asked.

"She asked me to meet her in here."

"Hm," Fran said.

There was less going on at the garage than at the luncheonette. The door swung open and Mae Cadle leaned out, hanging up a sign, CLOSED, then disappeared.

"Rafe must've finished working on that Hubbard Pierce," Al said. He switched on the neon outside the luncheonette. "On it all day long."

Then they saw Edie Cadle come out. She looked in both directions and then walked quickly across the road to the luncheonette and came inside. Bobby got down from his stool.

"What's the matter?" he asked. "You've been crying."

"All women cry, boy," Al said; "you'll learn that soon enough."

"Please, Bobby," Edie said, "I'd like to go—right away."

The Hanters watched them leave and hurry to Bobby's car and drive across the bridge toward Subberton.

"Poor kids," said Fran.

"What's poor about them, especially him?"

"I only meant it's hard to be young."

"Well, no harder than being old like us," Al answered her.

The evening rush started then, and for well over two hours the Hanters were too busy to talk, Al at the grill and Fran doubling at the counter and hopping it out to the cars that wanted curb service. It wasn't until shortly before eight that there was a lull again.

Fran kept busy. She found a bottle of Mr. Clean and a cloth and, standing on a box, started to wipe grease from the menu board over the grill. Next to this hung a framed color reproduction of a photograph of President Kennedy, which had been there long before the assassination. The Hanters had been and still were "Kennedy people," just as in the thirties or forties they would have been "Roosevelt people" and would, no doubt, have had a picture of F.D.R. where the one of J.F.K. hung now. This did not mean that they went along with everything J.F.K. had advocated. They did not serve Negroes willingly, for instance; they served them, but in a way that made it clear they were doing it because they had to. Al had never gone out of his way yet to please a Colored, often, in fact, handed out an overcooked or oversalted hamburger, in the hope the Colored would get the idea and next time give the luncheonette the go-by.

"Hey, Fran," Al suddenly said in a sharp voice. "Get what's coming."

Fran looked, seeing a dark, good-looking man getting out of a pink Cadillac, which he had carelessly parked across the drive-in marks customers were expected to observe. Even from this distance, she could see he had diamonds on both hands.

"He's the one brought Edie Cadle home the other morning," Fran said.

"He did, huh? Well, he looks more like what Edie Cadle'd be going out with than that Ingle kid," said Al. The man was all in white—white, monogrammed silk shirt, white linen pants, sharp white shoes.

"You should have heard Rafe Cadle light into him," Fran said, getting down from her box. "There's dirt between those two."

"Dirt? What kind of dirt?"

"I don't know, but there is."

Both looked indifferent as Acie Stanes came in and took a seat at the counter. Acie could pass for white almost anywhere, but not with Al. To types like him, he didn't give out with his "What'll it be?" but, in the manner of many small men, raised his chin in a questioning jerk that plainly said, "You—who are you and what do you want?"

Acie got the pitch. He sat twisting his rings, taking in the jukebox, the menu, the grill with dogs and burgers waiting.

"You got a license for that jukebox?" he asked Al, as an opener.

"If you want to play the box, just put your money in," Al answered.

"That's not what I asked," Acie said softly. "I asked, you got a license for it?"

"Who wants to know?"

244

"Just answer the question, man."

Al's attitude changed slightly. "I don't own that box. It's taken care of by the people own this place."

"So you don't own this place?"

"No," said Al.

"That means they own you," Acie said, in the same soft voice. "You know their names?"

Al was getting uneasy. "Matter of fact, no, I don't." He waited, his temper rising. "I don't tell my business to the likes of you."

Fran came out of the kitchen. Acie smiled at her. "Well, now," he said, "maybe it's time you found out. Man, *I* own that box. I got a right to ask you anything I like. Meantime, how's about a pair of burgers? In butter. No onion."

Al and Fran exchanged glances.

"That's better," said Acie, seeing he had made his point—respect for him had formed. Al put two burgers on the grill. "Butter, now," Acie reminded him.

"I heard you the first time," Al said.

Acie turned his attention to Fran. "Nice place, the Corner."

Fran said nothing.

"I said, the Corner's a nice place."

"Is it?" Fran challenged.

"Looks to be," said Acie, looking straight across the road at the Cadle garage.

"I hear you're a friend of Rafe Cadle's," Al said.

"Who gave you that idea?" Acie asked.

"Well, my wife, she says she saw Rafe talking to you the other morning."

"You got that?" Acie said to Fran.

Fran nodded.

"Well, if you saw that," said Acie, without looking at her, "maybe you've seen Edie Cadle tonight."

"She—they went out of here a couple of hours ago," Al said, trying to get rid of it.

"Al, shut up!" Fran said.

Al gave Acie his burgers. "The way you like them?"

Acie didn't touch them, only looked at them. "You say Edie went out of here? Who with?"

This time Al didn't answer.

"You." Acie turned to Fran, looking her in the eyes. "Did she?"

"Yes, she did," Fran replied. Respect had turned to fear.

"Who was she with?" Acie got up and struck the counter. "Don't make me ask again. Who was she with?"

"A boy, one of the boys from around here," Al supplied.

"No name?" asked Acie.

"We don't know his name," Fran said.

"Yeah," Al said, "just a kid, about her age."

"Meaning I'm not her age," said Acie. He went over to the juke-box and kicked it on all sides, shattering the glass. The lights winked out. "Look, little white man," he said to Al, "I don't like to find my equipment in this shape. You gotta pay me for this box."

Fran and Al stared.

"I don't like the looks of this place," Acie said. "You two better watch it. And if Rafe Cadle comes in, you can tell him I was here."

Fran stared at the monogram on the white silk shirt. "He—I mean Rafe Cadle—he almost never comes in here. But if he does, who shall I say?"

"Tell him Acie Stanes. He'll know. Too bad your box is busted. I feel real sorry. I feel so sorry I'll pay you for those burgers I didn't eat."

"No charge," Al said. "On the house."

"You're getting the idea," Acie said, and went out.

"Jesus!" Al said, wiping his face as he watched Acie drive off. "Jesus *H*. Christ!" His voice was high, almost cracking.

"Coward," Fran said. "When *I* don't charge, give trust, it's wrong."

"That wasn't trust."

"Then what was it?"

"Small graft from a policy operator. We're lucky it wasn't a few hundred bucks straight over the counter."

"I still say you're a coward."

"*You* better learn who we're working for," said Al. "They can pin you to the wall if they've a mind to."

" 'They?' Who's 'they'?"

A look of defeat crossed Al's tired face. "I've never known who 'they' are, and I don't want to know, either."

"Like he said, 'little white man.' "

"That's what he said and that's what I am. I just want to stay little and make it go."

The crushed way he said this turned Fran's contempt to pity. "Gosh, Al," she said, "I've always known there are people running us from up top, but I didn't know it could do this to you."

"Shut up," he said, turning away. She saw his hands were shaking. "You talk too goddam much."

"Al," she said. She went to him and put her arms around his cramped, bony shoulders. "I love you, you know. You know that, don't you?"

"You got to cool off some more from that road stud before I want any of that," Al answered.

BOOK

FOUR

CHAPTER 1

In the Bertolt Brecht-Kurt Weill opera, *Rise and Fall of the City of Mahagonny,* The Speaker at one point declares, "Those who truly seek are disappointed." Though towns like Olympia and its satellite village of Cope's Corner, indeed all of Bucks County, were full of seekers, they possessed no Brecht. It is possible that Brecht would have liked the area—as a place from which to flee to one of his Alabamas or Georgias, or to Benares. In a way, the county was not unlike Brecht's Mahagonny, that city of nets that is a caricature of a freedom permitting all to live as they please. But Olympia was the reverse of the coin, less a caricature than a self-conscious American town in which everyone tried to live as he was supposed to. Many truly came to seek "the Olympia way of life" (as anyone paying school and road taxes could tell you), but many also left. A curious expression crossed the features of these defectors when asked why they were selling out, and often they did not reply, perhaps because they did not know. If pressed for reasons for their running, as was Jim Mahoney in *Mahagonny,* their faces became even more perplexed. Were there not gin and whiskey? (In too great abundance.) Peace and harmony? (What peace and harmony?) Fish to catch? (The shad in the Delaware haven't been running for years.) Cigarettes to smoke? (My wife and I are trying to give them up.) The sleep everyone needs? (We can't sleep for the stone trucks from the quarries.) Swimming? (The Swimming Club discriminates.) And forgetfulness? (Ah, we wish we could forget!) The dichotomized face of the questioned one silently indicated, as Jim Mahoney did verbally: *But something is missing.*

To no avail were further cajolings, as in the Brecht opera—the beauty of the countryside, the talk of men, the quiet and peace of mind, the simple existence. The whilom resident, whose wife so optimistically at first had welcomed the Welcome Wagon, had sat on P.T.A. boards, explained himself in letters written to valley newspapers, had become a father, perhaps mayor, supervisor, planning commission member, transporter of cakes to the bake sales, churchwarden—the disillusioned daddy with wife and children moved on. He probably tried not to hear the cry above the tinkling pianos of Monkeywrench Alley and Lunchbox Lane, "This is eternal art!" as Brecht's Jim Mahoney, Jacob Schmidt, Pennybank Bill and Alaska-Wolf Joe heard it in Mahagonny; more than likely he was behind a stone truck, trying to make out what his wife and kids were saying, and managed not to hear it.

The communications industries, with their high percentage of failures, misfits and drunks, had contributed heavily to the county's assortment of excited newcomers, who hoped they at last had found a solution to debt, aging, disillusion—a new life, with all the *Mahagonny* inducements as lagniappe. The weekly Olympia *Sentinel*, wailing wall for the community, often implored its readers to write in and suggest what the thing or things missing might be; but letters in reply were vague, revealing only that the strained optimists writing them stemmed from that business civilization which has atrophied not only men's souls but also their capacity for rebellion. They had learned the Cocktail-ABC, had read the easy, Do-It-Yourself recipes for Life in the *Reader's Digest* and had believed them; the *Sentinel's* journalese, also, adhered to its brainwashed prose and offensive-to-none clichés. Dr. Ingle, who had dried out more than one of these in-process-of-reinforcing-the-optimism daddies (or mommies), had a phrase to describe them: "Scratch an Olympia drunk and find the Madison Avenue patina of five years ago, tarnished."

Something was missing; perhaps that segment of the American Dream the county was said to embody had folded, like the area tent shows, or perhaps Norman Mailer had finally done it in. The Olympia disillusion, which followed on the heels of dismay on discovering that the insisted-upon sweetness and light was a lot of horse manure, sometimes was temporary, even funny. Often it took the form of a seventy-two-hour hard fall from the wagon of grace the town at first represented; at other times it was terrible to see or hear about, as when there was a seemingly inexplicable suicide, achieved by the classic barbiturates, the gun brought home by Daddy from the war, drowning. (The canal was better for suicide than the river, because deeper; drowning oneself in the Delaware, except when it was in flood, involved lying flat and only partly submerged on its sandy bottom and sucking in resolutely.) The day-and-a-half lushing it up at the White Hare or the Ferry Slip or The Wharf was construed by some as amusing, but the local Alcoholics Anonymous did not find it so. Old residents learned with horror of these dwellers recently come and now gone forever, suspicion dawning that these things could, conceivably, happen to themselves. Something was missing, but what? Maybe it was not what was missing, but something of which there was too much.

Was it the growing roster of juvenile delinquents? The nightly depredations of both public and private property? The lack of a sewage system? (Sewage had nothing to do with morals, or did it?) The increasing sales at the state liquor store, not to mention the bottles carted from New Jersey, where selection of brands was wider? The preponderance of homosexuals? The rising percentage of knock-up brides? The marijuana scares that broke out once or twice a year on Monkeywrench Alley, only to be quashed and forgotten? The fall in church attendance? The unpleasant fact that virtually every business in Olympia had been burgled—many repeatedly—while only one per cent of these robberies were solved? Such scandals as that of the son of a local citizen, who, playing with Daddy's Luger, accidentally shot and killed the baby-sitter? (This, too, was quashed, for the boy's sake, the court implied; punishment wouldn't return the baby-sitter to life.)

These traumatic happenings were evidence, even to older residents, that either something was missing or there was too much of something. But they had suspected the drunk before he (or she) reached public saturation, had considered the suicide odd and an outsider anyway, and the boy who killed the baby-sitter spoiled and undisciplined; the dredging of the canal, the analysis of the barbiturates and the Luger laggardly confiscated were anticlimax. Equally disturbingly, they were not convinced that the horror of what sometimes happened was final and complete. Nembies were for sale by the handful, in front of the drugstore from which they had been stolen, along with sticks of Mary Jane; anyone could drive, walk or run to the nearest canal bank; and if there was one Luger, there were others.

Things, of course, as elsewhere, were seldom what they seemed. Like the Wild West Colonial renovations of Main Street houses and shops (stained pine projections tacked onto white clapboards of late "carpenter" Gothic), what went on out back was rarely what went on in front. (Where, Susan Ingle's bridge group complained, *was* the Historical Society, which wanted all to remain as it was, when these monstrosities went up? Not that they would have belonged to the Society themselves.) Stories of what could and did happen filtered into county intelligence via the police, the local doctors, and people who had been observers or involved. Old stuff was the wife of one local tradesman, who got squiffed at parties and tried to make the hostess or one of the other women present; recently she had been hospitalized, and the nurses reported they couldn't keep her hands off them. She was as much a part of local lore as the rich, elderly Quaker, suffering from satyriasis, known as Foxy-Loxy, doubly named because he was a grandfather and had features of marked Semitic cast. He crashed queer parties and then, six martinis to the wind, proceeded to berate the town for tolerating fairies, and his hosts for having no women present; Foxy-Loxy was hell to get rid of, but it could be done by decoying him to his car, with a pretty boy as bait, who then scuttled back to the party, leaving the old boy to smash his car through the bushes to the road and get home as best he could. Behavior of this kind was symptomatic, perhaps, of the fascination male homosexuals (especially handsome ones) held for certain men of the town; however much they might disapprove of *les boys*, they couldn't help wondering whether in some way they didn't cop more sensation than they themselves did. One ugly town father, in need of release, one night had taken the bull by the horns and telephoned one of the better-looking of the boys. "My wife's away," he had announced, after saying who he was, "and I'm standing here with a hard on. Why don't you come on over?"

His invitation was declined, without thanks: "Daddy, I'm a size queen, if you don't know; besides, I've heard all about you from your wife." The man extending this invitation reckoned without the peculiar freemasonry of *les boys:* they put the bitches' curse on him within the hour and from then on boycotted his business, economic withholding being one of the most potent revenges. But here and there, to be fair, were evidences of the sweetness and light so editorialized about. One lady weekly drew up to the Co-op in her Silver Cloud and sent the chauffeur in with tarragon picked from her herb garden; the proceeds, she explained, would pay for an extra day or two next winter in Florida. Another, a pillar of the Historical Society, was given to leaving her card in the mailboxes of people whose architecture or plantings she disapproved of. "A very ugly porch," she would scrawl across the card; "why not remove it?" Or "That burdock should definitely come out. Let me give you a few cuttings of my climbing hydrangea." And added her telephone number.

This was, possibly, part of the too much, not the missing. Still, something was missing, and Dr. Ingle, for one, had his ideas about what part of that was, as did others. It was next to impossible for an aggrieved taxpayer to report nuisances or violations with any guarantee that the laws governing them would be enforced. In the days when Ingle still had hopes of doing something about the stench of exhaust from the Cadle garage and the oily waste that smoldered in the oil drum out back, he learned, he said, that there was one law for the poor and another for the rich. His complaint had been filed formally, and the Board of Health had sent an investigator, but not until all had been prepared for his arrival, news of which had reached Rafe through one of his daughters, who had a friend working in the health office. When the investigator showed up, Rafe was shaved and in fresh clothes, Mae had changed her dress, not a car was running, the oil drum was empty and turned on its side. Rafe and the investigator discussed the complaint over a few beers.

"Who tattled on me?" Rafe asked.

The investigator, against all rules, revealed that Ingle had been the complaining party.

"Bastard," said Rafe. "Nuts as the nuts he treats at that clinic, if you ask me."

"He says there's this smell of exhaust."

"Can I help cars running on the road?"

The inspector sniffed.

"What you're smelling is probably a groundhog," said Rafe. "Damn things are all over the place. I've been gassing them, maybe I got one."

"Gassing them? Maybe that's the odor complained about." The Board of Health man wrote *Possible dead animal* on his report sheet. "I suggest you try to find that groundhog, Rafe," he said sternly. "Those things stink to high heaven once they're dead; even a mole or a small snake'll stink, dead."

"Yes, sir," Rafe answered, straight-faced. "I'll get out there and start digging for that hog right away."

After another beer, the inspector left. Rafe did no digging, and next day the cars were all running and a fresh batch of waste cooked in the oil drum, as usual. The Board of Health, when Ingle checked to find out about the inspector's call, reported that there was the possibility of a dead animal on the Cadle premises, but that no violation had been found. When Ingle further protested, it was suggested he write to the zoning board, which, in turn, replied that it had no authority in such matters, that the garage had been an existing business when the code rules of 1953 were drawn up. They felt that if Ingle reported anything he wished to complain about to Willie Bentrup, the township cop, it might get results; Bentrup was up and down the road all day, was a friend of Cadle's, and could give him a strong hint. Bentrup reported back that the dead groundhog had been located and disposed of. If Ingle had any other objections, he suggested trying the Board of Health. After more of this jumping in and out of the bramble bush, Ingle consulted his lawyer.

"You can file through the state courts," said the lawyer, after hearing the whole story. "I strongly counsel against it. Move. I've heard of stones being hurled, and stones carry no fingerprints."

That was the year the Ingle hedge went up, not that it did much good; and it was not bramble, but yew.

Most Fringe dwellers living on the hillsides of Cope's Corner still had privies, and many of them were shocking. Efforts of neighbors to compel one violator, who had a surface outhouse, to dig the customary trench beneath the seats, had met with no success whatever.

"Why, that's a *country* smell," he said, when he had listened to the complaints that extremely hot weather or downriver winds made his privy offensive. "That stuff always was hard to get rid of. I'll dig it out, if it'll make you feel any better."

Like Rafe Cadle's promise to Dr. Ingle to slap a coat of paint over the painted cigar and 5, this was never fulfilled, though the man did accept from the complainants a gratis sack of lime, so things would be a little less high on the hill. Something was added, rather than missing, in that case.

The tourists had the best of the countryside, Susan Ingle said, especially of Olympia. The walk of some became a swagger the minute they crawled out of their cars, and the lips of others began at once to phrase commentaries on how quaint it all was, and, "Look! That man we see on TV in the winter, he's here in person, in that play we missed in New York ten years ago!" "Come on, Morris, we're going to look for that real oil painting for the master bedroom, remember?" "But, Ma, my feet are tired." "All right, you sit on a husband bench and wait, and I'll buy the painting." "Now, don't get anything too abstract." "It's all abstract now, you know that, Morris." And off the wife would go, exact measurements and color swatches of curtains to be matched in her hand. Like Alice confronted with the small cake, marked EAT ME, Ma had nibbled at the "Art Knows All, Sees All, Tells All, Solves All" premise of Olympia, though not everybody (like Morris) finished the cake or digested what he had bitten off.

The art galleries, which crowded the streets of Olympia, had changed in the last five years, in a desperate effort to mirror the spirit of the times; but time's overtaking by time, the permanent revolution in art in New York and Paris and London, which they tried to latch on to, often made it all seem a little like the Red Queen in *Through the Looking-Glass;* it took all the running they could do, forward and backward, to keep in the same place. Whereas once "American primitives" were pushed, now the striving was for *à la mod,* metropolitan chic. Dozens of artists in the area who had never had a Philadelphia show, much less a New York one, found it not too difficult to approximate the puns of Rauschenberg and Rivers and Oldenburg and other celebrated

257

"pops." It could be said that all three artists, in almost literal copies made by Bucks amateurs, had done very well in Olympia. Louise Matthiasdottir, too, had been a breeze to imitate, with her cold palette, simplicity and student-size canvases; indeed, last year, someone who called himself Birger Akermark had done more than well, painting *big* "Matthiasdottirs." But now Marisol's frozen-faced toys were presenting problems; they were difficult to "run up." "Pop" art, of course, was already "out" at Olympia's Left Bank Gallery, as *out* was no longer "in"; the gallery, perhaps symbolically, was on the right bank of the river as it flows seaward.

The Left Bank boasted connections with London and Paris galleries, but what appeared on its walls were "the new mods"— young Philly beatniks, who had learned the secret of Xerox copies of newspaper blowups, how to make life-sized, cardboard cutouts of snapshots of friends (the grainier the better, and easier, after all, than casting friends in plaster, as George Segal did). They knew, also, about enlarged printed circuits, microscopic proteins magnified to vast proportions and transferred to canvas with house paint, and, in the already "over" catchphrase of the summer, what-have-you.

Just as the village of Cope's Corner tried for "artistic living in a William Penn setting," so Olympia's galleries strove for the witty insolence of a youth already middle-aged. Nothing went out of style more quickly than the ephemera of last season; the Red Queen was in constant crisis, deciding what was "over" and what was not. A Franz Kline looked perfectly terrible, baking in the sun of the Left Bank's display window; it wasn't a real Kline, even if it *had* been copied, exactly (by projector) from the Sidney Janis poster for Kline's 1957 New York show; but the couple who ran the place left it there, to show they were nothing if not eclectic— the Red Queen relaxed from time to time. Last week's artist, who resembled Martin Milner in an oldish way, had been on hand, keeping gallery, so the artist could be seen and believed; he had presented (as the catalogue noted, "frankly") strips of movie film printed, row upon serried row, on photographic paper; these prints had been made from positives, so a certain negative result was inevitable, as were repetitive motifs and a confusing texture. That show hadn't done at all well.

But this week's offering at the Left Bank exploited "Themes in

Nature Felt in Ourselves," collages by a new valley artist, Elberta Dawes. (*Kitsch*, like collage, was eternal, too.) These were fashioned from old *National Geographic* color pages of exotic flora and fauna, all varnished to a high gloss. They had fancy, literary titles, inscribed into the varnish, so nothing would get mixed up. "Journey to the End of My Orangeade Feet" was one title the owners of the gallery, who were fronting for Miss Dawes, liked especially; this artist had declined to appear, and all negotiations with her had been conducted by mail. The gallery told prospective buyers these works were as significant a turning point in "painting" as "Toasted Susie is my ice cream" had been in literature; that was the spiel, until a very tiresome local collector, Avery Mulford, reminded the gallery that Larry Rivers some years before had permitted a friend to inscribe on one of his works the legend "My farthest feet are deepest orangeade."

The Left Bank owners were quite put out when they heard this. "We are trying to get away from Rivers down here," they said; "these pictures are nothing like Rivers'." Both together moved to various examples of the Dawes work, explicating. "Don't you think the feeling for replication is remarkable? It's an overt expression, of course, of the shudder and shock to which all of us are exposed every day." A large stone truck lumbered by, and the owners waited until Mulford could again hear. "The style here is everything."

"I should have thought the titles were everything," Mulford replied, reading them.

"But, surely, you see the turmoil that went into this work?"

"Yes, I see the turmoil; I also see the effort. The work, if that's what it is, is clogged with it."

The gallery did not like Mulford; he had never been willing to lend any of his drawings or paintings for local charity causes, though his collection was known to include examples of surrealist and neoromantic artists, Dali, Tanguy, Tchelitchew, Matta; the Left Bank's owners (who kept up) had seen his Tchelitchews recently at the Huntington Hartford Gallery of Modern Art in New York.

"But you, Mr. Mulford, collect the 'Prince of Bad Taste,'" the gallery couple said, to punish him for being a nonlender and spoil-

259

ing their belief in Elberta Dawes. "That was Tchelitchew's own estimate of himself."

"But what wonderful bad taste," answered Mulford. "I wish you had a few Tchelitchews."

"We wouldn't turn a Tchelitchew over."

Nevertheless, the Left Bank scolded Elberta Dawes (by mail) for having duped them, and took her show down two days early.

By dint of ruthless weekly changes of these facetious *à la mods,* the modern Olympia galleries gave the Old Guard locals, still doing Maine seascapes in the summers and valley snow scenes in the winters, a run for their money. But a much more pernicious competition came from a source that was obscure, paid no gallery rent, and worked in hidden ways.

There were always trooping through the galleries and antique shops and junk shops of the valley bargain hunters, sometimes themselves painters, on the lookout for a Blakelock or a William Sidney Mount, an Eakins, or, with great good luck, an Edward Hicks; all these artists, at one time or another, had been known to turn up. If, by chance, one of these hunters came across canvases depicting some unidentifiable object in uncertain flight between reality and possibility, he likely as not took it for a Jack Tworkov, bought it, and hoped to parlay it into something he really wanted. There were many "abstract expressionist" efforts about—as accurate a description of them as any other—revealing the inner turmoil that impressed the Left Bank Gallery, and the effort Mulford had noted. Many seemed only half painted, but wasn't Tworkov known for his "unfinishedness"? Wasn't everything now, from the Return of the Figure, the New Realism, Cool Art to what-have-you left partly undone?

Within the last year, however, some very unlikely names had begun to appear in area shops—Vuillard, Pissarro, Boudin, Monet, Van Gogh; even the prowlers after bargains, many of whom were knowledgeable, like Mulford, could not entirely dismiss the possibility that such items could filter into the valley; people died, estates were settled, art was lost for years in barns (never forget Fragonard!) and was stolen every day. A Vuillard that had been found had been authenticated by no less an authority than New York's Dr. Zantvoord, who, as everyone knows, is to modern art what Berenson was to the Renaissance. This did the other Vuillards, Pissarros, Boudins, Monets and Van Goghs, which just might turn up, no harm, and gave even serious collectors courage and second thoughts. Almost anybody who had leafed through *Time* and *Life*, not to mention those who faithfully read *Arts Magazine* and *Art News*, knew the names of these artists of "The School of Paris" and what their pictures should look like; and not a few dreamed, secretly, of keeping an eye on county shops, with a view to becoming little Karoliks.

The transactions surrounding drawings and sketches and paintings by these artists had the paced inevitability of a *nō* play. The searcher, tired and dusty-handed from pawing through Victorian oleographs and nobody canvases, suddenly froze, then looked around furtively. The find was, if authentic, a minor example, true—perhaps a sketch for some great canvas known to everyone— but it would have a look of authenticity, and, on inspection, would be found to bear a faint signature (decipherable as Vincent, or Boudin, or any of the others). The lucky bargain hunter, naturally, concealed his excitement as he carried his discovery to the shop dealer and casually asked the price.

"I haven't the faintest idea," the dealer would reply, in classic response. "This came in only this morning, from an old house on the Philadelphia Main Line. Haven't had a chance to really look at it or put a price on it." The dealer would adjust his glasses. "It seems to be signed Vincent—ever hear of Vincent? I never did. It's nobody from around these parts—I know all the local names, Hicks, Eakins."

"No, never heard of Vincent," the finder would answer, breathing easier, sure now it was a Van Gogh. "But how much is it?"

"Prettily done. And old, seems like. What'll you give?"

"Fifty?"

The dealer would pause; anyone who would pay fifty for a scrap of old paper would pay a hundred. Done, of course, at a hundred, but with the understanding that the dealer made no representations and, since he worked on close margins, couldn't be bothered with returned merchandise. The delirium of the buyer lasted until any of the New York authenticators, like Dr. Zantvoord, laughed in his face. "This artist may have been named Vincent, but not the Vincent you hoped you were buying." The "Van Gogh" was junk, plain and simple, and the sucker had no redress.

These "treasures" were planted every other week or so in the area; not all were advantageously disposed of, and they disappeared, if there were no quick takers, whence they had come, no one knew where. But some of the deals were considerably larger than those of the "Vincent" kind. Teddy Hubbard, who had a sharp nose for the "over" thing that had not yet "returned," was not above turning an easy dollar, if he ran across something he could unload on a client or fellow decorator for a profit. True, bargains were becoming fewer every day, but now and then windfalls did occur—it was he who had smoked out the Vuillard, the one that turned out to be genuine, and which the good Dr. Zantvoord had placed in a New England museum, splitting a very handsome profit with Teddy. No doubt it was because of this first success that, when he came upon what seemed a Modigliani fallen on evil days, he had been taken to the cleaners.

It had showed up in a shop near Ohmerstown. It was, indubitably, a portrait of Mme. Hébuterne, and examination revealed that the canvas on which it was painted bore the imprint of a Paris dealer of the pre-World War I period. It was signed, clearly, in the upper right. Teddy had gone through the usual dissimulations with the dealer, but the dealer came right out with it.

"This belongs to an old lady who knows what she's got. She wants three thousand for it."

Teddy Hubbard pursed his lips. As a man who carried a comfortable sum in his "mad" checking account, he was in a position to buy it; he also knew how much money three thousand is. "Of course, at that figure, I'd have to have it authenticated," he said.

The dealer bridled. "You mean, take it away? Oh, no; anybody who'd want this would know it for what it is. Matter of fact, I've already got a man interested in it; he's coming back tonight."

Teddy hesitated.

"The old lady says it's by somebody very famous," the dealer went on, embroidering the provenance. "It's signed Modgilli." Mispronunciations were a *sine qua non* of these dealings, part of the disclaimer of responsibility. "The old lady got it from her nephew, who knew this Modgilli during the First War."

It was possible. "Very well," said Teddy. "You'll take my check?"

"I'll only take a certified check." The dealer made it hard. "The old lady wants it that way." Tantamount to No Returns.

Teddy hurriedly drove down to the Olympia Bank, got the certified check, and was back in Ohmerstown in an hour. He carried the painting away in triumph and, next day, drove up to New York to show it to Dr. Zantvoord.

Dr. Zantvoord took one long look. "Where did you get this?"

Teddy told him.

"You poor man," Dr. Zantvoord said. "This is patently a fake, so patent a one that I can tell you the name of the woman who painted it."

"*Woman?*" cried Teddy in a rage.

"Yes. A beauty shop owner, Elberta Dawes by name. No one knows where she lives. She paints nights, as a hobby. She's quite adept, as you see, and talented. Last week I was called in to give an opinion on not one Boudin, mind you, but *a pair!* They were by the same hand. You should see her Monet haystacks. They're not bad at all."

"I don't want to see them!"

"I suggest you return this dreadful thing and demand your money back," said Dr. Zantvoord. "I have sympathy for you; there will be no fee."

There was no returning the "Modigliani," though Teddy eventually did unload it, not at a profit, but he recouped somewhat. He was not the only one who had been duped by Miss Dawes's eclectic brush; Avery Mulford, although he would have died had anyone found out, had bought a "Modigliani" Hébuterne, equally expensive, equally fake. But to Mulford's glory as a collector, and as a man, be it recorded that he burned his.

There was no getting at Miss Dawes. Neither she nor her outlets made any claims to authenticity; no one had ever seen her; and the vanity of the few serious collectors she temporarily fooled protected her—they wouldn't have breathed her name had they known it. Besides, the Dawes "Vuillards," "Pissarros," "Boudins," "Monets," "Vincents" and "Modiglianis" gave pleasure to the many "little" collectors and tyros, who, whether or not believing in the "Pissarro" sanguine they had found, or the "Monet" sketch of haystacks, proudly hung them on their walls. After all, they were signed, however apocryphally, and lent the "connoisseur" touch now considered desirable. Whatever else was missing in the county, it was not "The School of Paris" as produced in quantity in a beauty shop somewhere, junk or art, depending on who bought it and was disillusioned, or who bought it and was made happy.

Nor was less pretentious, and unsigned, junk lacking. Everywhere was the clapboard saltbox, whose owner had converted downstairs rooms into an "antique" shop; no structure was too humble to house, in summer, the "collectiana" which, ten years before, would have been carted to the town dump; once abandoned but recently renovated railroad stations, basements, shacks at the lower end of town, offered trays full of advertising cards of the 1900s, spatterware cooking pots, patent medicine bottles, old tobacco tins, Mother's Oats premiums ("They're collecting these now, you know"), cherry pitters, apple corers, butter molds, pudding "shapes," sun-weathered sleighs with the upholstery ripped out, plush picture frames, tin cookie cutters, hair wreaths in walnut frames, moldy corsets. No street was without its "antique" shop, and one enterprising lad, in an effort to outdo his competitors, hung out a shingle promising DIVINE JUNK—one of Olympia's many *idées reçues;* it had been inspired by the name of a shop in Westport, Connecticut. If you wanted an authentic curling iron, a genuine 1905 ladies' silver buttonhook (for high buttoned shoes), the shoes to go with it, a bit crinkled and cracked, to be sure, but "antique," a chipped, Tiffany vase (pronounced *vahz*, if marked over five dollars), reproduction candy jars with *real* peppermint-striped candy in them, Olympia was for you.

Teddy Hubbard was assembling, on the third floor of his house, an "Ugly Room," the germ of the next promotion he would try to sell the fashion magazine ladies. He knew the ugly perhaps as well as anyone living around Olympia, and already the room held a four-foot cross made entirely of matches and seashells, two chairs whose frames were fashioned of buffalo horns (fugitives from Denver, without doubt), an almost life-size plaster statue of the Duchess of Windsor in her wedding dress, paintings by true *naïfs,* which looked like what they shouldn't, six pictures of surgical trusses painted on glass, with tinfoil insertions—"Too much for your aging mother," as Teddy himself would have said, describing what was to be found for sale in most county "antique" shops. "All strictly low camp, not a piece of high camp junk in the lot."

These seas of *objets trouvés* in part accounted for bitter complaints from some businessmen, who charged that the area was attracting the wrong kind of tourists, "tacky" (to use Susan Ingle's word for them) and with little money to spend, encouraging the atmosphere the Wild West Colonial renovations invited, a snake eating its own tail. Art, too, had failed the valley, evidently; local barns, that once had tried to put "The Delaware School" on the map, had almost given up and had reverted to exhibits of needlework and housewife painters, whose efforts sold easily, marked twenty to thirty-five dollars. The judges seemed never to get things right, pictures they had rejected later being acquired by important national museums, while those they had accepted and hung were still hanging—in local restaurants; "Vuillard," "Pissarro," "Boudin," "Monet," "Vincent" and "Modigliani" had strange bedfellows.

If, however, you wanted period American furniture, it was necessary to poke into such troves as that of the Misses Bowyer, whose antiques were genuine, if not for sale; or one of the shops out on the highways, where chest-on-chests and Sheraton side chairs, plate warmers and lazy susans, cradles and Hessian Soldier andirons rubbed shoulders with sets of wedding-band china, Toby jugs and Rockingham invalid feeders.

One of the better dealers, a Frenchwoman far out on the road to Ohmerstown, had "Continental" things. She was not too far out for the afternoon ladies; they drove hopefully out to her shop by dozens, as they did to Miss Flora Augusta Bowyer's, but with different results. The Frenchwoman's antiques were equally as genuine as Miss Bowyer's, but of another kidney and for sale. But the ladies didn't care for what they found there.

"What kind of rug is that?" one shopper would demand to know of the Frenchwoman. "Or is it a wall hanging?"

"An Aubusson, madame," the Frenchwoman would reply. "A carpet."

"*Carpet?* Well, how much is it?"

"Two thousand and five."

"Dollars?"

"Dollars."

The shopper would turn to her companions, a little ill at ease in their slacks and shorts among relics of the *grand siècle.* "Why, it doesn't have any nap. I never liked rugs without a nap. And what's that thing?"

"A *prie-dieu,* madame."

"You mean like for reading on your knees?"

"For prayer," the Frenchwoman would explain. "One places one's missal here, as you see."

"What I'm really looking for," another of the slacked or shorted ladies would say, "is a genuine Philadelphia highboy. You have any American things?"

"Perhaps, madame, you should try in Philadelphia." And, looking the ladies up and down, the Frenchwoman would shepherd them to the door, getting her own back by inquiring if they had not noticed her sign, TO THE TRADE ONLY. "I sell to dealers, you see. Good afternoon." It was her conviction that there should be an officer stationed at the bridges leading into the county, to request women not to reveal their upper legs, as, at St. Mark's in Venice, a verger requires women to cover their heads before going inside. *Les femmes variqueuses,* she dubbed these time-wasting shoppers, topping Susan Ingle's "tacky"; but equally often vein clusters were *variqueux.*

French furniture, in its grander manifestations, was still suspect in most of the county, and virtually treason in Olympia; only a few of the rich or decorators had it. But "provincial" (neither French nor Italian but straight from Grand Rapids) and Victorian, forever being discovered in horsehair Belter sets, were acceptable. Now and then a shrewd acquisition was made by Susan Ingle; she liked Second Empire, in its American adaptations, and had little competition from women searching for pine milking stools and the eternal cobbler's-bench coffee table, which would go on forever. One piece Susan Ingle knew she would never get was one owned by the Misses Bowyer, which stood in the middle of Miss Flora's shop, a great Directoire bed, adapted, it was said, from l'Aiglon's *crèche.* "Not for sale, *of course!*" Miss Flora always said, as though the customer inquiring were insulting her. "You see, it was Our Mother's and Our Father's; they both died in it, as my sister and I expect to die in it." And that was that.

Much of the business transacted was between dealers, of course, for whom acquiring stock was a constant problem. A set of cherrywood chairs would be found in one shop one week, in another the next; this shifting about was done not entirely in the hope of selling the merchandise; dealer envy was rife, and there was often bad blood between shop owners for weeks, if one had outbid another on some prestigious item, say, or made it first to an attic full of Saratoga trunks filled with old bustles and top hats.

One of the most spirited auctions lately conducted in the county had been an estate sale of the effects of a deceased spinster of ninety-four. She had been a somewhat grand old lady, a true hoarder, and had never thrown anything away. Her eleven dinner services (including one of Sèvres and another of Imari) had gone to the Frenchwoman, who resolutely outbid New York dealers who had come down for the sale; they were to be shipped to Paris, she said as she left the sale, where they belonged. What local dealers took back with them to their shops were the segmented, kidskin dolls of the old spinster's childhood, her cooking pots, complete sets of Émile Gaboriau and John Fox, Jr., and straphinges removed from her barn. Two boxes that came up toward the end of the sale—one of saved letters, another of old photographs—were acquired for next to nothing by the novelist who was said to write about Olympia, and a friend, who was making a collection for the Bucks County Historical Society. The saddest transaction of all, however, to many who had known the old lady, involved a carton of her saved cosmetics of former years, envelopes of Papier Poudre, flacons of Imperial Russian Violets, Poudre Melba, Parfum Mary Garden.

"Now, here are some lovely mementos, all unopened, in the perfect state in which she put them away," the auctioneer announced, as though alluding to *editiones principes*. "Probably the perfumes are as fresh as the day they were bottled, even might be good to drink, who knows?" (Auction room titters.) He tried to extract the stopple from one of the bottles.

"*Stop!*" cried a voice. "Don't open those bottles! I bid ten dollars for the lot!"

"Fifteen!"

"Twenty!"

"Thirty dollars!"

The bidding continued furiously, the contest being conducted between Teddy Hubbard and one of the diplomate psychiatrists of Tuliptrees, a young man with an intent face and horn-rimmed spectacles. Teddy saw the determination on his rival's features, and though he liked to win and had his "mad" checkbook with him, dropped out at ninety-five. The lot was knocked down to the psychiatrist for a hundred. (Dr. Ingle, luckily, never heard of this; if he had, he might have been obliged to re-evaluate his colleague in the light of his curious predilection.)

"End of sale!" announced the auctioneer.

Teddy was inconsolable, less over losing the carton of old-lady artifacts than because a set of Elsie de Wolfe boudoir pillows, embroidered with her mottos, *Never Explain, Never Complain* and *Don't Worry, It Never Happens,* which he had known the spinster to possess and wanted for his mother, had been abstracted from the sale by a relative at the last minute.

Something was always missing at sales, as it was missing in Olympia and the Corner and the county itself—and Brecht's Mahagonny. Perhaps it was part of Scott Fitzgerald's "the story of the moon that never rose." But the story went on, as stories do, and, whatever was in short or in long supply, the moon rose high over the county this summer night, drenching landscapes, revived by rain after days of scorching heat, with a brilliance that flooded peony and mandrake, rose and the common stinkhorn, veronica and deadly datura alike.

C H A P T E R   2

Edie had sat stiff and expressionless as Bobby drove across the bridge into Jersey. She looked shattered. He turned the car upward into the hills, toward the narrow back roads, surfaced with red clay, hard-packed by the dry summer. It was cooler here than in the valley, though the rasp of cicadas still told of the heat, and the air rushed through the car windows, hot on their faces.

"What was that about, at the luncheonette?"

She sighed and, moving close to him, let her head fall back on the seat. "More of the same, only worse."

"Was it like what you told me yesterday?"

"Part of it, yes. But I don't want to talk. Can't we just ride for a while? Give me a minute, I'll soon be all right."

"Okay," Bobby said.

How could she tell him about what had happened, about her day? As early as the late morning, when she had taken her sunbath in the back yard, she had felt Rafe watching everything she did. He had driven the Hubbard Pierce-Arrow into the rear of the garage, and she had heard the reluctant, squealing turnover of the old-fashioned motor as it was started up and the soft rise and fall of the tappets as it idled. The battery was low, she had heard Rafe mutter to himself; but other cars were running, too, and the smell of the hot exhaust drifting into the yard made her a little sick. Almost as regular as the Pierce's motor were sounds as one beer can after another was opened, drunk from and drained and then thrown clattering into the waste barrel. She could hear her mother upstairs, coughing and complaining about the fumes.

"Hey, Rafe!" she called down the stairs. "Can't you shut some of them damn things off? I can hardly breathe up here!"

No answer, only the car noises, the exhaust continuing.

Shortly after that, when Rafe had begun to straighten the Pierce's bent fender, the hammer beating on metal had been too much and Edie had gone inside.

"Gets me," her mother said, "how he'll stop everything he's started, just to work on that old piece of junk of Teddy Hubbard's!"

"Oh, who cares?" asked Edie.

"*I* care, that's who! The stink around here gets worse every day!"

Edie had gone into the bedroom and closed the door. She had heard her mother as she made the midday dinner calling over and over for her father to come upstairs. When at last he came, beer can in hand, there had been an outburst.

"Why, you're drunk as a skunk and it's only past noon," her mother said. "God damn it, Rafe, if you're drinking like this at this hour, what in hell will you be like by night?"

"Wait and see," came the answer.

"Eat your food."

"Don't want none of *that* food. I'm going across the river and get me a couple of pints of whiskey."

"*Whiskey?* Daytime? You're crazy!"

"We'll see who's crazy," Rafe said and, as he left, pointed a finger. "No using that phone," he reminded her; "if I find out you make any calls—"

"Yeah, you!" cried her mother. "You'll beat the both of us!"

"And I will."

"You might get a big surprise one of these days, Rafe Cadle. There's people you can go to nowadays, people I can call up, who'll come and take you away and put you where you belong!"

"You try any of that and you'll be dead before they get here."

"You filthy, drunken pig!"

"I'm going to get drunker," Rafe promised as he went out.

Mae took advantage of his short absence in Jersey to suggest that Edie make her call to Philadelphia while the calling was good and cancel her date with Acie Stanes. "I'll stand by the window and watch—he'll never know."

"Forget it," Edie said. "I have."

"But what if he comes here?"

"What if he does?"

Her mother blanched. "You know how that gets your Papa-Daddy upset."

"I know better than you."

"Go on, Edie, call him."

"If I call anybody, it won't be Acie," Edie said.

Rafe was back in no time with four pints in a sack. They could hear him downstairs, banging around, racing the motors, kicking the oil drums, could hear the tap turned on and off as he made his drinks.

"He's going to be drunker than *I* ever seen him," her mother said, midafternoon, as she watched from her window. She could see Rafe stagger out when there was a customer, jam the hoses into the tanks, half the time missing and spilling the gas on the ground.

"Well, I'm glad I won't be here," Edie said from the bath, where she was doing her hair.

"Honey, you're lucky," her mother said. "You found yourself a nice, clean boy, and you hang onto him, hear?"

The hammering downstairs got louder; they could tell Rafe was really tying one on this time.

"I'm going," Edie decided, "even if it is early," but before she could get to the stairs she saw Rafe staring at her over the banister. His hair was matted with sweat and he had his shirt off because of the heat and his hands and arms were covered with oil. He came lurching up the stairs.

"Well, I'll be damned!" he said. "Fixed up like you're going to a nigger wedding! You ain't fooling me—it's that Acie you're so all-fired fixed up for!"

Edie tried to get past him, but Rafe put an arm against the wall, stopping her. "Niggers are good enough for you, but not somebody like me. Huh? Is that it?"

"Papa-Daddy, please let me go!"

Rafe lunged toward her. "Lemme see your little titties!" he said thickly. "I can see them through your dress, but take them out and give us a good look!"

"Rafe!" cried Mae, getting up from her chair. "You stop such dirty talk! You ought to be ashamed!"

"Yeah? Why?" Rafe turned to challenge his wife. "Man can see his kid's titties if he's a mind to, can't he? You're not going to stop me, you old sack of water!" He took the pint bottle from his hip pocket, drank, and wiped his hand over his mouth. His eyes were blurred. Mae had seen him almost this bad before and could judge to the minute how long it would be before he fell onto the bed and passed out.

But Rafe still had a little way to go. Turning to Edie, who stood shivering against the wall, he said, "Going to give it to that nigger, ain't you? Well, let me tell you something—you give it to that nigger and I'm going to kill him and beat the shit out of you! *Hear that?*"

"You come and lie down," Mae said, taking Rafe's arm. He turned toward her, head lowered, then wrenched away.

"Fuck you, bitch!" he said. "Everybody around here gets it except me—I'm going to—"

"You're going to lie down on that bed until I can get some strong coffee in you," Mae said. She saw he was almost finished.

"Coffee?" Rafe laughed. "This is what I want!" He reached again for his pint, unscrewed the top, then bottle and top fell to the floor.

Mae took over. She pushed him toward the bedroom and Rafe fell across the bed.

"Ah, you bitches!" he said. "I'll get you, the both of you!" Turning on his stomach, he fixed Edie with a stare. "I'll begin with you. Time you had a good belting. Never should have stopped beating you, then you wouldn't be passing it out to every buck—" He broke off. "That Ingle kid—is he getting it, too? Just let me catch him around here, he'll never forget it!" His eyes closed.

"I guess that's it, for this time," Mae said. "He'll sleep it off, but you'd better go anyway."

"But I asked Bobby to pick me up here."

Mae was expertly straightening Rafe out on the bed, lifting up his feet and swinging him around. "Well, you pick up that phone and call Bobby Ingle and tell him not to come here." She watched Rafe as she talked; his stertorous breathing was already turning into a snore. "I think he's out, but you never can be sure with him —he just might get up and start all over again."

Edie had gone to the phone and called Bobby. . . .

"I'm sorry," she said, coming out of it, taking Bobby's hand. She looked into the mirror for assurance that she was all right, found it.

"You making it?"

For answer, she turned and kissed his cheek and then, in a desperate instant of affection, found his mouth.

Bobby slowed the car. All was possible now.

"I want to peel the day away from me and cut loose," she said.

"So do I. Let's cut!"

"Let's be crazy!" She settled herself beside him, her arm laced in his.

"What we need are some giggles," Bobby decided. He stopped at the next shopping center they came to and went into the liquor store for a pint of vodka and a beer-can opener; the next-door supermarket provided the requisite splits of grapefruit juice.

"Why do you suppose they're called giggles?" Edie asked, when Bobby had brought the makings to the car; she took a swallow of the vodka, chasing it down with the grapefruit juice.

"Maybe because they make you giggle."

"I need to giggle."

Bobby's swallows were longer than Edie's. "And I have the giggles. What shall we do first?"

"Whatever you like."

"A few more of these and then a couple of club sandwiches? There's a hootenanny up at The Rock."

"Wonderful," she said, matching his mood.

The Rock once had been an expensive country restaurant, but

272

the turnpike had bypassed it; now it catered almost exclusively to people of Edie's and Bobby's age, who brought their liquor with them and either drank in their cars or at the tables, depending on which night it was. Saturdays the place was carefully policed, but on a weekday night, like this, anything went. As Bobby parked, they saw that the place was brightly lighted and jammed, and, on entering, they were greeted by Heavy-handed Harry, the owner; when the combos were resting, he would often pick up his guitar and do impersonations of Elvis and Sammy and Tommy and Frankie.

"You got your stuff with you?" he asked.

Bobby placed the vodka beside a leg of the table and ordered grapefruit juice setups.

"Man, that does take me back," said Harry, "only it used to be gin."

"Let's dance," Bobby said, extending a hand to Edie, and they joined the others on the crowded floor, so crowded that all they could do was hold on to each other and move slowly. Her eyes met his and at the same moment he leaned down and kissed her.

"Mm," she said, "we fit."

"We do, don't we?"

She moved in rhythm with him, arms around his neck, eyes closed. He could feel her breasts pressing against him. Her hair smelled of flowers.

"Look," he said, after the combo had signed off and Harry took the platform, "let's go. Let's be alone."

"All right."

Back in the car, Bobby had another drink, but Edie refused.

"I've had enough," she said.

"I know a place." Bobby knew the back roads as well as the lines of his hand. He drove slowly, savoring the delay, parking where a narrow path led through the trees to a small clearing in a glen. He took the robe from the back of the car and threw it over his shoulder. The moonlight streamed through the trees above them, and everywhere were cries of night birds and the fragrance of deep forest. A soft night breeze had sprung up, and when they reached the clearing the fresh wind stirred the grass. It was all breathlessly beautiful and they paused in silence before Bobby spread the rug.

"If only everything could be like this," she said.

"It can be, for now."

He kissed her softly, seeing the thick lashes that lay on her cheeks, and when they lay down together found each other in a long embrace. Her black hair made a pillow for her head.

"Don't make me wait," he said.

She did not answer, but he saw her smile in the moonlight, and his hands moved to her blouse. She rose a little, letting him draw it over her head. Her skirt, too, was light, and unbuttoned easily.

"Edie," he whispered as he covered her with kisses. "You're even more beautiful than I'd dreamed."

"But I want to see you, too," she said.

He stood up, slipped off his shirt and let his slacks fall to the ground, kicking them aside. Her breath came more quickly when she saw him and she held out her arms, drawing him down and clasping him to her.

There was only one awkward moment when, seeing him fumbling in the pocket of his slacks, she said, "You don't need to use that with me."

"Don't I? You didn't really tell me yesterday."

"I'm telling you now."

She was soft and taut beneath him and wonderfully slow. Her breasts flattened against him as he held her and he could feel her nipples, hard and abrasive against his own. He was a little too quick for her, but this seemed not to bother her.

"Don't worry, there's more," she said.

"I was too ready. If you knew how I've thought about this. You."

"I know. I've thought about you, too. You *are* that color all over," she said, stroking him, pressing the bulge of his shoulders. "Even in this light I can see that."

"Do that," he said. "Drive me crazy."

"That's what we decided."

"Yes. Don't stop."

It was a sudden movement and sighing in the treetops that made him suddenly sit up. The wind had been there for some time, but neither had heard it. Then a flash of lightning tore the sky and a thunderclap followed. A swift gust of wind brought the rain down with violence. Quickly they pulled on their clothes. The rain was

274

coming in torrents now, and by the time they reached the car they were drenched.

"Do you care?" he asked, laughing.

"No. I loved it."

"Here, let me dry you." He rubbed her hair with a corner of the blanket beneath which they had run, patting her dry before he dried himself.

"It seemed so short," she said, as they sat in the darkness; the moonlight had given way to black, streaming rain outside the car.

"Edie!"

Her mood had changed; she shivered slightly. "It's because I don't want to go back," she said. "I can't go back."

"We don't have to go back yet."

"But when we do, let me out anywhere. I'll make it by myself— to anywhere, so I don't have to go back *there*."

"You know, that's what I feel all the time myself about going home. It's like a warm grave above the ground, all comforts, everything, everything but what I care about. I feel the same way you do."

She smiled crookedly. "That leaves both of us nowhere to go. What time is it now?"

"After two, I think." Bobby checked with his watch by the light of the dash. "Almost two-thirty. Let's not go back."

"But sooner or later—"

"Let's forget that." He thought a minute. "Will you do what I'd like to do?"

"What is it?"

He started the motor and backed out onto the road. "We could go over there," he said, indicating a fuzz of light surrounding a motel. He slowed, laughing. "Do you know the one, 'Matthew, Mark, Luke and John, all four had a big hard on'? Well, I'm all four."

"Let's do," she said, laughing with him.

He had all the fears—they were too young, under age; they weren't married and looked it; they would be turned away. The man who came forward out of the motel was dark and the neon of the sign made him look like a man from Mars.

"Yeah," he answered, when Bobby asked if there was a room.

"We got one left—you'll be the last before I turn on the No Vacancy sign." He switched it on from a box next to the office door. "Overnight?"

"Yes," Bobby said.

"It's a double bed."

"My wife and I don't mind."

"Sign the register." Bobby signed "Mr. and Mrs. Robert Ingle, Jr., San Francisco, Calif." It looked great.

"Fourteen dollars," the motel man said, and Bobby paid; it left him with a single dollar. "Check-out time three o'clock tomorrow." Tired after his long day, the owner swept them into one of dozens of identical cabins stretching back from the highway. "Phone there. If you need anything. Good night." And he left.

Edie hadn't said a word. She stood beside Bobby, hands at her sides. "You're good at this, aren't you? Your first time?"

"Yes. Are you afraid? Because you've never done this before?"

"Do you want the truth? I have."

"I don't care." Bobby locked the door and drew the curtains. They stared at each other across the double bed, turned down, fresh sheets white in the glare of the bulb hanging above it. Edie found the switches, cut off the overhead light, and turned on the lamp by the bed. Then she went into the bath. By the time she came out, Bobby had had the last swallow of the vodka and had convinced himself he could forget about not getting home, his mother's car, all of that. Tomorrow—no, today—was another day, and the next tomorrow he would meet as it came.

Nothing in his morning fantasies about Edie, or what happened in the glen before the rain, had prepared him for her tenderness.

"I've never felt like this before," she said. "You're not like the others."

"It was wonderful, you mean?"

"Yes."

"I'm glad I'm good at it. So are you."

"I'm only this way when I'm with someone I like."

"Have you been with many?"

"I guess you'd call it many. You see, I've never had a girl friend, to compare notes with, so I don't know. But I always did it if I felt like it with anybody I liked. Are you jealous?"

"No."

"If somebody else were with us now, you wouldn't mind my being with him?"

"What if it were another girl, would you mind? Did you ever do that? With two?"

"Once or twice. Did you?"

"Never with more than one girl, only with other guys watching. And that's no good, unless you're the first one. Low man on the pole is the end."

"I never did that," Edie said. "You know why I like you? Because you don't ask me to do anything I don't want to do."

"Don't I?"

"But of course I'd like to try everything with you."

"Would you? So would I, but that takes time."

"What do you like most? What we did just now?"

"That, yes. But could we do this? Have you ever?"

"Once. I'm afraid I wasn't very good at it."

"I can tell you like it."

"Of course. Because I like you. . . ."

"Oh, that was really it," he said; "you really turned me on. I'll be tired now."

"So will I. We made it all the way."

"Give me your hands. They're little."

"Little in yours. Hold me like this. I want to sleep like this."

"Edie."

"Mm?"

"We're crazy."

"I'm glad."

"Good. Sleep now."

They slept.

He had an ecstatic sensation of floating upward and dropping. . . . He was lying in the motel bed, Edie's place beside him deserted, the sheets rumpled where she had slept. A rancid, metallic thirst had dried out his mouth and he was hungry. He remembered the single dollar in his soggy, wrinkled slacks, hanging from a peg on the wall. Morning? Or late morning? Or later than that? His watch confirmed it was almost noon.

Edie came out of the bath. She had dressed and done what she could to smooth the wrinkles from her blouse and skirt, but with little success. She smiled.

"I guess this is what it's like. Afterward," Bobby said.

She came to him and tweaked his nose, running her fingers through his hair. "I'm glad we did it, aren't you?"

"Yes. Now there's the hell to pay." He looked dazedly about. "I'd better phone home." He lifted the receiver and, after a delay, gave his number.

His mother answered. Her voice was flat. "You're all right?"

"Yes. The car's all right, too."

"Where are you?"

"Not far. I'll be home in an hour." He hung up, then took the receiver from the hook again and offered it to Edie.

"No," she said; "I'll have to do it another way."

Bobby quickly dressed and they checked out. The motel man's wife was on duty and watched them go without curiosity. When they were driving down from the highlands to the valley, Edie said, "You'll have to leave me out on this side of the river. That'll be easier for us both."

"It doesn't seem right."

"Nothing's right. I'll work it out somehow."

"When can we be together again?"

"When you like—only let me call you, things being what they are."

He stopped the car and she got out. He could see her in the rearview mirror as he drove onto the bridge. Then a truck loomed behind him and she disappeared.

The Ingles' evening with the Braithwaites had been a shadowy thing altogether. The weather was humid and very hot, with streaks of cirrus clouds around the moon, and a white mist hung over the river. Susan Ingle had always to remember what Mrs. Braithwaite's Christian name was, and that for this one night of the year they were on first-name terms. Dr. Braithwaite, considerably younger than Dr. Ingle, never felt himself off duty and carried Tuliptrees with him wherever he went, like a snail dragging its slime. Inevitably, Tulip One and Tulip Two and their patients came into the conversation, and the shop talk Susan so dreaded erupted; though she kept up what she hoped was pleasant chatter, she couldn't help hearing bits of diagnoses and clinical jargon.

"Retaliation drinking is in the picture, of course," Dr. Braithwaite said; "she feels unrewarded by the community and is having her revenge on it."

"I disagree," Ingle said to this; "I think it's assuagement drinking with her—of the kind to be expected in a community that is failing and losing appeal. . . ."

The Ferry Slip, in Olympia, where they had cocktails and dinner before going on to the Playhouse, was crowded, and Susan and Mrs. Braithwaite were distracted by the entrance of a woman who seated herself at a banquette in one corner, near enough to them so that they heard her order a sandwich and buttermilk. The woman wore a suit, flat walking shoes and carried a large handbag; her hair was long and straight, dun-colored, and hung to her shoulders; and, though the Ferry Slip was anything but brightly lighted, she did not remove her very large, dark sunglasses. Not only Susan and Mrs. Braithwaite found themselves staring; people at other tables were watching the woman too; only the two psychiatrists, lost in their speculations about the woman who believed she was Elizabeth Taylor, seemed oblivious.

"Why, it's impossible!" Mrs. Braithwaite said to Susan. "That can't be who it is!"

Susan put on her spectacles and looked long and carefully at the woman. "If it isn't, she's the spitting image of her. Who else could it be?"

"Well, of course, women have been dressing like that, trying to look like her, ever since I can remember," said Mrs. Braithwaite.

"Why do you suppose she's alone?"

"That was the whole mysterious thing about her, that she was always supposed to be alone."

"Oh, no," Susan said. "Long ago, when we would go to New York for a week in the winter, we would see her walking. There was always a man with her, one of those men with overcoats that are too long and black homburgs. Helmuts, we called them." She studied the woman. "No, that's not her, because she wouldn't come here."

The woman in the dark glasses seemed impervious to the stares she was getting, and when her sandwich and buttermilk arrived, ate slowly and with composure.

"The outlook is doubtful," Ingle said to Braithwaite. "Schizophrenia, clearly; she's in the acute, early stage and her conviction that she is Elizabeth Taylor is merely symptomatic."

"I quite agree," Braithwaite said.

"No, I'm convinced that's who it is," Mrs. Braithwaite said, coming back to it, breaking through the Tuliptrees talk. "It *has* to be—the way the hair falls over the forehead, the movement of the hands, everything."

"I still say she'd never come *here*," Susan replied.

"Who are you two talking about?" Ingle asked.

Susan pointed the woman out.

"What's so extraordinary about her?" Braithwaite asked.

"Really, dear!" his wife said.

"Is she someone I should recognize?" asked Ingle.

"You men are impossible," Susan said. "Don't you see?"

"I wish you'd let us in on the secret." Braithwaite laughed. "Who is she—or is she anybody?"

"If you don't know, it wouldn't be any use telling you," his wife said.

The woman had finished her sandwich and rose. As she moved across the restaurant, with a curious, light, drifting walk, every eye followed her. When she had gone out, Ingle raised his shoulders in a shrug.

"A woman of a certain age. Sixty, I'd say. Considerably underweight and, quite possibly, anemic."

"A common somatotype of the Scandinavian countries," added Braithwaite.

Susan and Mrs. Braithwaite exchanged looks. "Hopeless, both of you," Susan said. "Dick, why don't we have another round and then order?"

The Playhouse part of the evening was even more shadowy. The play, a relic of gangster-prohibition humor, with the inevitable chorus girls of the twenties, was frantically paced. The audience, for the most part elderly, was stolid and unresponsive, accepting everything but evidently feeling neither pleasure nor boredom. The comedian and his colleagues were knocking themselves out but getting no laughs. The whole thing had palled on the Ingle group from the rise of the curtain.

"Those are *not* costumes of the twenties," said Susan during one of the chorus girls' numbers; "those are beach pajamas and thirties."

"Isn't he *fat?*" asked Mrs. Braithwaite at the first intermission. "Why, on TV he looks like a skinny kid." She turned to Susan. "I know this is your treat, but don't you and Dick feel you have to stick this out because of us."

"Oh, come on, darling," Braithwaite said, "it's not that bad."

"I'm afraid it's all a little too Old Testament for me," his wife answered.

"Darling, please."

"I didn't say Jewish, I said Old Testament."

"That's even worse."

"I'm glad you said it first," Susan agreed. "Why don't we leave? Okay with you, Dick?"

All four trooped out into the Playhouse yard.

"Well, summer theater," Mrs. Braithwaite summed it up.

"When I think how it all used to be!" said Susan. "Once everyone wore black tie, or at least jackets. Now look at them! Don't you just *hate* men in drip-dry nylon shirts like that? Short sleeves, with their old, gray, hairy arms?"

"Don't you just hate men?" Braithwaite put in, overhearing.

"Sue," said Ingle, as they walked toward their cars, "you know this means asking them back to the house for a nightcap?"

"Yes, I'm up to it."

Once back at the Ingle house, Braithwaite and Ingle went more deeply into Tuliptrees problems, while Susan and Mrs. Braithwaite discussed the routine subjects common to all women, the cleaning of silver, whether or not cedar closets were enough or moth flakes were needed as well, nylons. When the Braithwaites said good night, Susan announced she would lay out a few games of solitaire, to compose herself for sleep.

"It went all right, don't you think?" she asked. She conducted her pantomime of small activities carefully executed: opened the cigarette box, took one, lighted it, blew out the match, inhaled, found her deck and shuffled it.

"Yes, all right," Ingle answered. "I was surprised you chose to walk out on the show and talk instead."

"I couldn't imagine not walking out on that. It's really not at all the way it used to be, is it, Dick? Do you remember when they had Gertrude Lawrence in—what was that thing?"

"I remember."

"But those men in those shirts, with all that gray arm hair!"

"Sue, I have gray hair on my arms."

"I didn't mean you."

"Things can't stay the same. You can't expect Gertrude Lawrence in this year of grace. She's been dead for years."

Susan put down her deck. "Like so much else."

"Something upset you tonight. Was it that woman in the restaurant?"

A sudden rigidity in Susan's movement told Ingle his guess had hit the mark, but she said, "Nonsense! That couldn't have been who we thought it was."

"Neither of you would say who you thought it was."

"No." Susan began to lay out her first game. "One more thing that was wonderful that's gone."

"Why don't you come to bed?"

"I thought I'd wait up for Bobby, since I'm not tired."

"Don't you think it's foolish to wait up for a boy his age? If he can go out by himself, he can get back by himself."

"But I'm worried about him. Aren't you?"

"Not in the way you are. We've got to let him go sometime."

"You go on up, I won't be long," Susan said. When she did go upstairs, some hours and twenty cigarettes later, it was not to sleep. She lay awake a long time, imagining every catastrophe that could overtake a son who had never before stayed out all night. The police, whom she called, were courteous but uninformative, and at last, after daylight, she fell asleep. Bobby's telephone call woke her, and she was dressed and downstairs when he came in.

"I suppose there has to be a first time for everything," she said. "I've called your father to say you're all right. And the police. We were worried to death."

"The *police?*"

"We thought you might be in trouble, or have had an accident. You could at least have let us know."

"I did as soon as I could. I'm sorry."

"You don't look it. You look hung-over and awful. Edie Cadle's mother called here; she was worried, too."

"Oh," said Bobby dully, "and what did you tell her?"

"There was nothing to tell. Now you've done this, I hope you're satisfied."

"I'm not ashamed, if you mean that."

"Maybe we've said enough. Go on upstairs and shave. I'll have Mrs. Schaaf bring you some coffee." She went to him and put her arms around him. "I guess you're not my little boy any more," she said, breaking into tears, kissing him on the cheek.

Bobby turned his face away; his mouth tasted too terrible to kiss back. Then he went upstairs.

CHAPTER 3

Tavio said, "Why haven't you taken care of the garden? Why do you have a large garden if you don't take care of it?"

Miriam stood at the kitchen table, preparing yet another meal. The question, like most of his others (he was maddening in the things he asked), trod on areas she was exhausted from discussing. She waited, feeling the suffocation of anger repressed. "Death makes everything stop, including gardens" was all she could think of to say.

"Did Cort care for the garden?"

She bit her lip. "How dare you use his name!"

"You use it."

"I was his wife. You didn't know him," she angrily replied.

"I think I'm beginning to know him very well," Tavio said.

The man's insidiousness was unbearable. For the many hours of the day (they seemed chopped up and flattened out, in interminable intervals of confusion) she had been trying to put a bearable complexion on it, to take him at the value at which he first presented himself, but those other personalities, of which he had warned her, kept breaking through. There was the Tavio of silence and charm, of great tenderness, mercurially changing into another personality entirely, questioning, insisting, belaboring. He was perverse and willful, his words often having no relation to himself or to her; when his actions seemed clearest, their meaning was a cipher, deepening the loss of self she felt more and more each hour he stayed.

It had been possible for her to endure him on the assumption that at any moment, any scrambled hour, he would be leaving, taking his newspaper bundle with him. But her own fascination with him kept intruding, equally perversely, against her will. She had hoped, after their time in the bed in which she and Cort had slept, that he would go of his own accord, settle it for her forever; but she knew he was staying because of her own lapses, giving in to him. She understood that his intrusions on her memories of Cort were deliberate, that he had calculated them to be a way of breaking her even more to his will. This, she supposed, was what the bird experienced when the snake fixed it with unblinking eye. The truth was that she hated him, despite his sexual appeal; as the hours disintegrated, his hard, chiseled features took on a blurred vagueness that made him seem someone else. Whenever she looked at him directly, it was as though she had been commanded to recognize someone she had never met. It was not his aura of fantastic handsomeness that drew her to him, though that undeniably was part of it, but it detracted, too, for in his beauty lay the roots of her guilt, her agonizing unfaithfulness to Cort. It was, in part, his quality of having come out of nowhere and also, of course, his animal enjoyment of her, which had in it more comparisons than she had at first suspected; for, though she was new to him and a mystery (because "a lady"), it was evident she was one of a long sequence of women. It was his combination of nerve and naïveté that destroyed her defenses.

Sometimes he was primitively childlike. He had asked, when showering in the bath off her bedroom, about the soaps, the brushes, the sponges, which she took for granted but which seemed to him fascinating toys. "Why is this egg-shaped?" he asked of a cake of soap.

"I suppose because it's bath soap."

"Oh, is bath soap different from plain soap?"

And when she found him in the studio, soberly turning over canvases, he said, "This one is most like you—your breasts are like that. He caught you perfectly."

"I don't discuss my husband's painting," she had replied hotly.

"Why not? I thought that's what art's for, to talk about."

Her anger had excited him; he had put down the canvas and once more locked her in that embrace that was becoming more soporific each time she endured it.

As he straddled his chosen kitchen chair, watching as she prepared food (as though her function included kitchen duties as well as those of the bed), she saw he was no true primitive. He was, as he several times said, younger than she; but he was diabolically knowledgeable in the ways of intrusion. Looking at him, she thought of those classic heads of antiquity, in which the eyes are missing, more deadly in their gaze than any living face, because expressionless. His life had been, to hear him tell it, an open book, so simple his recounting had required no time at all, only repetition. Its desultory family figures, street corners and candy stores and baseball diamonds, he invoked with an almost cinematic immediacy. She could see the parents, and the grandparents behind them, the less handsome brothers, the plain sisters (one with a mustache), even the parish priest. And the girl, Maria Anna, whom he had deserted in a violent *volte-face*. And all the time she saw him: a mute Villon with no Paris, no rooftops down which to slide, wandering and aging, but trying to win over age by choosing only women older than himself. And she could fill in the background blanks—the working-class table always reset after supper for next morning's breakfast, the oleographs of the Virgin and the eternally bleeding Sacred Heart, the wash pants on the clothesline, the compulsive daily washings of the poor. As he explained himself, she felt like a caseworker waiting to write significant observations in the report after her client had gone. I have been brave and courageous and have done what other men have feared to do, he seemed to be pleading for her to believe; the world I deserted was hideous, as I am beautiful—a throwback. I intend to catch the boat the others have missed; I am noble because I am a savage. But there were the odds and ends, like overmuch cloth in a badly cut suit—"You aren't my first lady, I know about women like you." He cared nothing for money, often gave it away, as he had done the night in Olympia, of which he gave her a detailed account. Life histories of others clung to him like barnacles—"The stories I could tell you!"

As she remembered these things she worked on, cutting meat and bread, boiling coffee, of which he seemed very fond, demanding it at all hours.

"Look!" he cried suddenly, and she turned. He flung open his shirt. The roses, he told her, had been the most painful ordeal of his life. It had taken the tattooist in Saigon two weeks to do them; he had considered them his masterpiece.

As she listened, nodding but remaining silent, she knew the threat to her sanity was temporary; in the last few hours she had experienced a reintegration of herself; she was less captive now than he; there was a limit to the times he could make himself believe himself and what he said. She sighed, and determination to fight against him—and herself—again returned.

"This must be all, this time," she said, setting his plate down before him. She did not sit down.

He looked up at her, instantly calm. "Why?" And seeing that she stood, did not intend eating with him, he got up and walked out to the terrace, his plate in his hand. He moved easily about the house now, as though it were his own; their relationship had assumed a certain formality: he paused at doorways to permit her to pass first, stood until she was seated. Food seemed to segment each encounter, break day into fragments.

He held the door for her now, a command to follow. Outside the chairs were widely placed; she welcomed this, taking the one farthest from his.

"Why?" he asked again.

"Because I say it must."

He proceeded to eat. "You didn't answer my question about the garden," he said between mouthfuls.

"I'm not going to answer it."

"I could get it into shape in a week."

A week! Once more the nightmare descended.

"No, you must go now, today," she said.

"Why now? You know there's more for us."

"More of what?"

"Call it what you like—I always know when there's more for me to take away."

She frowned. "What is it you want to take?"

"More of myself." This was the kind of thing he said to which there was no answer.

She closed her eyes. This can't go on, she thought. I'll slip away when he's sleeping, and stay away until he has gone. Or I'll manage to get to the phone and call Rosa. For the space of time her eyes were shut, she tried to believe it was the day before he came, with all the safe surroundings of her world about her. But the surroundings no longer worked as protection, only as objects of his curiosity and questioning. *Questions, questions, questions!* She opened her eyes and saw he had finished eating and had again pushed his plate away toward her, and was ready and impatient for the next thing.

The sun was very bright on the flagstones, and in the shade of trees by the canal crows coughed and conducted their quarrels. A quick, darting movement, where grass grew between the stones at her feet, caught her eye—a small, ovoid bug, a beetle, iridescently green. It streaked back and forth on some mysterious insect errand, skating from sun to shadow so rapidly her eye could hardly follow; one instant its viridian-gold track would cross beyond her feet, the next disappear into the shade. She sighed. A deep, irregular inhalation rushed into her, she held her breath, and then, as instantly as she had seen the green bug, great sobs overtook her and she wept.

"What's the matter?" Tavio asked, alarmed, rising and coming to her.

She shook her head angrily, to show she could not answer.

"Tell me," he said, touching her.

She drew away as though grazed by fire.

"What is it?" he again demanded to know. "Is it that I've been too much for you?"

She stared up at him in hatred, tears streaming from her eyes. "Why would you think it had anything to do with you?" she lashed out at him. "I hate you, loathe you! If you knew how much, you'd go!"

He shrugged. "Nothing happened that I could see." He studied her for evidence. "One minute you were all right, the next—this."

Again she moved her head, trying to discourage his questioning.

"Tell me what it was."

"Some things can't be put into words." She saw that her outburst had affected him more deeply than any other thing she had said or done; but she felt the familiar mechanism working in her—he could draw from her anything he liked, simply by insisting and waiting. She said, "There was a little green bug. Did you see it?"

"Just now?"

"Yes."

"Sure, I saw it."

"It was something you couldn't understand. My husband always called it the summer bug. He was fond of saying that when it came, the summer was really here. He used to sit and watch for it, wait for it to come. Now, when I saw it again, I remembered."

"Is that all? Is that why you went all to pieces?"

"That's why." She dried her eyes.

"You know," he said, "I'm beginning to see what you mean—Cort must have been quite a guy."

"Don't call him that!"

"I'd like to see all of his pictures, have you tell me about them, talk with me—"

"I don't want to show them to you. Or talk about them!"

"Oh, no? Why not?"

As if the phone had read his mind, it rang insistently in the studio. She went to answer it, Tavio closely following. She spoke minimally, as naturally as she could, guardedly.

"You have a life I'll never know about," he said, after she had hung up. "Or was that about me?"

She stared at him.

"Who was it, then? Tell me who it was."

"My husband's dealer. He and his wife are coming for the weekend. Saturday," she added, before she thought, then was glad she had told him. She repeated it, watching him.

He shrugged, as though days of the week were all the same, then said indifferently, "By then I'll be gone."

Dear God! she thought. *Thursday, Friday* . . .

"Did Cort get paid a lot for paintings like these?" he asked, going to a row of stacked canvases, tipping them forward, one by one, toward the light.

"Yes."

"Like how much?"

"Depending on size, excellence. Ten, fifteen thousand."

"For *one?*"

"For one," she said, exhausted with it, with him, everything.

He looked awed and impressed.

There was always this time of day, when the light filtering into the studio from outside seemed both shadow and sun, without chiaroscuro. The tall north window, with its many panes, became a design of rectangles admitting an impartial glow, picking out the countless objects of a painter's world—easel, squeezed paint tubes, dried grasses in a jar, turpentine, varnish . . . *mahlstick!* She could see Cort moving among his works, preoccupied with what would come from him next, something minted new or something lost forever, entirely detached, absorbed in himself. This was the hour of black sun, with the house peaceful and quiet, because he was at work. . . .

"Miriam!"

Again she felt the hot tears on her cheeks as, bored with flipping canvases, he came toward her.

"Cort!" she said beneath her breath. "Cort! Help me!"

"I'm not Cort. I'm Tavio!"

She turned her face from him. "Don't!" she begged. "Not again, not now, not here!"

"Say my name!"

She forced herself to say it. And the wave of shame and ecstasy flooded through her once more, like blushes from the heart. This time, at least, was one more time toward the time when there would be real time again and it would be over quickly. She lay back on the studio sofa, rigid as a sacrifice, and permitted him once more to exhaust himself, face turned from him in a bitter smile, violated but unsubdued, learning the destruction of sensuality by sensuality itself.

> *One, two, three, four!*
> *Hang up your Midsummer Men!*
> *One for Harry and one for Larry,*
> *And two for Bob and Ben!*

Miss Emmeline Bowyer hummed as she held at arm's length the flesh-colored stockinette on which she was sewing, and examined it and found it good. She had always been deft with a needle, but it had been years since she had used one, and her longsightedness didn't make fine stitches any easier. But difficult or not, what she was fashioning was a pleasure. He was emerging rather nicely, she thought, a doll-like little man, made from odds and ends from her sewing box. The head consisted of a darning egg neatly encased in the stockinette, with jet buttons for eyes, a bit of red silk for the mouth, and the body was long and gangling, arms and legs stuffed with cotton batting. Where the legs began, she had added two larger buttons and fringe, for his pencil and tassel—her very own Midsummer Man. And hang him up she would, from a branch of the apple tree, as soon as Flora had gone off to Olympia in the taxi, to do the weekly marketing and shopping.

> *Sweet Saint John!*
> *Upon your Eve I pray—*
> *Show me the Midsummer Man*
> *Who'll steal my heart away!*

The refrain held in it the whole of the panorama of Midsummer Day, a day in a thousand, in which the flowers had dripped heavily into the canal and river, as if in deference to the spirit that permeated the Corner. It seemed as if the hot mist, left behind by the night's rain, was vibrating to the lilt—not a surprising thing, since it was the Midsummer Man's day. Miss Emmeline could almost feel the charm working in the secret talk of the cicadas, high in the trees. *The village seems asleep or dead*—the line came to her from the years when she sang and played the piano—*Now Lubin is away.* That must be Haydn.

She could see the Cadle garage and the hated luncheonette baking in the late afternoon sun; the Ingle house, too, looked hot, but gave out no vibration of life—but, as Flora said, it was when things seemed most quiet that it was best to be watchful. She took up the glasses from the windowsill and focused on the Glidden house: all shuttered and more secret than before, now those rhododendrons had been planted. *But let concealment, like a worm i' the bud, Feed on her damask cheek.* . . . Words of songs were so often right. Was the Midsummer Man being concealed by Mrs. Glidden? It was probable. . . .

Oh, for time and strength in which to fashion all four of the Midsummer Men in the old rhyme! But making even this one had been a feat, her hands being as shaky as they were, and Flora's ins and outs obliging her to conceal her handiwork hastily beneath the bedcovers, and always the danger Flora would smooth the bed or fluff the pillows and find him. When Flora's taxi came would be the moment to creep downstairs, carefully and quickly, steal out into the garden and hang up—Harry? Larry? Bob? Ben? No, I'll call him Lubin, as in the song, she decided. Then would be the time to name over the orpine flowers in the beds—succulents, sedums, livelong—and touch them, one by one, in the ritual that would bring to her the man who would steal her heart away. *First the blue and then the pink. Hark for the bell, look for the Man with the tassel.* . . . That it was, perhaps, a little late, long past the midnight hour, did not bother her. After all, she was doing the best she could (*against them!*) and she was very old, and even to be contemplating the dangerous descent of the stairs and the tour of the garden would make up for any tardiness.

> *One, two, three, four!*
> *Hang up your Midsummer Men!*

The refrain was insistent in her ears, almost as loud as the jazz streaming from the luncheonette jukebox. Then, in a single effort of last stitches, she added ears and toes, pulled the thread and knotted it, snipped off ends: there he lay on her knees, as neat a little fellow as ever she had made in childhood under her English governess's supervision. And in the nick of time—Flora was ascending the stairs, Spot preceding her, his small, almost catlike paws announcing her heavier tread. Miss Emmeline quickly hid the doll beneath the sheets.

Fortunately, there was a diversion—*peck-peck-peck, drrill!*—the irritating woodpecker that had been hammering at the house intermittently all afternoon.

"Flora," said Miss Emmeline, "do speak to that bird!"

Miss Flora lifted Spot onto the bed and settled him; he looked tired from the heat and breathed hard. "I think he's been fighting *them* off," she said, before going to the window. She clapped her hands several times and the woodpecker flew away. "He's not the least bit afraid of me," she complained. The woodpecker had settled on another window cornice. "It doesn't let up a minute. Stones going, ferns and flowers disappearing—even the birds don't want us to have a minute's peace!"

"I know, dear, I know!" They had already had the daily recapitulation and summations of last night's depredations; Miss Flora had exhibited her poor hands, palms cut by the broken glass in the flower beds, and had relayed the news that the yellow rambler rose on the front wall was being systematically sprayed and poisoned by Dr. Ingle, even as he stole yet another stone.

"Now, I've put up the 'Closed Wednesday Afternoons' sign on the door, I have the list. Everything, I *think*." She read it out, in case Emmeline should have a last-minute request. She didn't. "I don't think any ladies will come while I'm away, but if they ring, ignore them. I'll have to lock you in, of course."

"Oh, I shall ignore them," Miss Emmeline promised. "Now, do take care and tell the man to drive slowly."

"I always do." Devoted and faithful to her sister as she was, Miss Flora secretly looked forward to her Wednesday outings and being, for a little while, by herself. "I'll just plump your pillows."

"Please don't trouble, Flora!"

Miss Flora plumped them anyway, but luckily didn't straighten the bed sheets. She lingered, not wanting to alarm her sister, but not wanting to be remiss, either. "It is Midsummer Day," she warned, "and of course lunacy is about. In case anything *extreme* should happen, there's only one thing to do—cry help out of the window."

"Yes, Flora," Miss Emmeline meekly answered. She sat back against her pillows with a self-satisfied expression. So far, so good. She patted Spot, who whined when the taxi drew up and drove away. *One, two, three, four!* With an agility that would have surprised her sister, she got out of bed and went to her closet to find something to wear. A real dress, after years of peignoirs! Getting into it took time, but then, the Midsummer doll clutched beneath one arm, she began the descent of the stairs. She had to stop for breath on the landing, looking about, seeing the familiar stock in the shop, unchanged over the years.

Miss Flora had been as good as her word. All doors were locked and keys removed. It was necessary for Miss Emmeline to descend to the basement and literally *force her way,* by tugging and pulling at the boards laid across the doors through which coal was delivered, up to the garden. She stood at last, panting in the daylight, saw the apple tree from a fresh angle. With deliberate tread she walked toward it and hung the Midsummer doll from a lower branch. She had to hold the branch a moment for support, before she made her rounds of the orpines in the flower beds, but after a time she managed, bending over to name and carefully touch them in order.

She named over the blues, then the pinks. "Meteor, Carmen, Ruby Glow. And gray-green, silvery-gray, for good measure." She paused. "Acre—I know you, yellow, we planted you on Our Father's and Our Mother's graves."

Though she hadn't been aware of any but usual Corner noises— magnified, of course, because she was outdoors—the tinkling bells and silvery sounds were unmistakable. Her first thought was that she should go back into the house, to investigate. Had the telephone gone mad? Was Flora trying to reach her from some wayside smashup? Were kite lights being flown, *even in daylight?* Was it a warning that the hot lead was about to come down? Or were the Whites disintegrating, being taken over by the Coloreds at last? Russians? She walked back to the wall and the apple tree, snapping her eyes open and shut several times, partly from feeling faint after having bent over the flowers, partly because she could not believe her eyes. Ah! There was everything to be said for doing things the old ways. The Midsummer doll turned on his string. The charm was working. It was Gypsies!

CHAPTER 4

The tinkling bells Miss Emmeline heard were the only warning the Gypsies gave. They must purposely have chosen the slow hour of late afternoon to arrive, the time when the roads leading to and from the Corner were lightly traveled and few cars were parked outside the Cadle garage and the luncheonette lot. They came by way of Horsefly Run, a little-used back road that ran through the hills to Olympia, which opened onto Old Hessian a few hundred yards uphill from the intersection.

Fran Hanter saw the caravan even before Miss Emmeline because she was outside washing the luncheonette windows. It was hard work in the humid heat. "Al, come quick!" she called. Her voice had an urgency that brought him running from the rear of the building, where he was cleaning out the rest rooms. "Do you see what I see, or am I going absolutely nuts?"

Al's glasses, as usual, were steamy, but he confirmed what she saw. "Do I see them? Jesus H. Christ, there must be a hundred of them! Yep, that's the way they come when they come, not on the highways but through little roads like the Run."

"But they came so *fast*," Fran said, wiping her forehead with her apron. "I saw them in the glass and when I turned around, sure enough, there they were."

"And all over the place already—they're at Cadle's, too."

"You better get on that phone and call Willie Bentrup, tell him to send out a radio call. We don't want Gypsies here. You want me to lock up?"

"No, let them come on in," Al said. "Better than having them break the place down. It's business—I guess that's how we'll have to look at it, since we're a public place."

"But there just *aren't* Gypsies any more!" Fran exclaimed, still not believing the caravan that continued to pour down Old Hessian.

Al ran toward the phone.

The first vehicles to draw up were motor-drawn trailers, some of them spanking new, and, after the motorcade had settled around the grass quadrangle, came open carts and old, round- and square-roofed, lumbering wagons, containing still more Gypsies. There were pet dogs following behind, and some wagons had goats tethered to their rears and mares and foals in tandem. All at once Gypsies were everywhere. One very large wagon halted by the apple tree, so the horses could drink from the stone trough. The families in the trailers seemed to have plenty of cash; they found the Cadle place especially interesting; gas tanks were being filled as fast as Rafe could get around to them, and Fran and Al had no choice but to let the Gypsy kids play the new jukebox,

294

which had arrived that morning, and take the orders of their parents and fill them. The wagon Gypsies held back somewhat, as though waiting to see how things would go before getting out cranes and kettles for cooking.

A buxom, dark woman in a red polka-dot dress, wearing large earrings and quantities of gold coins around her neck, saw Miss Emmeline standing by the wall and jumped down from the wagon by the spring and came forward.

"Hello, dearie," the Gypsy said, smiling at Miss Emmeline. "What's your name, little old lady?"

"I won't tell you my name," Miss Emmeline answered. "Please go away."

The Gypsy saw the Midsummer doll dangling from the apple branch and looked intently and questioningly into Miss Emmeline's eyes. "Be ye one of us, then?" she asked.

Miss Emmeline's lip trembled. "I live on these premises," she warned the Gypsy, "though nobody any longer remembers who I am."

"How about a true *dukkering,* to tell you who you are?"

"Duk—I don't understand."

"Read your palm and tell your fortune," the Gypsy translated. "I have the second sight." She reached out and touched Miss Emmeline on the forehead, nose and chin. Miss Emmeline slowly extended her hands across the wall. The Gypsy took them and first held them against her breasts. Miss Emmeline could hear through her fingers the Gypsy's big, strong heart steadily beating. Then the Gypsy spread the old, spotted hands, examining the palms. She read the left, frowned, then did the same with the right. "Fate line thin and dim. Long, uninterrupted life line. Your heart line is islanded, and you have no sun line at all. You have a white hand, lady dear," she summed it up.

"A *white* hand?" quavered Miss Emmeline. "Why, of course my hands are white!"

"Your palms are like untrodden snow," the Gypsy said.

Miss Emmeline began to shake all over. "What does that mean?"

"It means that nothing's ever happened to you," said the Gypsy, "and nothing ever will. Shall I do you in the cards? I have the true tarots."

"No, no, please not." Miss Emmeline retrieved her hands and drew back. She began to cry.

"Don't take on, lady," the Gypsy tried to comfort her. "Lots of people, when their lives are read, feel this way. Many have white hands."

"Oh, it's so true!" Miss Emmeline said through her tears; all barriers went down before the Gypsy. "I was always the plain one, I never had a chance. I nursed Our Father and Our Mother with nothing for myself, ever. Now I'm the old and sick one." She wiped her eyes. The Gypsy clearly wanted to be paid. "I'm afraid I have no money on me, but I'll give you this." She stooped, picked a branch of sedum and held it out to the Gypsy.

The Gypsy's eyes widened. She looked again at the Midsummer doll, then at the cluster of pink flowers Miss Emmeline offered. She made a sign with her fingers. "No," she said, drawing back, "I take nothing from you!"

"Emmeline! Emmy!" came a voice frantically calling from the direction of the bridge. Miss Flora was leaning from the taxi, jammed between two cars, only two of the many that were banking up on the bridge. She saw there was trouble and, getting out, came running. "Emmy! What are you doing out of bed and *downstairs?*" Then, turning to the Gypsy, she looked her up and down. "Who are you?"

"Only an honest *chie*, lady, who makes her way by *dukkering*."

"She read my palm, Flora. She said I have a white hand."

"What nonsense have you told my sister?" Miss Flora demanded.

The Gypsy would try for money from Miss Flora, evidently; she held out her hand. "Cross my palm with silver and I'll tell you."

"Never! No money!" cried Miss Flora, and she went inside the gate and banged it shut.

"*Yn iach,*" said the Gypsy in farewell, again making a sign.

"Come, Emmy." Miss Flora took her sister gently by the arm and led her into the house. "Emmy, Emmy!" she scolded, more gently this time. "Why ever did you risk the stairs? Why, you might have *broken your hip!*"

"I wanted—I made a Midsummer Man to hang up—"

"I told you that was nonsense!"

"But I want to see the Midsummer Man!" Miss Emmeline wailed.

"Dear, that's all in your mind. There's no such man."

"But *you* saw him. And last night, when Our Governess was here, she said—"

"That wasn't Our Governess, that was Miss Hankins. . . . Take the stairs slowly, one at a time. There." It took quite a time for Miss Flora to get Miss Emmeline back into bed and settled with Spot beside her; she was prostrated by her experience.

"Are they Russians, Flora?" she asked breathlessly.

"You saw they were Gypsies." But the seed of doubt had been sown. "At least, I *thought* they were Gypsies."

"But Russians are Gypsies, aren't they? Egyptians from Asia?"

"Rest, now," Miss Flora said. "I'm going to call the state police, and if they don't come this time, I'll go straight to the top, to Harrisburg and the governor himself."

"And I'll watch for the Midsummer Man."

With this, Miss Emmeline dropped off to sleep, and Miss Flora once more took up the skeins of persecution.

Al Hanter didn't make it to the phone in time to alert Willie Bentrup; the Gypsies were so thick it was all he could do to get behind the counter and start filling orders. It must have been, he later figured, one of the people downroad who called Bentrup to report the invasion. Or maybe it had been that crazy coot, Miss Flora Bowyer. Fran, in spite of being rushed, got quite a kick out of seeing the other Bowyer sister having her palm read; it was the first time she had seen Miss Emmeline, so perhaps it was true, as people said, that there was a third and even crazier sister kept secretly in the attic.

Some of the wagon Gypsies started to pitch tents and set up cooking paraphernalia. The younger women, baskets over their arms, began to hawk cheap jewelry and laces, some going downriver knocking at doors, others trying for customers in the cars that were lined up, twenty deep, behind the stop signs, unable to get through. Some of the men, tinkers, went ahead, stopping from house to house, asking for knives to be sharpened or pots and pans to be mended. Older women stayed by the wagons and trailers with the children, of whom there were swarms, sometimes as many as six to a family.

By the time Willie Bentrup reached the Corner, the intersection was so crowded that he had to park his squad car in the

297

Glidden driveway and go the rest of the way on foot. The Gypsies were well enough behaved; it seemed not to occur to them that they might be found strange by the villagers; the quiet, easy way they moved showed that. It was people in the jammed cars blowing horns and yelling to get through causing most of the noise. After several inquiries, Bentrup found the Gypsy chief, a large, calm blond giant of a man, with skin burned russet by the sun.

"You the head man?" Bentrup asked.

"I am the *shevengro,* yes," came the Gypsy's reply.

"What's that?"

"I take care of my people."

"Well, you can't take care of them in *this* village," Bentrup told him. "There's state and county and township laws against pitching any tent or parking any trailers. The sundown law. We've got laws against pilfering, too."

"No one is pilfering."

"How do you buy those things, then?" Bentrup jerked his head toward the *shevengro's* bright aluminum trailer. "Something paid for that, or did you just pilfer it?"

"My people do odd jobs before and after the fruit picking. This is picking time now," the *shevengro* said with dignity.

"Not around here they don't pick. Where were you before you came here?"

"We were picking down Trenton way."

"I'll give you exactly one half hour to get everybody out of here—wagons, trailers, the whole kit and kaboodle. Now, get these tramps moving!"

"They're not tramps," answered the *shevengro* with patience. "They are *mumpers*—"

"I don't want details. Get a move on out!"

The *shevengro* gave Bentrup a long, bitter look. "Maybe we'll meet again, someday."

"Just clear out," Bentrup repeated, moving away. The kids milling around and the girls touching him and asking to tell his fortune bothered him, and without his squad car he felt his authority diminished. He made his way over to the Cadles', where he could phone in his report and wait for the Gypsies to leave.

It took him only a few seconds to see that Rafe was in the

298

middle of one of his bad drunks; he was worse than Bentrup had ever seen him. Rafe had hollow legs; his tolerance for alcohol was high, so high that Bentrup often wondered what would happen the day Rafe's legs filled up and he really came apart.

"Christ, Rafe," Bentrup said, "you're stewed to the balls!"

"Christ yourself," Rafe answered. He was in a foul mood. After the Gypsies' cars had been serviced, he had further fortified himself; a freshly opened pint stood between the gas pumps. "Why in hell don't you get these fucking niggers out of here?"

"They're Gypsies, Rafe, not niggers."

"All the same to me."

"Why don't you go a little easier on that stuff?" Bentrup suggested.

Rafe scowled. "People drink because they can't stop drinking. You mind your own business."

Bentrup asked to use the telephone.

"Got no more phone," Rafe said. "Ripped it out this morning."

Bentrup had to stand where he was, watching the Gypsies' departure. It could be seen that the *shevengro* had given the order to move fast. The wagon people were packing and hitching their horses; the silver bells on the whiffletrees made blurs of bright sound in the warm summer air. But they were waiting for the hawkers and tinkers to return from down the road, as well as for the trailers to lead the way.

"In all my born days, I never seen nothing like this at the Corner," Mae Cadle called down from her window. "That's what's happening to this country, no law and order. What we need are more police."

"Well, I'm getting them out as fast as I can," Bentrup answered her. He could see Edie standing behind her mother, a terrified expression in her eyes. "What's with the kid?" he asked Rafe.

Rafe's eyes were now beyond being bloodshot, having reached a stage where a brownish film stretched across them, with darker brown blots at the corners. "I'm fixing to give that kid a good hiding, that's what's the matter with her," he answered. He turned and looked up at Edie. "Alley carrier!" he shouted, pointing a finger, then turning again to Bentrup. "What's a man to do with a filly's out night after night, letting every Tom, Dick and Harry slip it to her?" He answered his own question. "All he can do is beat the life out of her, it's the only thing cures what's wrong with her. Bare-assed, too."

Bentrup turned away; he didn't want any more of this. The Cadles' private life, public as it often was, was something he tried not to think about. And he had other things to do. But Edie's expression lingered in his mind; he couldn't forget it.

The Gypsies seemed to bring out the most surprising reactions in everybody. Not only people living around the quadrangle of grass were bothered by them; villagers from downroad and from the Fringes, who hadn't seen them arrive but had heard the commotion, flooded up to the intersection.

Don MacFinden and his father and father-in-law were among the first to walk up the road to see what was going on. They had left the young MacFindens' house against all the protestations of Nancy's mother and Don's and Nancy herself; Nancy had set up a barbecue in the garden and had just taken the steaks off the grill.

"This never could've happened in the old days," the elder MacFinden said, when he saw the Gypsies. "We'd have had a kettle of tar boiling by now, and those bastards would've beat it so fast we wouldn't have had to rip open pillows for feathers, much less cut rails to ride them out of town on."

Nancy's father said nothing.

Don said, "Aw, come on, Dad, let's go back. Who cares about Gypsies? I've got hundreds of slides to show, and we'll never get through them if we don't start early. I've got the projector and screen all set up."

"Besides, Nancy's holding those steaks," her father reminded, and the MacFinden contingent returned to the house. Nancy put the steaks back on the grill, which resulted in their being overdone, the way the elder MacFinden hated them, so that part of their evening was already spoiled.

The Hubbard ménage had got wind of the Gypsies soon after they arrived, and early on Miss Hankins had given Mrs. Hubbard an extra tranquilizer, figuring it could do no harm, since the old lady had been feeling nervous from the heat anyway. Miss Hankins herself felt peckish, but hot tea was her salvation in all weathers.

Teddy Hubbard had been very explicit about keeping his mother quiet; he wanted her fresh and well for the party.

"I've always been told Gypsies bring bad luck with them," Mrs. Hubbard said, before she lapsed into her tranquilizer doze. "I'll never forget the realistic way Gerry played *Carmen*—Carmen was a Gypsy, you know; rather a nice one. Her card scene—"

Here we go again, Miss Hankins said to herself; if I have to hear that record about *toujours la mort* once more, I'll bloody well *scream!* But aloud she said, "Yes, dear, Miss Farrar must have made a wonderful Gypsy."

"And a wonderful Butterfly and an even more wonderful Zaza and—and—" Mrs. Hubbard was fading. "Now, you won't go out and leave for your walk until the Gypsies have gone?"

"I wouldn't walk to the window to look at a Gypsy," Miss Hankins promised. "In England, of course, we take Romanies for granted; but our Gypsies are practically respectable, you might say."

Bo was more interested in the Gypsies than either Miss Hankins or Teddy. He was lying in his room, sulking, nursing the black eye Tavio had given him, leafing through back copies of *One,* the magazine for homosexuals, *Man of Our Times, Physique Pictorial* and *Trim Studio Quarterly*, of which he had a definitive collection. One he held showed with graphic vividness a massive motorcycle man in leather jacket about to paddle the rump of a very buttocky bar-bell boy; Bo liked pictures of spankings, boys with heavy boots and hammers, boys in chains. But today the little magazines weren't doing a thing for him; they only made him remember Tavio. When he heard the noises at the intersection, he was glad for the diversion and ran out to see what was happening. Teddy was cutting back the big wisteria vine on the porch, gardening gloves and rose spray nearby, ready for the next garden chore.

"Well, it doesn't look so bad with the black eye makeup," Teddy said to Bo. "Unfortunately, there's no makeup for Pierces that have been crashed into by people who come home drunk and beat-up."

"I didn't crash into it, I only grazed the fender," Bo answered. He was never going to hear the end of it; it was almost like being one of the boys in the little mags, the one always at the end of a chain.

"I thought you were tired and wanted to nap," continued Teddy. "Now you're up, I could use a little help. Why don't you get the bouligny shears and get going on the other end of this vine?"

"I'm going up to the intersection."

"It's only Gypsies."

"*Only* Gypsies!" Bo was really sent. "I've never had a Gypsy."

"You've had everything else. I'd stay well out of that rumpus, if I were you."

"Oh, you're such a killjoy!" Bo told him. "*You* wear your gardening gloves and spray your roses, *dear. I'm* going up to where there seems to be a little life."

Bo's contention that everybody was everything and negotiable seemed, for once, to be borne out. He had no trouble finding what he perpetually searched for, a glad-eyed Pan, with curly mop and simply heavenly rags. The Gypsy was quite amenable to going into the stand of locusts and sumac between the Cope's Corner Inn and the Glidden house, for a price. Bo, in his imagination, invested him with phantom horns beneath the mop and, even, a rudimentary tail. But the price turned out to be rather higher than had been arranged; Pan, once he had obliged, not only took the money, but, being both older and stronger than he at first appeared, relieved Bo of his gold Cartier watch and both his brown diamond and seal rings.

Bo's expensive adventure took place at the height of the Gypsy confusion. At about the same time, when everything was at its noisiest, Acie Stanes drove his pink Cadillac into the middle of it all without being noticed by anyone except Mae Cadle. Mae had reached a point of terror about Rafe earlier in the day, and was beyond fighting against what she knew was later to come.

"Edie," she whispered, drawing her to the window and pointing, "that's him, isn't it?"

Edie, who had put in a day at least as terrifying as her mother's, nodded. She had managed to get into the house that morning without Rafe's seeing her, but when he came upstairs for the midday meal, all hell had broken loose; it had been all Mae could do to keep him out of the bedroom. "That kid's not going down those stairs until I give her the strapping she deserves," Rafe had

302

said flatly, and meant it. "And no phone calls. Mae, *I* heard you sneaking out last night, to call up that Mrs. Ingle." That was when he ripped out the phone cord. Shortly after that, he'd started on boilermakers.

"Honey," Mae said, "you've got to get out of here somehow, no matter how you do it. Get out and stay out. Maybe by tomorrow I can cool your Papa-Daddy down. He's gone back inside, for more beer."

"But what about you, Mom? You ought to get out too," Edie said. "If you knew Acie, well, we could both run for it."

Mae looked out at the pink Cad with Gypsies swarming around it. She could see Acie in his bright silk shirt, looking hardly a day older than she remembered him. Lowering her eyes, she saw her white, lumpy legs, her swollen feet in their old green wedgies. "No, forget about me," she said. "I've handled Papa-Daddy before, I'll handle him again."

"Oh, Mom!" Edie cried. "Come with me!"

"No. You go. With you gone, he'll ease up, I know."

Edie hesitated a last second, then kissed her mother and ran for it. Her mother's voice followed her: "Promise me, you won't let that Acie lay a hand on you!"

"You always say that about everybody."

"But don't, honey," Mae begged. "Don't!"

Edie was so scared as she crept down the stairs she wasn't sure she could make it. She wouldn't have, either, if it hadn't been for the Gypsies outside, because Rafe just missed seeing her as he came out of the garage's rear. It had been right to go—he would ease up now, as her mother said. She pushed her way through the crowd to the pink Cad and got inside, breathing a sigh of relief. No matter how rough Acie might be about standing him up, nothing could be as bad as being locked in the bedroom and breathing the exhaust gas and hearing Rafe drinking and cussing downstairs.

"Well," Acie said to her. "What makes you think I came for you?"

"Didn't you?"

"You got your wires crossed yesterday, or did I?"

"I tried to phone you," Edie said, "but I couldn't. Acie—don't make me explain; we can have our date tonight."

Acie did not smile. "Better late than never?"

"Let's get away from here," Edie implored, and Acie, imperiously honking, backed through the Gypsies, turned around, and drove across the bridge.

"Girl, we got things to settle," he said then. "You want a stick?" He held out a freshly rolled Mary Jane.

"No." She saw Acie was already high.

"Yeah," she heard Acie say. "I got plans for you. I'm *way* up there, girl. I can look down and see those steeples and people and hear all that juke floating up to me, just like I owned the earth. Everything is my turf tonight."

Edie knew then the kind of night it would be.

The Ingle household reacted slowly to the Gypsies. Susan Ingle was playing bridge in Olympia, where news of the trouble at the Corner became known only after sundown when the bars began to liven up, and Dr. Ingle was at Tuliptrees. Mrs. Schaaf, perhaps alone of all the Corner people, was not upset; she gave the tinker who came to the door the kitchen knives to sharpen, and he sharpened them well and returned them in a few minutes, as promised. Bobby Ingle, as tired as he had ever been in his life, had a hard time getting awake. The shouting and blowing of horns penetrated his sleep and he opened his eyes, trying to think what it might mean, but then sleep again overtook him and he turned over, burying his head beneath the pillow. But the noises still came through. At last he got up, found Mrs. Schaaf, and asked what it was. By then the sounds coming from the Cadle place were so loud that he knew the trouble Edie dreaded must have come. He quickly dressed and ran out to find her. The garage was closed tight, though he could hear a violent fight going on inside; things were being thrown and smashed against the walls and floors. After repeated knockings, a window went up and Edie's mother leaned out.

"Edie's not here," she said; her hair was in disorder. "Boy, you better make tracks away from this place—it was you kept her out all night and got her daddy wild!"

"Do you know where she went?"

"Anywheres to get away from this hellhole! Go on, go! Terrible things are happening here!" And the window slammed down.

The trailers were moving up Old Hessian and the commuter traffic was unsnarling. Willie Bentrup, who had stood in the center of the quadrangle, to make sure the Gypsies all went, was relieved to get back to the squad car, still parked in the Glidden drive. There he saw the good-looking Eye-tye, standing by the mailbox. Feeling that a seal of approval had been placed on him by his having worked for Mrs. Glidden, Bentrup braked as he drew out.

"Hi," he greeted Tavio. "Ever see anything like that before?"

Tavio looked at Bentrup with the lack of expression he used on all cops. "Sure, I've seen Gypsies before."

"Well, we made them haul tail in short order."

"I saw you talking to the *shevengro*."

Bentrup looked at Tavio more closely. "Say—that word. How come *you* know it? You one of them Gypsies, too?" It occurred to him the Eye-tye might not be Eye-tye at all but a front man, sent on ahead, and to blame for the whole mess.

Tavio didn't reply, only continued to look at Bentrup expressionlessly.

"You know, you don't want to hang around here too long yourself," Bentrup warned.

"I come and go as I like."

At that moment Bentrup got a radio call—the Gypsies were up on the highlands now, still looking for a campsite for the night, and fresh complaints about them were already beginning to come in. Bentrup sped up to the intersection and turned up Old Hessian.

Tavio walked slowly after him, toward the spring and the apple tree. The Corner was as quiet now as it had been full of noise a quarter hour before. Tavio reached out and touched the doll, still hanging from the apple branch; it swung back and forth in the fading daylight. A sharp yap from the house behind the tree, from which the woman had called out to him his first morning in the village, caused him to look up. There, behind a screen, he could see a dim face with a pair of opera glasses held before the eyes— the face of an old woman, perhaps the one who had called to him, or one like it. The small white dog barked again, and the old woman raised her hand, like a claw, and waved. She seemed to be trying to say something to him, though he could hear no words. He raised his own hand then, in his thumb-and-forefinger

305

circle, and could see the old woman smile. Then he turned and walked back to the Glidden house.

Whatever the disappointment about the overdone steaks cooked on the MacFinden barbecue rack, the showing of the slides began well enough. Don started off with the pictures of the rice throwing at the plane at Idlewild, following with the change of planes at Miami and the arrival in Yucatán. Then came, in carefully arranged sequence, the jungle ruins at Chichén Itzá, the Mayaland Hotel, Mérida and Kabáh, Mérida again and then Uxmal.

Don kept up a running commentary, with Nancy prompting when he forgot some name or detail of time or place. It was a toss-up whether Nancy's parents or Don's were the more entertained. Nancy's mother thought the colors of everything wonderful, and her father suggested they might do well to follow the identical itinerary when they took their next winter vacation. Mother Mac felt it was all very pretty, but wondered about the comfort of the hotels and whether the water was safe to drink; there was always the water, and Nancy was a riot on the subject of the Enterovioforma. Some of the pictures evidencing the phallic worship of the Mayans were perhaps a bit much for the old folks, but Don was careful to change slides quickly when there was a well-articulated shot of the many fertility symbols or a rain god with phalluses sticking out of his ears.

After a while, he let Nancy take over the travelogue; somehow he was not finding it easy to keep his mind on what he was doing. He inserted the boxes of slides in proper order, that was easy enough; the projector was automatic. But what was really on his mind was the C.T.A., and worry about how it was going to work out for him and Nancy. It was astonishing how large and obtrusive a small, white cardboard box could seem, when you didn't want it to be seen. He had gotten the C.T.A. and box into the house without Nancy's noticing by the expedient of carrying it in a rolled newspaper, going at once to his own bath and concealing it in the medicine cabinet, behind several cakes of soap. But all day long he had fretted that Nancy might come across it, and what would she think?

It was during the Uxmal slides that he had made the boo-boo—Don could have sworn he had edited out the shot of a group of large phalluses, rearing starkly up from a field beneath the larger temple. But there they were, bigger than life, and were on the screen a good half minute before the old folks realized what they were.

Don's father took it all right, throwing back his head as though he had a whiplash and laughing, slapping his knees, but his mother was clearly offended.

"Son," she said, getting up in the darkness, "I think we've had enough for one night. Really, Dad, I'm ashamed of you!"

"You know what they are as well as I do," the elder MacFinden said.

Don by then had changed the slide. "You can't go yet," he said. "Why, there's all of Mejico City and Oaxaca and Monte Albán and Mitla—"

"I think maybe we should let the rest go until another night," Nancy's father put in. He also got up.

"So do I," Nancy's mother said.

There was nothing to do but cut on the lamps, so everyone could see to go. In a way, Don didn't care too much, because now there would be time for him to have a few drinks with Nancy and, if all worked out as he had carefully planned it, give the C.T.A. a try. But when they were alone, Nancy refused the drink he offered.

"Oh, come on, doll," Don urged. "Just one?"

Nancy yawned. "I don't feel like it."

"Is it because there's no more tequila? Because if it's that, it's early, I've time to drive across the river and get some."

"It's not that."

"Oh. Don't tell me you were bothered because that Uxmal shot got shown by mistake?"

"No, not bothered really."

"It didn't bother you when I made the shot at Uxmal."

"No, but tonight, when I saw it, I was a little upset."

"But why?"

"I don't know why. Darling, let's don't have a post-mortem on it. Let's forget it and go to bed."

"Okay by me," Don said. "Won't change your mind about a drink?"

"No, I'll go ahead," Nancy said.

Don had a couple of bourbons by himself and got ready for

the ordeal, but when he came out of his bath, the C.T.A. concealed in the pocket of his dressing gown, he found the bedroom in darkness. Perhaps that was all to the good, really, the best kind of luck, because he hadn't really figured out how he would manage preliminaries and then slip the thing on without risking having Nancy see him do it.

"Are you awake, doll?" he called out softly.

There was no answer from Nancy, only her breathing, even and regular, in the bed beside his own. Don hesitated. Never before had she gone off to sleep so quickly; it was still the honeymoon time—the time to make love, then lie awake afterward and talk. She had seemed tired, and perhaps was. Now he thought about it, the Uxmal slide had disconcerted him, too. When he remembered the gigantic phalluses in the field below the temple and the joke the guide had made about them, he couldn't help thinking how ironic it was. "These were brought by the archeologists from another site. The Christians mutilated the statues to which they belonged," the guide had explained. "Perhaps they planted them here in the hope they would grow." Don wished his problem were that simple. He returned to his bath, replaced the C.T.A. in its box, again hid it behind the soap in the cabinet, and gave up the day.

CHAPTER 5

Bobby Ingle was shaking all over when he got back to the house. He had had no experience of the kind of violence he had heard behind the thin walls of the Cadle place, violence he could still hear, even through the closed windows on the north side of the house. After a short time it subsided, and he tried to forget he had heard it. He was hungry and, since Mrs. Schaaf had gone, cooked himself a plate of eggs and then went back to bed and tried to read. But he couldn't get through a single sentence for thinking of Edie, worrying about where she had gone to get away from the terrible life she had told him about, and what he was going to do about her. There was no question of phoning her—". . . *only let me call you, things being what they are*" had been her last words to him. A depressing anticlimax to his day, which hadn't been a day at all but an extension of his night, took place when his father came home. Bobby listened as he came slowly up the stairs, quickly switching off the light at the head of his bed. He heard his father pause. It wasn't that Bobby didn't want to see him or feared scolding or punishment (the permissive Ingle policy of upbringing excluded both, and Bobby had long since learned this), but what had happened with Edie had been complete and he had nothing to say about it. His father knocked anyway.

"Come in," Bobby said.

"I hope you weren't asleep?"

"No." He turned the light back on.

Ingle came to the foot of Bobby's bed and sat down. He looked tired. "I wasn't sure you'd be here. Why didn't you phone us last night that you wouldn't be home? Your mother stayed up all night worrying."

"She told me. I suppose you want a rundown on why I stayed out?"

"I don't need a rundown. I may have had five analytic hours today, but I think I can fill in what you did without explanation from you. Edie Cadle, of course."

"You knew that."

"Yes, I knew."

"You were all for my seeing Edie, when we talked about it the other night," Bobby reminded.

"I certainly considered her a better alternative after what you told me," answered his father. "But did you have to stay out all night?"

"It simply happened that way."

Ingle nodded. "Yes. But staying out all night at your age brings certain unexpected complications. Mrs. Cadle telephoned here; she was worried, too."

"That must have killed Mother—having to talk with somebody on the Fringes."

"Well, it bothered her, and it's not surprising it did, considering the relationship between the two houses." Ingle paused. "I wonder if you've any idea how much I could tell you about the Cadles?"

"I know you're doing the study."

"Have done it—the story's almost over, Bobby."

"It's awful over there. You should have heard it tonight. Dad, I want to take Edie out of that."

"You haven't been able to take yourself out of anything yet."

"I know that," Bobby admitted, "but this is different. Edie's not like other girls I've known."

"She was until a few days ago."

"Yes, but then, I don't know, something happened between us. I saw her out in her back yard taking a sunbath. She smiled, and I smiled back. And then everything was different. She makes me feel something I've never felt before."

"You mean you think you're in love with her?"

"No. Who knows what love is? It's that I think about her all the time, and when I'm with her I'm glad to be alive and when I'm away from her I'm miserable. Like now."

Ingle looked at his son, for a moment trying to see him with an analyst's dispassion. His somatotype was of the commonest—2-4-4, balanced mesomorph-ectomorph, probably 10-level, lean, far stronger physically than his brother Houghton. His IQ, too, was higher, consistent with the theory of increase in intelligence from first- to last-born in a family; and, having been born in autumn (a "cold-weather conception" baby), all chances had been weighted to his advantage. A fraction over six feet tall, weighing around 160, he would gain little weight as he grew older and was likely to be long-lived.

"You know, Bobby," Ingle said, "you're going to live a long time, probably. You're nineteen. There are other girls in the world, millions of them."

"I told you, she's not like other girls," Bobby said stubbornly. "And I don't want to spoil this by talking about it any more."

Ingle understood that. He said, "Before you do anything, I hope you'll think carefully."

"Not that I know what I'm going to do," Bobby typically answered. "All I know is that Edie's all I care about."

"Yes, I see that—or that you think that." Ingle stood up. He started for the door, then turned; he was conscious of his own tired soma, needing sleep. "I suppose it's no use asking you to think what your doing this means to your mother and me? I know

310

you'll not believe this, but I never in my life stayed out all night."

"Not even before you married Mother?"

"Not even then."

"But there must have been a first time for you—Mother said when I came in she supposed there had to be a first time."

"And I didn't carry safeties around with me either, much less a complete set of prophylactics."

"But, Dad," Bobby said, "that was then. That's all over now. You can buy all that stuff at any of the highway diners—everybody has sex now, whenever and wherever they need it. It's like talk."

"There were those in my generation who said sex was no more important than talk, too," Ingle said.

"It's not like talk."

"I'm glad you concede it's more important."

"I don't concede that it's either more or less important. It just *is*. Dad, I'm no different from anybody else about this."

Ingle sighed. "All right. Talk to me this way, if you like. In a way, I'm glad you do. But please try to shield your mother from some of this, the details; she's not interested in hearing them."

"Well, for someone not interested, she asks a lot of questions."

As Ingle watched Bobby, aware of the impassioned precision of his observation of him, discouragement suffused him, as it sometimes did at Tuliptrees, when he realized there was nothing he could do for a patient and even compensating him was out of the question; the personality slipped and stirred restlessly, in a pattern entirely discrete and its own, unsusceptible to suggestion or help. Bobby's thoughts moved beneath the outwardly calm, blond surface he presented, directing him this way and that, like a paramecium under a microscope, and he was driven and directed by them as sand shifts wetly in a quagmire.

"And tomorrow," Ingle said. "What about tomorrow?"

"I'll decide tomorrow what to do tomorrow."

"You said you wanted to take Edie out of her situation. How?"

"I'm thinking about how—or I was, before you came in."

"You have no money, for one thing."

"Money's not everything."

"Isn't it?"

"You've often said it's not."

"Unless you haven't it." Ingle stood in the doorway, one hand on the knob. "All right," he said, "go back to where you were before I came in. But first tell me—what was this about Gypsies in the village?"

Bobby told his father what he knew. Ingle listened carefully, nodded. "Sometimes I think those old sisters up by the bridge, the Misses Bowyer, may not be as crazy as they seem. Or are crazier than anything I know about. Did you see that doll hanging over the spring?"

"Doll?" Bobby looked blank.

"Some kind of fetish, made of stockings and buttons."

"I didn't see any doll."

"Maybe the Gypsies left it. Or I imagined it. Well, good night."

"Good night, Dad. And thanks."

"For what?"

Bobby shrugged. "Oh, I don't know. Thanks."

Ingle closed the door and went to his own room. Before he switched on the light, he let his eyes focus on the cigar and 5, painted on the Cadle wall, which he could barely make out in the light that came from the lamps above the intersection. The Cadle place was quiet, but there was an illusion of glow where the cigar turned to ash, and the 5, with its one-two-three, dark-light, lighter-than-dark brushwork seemed to move slightly, to have a life of its own. Cupid's Jack-a-lantern, he thought bitterly—Sheridan knew about quagmires. It's all there, if I could have seen it. God, how I tried! He undressed, put on his pajamas, brushed his teeth and, before getting into bed, opened the window wide. The susurrus of night insects and Corner sounds seemed to clog the window screen with a fine, white, airless down, shutting out life. He felt helpless, not only tired from his day and the talk with Bobby, but inert, aware of a surge of self-judgment rising in him like dark water to his throat. I did it all wrong, he thought in the darkness. But where, *where* did I blunder? Then, mercifully, he dropped asleep.

BOOK
FIVE

CHAPTER 1

It was almost morning when the lights finally went out at the Cadles'. All through the night they burned above the gas pumps, and the CLOSED sign hung crookedly in one window. In the workshop, Teddy Hubbard's Pierce-Arrow could be seen, pristine beneath a cluster of naked bulbs, towering above smaller cars around it, its white body, red upholstery and nickel-plate trimmings making it seem a fugitive, brightly plumaged bird, held prisoner by some squat, dun-colored species.

The garage was not the only place in the Corner that kept lights on all night; the Hanters, when they closed the luncheonette, left the neon blazing, and at the Misses Bowyer's, the two big spotlights attached to the rear gable switched on and off, trained on the garden. The Cope's Corner Inn, too, an early closer, stayed open later than usual; news of the Gypsy caravan had brought heavy trade to the bar, though everyone knew a campsite had been found and it would not return. By the time Willie Bentrup stopped by the luncheonette for his regular Danish and coffee, the Gypsies were stale news.

"They camped up outside Doylestown somewhere. Some Quaker felt sorry for them—you know Quakers—and said he didn't care if they spent the night on his land, as long as they got off by daylight. So they're gone. They're somebody else's headache now," Bentrup told Al Hanter. He took off his cap and mopped his forehead. "Where's Fran?"

315

"Slept late," Al said. "She'll be in in a few minutes. Better be, because I got to go to the can."

"Go on, I'll watch the place for you," Willie Bentrup offered.

"I can wait. In this business you learn that." He served up Bentrup's Danish, with plenty of butter, the way he liked it, and his coffee, with an extra measure of cream.

"I heard Fran's mother's not too good."

"On her way out. Any day, any hour, now."

"Well, we all gotta go sometime."

"Except me," Al wisecracked. "I gotta wait for Fran. No, seriously, Willie, I hope when I go it'll be some other way. The old girl's been in bed two years. Bedsores. Down to seventy-nine pounds. Murder's better."

"Must be expensive."

"It'll take every red cent the family's got to get her laid out. And then some. I'll probably have to bury her."

"Tough," Bentrup sympathized.

"It's all tough," Al said. "Money's always tough."

"But not as tough as before the war," said Bentrup. "Remember before the war? Jesus! Then I became a V-12 boy, always broke then, too. Whenever there was leave, we'd all pitch in a buck, toss it onto the barracks floor, and sit around in a circle and jack off. Man who could shoot farthest won the pot."

"Those were the days. Sometimes I wish I was back in the service. Why, when I was at Dix—" The phone on the wall rang and Al broke off to answer it. "Funny," he said, returning to lean on the counter opposite Bentrup, "sounded like somebody hung up when they heard my voice."

"Crackpot, maybe," Bentrup said. "Say, Al—remember that little piece won the Miss Olympia beauty contest couple years ago? The one supposed to be going on the stage or in the movies, or maybe it was TV? Redhead, kinda little, but built?"

"Folks lived up the road a piece?" Al remembered.

"Yeah, her. Well, she's back, peddling it."

"Didn't make the movies?"

"Guess not. Handing it out for free, on the canal bank. Four ways, I hear."

"Well, now, I've heard of the three *main* ways, but what's the fourth?" Al asked.

"Telephone fuck—between the tits."

"A telephone fuck is you stick a tit in each ear so you can hear yourself come. The other's a *fiddle* fuck."

Bentrup smiled sourly; Al had upped him and he didn't like his stories upped. "I hear there's really twenty-eight ways, but for the life of me, I can't figure them past nine or ten—" He stopped as Fran Hanter came in the door. "Oh, hi, Fran."

"Hi, Willie. Get rid of those Gypsies finally?"

"Another day like yesterday and I'll turn in my badge. Christ, what a day!"

Fran got into her flat shoes and tied on her apron. "So what happened besides the Gypsies?"

"Well, those crazy Bowyer women called up the governor's office in Harrisburg. Got through, too, not to the Gov himself, but some kind of secretary or something. They filtered the complaint down to us."

"What was it this time?" Fran asked. "More rocks disappearing?"

"No. Seems the Russians are really on their way." Bentrup winked.

"No kidding!" said Al.

"Yep, they're flying around in a big spacecraft you can't see, only hear, right over the Bowyer place, getting ready to pour hot lead down on us all."

"Those poor old things," Fran said. "Till yesterday, when the Gypsies were here, I never believed there could be two of them. But there the old one was, having her hand read, big as life."

"From the number of complaints on file, the place must be stacked with old ladies," Bentrup said. "They're not the only ones. Some nut called my wife to say there was a little man hanging from the apple tree."

"There was," Fran confirmed. "Kind of a funny doll made of old stockings."

"Well, it's gone now," Bentrup said. "I guess it takes all kinds."

"It sure as hell does," Al agreed. "You get any complaints on the Cadles? Christ! Rafe was taking the place apart last night, from the sound of things, but I guess Mae's got him quietened down by now. And the 'Closed' sign's out."

"Well, that doesn't sound like a heavy day to me," Fran said.

"Oh, there was more," Bentrup continued. "That old army

colonel, the old guy that lived all alone in that big stone house near Ohmerstown—he strung himself up. They found him late last night. Dead at least two weeks, the coroner told *me*, but I guessed it was longer. Had to take what was left away in a sack."

"But why didn't they find him before?" Fran asked.

Bentrup shrugged. "He didn't have anybody, lived there all by himself. He'd still be hanging there if somebody hadn't stopped by the house to ask directions. Stone house, odors don't leak out like they do from a frame house. But it was still fierce."

Fran shuddered. "I don't see how you can eat."

"Talk about nuts," said Al. "He was the nuttiest!"

"Lots of those old colonels are nuts," agreed Bentrup. "This one was a John Bircher—used to mail out all kinds of Jew literature."

"Jew literature? What's that?" Fran asked.

"Well, pamphlets against the Jews. They're really winning. It's all just a big Jewish plot down in Washington. They got all the money. The meek shall inherit the earth. Like that."

"The meek don't inherit a thing, I can tell you that," Fran said.

"This colonel, he mailed out nigger literature, too."

"Don't talk to me about niggers!" Al said. "Look at me. I'm no Jew *or* nigger, and I got from nothing. All their foreskins should grow back, yet, if you ask me—"

"Al, you stop talk like that!" Fran said.

"Well, somebody somewhere owns me—you, too—and we don't even know who. Could be some Jew or nigger. I tell you, Willie, when high yallas start coming in here and giving orders and kicking in my jukebox and making me buy a new one, it's time somebody sent out literature."

"That happened in here?" Bentrup asked.

"Other day. Oh, the new box is already in and paid for; they saw to that. Cash on the line."

"Who's 'they'?"

"That's what I'm telling you, Willie, I don't know."

"You shoulda called me," Bentrup told him.

"You think I'm crazy?" Al gave Bentrup the rest of the story about Acie Stanes's visit. "And this one's got a pink Cad and silk shirts with monograms *and's* screwing Edie Cadle—"

"How do you know that?" Fran objected. "Edie was in here with that Bobby Ingle."

318

"She's screwing him, too, if you got eyes. Everybody screws her, like they always screwed Mae and the other Cadle daughters."

"You haven't got a good word for anybody," Fran said.

"So his name was Acie Stanes, was it?" Bentrup came back to it.

"You know him?" Al asked.

"He's a policy operator from Philly. An ounce man, too."

"Christ! Try and win!" Al said.

"He's a friend of the Cadles," Fran said. "I can't figure it."

"I wouldn't call it friend, Fran," said Bentrup. "I know that much. But I can't figure it either. What gives with them Cadles?"

"Don't ask me," Fran said.

"Fight all day and fuck all night, they sound like," said Al. "Well, I ain't throwing no stones at Rafe. I got a glass house, too, I been dressing in the cellar for years. Like you say, Willie, it takes all kinds."

"It sure do," Bentrup said.

"There's mostly one kind of people around here, though," Al went on, since business was rushing by. "Now, you take all these tourists—not one in a hundred's got more than the price of hamburgers and Cokes, and yet there they are, all over the county, gawking. Rubbernecks. Not spending if they got it. Down in Olympia people running businesses will tell you they never *seen* the like of the kind of people that's trekking through the stores. Sometimes wonder if they're people. Fifty, seventy-five cents they spend, maybe. Dragging their asses around looking for *what?* What in hell do they think they're going to see? A couple of old stone houses and that funny playhouse made from a barn? A river with hardly any water in it except at flood time?"

"I've never been in that playhouse," Fran said with pride.

"Me neither," said Bentrup.

"So what is there around here?" Al demanded to know. "A lot of stuck-ups living like on top of flagpoles, nobody ever sees anybody else, just us working folks, waiting on custom."

"Well, they say these restaurants are famous," Bentrup suggested, remembering the Olympia Chamber of Commerce brochure. "They must be good, they get five, ten bucks for *one thing,* drinks, vegetables, dessert, everything like that extra. I hear some of these famous people, they don't mind dropping a century note a night."

319

"You ever been in one of those restaurants?" Al asked.

"Only to chase trouble. People who can't pay their tabs, or get drunk and fall in the canal and have to be fished out."

"Well, *we* can tell you," Fran said. "Before we had this stand, I waited table in each and every one of them, one time or another. Al, he cooked in a few, too. We wouldn't put the stuff they served in our mouths, I can tell you. We ate home."

"I never saw any famous people," Al said. "Celebrities, supposed to be so much. Just a lot of actors with no jobs and those people they call writers—lots of them. Never heard of them. From the way some people talk, you'd think Sinatra drops in here for cocktails."

"He drinks Jack Daniels," Fran supplied. "I read it in a book."

"*She* reads the books, not me," continued Al. "Remember that one place we both worked, Fran? Where they used the baked potato skins that came back to the kitchen over and over with some cheese guck in them? Pommes Olympia, they called them. *Pommes* is frog talk for spuds, Willie. And the barman had orders to save all the cherries and fruit from drinks people didn't finish. Everything left on the plates got ground up and went into the Russian dressing. Fifty cents extra."

"On iceberg that'd probably come back too," Fran added.

"Iceberg?" Bentrup wasn't following.

"Lettuce. You can use it over and over, till somebody eats it. But that isn't the half of it," Fran said. "So they get this five, ten dollars for what they call chefs' specialities. Huh! Al used to make them as easy as he makes red-eye gravy. Canned soups, canned vegetables, store-bought rolls, margarine instead of butter. Sprinkle a little rosemary over whatever it is—makes Pommes or whatever-it-is Rosemary. Ever notice how all those places've got a candle guttering on the table? Keep it dark, then they can't see whether the steak's rare, medium or cooked to death. When customers used to complain to me that the rolls were cold, I'd tell them, 'Honey, I know. Hold them over the candle, that'll warm them.'"

"It don't matter what they serve," Al said. "These tourist jerks will eat anything. It's all eat and run anyway. No steady custom. Nobody, hardly, ever comes back, so why knock yourself out? Excuse me." He went at a fast walk out the rear door. Fran and Bentrup could hear the door of the rest room bang.

She sighed. "I don't know," she said. "Something's the matter with this place, me, everything."

"Yeah?"

"Sometimes I think I'll go *crazy* with all the noise and people who come in here. Never a minute of quiet."

"I know what you mean," Bentrup said. "The way it seems to me is, there's too many people now, with too much time and going too many places too fast and too often. I sometimes wonder who in hell they all are."

"People!" Fran said.

A great, empty truck, so long that it was having difficulty negotiating its way around the grass quadrangle without backing, at last made it and went grinding and clattering up Old Hessian, leaving behind a thick, black cloud of exhaust.

"Those things are the worst," Fran said.

"Now, don't start on how I should go for the big trucks. I'm a township cop—it's for the county and state boys to do something about those things if they're going to."

"They're not going to."

"Well, this whole country's going to the dogs," Bentrup summed it up. "It's not just here, it's everywhere else, too."

"The trucks, yes; they're trucks," Fran said. "But there's something the matter with *people*. Not just the ones come in here. You take this village. Take it house by house. Take the Cadles—"

"You take them. I've had them, for a coupla days anyway."

"And those Ingles. They say he's a doctor, a headshrinker, but he looks kinda crazy to me himself. And his wife's even crazier. There are the Bowyer sisters, nutty as fruitcakes, both of them."

"Or the three of them," Bentrup said. "I hear there's one in the attic, flat like a board from lying down, that they've kept up there for years. Kind of a spare." He laughed.

Fran was serious. "Listen to me, Willie. How about that Mrs. Glidden, supposed to be such a lady? A lady widow. You know what's been going on over there?"

"Yeah, all the cops know about that Eye-tye."

"You do?"

"Well, we kinda remember he's there, and watch it."

"I can tell you about him," Fran said. "He was wonderful. He knows about it all being wrong and no good, even if he was a bastard to me. He's looking for the next river and the sea."

Bentrup frowned. "Fran, are you okay?"

"Of course I'm not okay. I'm as bad off as everybody else we're talking about," she answered bitterly, her eyes very bright.

"Well, I heard you're upset about your mother—"

"Yes. She'll go today, maybe. I hope. It was so bad at home, none of us could stand the end. She's in a coma anyway." She swallowed, waited. "But to go on down the road—how about those Hubbard people? What are they?"

"Two queers. One rich. One he keeps in a gilded cage, you might say. An old lady, Hubbard's mother."

"And that poor English nurse of hers, talking to herself."

"Fran, that's life. And it's not all crazy. There're the young MacFindens; they're all right."

"Give them time, they'll soon be like everybody else—like Al and me. Hating each other and loving each other so much it seems all one and the same. Shackled together, like with chains."

"Fran, girl, you need a rest from this place," Bentrup said.

"What I need is a man, a real man!" She laughed. "I've had a few, did you know that? It hasn't been all Al. That Tavio—I'll never forget him."

"That Eye-tye?"

"Yes, him."

"Christ, Fran! You shouldn't be telling me this stuff—" Bentrup stopped; to his relief, the loud flatus of the Olympia "siren" was shuddering up the valley. "Oh-oh," he said, getting off his stool, "that sounds like four longs and two shorts."

"A fire?"

"No, not a fire. Disaster, though."

"It's disaster somewhere all the time. Old colonels, old crazy sisters. Well, see you, Willie." Bentrup went out and Al returned from the rest room. "Al," Fran said, "you didn't tell me—has there been a call from the hospital?"

"No, I'd have told you. The phone did ring, but it was a wrong number or something. Anyway, they hung up when I answered."

Fran stood up. "I'm going to call them." She went to the phone and dialed. Al only half listened to her; it sometimes took a while, getting through to the floor nurse, then the round-the-clock nurse. He heard Fran's voice break. She slowly put the receiver back on its hook.

"Well?" he asked.

"She died an hour ago. They said they tried to call here." Though her voice was shaky, she was not crying.

"Gosh—I'm sorry," Al said.

"You're not sorry. Why pretend?"

"You want me to go with you?" Al was already taking off his apron. Fran didn't answer. She went to get her purse from below the cash register, slipped into her other shoes. "Well, do you or don't you?"

She turned. "You'd better stay here and keep things going. It's us who'll have to bury her."

"I thought it would be."

"I'll be back," Fran said in a voice that was suddenly hard and dry. "We're stuck with each other. Stuck like two frozen, uncooked hamburgers you can't pry apart to cook. But we're no good apart, we've got to go on together. Just don't tell me things like you're sorry." She walked to the door and went out.

It was only when she had gotten into her car and started the motor that Al, who was watching, saw her break into tears. He didn't see her drive away, because a customer came in. By the time he had served up what was ordered, Fran was gone.

Mae Cadle had been in a state of panic all day Wednesday about Rafe's drinking, and his watching Edie and threatening her had driven her almost crazy. The Gypsy crush hadn't made her feel any better, either, nor had Bobby Ingle's knocking on the door, coming, as it did, after her row with Rafe and trying to get him to pass out.

What was the real matter, of course, was Acie Stanes—she had started shaking all over when she saw him, and though she hardly ever took anything harder than her Diet Cola, sneaked a couple of stiff ones from the pint Rafe left standing on the bedroom dresser. The drinks steadied her, but not much, and she sat down in her rocker and, to get her mind off everything, turned on her radio, keeping it turned low to her favorite Philly station. A revival meeting was in progress. "Come on, sistern and brethern," the preacher was calling out, "come right up and testify. Jesus is here waitin' for you. Come before it's too late!" They were singing Mae's favorite hymn, too, "Shall We Gather at the River?" and it put her in a mood. But no matter how she tried, she couldn't get her mind off Acie, sitting in the pink Caddy, surrounded by the Gypsies. Whether it was that she couldn't see as well as she could once, or that her memories of him were strong, he had looked to her the same as he did those sixteen–seventeen years ago, those hot, summer months when she'd hardly be able to wait for him to get down off the stone truck and come inside with her. What scared her so was that she kept thinking of him without any clothes on, of the tight, black, kinky curly hair he had down there, not like white men had, and what hung beneath it. She'd found out right away why Colored women would put up with almost anything from men they lived with or were married to, just to have that thing in them at night. Acie had made her feel something she'd never felt with Rafe or any other man, no matter how she tried, closing her eyes and pretending it was him when it wasn't. He'd been full of tricks, too. *And now Edie. . . .*

"But that's sin, can't think like that, deadly sin!" she muttered to herself, and the chant of the revivalist preacher came through to her clear and loud, like in the old days, when she really believed and used to feel the spirit in her. "Now, I want each and every one of you, sistern and brethern, to go on up to New York to the World's Fair. Don't go to them sinful places, where they show you how to blow God's world to atoms, go to the place where the Blue Peter is. It come from the Pope, but don't let that bother you, it's our sweet Jesus Himself lying in his own Mother's arms. Remember, the Blue Peter." Huh! Mae thought to herself, I'll never get to the World's Fair or anywhere else! Her mood softened and deepened. She'd be to blame for what Acie might do to Edie, his very own daughter! Suddenly she began to cry, rocking herself from side to side in time with the singing, holding her elbows close to herself with trembling hands. Tomorrow, she promised the preacher, she'd get on a bus, somehow, and go to see the Blue Peter and throw herself down and beg to be washed once again in the blood of the lamb. The promise brought the old-time spirit

324

flooding back into her, stronger than she'd ever felt it. Throwing herself onto the floor in front of the radio, she prayed, "Oh, sweet Jesus, forgive me, a hardened old sinner," taking her prayer straight from what the preacher was saying. "Help a poor, miserable sinner that's strayed from the true way and wash me in your blood and make me pure! And take care of my little girl and bring her back home safe to me," she added.

She was crying and praying so hard that it took her quite a while to realize there was somebody knocking and calling at the downstairs door. Getting up painfully, she went to the window and called down, "No more gas or service tonight. Can't you see that 'Closed' sign?"

"But I want to see Rafe," replied a voice, which she recognized as belonging to Teddy Hubbard. "Is the Pierce ready?"

All at once Mae saw sin, cold and clear. "*I* don't know if it's ready and don't give a *damn* about your old Pierce!" she said.

Teddy Hubbard tried to be patient; he saw she looked drunk and all mussed up. "I wouldn't bother you, but I tried to get you on the phone, and it must be out of order."

"Oh, it's out of order, all right—Rafe ripped the cord right out. He's not coming down tonight, he's dead to the world."

"Oh. Well, when he wakes up, tell him—"

"Tell him yourself," Mae said. "You—you—!" Those drinks must have been stronger than she thought; she couldn't think of the word.

"Mrs. Cadle, is anything the matter?" Teddy Hubbard asked.

Mae glowered down at him. "What would you and your likes care what might be the matter with *respectable* people like us?" she demanded. "All you care about's that big piece of junk down there, that you use to ride around your tee-nancy friends to the shame of the whole place!" The word she searched for came to her, blazing with sin. "Morphadite!" she cried. "Taking away some girl's chances of getting a good husband! *You're* the reason there's so many old maids, you and your morphadite molly friends!" She laughed. "Doing it with each other!"

Teddy Hubbard knew when he was licked. Turning, he started walking down the road toward his house. But Mae's words were for the whole village. "Morphadite!" she screamed after him. "Why don't you try it with a girl sometime, maybe you'd like it, maybe it'd make a man out of you!"

Teddy rarely lost his temper, but the sight of his Pierce inside, where he couldn't get at it, made him furious. He stopped. "Or *you, you* could try it with a girl—it might make you into something besides an old bag with balls!" he flung back at her.

Mae slammed down the window. Luckily, Rafe had snored through it all. He was really out, sawing away, sounding sometimes like all the cars downstairs being raced together. R-r-r-*ruh!* R-r-r-r-*ruh! RUH!* came his breathing, just as though he had his foot on an accelerator. Mae was bushed, and after having herself a little something from the fridge, she closed the door to the bedroom and settled down on the Castro, to worry about Edie and wait for her to come in.

She must have fallen asleep then, because the next thing she knew it was daylight, and she could hear Rafe's waking-up yawns in the bedroom. It took him a while to get to his feet, but then he opened the door, whiskey bottle in hand. He looked horrible.

"You been at my bottle," he said. In the past, Rafe had been on all-day drunks, and day-and-night drunks, but she had never seen him like this.

"I only took two or three little swallows," Mae defended herself. "Because you're like an animal, that's what you are! Drive any woman to drink, not just me!" He didn't say anything to this, but went into the bath. She lay listening to him as he urinated—the amount of beer and whiskey that man could hold inside him! He peed like a horse, a steady stream. Usually, in this state, he staggered back to bed and slept another hour or so, but this time she didn't hear him go back to the bedroom.

"Don't think you're going back to sleep," he said to her from the doorway. He took another drink, finishing the pint.

"Who could sleep in this place? My God, Rafe, don't keep on drinking that stuff!"

He came toward her, the filthy, grease-covered clothes he had slept in hanging on him. "Don't you come near me, Rafe Cadle!" Mae warned him. "Stay away from me!"

"Why?" Rafe asked. "That's what a wife's for, when a man feels like it."

326

"But you— We haven't—"

"Move over, you bitch!" Rafe commanded, getting into the Castro beside her. In the gray daylight he saw her, breasts sagging beneath her shapeless brunch coat, white, doughy, blue-veined legs sticking out of the sheet. She tried to hold the brunch coat to her, but he ripped it from her, leaving her naked.

"No!" Mae protested. "I don't want anything to do with you after the things you've said and done to me. Dirty pig—you stink!"

"Hold your breath if you don't like it," Rafe said. "Come on, old lady, you used to be nuts for it. You're not too old for the nook!"

He was strong as ever; she had no strength against him. He held her down to the bed until her shoulders ached and her arms were limp from trying to fight him. She felt his belly against hers and then the familiar slide of him into her. He held it there. The terrible thing was that, after all the spirit she had felt in her before going to sleep and all her fighting and thinking she'd hate it, she was as crazy about it as ever. It had been so long.

"Oh, Rafe," she said, "Rafe!"

"No complaints now!"

"Rafe, be good to me. Like you used to be!"

"I'll be good," Rafe said, starting to pump her.

"I mean, be *nice* to me—" No matter how crazy she was about his being in her again, his breath was so foul she had to turn her head away.

"You oughta know what's good and what isn't," he said to her between strokes. "Christ knows, you've had enough of it with the others to judge."

"Oh, Rafe!"

"Say I'm good."

"You're good. You always were!"

"Good as Acie?"

"You bastard! Don't talk about him!"

"Why not?" He kept steadily pumping. He knew her like an old map; he was driving her crazy, no matter how she was hating what he said. "Come on, tell me. Am I as good?"

"I wish you'd stop talking!"

Rafe stopped to rest; nothing like giving it out slow. "I always wanted to know what it was about him. What did he have I don't

327

have? Little hands waving around on the end of it or something?"

"Bastard!"

Rafe started up again. "Think. You can remember," he urged.

"No, I can't remember! Oh, Rafe!"

"Uh-huh. A little rest has done you good. The same old places are there, and I'm finding them."

"You sure are! But please, don't talk—"

"Like that one?"

"Yes! Yes!"

"That's my old lady!" He was letting her have it deep, taking his own good time, but holding himself well in check. He had her right on it, several times, but each time he got her to the brink he stopped.

She was grinding wildly. "Now!"

"Just you lay still," Rafe said. "You haven't told me about Acie." She was turning her face from side to side, gasping, trembling all over. Even in the old days, he'd never had her any wilder, any more screaming for it than this. "Well?" he asked.

"What do you want me to tell?"

"Was he as good as me, better than me?"

"When it's like this a woman can't tell. It's all the same—"

"Oh, no," Rafe said, "it's never the same, don't give me that. A man likes to know."

"I— I told you I can't remember."

Rafe grasped her, not letting her move a muscle where it mattered. "So you can't remember?" He was close to his climax, but he was going to make her answer. He got her there again, held off, then felt her go limp and furious beneath him, her rhythm lost. "You going to answer me or not?"

"Shit!" she hissed at him. "You shit! Getting me that far, then making me lose it—"

"No answer?"

She said nothing. Rafe couldn't have held off another second, whether she answered him or not, he came in a flood of rage, then lay atop her, sweating and breathing heavily, after a minute rolling away from her onto his side.

"God!" she cried. "How I hate your guts!"

"You wouldn't tell me. Tell me now." Rafe was still horny and could have gone back and fixed her up, would even have liked it himself, maybe.

But she said, "I'll tell you this much, Rafe Cadle. Nobody, not Acie or anybody else, ever left me like this, hanging."

"Well, you can hang," Rafe said, getting up from the Castro, returning to the bath. "And you can get off that big ass of yours and make me my breakfast. I'm hungry."

Rafe could drink like he did because he always ate. Much as she hated him, she knew if she crossed him now, it might get worse. She made him coffee and fried his eggs the way he liked them. He had a terrible hangover, but he had shaved.

"At least part of you's clean," she said to him. "Why don't you wash the rest and change your clothes?"

"Why the hell should I?"

"If only for the customers."

"I'm clean enough for what I have to do," Rafe answered. "A grease job on the Hubbard Pierce." That meant using the old-fashioned, hand grease guns he kept for the purpose, the crankcase splatter, the distillate he would use for the wash job. He squinted at Mae. "That question you wouldn't answer—that wasn't the only one. There are others, lots of them."

"Like what others?" Mae spat at him.

"Where did Edie go?"

"I don't know."

"You know."

"Even if I knew where she *went,* I wouldn't tell you. I hope she's got sense enough not to come back here."

"She'll come back. She'd better. Well, later you're going to answer my questions. All of them."

"Yeah? When?"

"When the time comes."

"I'm going to get out of this place!"

"Oh, no, you're not."

Mae looked apprehensively at the phone wires, ripped and lying on the floor. "I'll figure a way. I'll get out somehow."

"I'm going to be right downstairs," Rafe warned her. "You try." He balled up his right fist and brought it lightly to within inches of her jaw. "You just try."

Spot, the Misses Bowyer's dog, customarily spent hours of every day lying in front of the red shale wall, often in the road itself. He was not a very bright dog and owed his survival less to nimbleness than to the carefulness with which motorists slowed for the bridge and exited from it; if Spot had ever been nimble, he was no more, and lay wherever there was a patch of cool shade, letting cars and pedestrians make their way around him. Spot had a forlorn expression, as if he was aware of being halfway between jackal and wolf, unable to give his whole allegiance to either Miss Flora or Miss Emmeline. When he was not being walked or washed by Miss Flora and was settled upstairs on Miss Emmeline's bed, he attended only to her, and Miss Flora did not exist; downstairs he was Miss Flora's, and behaved as though he owned the world, lying in his road, indifferent to the drivers of cars and trucks who, seeing him at the last moment, braked and swerved around him, cursing. Sometimes Spot raised his head and feebly wagged his tail in recognition, but no more than that. It was his right to lie in the road, his attitude conveyed, and Miss Emmeline, when arguing with her sister the advisability of letting Spot lie where he pleased, supported him. "After all, we own to the middle of the road and the state passed through with our permission. Our Father told me that, when he conveyed the property to us and explained the survey papers."

"The state!" Miss Flora's voice was bitter. "Don't speak of the state of Pennsylvania to *me!*"

"Perhaps if you telephoned the governor again," Miss Emmeline suggested. She looked wan and tired; the Gypsy had worn her out; she had not been herself since.

"The governor absolutely refused to speak to me *personally*," Miss Flora said, "and none of the idiots he kept sending to the phone made the least sense. Little secretaries. I explained that the Russian machines are *quite* audible, not that any attention was paid to my warning. It goes to show. Probably it was equally impossible to warn Hindenburg about Hitler."

She had reason to be bitter. For all her efforts to bring what was obviously happening to the attention of the authorities, she had had no thanks and, moreover, no results. No one had come, not even Willie Bentrup, which would have been the least, *the very least,* the governor could have done.

To add to the Russian anxieties, it was proving an unusually noisy day, even for the Corner. The heavy traffic buzzed in the glass foliations of the Venetian mirrors downstairs in the shop, and jets breaking the sound barrier caused vibrations in the vitrine in which the Waterford glass was kept. Diversions, quite possibly, of fifth columnists obscuring what was really taking place. But even so, the Russian machines were flying overhead, the sound they made of so high a frequency, evidently, that only a dog could detect it—Spot had registered it and responded to it all night, whining and whimpering. And there had been the jukebox blaring till all hours in the luncheonette, not to mention that dreadful Cadle woman screaming drunkenly from her window. Miss Flora had rung the Cadle phone, to bring the woman to her senses, but the operator had reported the line out of order— obviously untrue. Lies were everywhere, and the depredations continued—new stones missing and the yellow rambler rose that had adorned the wall for many years was wilted, probably dead at last, from Dr. Ingle's relentless spraying with his poison. The rose, clearly, was not the only thing he had sprayed, for tiny apples, hardly formed and no larger than marbles, had begun to fall from the apple tree even before dawn. All day Miss Flora had raised and lowered windows, unable to decide whether letting in air and noise from outside was better than enduring the cool, damp stuffiness within.

"Where is Spot?" Miss Emmeline cried suddenly; she had not had her sleep, and was feeling nervous. "I want Spot!"

"Spot's lying in the road, alert to warn us," Miss Flora said. "He's not much protection, but all we have."

"We should have him with us here. Then we can all go together. Do you remember Our Governess telling us how, when the Zeppelins flew over London, the nannies would stand by the cribs, so if there was a direct hit—"

"That was the 1918 war, Emmy; this pouring of hot lead will be different." Miss Flora rose. "Spot's not had his bath. It's not safe to use the pump, so he'll have to do the way he is."

"Flora, do hurry!"

When Miss Flora got downstairs, Spot was nowhere to be found. She looked up and down the road and everywhere in the garden, calling until she was hoarse, but there was nothing to do but go back upstairs.

"I couldn't find him, Emmy."

Miss Emmeline began to cry. "They've taken him! That's the way they start, taking people's pets!"

"Don't cry." Miss Flora tried to give comfort. "We'll probably hear him at the door any moment, asking to be let in. The gate's ajar."

"But is that wise?"

"The gate no longer closes—the latch has gone with the stones."

"Oh, dear! My Midsummer Man, and now Spot!"

"Emmy, be brave! Russians are no joke!"

"But what if we should survive the lead, Flora? We don't know who they will be!"

"The one who'll take over has a name beginning with K, though I suppose it's different in their alphabet. Where *can* that Bentrup be?"

"You reported that Spot has been taken?"

"Immediately."

Another of the tiny apples dropped from the tree. Miss Flora, usually so adequate, was beginning to show strain. To have been a taxpayer for years, and to have been refused the governor's ear! What it all came down to once more was the state police and Bentrup. She supposed Bentrup must be sleeping somewhere, in his squad car, because even when she had reported the noises emanating from the Cadle place, hours ago, he had not investigated. Miss Emmeline had been shocked by the shouting bout between the Cadle woman and Hubbard; though she had not been able to see clearly what happened, every word had been audible.

"I can't get that word—what the Cadle woman called Mr. Hubbard—out of my mind," Miss Emmeline said, coming back to it. "Morph— It was Morph-something. What does it mean?"

"Emmy, I don't know." Miss Flora had evaded the question a dozen times, but now she considered it would be wiser to discuss the word, frankly and openly, and close the subject. "I believe what she intended to call out was 'hermaphrodite.'"

"Oh!" said Miss Emmeline. "But is it biologically possible? We must ask Miss Hankins. She'll know."

Miss Flora let it go, there was so much else to worry about, such as the intermittent, flashing sheets of light, which seemed to come from sunlight striking the windshields of cars, but which, from long experience, both sisters had learned to disbelieve.

"The kite lights are flying again," Miss Emmeline observed, her voice quavering. She held up her hands. "That Gypsy said my palms were white. They're not white at all! Something is going to happen to me!"

"Of course, dear, she was wrong," Miss Flora agreed. "Now we know who they all were—you were right about that. Surely, other people must see and hear what we do?"

"Evidently they don't, Flora. They never have."

"Yes, we're all alone." Miss Flora sighed. "If even Bentrup won't come, help can hardly be expected from other sources. You don't think Cadle—" She broke off, remembering that the garage number had been impossible to reach earlier.

"Cadle is a monster, and his wife—*if she is his wife*—is worse," Miss Emmeline discouraged in a hissing tone. "*I* never considered she was any too white. The daughter—"

"Or the Hanters?"

"I should prefer the hot lead. She's a prostitute and there's no telling what he is. Flora, haven't you guessed why they bought our west lot? We were so unsuspecting! We should have known!"

"I suppose so." Miss Flora looked very tired. "There's Mrs. Glidden—she *is* by way of being a lady—"

"No better than that Hanter woman, really. I suspected those rhododendrons from the beginning. She must have known we *knew*."

"There are those young people, the MacFindens. No," Miss Flora answered herself. "They own quarries."

"That leaves Dr. Ingle," Miss Emmeline summed up. "*He's* been in league with them for years. Remember the stones and the roses!"

Miss Flora began to pace the bedroom. "We must try to alert someone." She turned. "Emmy, I have it! Do you remember the time we telephoned President Eisenhower?"

Miss Emmeline sniffed. "I remember the White House said he was playing golf!"

"He never called back, of course."

"Heaven knows what the present incumbent is playing at!"

"But I'm going to try anyway, Emmy," Miss Flora said. "It's all there's left to do."

"Have we the White House number?"

"Yes, I made a note of it—you recall we looked it up in Our Mother's *Social Register*." Miss Flora went to the phone and dialed o and gave the number NAtional 1414. A pause ensued. Miss Flora repeated the number. Another, longer, pause; Miss Emmeline could hear the operator's voice in the transmitter, crisply repeating something. Then Miss Flora: "But I *never* use code numbers, neither area ones nor any others! I gave you the White House number, and I expect you to put me through immediately. *Immediately*, do you understand? The fate of the nation may depend on it!" Another pause, after which a special operator came on, then another, until Miss Flora was out of patience. "No," she repeated, over and over, "I will *not* dial direct! You are a monopoly, a servant of the public—*and this is treason!*" She replaced the receiver, returned to Miss Emmeline's bed and sank down.

"What happened, Flora?"

"That was no use either. All I got was numbers and codes. Codes! As soon as I catch my breath, I shall go higher up."

"I don't think you can go higher up than the President," said Miss Emmeline. "And if you can't be put through to him—"

"It's too late anyway; *they've* taken over already."

"But what will we do?"

"Wait," Miss Flora said.

"If only Spot were here!"

More apples dropped from the tree. The apples continued to fall all day. Sometimes they fell singly; at other times Miss Flora and Miss Emmeline would be startled by the tattoo of clusters striking the earth together. Miss Flora closed the shop and tried to put her mind on preparing a last meal, but she wasn't hungry and her heart wasn't in it. Miss Emmeline had no appetite, either.

Ever since the phone call from Dr. Kidder there had been the lightest of gauze reserves between the young MacFindens. Nancy felt guilty for having doubted Don, guiltier still for having looked up Dr. Kidder in the Jersey directory, though, heaven knew, it was the simplest of curiosities, a wifely and solicitous enough thing to have done. Don knew the phone call had been a mistake, though Dr. Kidder's, not his, and a piece of bad luck; in future, he would take his father's advice never to tell your wife anything you didn't absolutely have to. "Old Kaiser Wilhelm had one thing right, when he said women should have only three interests—church, children and kitchen," the elder MacFinden had said before Nancy and Don were married. If only, after hanging up after Dr. Kidder's call, he had shrugged it off! But he had begun the white lie, becoming blacker each hour. He suspected Nancy was capable of taking his falsehood to the mat and tussling with it until she got the truth; irrationally, he blamed her for her suspicion of him, as he secretly blamed her for being so damned difficult to satisfy in the sack. Well, satisfied she should be, and next night, he had promised himself as he got into bed.

Nancy had been feigning sleep when Don came out of his bath and spoke her name. I wonder if this is what marriage is going to be like, she thought as she lay in the dark. Not yet really settled into a new house, and already she was sure Don had lied. Or fibbed—what difference was it? When the Gypsy commotion was going on and the men went up to the intersection, she had taken the opportunity to ask Mother MacFinden about the company doctors.

"I don't think it's doctors," her mother-in-law said; "there's only one, Dr. Bensberg. Why?"

"Oh, I somehow got it into my head it might be Dr. Kidder," Nancy replied, keeping it light.

Mother MacFinden shook her head. "I've never heard of any Dr. Kidder. As long as I can remember, the quarry doctor's been Dr. Bensberg. He knows all the steady men and the drivers, all about the policies Papa Mac carries and fills out the compensation forms when there's an accident."

"I see," Nancy said, dismissing it for another subject.

Now, at night, much came back to Nancy that she'd only half noticed in the daytime. Don had looked so odd, almost fugitive, as he came in—late—before the showing of the slides. He hadn't half eaten his steak, which was unlike him; but then, by the time the men got back the dinner was ruined anyway. And, though at midday he had been so excited about the slides, she had noticed his preoccupied expression as he sat beside the projector. She had taken over much of the commentary, and the inadvertent inclusion of the slide of the phalluses near Uxmal seemed to put the seal of disquiet on the whole evening. Don's suggestion, too, that she join him in drinks before going to bed had seemed a little insistent; after all, the honeymoon was over, or at least tapering off; they were supposed to be getting into the routines of ordinary living, and drinks before bedtime were a far different story from drinks before dinner. Before settling herself for sleep, she almost asked Don about it again, but not quite; after all, she had pretended not to be awake, and if she had spoken, he would have caught *her* out in a lie. Two lies, really, because she had denied him the sex she knew he wanted and needed.

Next morning, as she cooked breakfast and watched him tuck it in, making up his lunch pail the while, she was feeling a little sorry for herself. Other husbands didn't insist on lunch pails; they ate a sandwich at a hot dog stand somewhere. And all those limitations as to the foods she could and could not serve! Ham, beef, potatoes, pie, cake, but no chicken, turkey, lamb, liver, fish, greens —yellow vegetables only. When could she make and enjoy those aspics and mousses and other "made" dishes, in the preparation of which her mother had so carefully instructed her? She was a light eater and would have been happy with black coffee for breakfast, a salad for lunch and a nice casserole for dinner. Curiosity about the phone call still nagged her, and as she packed his thick ham sandwiches, she said, "Don, darling."

"Hm?"

"Where were you Tuesday night between leaving the quarry and coming home?"

"I wasn't anywhere. I had to stay late, to see about the driver who hurt his foot."

"You said it was his hand that he hurt."

"Did I?" Don frowned, remembering too late. "Yes, I guess I did. It was a multiple injury, it turned out—both hand and foot."

"And you were at Dr. Kidder's seeing about that?"

Don put down his knife and fork. "Who said I was at Dr. Kidder's? *I* didn't say it."

"But weren't you?"

"Well, yes, I was, as it happens. What about it?"

"Only that I think it's odd you'd go all the way up to Dutch Falls simply to discuss this driver's compensation."

"You've no idea how strict insurance companies are," Don said, trying to save it, getting in deeper every minute. "Verification, request for treatment, all that."

"Oh," Nancy said, clearly not believing a word of it.

Don looked at her quizzically. "Say, how did you know Dr. Kidder's at Dutch Falls?"

"He has a Dutch Falls telephone number."

"And how in hell would you know that?"

"I looked him up in the directory."

"And what if he is in Dutch Falls? What if I was there?" It was the very first time he had spoken to her roughly. "What made you go to the trouble of looking him up?"

"It wasn't any trouble—as soon as I found he wasn't a Pennsylvania doctor."

"Doll, what in God's name is this?" Don demanded to know. "Why the inquisition?"

"I'm simply worried about you."

"*Me?*"

"That you're sick or something and aren't telling me."

"And what does that mean, 'or something'?"

"I thought you weren't telling me the truth about Dr. Kidder's call. I couldn't help worrying, and while you were up at the intersection, before dinner, I asked Mother Mac about the company doctors."

"What would Mother know about company doctors?"

"She said the only doctor she'd ever heard Papa Mac talk about was Dr. Bensberg. She said she'd never heard of Dr. Kidder."

Don looked like an angry kid, the way he flushed, but he was not going to give in. "In our family," he told Nancy hotly, "the men take care of their end and the women mind their own business."

"All right," Nancy said, closing his lunch pail, looking at him almost defiantly, "but you can't blame me for simply *asking*."

Maybe Don should have let it go at that, but he didn't. It made him furious that Nancy had looked up Dr. Kidder. He said, because he had to know, "You didn't do anything stupid, like calling Kidder up, did you?"

"Of course not! Why would I do that?"

"Because you didn't believe me."

"Not that he would have told me anything. Doctors don't."

Don was sweating, though the air conditioning was running smoothly. "You still don't believe me, do you?"

Nancy said nothing.

"That's the way it is, isn't it? You think I've lied to you?"

"Not if you tell me you haven't."

Don ducked this. "Look, doll, for Christ's sake! Let's not get into a swivet over nothing. We've never quarreled, let's not start. How's about forgetting it?"

Nancy knew he was evading, but she agreed. "All right."

"And kiss and make up."

As she let him take her in his arms, she was half sorry she had brought the subject up. "Darling, I'm sorry about last night. I was tired."

"Never mind. It keeps." He nuzzled her hair. "Tonight we'll make the hay."

"You were tired too."

He released her. "Not very."

"You were snoring the minute you hit the pillow."

"Then you must have been awake, if you heard me." He stared at her. "All right, I wasn't born yesterday. I get the message." And, taking his lunch pail, he went out without saying goodby.

All during the day, Nancy kept thinking he would call, to say he was sorry, but he didn't. She kept going over and over the Kidder thing. Don had lied about something. You couldn't forget a lie. Husbands did not lie, unless there was something to conceal. Was he sick? Had he caught something serious in Mexico, along with the Montezuma's Revenge, from which they had both suffered briefly? There were terrible diseases that didn't show, like some kind of osteolysis or something she'd read about in a magazine, in which the bones of the body slowly disappeared. You saw people on the street one week, and the next heard that they had died. Young people, like themselves. If it had been anything but a "medical" lie, it would have been different. And the breakfast airing hadn't settled a thing: there the lie still was, unexplained.

Don's asking if she had called Dr. Kidder had planted an idea; she considered ringing the Dutch Falls number—but no, she couldn't do that. Nor could she discuss her feelings with anyone. Mother Mac-Finden would have gotten very upset, and her own mother, she knew, would have laughed at the whole thing and told her to forget it, which she tried, unsuccessfully, to do. All in all, she had a poor day.

But her day wasn't a patch on Don's. Once at Number Three, he started thinking about the relentless curiosity of women, wives specifically. Tell them one little detail, and they had to know it all. Maybe Nancy would start taking the house apart, looking for evidence, and find the C.T.A. Reason, of course, told him there were millions of chances against this happening. Still, she might decide to rearrange the bath shelves. Hell! It was then he remembered that the C.T.A. was less important than Nancy's having pretended she was sleeping when she was wide-awake, waiting until he started snoring. That one hadn't been hard to figure out: Nancy was tired of sex, because she was never satisfied. That was it. And there was only one thing to do, or rather two things—let her go without it for a night, punish her a little for her punishing him, and *then* let her have it, with full benefit of the C.T.A.

Back to the C.T.A. was a sweat, too. The formulation of the technique, the circumstances by which he would, at first anyway, keep the knowledge of it from her while using it, was a knotty problem. It would have to be dark, certainly, but that could be easily managed, though it would be a switch from his usual habits. He was highly oriented visually, he had early explained; he liked it with the light on. But would it be possible, even in the dark, for him to come to bed already wearing it? That would be simplest for him, of course, but that way danger lay: he would have, somehow, to keep Nancy from performing the ritual scrotal caress which he had taught her. Those elastics that held the thing on would be a dead giveaway, even if her hand did not stray to the C.T.A. itself. It had been advertised as tender to the touch in the prospectus, but from handling it, especially when it was lubricated, Don knew it would fool nobody. It was resilient, yes, but sprang back into shape at once when pressed, like the plastic fabrication it was. Carrying it in the pocket of his dressing gown, as he had last night, probably had been a bad idea; he had planned, after foreplay in the dark, to slip it on quickly and make the "unobtrusive" entry Dr. Kidder spoke of. But having tried it on first in his bath, this did not seem an encouraging possibility; it required real dexterity to get the elastics looped exactly right around his balls. Damn! By now, he was so browned off thinking about it that he wasn't going to call it scrotum any more, not to himself. It presented an almost impossible problem. He remembered the way the thing, which was convincing enough when in place, had come loose in Dr. Kidder's office and plopped to the floor.

Two alternatives to the headache presented themselves: one, simply to *tell* Nancy about the C.T.A. (not show it to her, but introduce the subject subtly and discreetly, playing it by ear, to see how she'd react); or, two, forget the whole thing and throw the C.T.A. as far as he could throw it and the hell with it. The trouble was, he couldn't make up his mind about either. If he discussed it with Nancy beforehand (subtly, discreetly, of course), she might go all to pieces; whereas if he was lucky enough to use it successfully once, she might accept it, as he had gotten used to that damned rubber-and-talcum-smelling pessary her gynecologist supplied, and which they had used at first before the control pills. As for getting rid of the C.T.A., that presented almost as difficult a problem as a *corpus delicti*. Throwing it, however vigorously and far—where might it not land? It was plastic and virtually indestructible. If he tossed it into the river or canal it might come bobbing up months later, washed to his doorstep by a spring freshet. He could always mail it back to Dr. Kidder, let *him* get rid of it. (It might even, if unused, be returnable to the manufacturer.) Or bury it? There, again, it could be dug up, perhaps by a child, who would develop some kind of neurosis about it. Could it be burned? Memory supplied him with experience of occasional plastics thrown into fireplaces along with debris by mistake: they had either proved invulnerable to fire or had curled into odd shapes— even more of a problem.

Well, he would have another day in which to think about it and come to a decision. That night, when he got home, he went at once to his bath, breathing a sigh of relief that the C.T.A. was as he had left it, undisturbed by Nancy's housewifery, undiscovered. Nancy was as cool as he was. After a quick supper, during which they exchanged not one word about the Kidder question, they both turned in. Don had made up his mind that he was not going to speak the first word of reconciliation, and dropped off to sleep quickly. But Nancy, who had made the same resolve, lay awake a long time. This time she had something new to cry about, not only the memory of the nights at Mérida and Chichén-Itzá, but a first marital quarrel, than which, she decided by morning, there is nothing more bitter. She thought Don might be lying awake, too, but couldn't be sure. She went to sleep only after dawn, and by the time she got up it was midmorning and Don had gone.

CHAPTER 3

As Miss Hankins stood at her tower bedroom window that morning, doing her calisthenics and deep-breathing exercises, she wondered how much hotter it could become. Hot tea, her panacea for all ills from chills to fever, no longer cooled her. She had been only mildly serious when she said to the Misses Bowyer that she had been too long on this case; but now she thought she might be better off to take a pulmonary patient spending the winter at Luxor, some old boy on his way out with bronchiectasis or emphysema, but with all his marbles—no more old ladies who couldn't tell snow from birds. Egyptian cases paid well, and Egypt might be fascinating—no hotter, at least, than Pennsylvania in summer, certainly drier. She might even catch a baronet and end her days with a handle to her name. ("Yes, m'lady." "No, m'lady." "At once, m'lady.") Miss Hankins' impressions of Egypt had been garnered from girlhood readings of Robert Hichens, and for a few lovely moments she saw herself in solar topee and veil, drifting along the languid Nile with a sexy dragoman in attendance, and perhaps—because she would be widowed by then, bronchiectasis and emphysema being the diseases they are—she might, just might, permit herself the prerogative of English ladies. . . . But all she could see, actually, as she breathed *in*, out, in, *out,* was the modern house of the young couple named MacFinden across the road; she had seen them once or twice, and they looked to her as though they'd be more at home at Little Tooting than in a structure that had cost, local rumor had it, close to six figures. Well, America, Americans. Her own American was rapping with her cane (*stick!*), ready for breakfast, and Miss Hankins, setting her jaw, went in to meet Mrs. Hubbard's mood of the day, whatever it might be.

It appeared to be somewhat abstract and on the whimsical side; she asked for her usual coffee, fruit and toast, and when Miss Hankins brought it, behaved as though something had been forgotten, regarding her with the oddest expression.

"Well, how are we today, really?" Miss Hankins inquired.

"How am I *really?*" From the moment she opened her eyes, Mrs. Hubbard was sure it was her birthday. She waited for Miss Hankins to make some allusion to it (after all, eighty-three!) but, when she did not, asked, with the peevish severity that characterized her mornings, "Miss Hankins, have you forgotten?"

Miss Hankins looked concerned; Mrs. Hubbard rarely used her name except in reprimand. "Why, no, dear," she replied. "We've had our first white pill, and the angular blue one and the pretty spansule you take with your breakfast and the *scored* red one—you *did* take your spansule?"

"Yes, yes, I took them all."

Mrs. Hubbard had many accessory ailments—spastic colon, gas, allergies. Miss Hankins always worried that her charge might conceal part of her medication among the toast she chewed but did not swallow, and dutifully checked trays when she carried them back to the kitchen. With invalids of Mrs. Hubbard's age you could never be sure they were not disposing of pills another way, throwing them into the *chaise percée*, perhaps. Mrs. Hubbard knew too much—her figure of how many Nembutals were needed to assure never waking up had made Miss Hankins doubly apprehensive. She kept all medications locked up, of course, but now she also counted remaining pills and spansules daily, as an extra precaution.

"Well, since you have no memory, I'll have to tell you," Mrs. Hubbard said. "You may wish me happy birthday."

"Your birthday's not until Saturday."

"It's today. Certainly *I* should know. It's my birthday, nobody else's."

Nothing would change Mrs. Hubbard's mind. All morning she talked about the dress she would wear that night and urged Miss

Hankins to begin doing her hair. "I think I'll wear my Harding blue. Or, no—on second thought, I think my Grace Moore blue is softer and more becoming. Is it pressed?"

"I'll press out whichever you decide on when the time comes." Miss Hankins hated pressing anything.

"Whatever happened to Grace Moore?" Mrs. Hubbard wondered. Miss Hankins grimaced at the question, fearful it might bring on a demand for a session of those tiresome, scratchy old gramophone records of Gerry and Caruso. "She burned up in an air crash."

"The poor dear! Mr. Hubbard and I never flew, we used the Cunarders," Mrs. Hubbard remembered placidly.

Miss Hankins strung her patient along. Odd, she had hated the very idea of the party at first. But there you were, invalids. At least she was feeling cheerful, wasn't going on about being sick of life and wanting to die, or making those strange, unanswerable commentaries about Mr. Ted's and Bo deWillig's relationship. Miss Hankins noted the exact medications of the last twenty-four hours, so she could suggest to the doctor that a good balance had been achieved, and that mood amelioration and psychomotor responses were better than usual. When Teddy came upstairs after lunch, she managed to have a word with him in the hallway, before he went in.

"I've tried to keep her quiet and she does seem in good spirits. She's a little nervous from the heat and her memory's playing her tricks. She thinks today's her birthday and that the party's tonight. I can't get it out of her head."

"I'll see what I can do with her," Teddy said. He went into his mother's room, went to her chaise longue and kissed her. "Now, what's all this about your birthday being today?"

"So you're not going to wish me happiness, either," Mrs. Hubbard said. "Oh, dear!"

"But her bladder pills have been working very well," Miss Hankins said. "I don't understand this sudden—"

"Teddy," said Mrs. Hubbard.

With great care and gentleness, Teddy lifted his mother from chaise longue to *chaise percée* and back. "You're both in league against me," Mrs. Hubbard insisted. "This *is* my birthday!"

"No, Mother, day after tomorrow. Saturday's the party."

"Oh, why will you both try to mix me up? You ask me to keep in a good mood and rest, and I do. Now you tell me I'm wrong about my own birthday!"

Teddy looked at Miss Hankins. "Dear, dear!" Miss Hankins reproved. "Temper. And we were so cheerful and bright till now."

"I wish you'd stop using *we* in addressing me." Mrs. Hubbard intercepted a wink Teddy intended for Miss Hankins and, unexpectedly, softened. "Ah," she said. "A surprise, is it? Well, I'll pretend."

Teddy had a further colloquy with Miss Hankins outside the door. "Since she's got it all mixed up anyway, maybe we can move the party up to tomorrow night. Though I dislike weekends that begin with the climax on Friday instead of the Saturday."

"I know what you mean, Mr. Ted," agreed Miss Hankins. "Shall I go along with her on this surprise idea, then?"

"Let her think what she likes."

"You see?" Mrs. Hubbard triumphantly said when Miss Hankins returned. "It's a surprise. I can always tell when people are trying to fool me. I wonder what it can be."

"We find out about surprises when they happen, dear."

"So we'll pretend it's *not* my birthday."

"But we can get ready, just the same."

"Yes, always good to be prepared. And it's rather like royalty, in a way, celebrating when convenient. I remember when I was presented—long before your time. Queen Alexandra was in her heyday—brown satin and diamonds to match. And Melba after dinner."

Miss Hankins had heard the story often. She was so sick of it that she decided to go down to the laundry and press out the blue dresses so they would be ready for the party, whenever it might turn out to be. Later, much later, when she had hung the Harding and Grace Moore back in the closet, was when things got really out of control. Mrs. Hubbard, who had been looking sly, suddenly remembered that, because of the many obit readings earlier in the week, the Sunday *Times* brides had been put aside.

Miss Hankins doggedly found the society section and read them out: "The bride wore an ivory peau de soie with a lace mantilla that had been her grandmother's. She carried gardenias and stephanotis. . . . The bride wore an Empire gown of white crepe and a tulle veil attached to a white crepe pillbox. She carried a bouquet of lilies of the valley and stephanotis. . . . The bride was attired in a gown of white net embroidered with Alençon lace over peau de soie. She carried a missal with white roses and—"

"And stephanotis!" finished Mrs. Hubbard angrily. "Must they all carry stephanotis?"

"They all seem to favor that."

"What's happened to simple garden flowers, and muslin?" Mrs. Hubbard wanted to know. "I was married in muslin—very smart. When Teddy takes his bride, I'm going to suggest that she carry something simple. No stephanotis."

"But Mr. Ted has no plans to marry, at least not at the moment," observed Miss Hankins with diplomacy.

"I am hard to fool." Mrs. Hubbard raised a forefinger. "The longer they wait, the harder they fall. *I* think, from the way he's been behaving, that he's found some lovely girl at last. I do have all those diamonds, simply wasting away in the bank box, and my pearls, too, which haven't been fed for years."

"Dear, I think you—"

But there was no stopping Mrs. Hubbard. "The diamonds are rose-cut, of course. I do hope Teddy hasn't gone out and bought a stone, when all he has to do is ask me for it."

Hankins, said Miss Hankins to herself, her eyes closed tightly, it's time to leave a case when it gets this bad. But manners and habit were too strong. Opening her eyes, she said, "Dear, I think we've had too many brides. I think your nap, now."

"Yes, I must be fresh. And I'm going to surprise Teddy, as well. When he introduces the girl of his choice to me, I'm going to offer her my pearls."

After settling Mrs. Hubbard comfortably, Miss Hankins put a hand to her hot forehead and, with the intention of pouring herself a tot of brandy, made her way downstairs through the dining room to the pantry. Her intention froze. Beyond the swinging door into the kitchen, she could hear Teddy and Bo in heated argument.

"*What* did she call you?" Bo was asking.

Miss Hankins heard an unfamiliar word.

"Women!" cried Bo. "Wives of drunken mechanics! In Sweden

the woman would be whipped like a horse! Surely, you are not going to take that lying down?"

"We have ways in America better than horsewhipping," Teddy assured him laconically.

"When do we leave for Cannes?"

"Only when I've finished the Long Island job."

"And then only by ship, I suppose!"

"Naturally."

"But ships are so *boring!* Why can't we fly?"

"Bo," said Teddy, "you can always eat and drink yourself into ten pounds of overweight, and then have it beaten off at your muscle beach."

"While *you* are on the phone with Kuhn Loeb, or is it Morgan?"

"What do you think pays for Mother Carlton?"

"I know. But *I* never have any money," Bo said bitterly, "and if you die tomorrow, where will *I* be?"

"Life's too short to start that one again," Teddy said. "You'd better get on with the food for the party."

"At least, there won't be any women there. I can't abide women at parties."

"You might remember that my mother's a woman, though an old one. The party's for her. Miss Hankins is a woman, too."

"They look like a couple of old drag queens to me."

"Bo, I've had about enough of that!"

"Oh, don't go on about it, just because *you're* old!"

Miss Hankins listened in pained embarrassment. There ensued a silence during which, for some reason she did not understand, the quarrel seemed to end. When Bo spoke again, it was of something else.

"I put in extra measures of gelatin in the blancmanges, to make sure they'll stand up when I unmold them. Don't you think the pink makes them simply too chic? Juice from the maraschinos. But do you think everybody will know what they're supposed to be?"

"If they don't, they'll be nuns," Teddy laughed.

"I always suspected nuns know as well as everybody else."

"The pudding's more important."

"If we could once, *just once*, have something besides fairy pudding," Bo complained in his Swedish singsong. "A barbecue. Cold cuts. But no! Fairy pudding, fairy pudding! I'm sick to death of it."

"At least you know how to make it, and it stretches. Considering how stinking you'll be when it's time to dish up—"

"Why wouldn't I be stinking? You're so mean. In Stockholm, anywhere else, a man with your money would have servants. I wouldn't waste my day making fairy pudding!"

"You know servants make Mother nervous. Stop bitching—you couldn't wait to run up that dessert."

Miss Hankins had been privy to many harangues of the kind. When she had first heard of fairy pudding, she had imagined it would be a frothy ice, light as gossamer, instead of the rather heavy casserole of noodles, canned tuna, capers and sliced black olives that it was. She had even eaten it, when shepherding Mrs. Hubbard during parties. She couldn't agree more with Bo, that something different would be a good idea.

At this moment the telephone rang. Miss Hankins, knowing Teddy would answer it on the pantry extension, pretended to have only this moment arrived. She held open the swinging door as he came through and joined Bo in the kitchen.

Bo stood at the sink, wearing a chef's white cap and apron. He was surrounded by open cans of tuna and the copper molds filled to the brim with the pink blancmange. "Hello, Hanky," he greeted her. "You're just in time to see the dessert before I put it in to chill. Aren't they divine?"

Miss Hankins looked coldly at the tall, copper molds. "I always thought shapes so much trouble," she said.

"But, dear, you must tumble to what they are. You're a nurse."

Miss Hankins had never dropped a hairpin since coming to work in the house, and Bo never tired of trying to break her down or of telling Teddy how "wise" he was sure she must be. Miss Hankins, straight-faced, said, "What I'd give my eyes for is a plain gooseberry fool, with a bit of Bird's Custard on the side."

"Really, Hanky, you're such a spoil-sport!"

"Hankins, if you please, Mr. Bo."

By then, Teddy had concluded his phone conversation and Miss Hankins returned to the pantry and poured herself two fingers of the house's best. Trust Bo to come in and make a remark about it.

"Brandy? At this hour?"

"I felt faint."

"Why?"

"I simply felt faint," Miss Hankins repeated.

Bo laughed. "Have another, then."

"I intend to."

"Where did Teddy go?"

"I wouldn't know." There were sounds in the garage, and almost at once the Mercedes appeared and turned into the road. Miss Hankins finished her second brandy and went out, across the dining room, to where the Inclinator waited. The brandies had done no harm. As she ascended, she wished Oscar Wilde could see what he had started. Hanky, indeed! Hankins, she instructed herself, you will give your two weeks' notice tonight. Oh, yes you will, m'lady. Indeed, m'lady, you will!

Dr. Ingle's Thursday schedule was lighter than on other days of the week, and, as was customary, he came home early. He found Susan in the living room, for once not playing one of her chain games of solitaire, but reading. She wasn't smoking, either. It was Mrs. Schaaf's night off and Ingle expected that after a couple of cocktails they would go out somewhere for dinner and that Bobby would join them—if he hadn't a date.

"How were the Tulips today?" Susan asked routinely.

Ingle kissed her. "Both One and Two quiet, even placid."

"I'm glad. I hate to see you working so hard, giving so much of yourself. I've put the martini tray out."

Ingle went to the hunt board in the dining room and put ice into the pitcher. "One for you too?"

"Of course. Is there some kind of drink that simply wipes out everything that's happened up to now, do you suppose? I wish there were—tonight I'd have it."

Ingle stirred the drinks, poured them and carried them into the living room. "Is it that bad tonight?"

"Well, isn't it?"

"Is he upstairs?" Ingle asked.

"He's been in his room all day, except for coming with me to Olympia when I shopped. He asked to."

"Did he talk to you?"

"He as much as said you'd asked him to be careful what he said to me. Well, he was careful. He said hardly anything. All he does is watch the Cadle place and phone over there."

"I suppose it'll be Edie Cadle every night now."

"I don't know. Dick, I know it's no use any more asking you to talk to him. I'm sick about it."

"I talked to him last night."

"And?"

"Nothing."

"Nothing about his staying out all night?"

"What we both knew anyway. I tried to tell him what he's getting himself into, but he only told me Edie's not like other girls and he wants to take her out of the situation. I asked how he expected to do it, with no money, and he came back with his line about deciding about tomorrow when it comes."

"Do you wonder I'm sick about it?"

"No. I'm sick about it too."

The telephone rang. Before Ingle could reach the downstairs extension, he heard Bobby rush from his room and answer it on the stair landing. "It's for you," he called down.

Ingle picked up the receiver—merely a question from one of the Tulip nurses about sedation for a patient. "Why don't you come on down?" he called to Bobby, when he had hung up. "We're having a drink and then we're going out for dinner."

To the surprise of both, he came at once. He was dressed as though to go out.

"Are you going out?" Susan asked him.

"No."

"Oh."

"Make yourself a drink, if you like," Ingle said.

"I don't want a drink."

Silence.

"I think you might say something," Susan said, after a long minute.

"What is there to say? You both know what I'm waiting for, why I'm staying home."

"I'd think you'd be sick of staying up in that room," said Susan.

"I am. But that's nothing new. I've been sick of sitting around the Corner and waiting for something to happen for years."

"Don't start on that again."

"You ask me to say something and when I do you don't want to hear it."

"Let him say what he likes, Sue," Ingle said. "Go on."

"I've done a lot of thinking up there."

"I suppose you have. What about?"

"Not making mistakes."

"What mistakes?" asked Susan.

Bobby raised his shoulders and spread his hands. "Look around. Something's the matter with this place and everywhere else I've been. From what I figure, the next thing will be my military service and after that a life of trying to be the dog that doesn't get eaten up by the others. Financial tie-ups, kids, mortgages—you're through at forty, tied down, and keep knocking yourself out for the kids until they lay you in the grave—ahead of the widow. Look at the old girls you play bridge with, Mother."

Susan let the "old girls" go by. "I'm not a widow."

"And even the grave's not tax-free," Bobby said; "only passing the buck to the kids for keeping up the cemetery plot."

"You used to have such good manners," Susan said. "You still have them, if you'd use them."

"I'm sick of what you call good manners, too. What are they but an admission that everybody has to pretend to fool everybody else? You spend a lifetime using nice-guy approaches, saying things you don't mean to people and wind up not knowing what they're like. Dad's supposed to know what people are like. My God, Dad, if you do, how do you stand knowing? I've seen some of the Tulip case folders."

"Not all people are disturbed or neurotic or psychotic," Ingle began. "Your brother Houghton—"

"Don't get onto old Hoot again. What Hoot decided to do with his life has nothing to do with me."

"But you've got to be trained for something, someday work," said Susan impatiently. "No one expects you to be like Houghton, but you'll have to take up something, some business."

"No business for me."

"But why not?"

"Because I've read a lot up in that room. I even know some of the jazz about it. Power controls. Spot checks. Created error programs. Being bonded. Supervision. Method procedures. No thanks, I'd rather be undercover."

"By which you mean what?" Ingle asked.

Susan interrupted. "None of this has anything to do with what's really the matter—Edie Cadle."

"I've been told to be careful what I say about that," said Bobby.

"Yes, I know," Susan answered. "Bobby, do you realize that if you were to marry that girl, you might have a *black* child?"

"The chances are thirty-two, sixty-four, even greater against such a thing happening," Ingle put in.

"Who said anything about having children or getting married?" asked Bobby. "I've been talking about *not* getting married, *not* having kids."

"Bobby—I've tried to accept that you have intimate relations with girls. Your father's made it clear—"

"How would either of you know if they're intimate or not?"

"I saw when you came in after being out all night how you looked. You'd felt *some*thing," Susan insisted.

"If we're talking about Edie, I got to know her better," said Bobby.

"We are talking about her," continued Susan, "and if you have intimate relations—"

"—there must be consequences?" Bobby asked.

"Of course there must be."

"No, no babies," said Bobby. "Remember?"

"I don't mean just babies, I mean emotional consequences."

"Well, if there are, I'm not going to be thrown by them."

"I think you are being thrown by them," Ingle disagreed. "And where, if you don't mind my asking, is Edie?"

"I don't know," Bobby said. "That's why I'm like this, because of something she said to me and because I can't reach her." He waited. "I took out my savings from the bank today."

"So that's why you asked to go into Olympia with me!"

"Yes, that was why."

"But that's only a few hundred," Ingle said.

"Yes, only a few hundred."

"Well," said Susan, "I can tell you that whatever it is you think you're going to do, that money won't go far. You'll find everything comes down to money."

"And Dad says money's not everything. I've had both versions from you for as long as I can remember."

"Both are true," Ingle said. "Bobby. What we're both trying hard to tell you is, don't do this rash thing. Your mother and I would never have had what we've had between us, the kind of life we've had, if we'd done anything so foolish."

"You mean, you've had happiness?"

"That is what I mean," Ingle said.

"And you, Mother. Have you had it too?" Bobby asked.

"Of course I've had it! Your father and I've always had it!"

"I don't believe you. I think you've been miserable."

"How dare you! Dick, are you going to sit there and let—"

"Yes, let him," Ingle said. "Go on. Why do you think that?"

"You really want me to go into it? Tell you?"

"Yes."

"Well, when I was still a kid—"

"You're still a kid to us—"

"Sue, let him say what he wants to say."

"I'm trying to tell you," Bobby said. "I think I was eight, or maybe nine. I had whooping cough and I started to cough and choke and couldn't make you hear me. So I got up and went out into the hall. Neither of you heard me. You were both in bed in your bedroom—before Mother moved into the front room by herself and you into your study. What you were saying at first sounded like so much gibberish to me, but then I began to make it out, though I didn't know what it meant then. I couldn't help hearing it. It scared me so I stopped coughing. Mother kept asking you where it had gone, what had happened to it. She was crying. I didn't know what she meant. I supposed it must be something that had been lost in the house. And then the bedroom door opened and I saw Mother's face, and she said, 'God help me, Dick Ingle, if I stay with *you*! It's gone, I tell you, over. *You* with all your mental screwdrivers'—those were the words exactly, *mental screwdrivers* —'you never knew what I'm all about, haven't the faintest idea. If you loved me, but you don't really.' And then I worked hard to remember it and I did. I still can recite it perfectly, as I've just done. Next day you both pretended everything was the same."

Both heard him out in complete silence. Then Susan said, "But all married people have troubles. If men and women let little things like quarrels make any difference—"

"This wasn't a little quarrel, Mother. And it wasn't the only time I heard it. Hoot used to hear it, too. It was always the same quarrel, about how it had been lost. When I began to understand that what you both pretended in the daytime was all a pretense, it cracked something in me. I've never believed in either of you since. I made up my mind long ago that I was never going to pretend one thing while feeling another. Or pretend one thing was something else. Dad, that was what I meant, my answer, when you asked last night if I love Edie."

"You're talking a lot of rot," Ingle said.

"No, I'm not. You both lead lives of making believe everything's okay and jake. You play these parts for each other. Dad, I've heard you, conning Dr. Gough and Dr. Braithwaite with all that square work about The Good Woman, and I've heard Mother with her bridge girls doing her big Southern Belle act. She even does it with me—you did your Antietam act only the other day. You're both of you made up of these parts you've made for yourselves. I've often wondered if you ever really look at yourselves, see how you look to others. Me, for one."

Susan was beginning to show strain and nerves. She had listened expressionlessly. Now she said, "You think we're phonies, is that it?"

"I didn't say that."

"But you meant it," Ingle put in. "Has it never occurred to you I've spent my adult life getting behind pretenses, to try to make people understand themselves, believe in what they are?"

"Yes," Bobby answered, "but how can you really be good at your job when you're so busy being somebody you're not?"

"I think you've said quite enough to your father," said Susan.

"I haven't said anything you don't know already."

"I don't know it!" Susan cried. "If you were like Houghton—he was always so loving! If your father and I've had our troubles, if he knew of them, he tried to understand and loved us the more!"

"That sounds like something from the end of Act Two," Bobby said.

"You're being pretty rough on us, for someone who's a failure,"

Ingle told Bobby cuttingly. "Why don't you turn that merciless searchlight on yourself? Think how you look to us!"

"I've tried," Bobby answered. "I've tried to swallow this family business—"

"What do you mean by that?"

"The assumption that the family as an institution works."

Susan's face was rigid. "Bobby," she said. "Bobby, please!"

"It doesn't work," Bobby continued. "Look around you. Dad, you see it all the time at Tulip. All those people strangers to themselves, strangers to husbands, wives, mothers."

Ingle was getting impatient. "Have you any idea how dull and stupid and boring what you're saying is? At Tulip we have people —a few of the very few people capable of helping others—"

Bobby laughed. "Yes, I know. I used to think people like you really *knew,* Dad. But when I began to notice the kind of people head men and head women marry, I changed my mind."

"I don't have to take that," Susan said, getting up.

"You apologize to your mother," Ingle said.

"I apologize—"

"And to me, too."

"Dad, I didn't mean you. Present company excepted always," Bobby said. "I meant kooks like Mrs. Braithwaite. I've heard you tell Mother yourself that she was somebody Dr. B. met while she was in treatment. A schizzy-schiz—your word for her, Dad. And Mrs. Gough, too—isn't it true that she has to go away every couple of years because she can't stand anything and goes all to pieces?"

Ingle said nothing.

"I'm not going on with this, Dick," Susan said. "Bobby, you've made us miserable, simply miserable! You make me wonder if I've done anything right."

"You did lots of things right, Mother, both of you. You've left me alone."

"If we leave you alone, it's because we've both tried to do everything for you and you won't have any of it," Ingle said. "We don't know what it is you want!"

"I want reality."

"You're standing in the middle of it, if only you knew it."

"I want to be myself and I'm going to be," Bobby stated, and with that both Susan and Ingle gave up and went out to dinner. Bobby stayed home, waiting for some word from Edie.

CHAPTER 4

By now, the intense heat was being taken for granted, as well as the high humidity that hung above the valley and seemed hourly to increase; people despaired it would ever rain again, ever again be cool.

Miriam went to the studio window, where a jar of peonies—the season's last, picked days before, by Rosa—withered. Her movement, merely that of crossing the room, disturbed the flowers, and as she reached for the jar, the petals of the peonies dropped instantly, as if flung, to the floor. Beyond the window she could see Tavio in the blistering sunlight, working at the far end of the garden; because of the great pink dogwood that drooped over the canal, she could see only his head, a handkerchief knotted around his hair to keep the sweat from his eyes. She thought, My God! This is Thursday—I have weekend people coming and he's still here! Dully, she stooped and swept up the peony petals and carried them and the vase to the kitchen, pouring out the ill-smelling water, set the vase on its accustomed shelf. She felt powerless to do anything; for the last day, she had moved from one small household chore to another, like an automaton. Tavio had, countless times, declared he would go, had seemed about to go—but here he still was. She had tried every bluff she knew, but nothing in the least would hurry him. Returning to the studio window, she watched as he cut out a creeper, balled it in one hand, placed it in the cart in which he had dumped weeds and grass cuttings. There was nothing she dared talk to him about now without waking up hostility. He was restless and bored with himself. Their spasmodic dialogues had flickered, like day lightning, through the summer hours; between waking and sleeping she watched him, listened, saying less and less, doing as he told her to do.

"Why do you stay?" she asked, watching his somber, black eyes as they regarded her. "There's nothing more."

"Oh, yes there is."

"But you said you would go!"

"Not yet," he always said; "there are the flower beds still to be edged, and the honeysuckle that needs clearing out."

"But I don't want you to work any longer."

Tavio only laughed.

She feared trying to deter him from working in the garden; his growing silences frightened her more than any of his talk at night or during the days before. She surmised that some new resolve was developing behind the veiled blackness of his eyes, his deepening watchfulness of her. His outbursts of hostility terrified her—he would suddenly appear at the doorway and unleash a string of accusations, as though a predetermined hatred existed in him and he was directing words at her designed to make her do something, take some action against him.

"You were getting ready to run out on me," he would say. Or "I heard you phoning—you've called someone about me."

She could only guess what he wanted her to reply; denial he wanted, certainly, and, exasperated, she gave it. "That's not true, I've called no one."

"Sure? You're telling me the truth?"

"And what if I had called?" she flung at him.

A pause. Then "You're pretty fond of your own company, aren't you? For the last day, you might have been alone here, as far as I'm concerned."

"If you knew how I wish I were alone!"

"You and all those dirty canvases. *His* dirty postcards of you!"

"If only you'd go!" she said miserably, his voice telling her another of his precipitous approaches was to follow. "No!" she cried, and stretched out her hands against him.

He grasped them and said, in the voice of an old lover, as though this were a game leading to a purposeful protraction of pleasure, "You like to fight me, don't you? It's more fun for you that way, isn't it? Did you fight like this with Cort?"

She closed her eyes and set her teeth—she could no longer beg him not to speak of Cort, only endure. And it was the same once more; he picked her up and placed her on the sofa and, suddenly placid, as though having possessed her only hours before made more time for them now, embarked again on what she recognized as a pattern in the way he took her—the ruthless baring of her breasts, burying his face between them, the slow descent to her belly, followed by the flinging slap of himself upon her. She let him do as he pleased, only her rigidity betraying she wanted it to be over, dropped into a nothingness in which she felt nothing. It seemed to her she had slept with him forever, that there never had been anything but this suffocation.

"Some like it fighting," he told her, having finished, as he pulled on his shirt and got into his pants. This, at last, gave her his weakness; he was tiring, slowly, but tiring nevertheless; the work he insisted on doing in the garden and wearing himself out in bed had begun to tell; he looked tired and spent. Now he spoke less of her, found his strength in boasts of how he was too much for her, how much he could do. But she could see her growing unresponsiveness disturbed him; the silences between them were lengthening; the cries of delight he had drawn from her at the beginning were no more.

All was hatred between them now, and the dream Tavio had had the night before sealed it. It was as vivid in Miriam's recall as though it had been a dream of her own. She had wakened and felt him trembling beside her, some terror erupting through his breathing, usually so deep and untroubled. The moon was inscribed in the circular arch of window beyond the bed, flooding the room with that particular full moonlight that has no color, only gradations of light and shadow.

"Maria!" he cried in anguish through chattering teeth. "Maria Anna! Anna! Maria Anna!"

"Wake up," Miriam said, shaking him, since he seemed to be choking, but though he opened his eyes and stared at her, she saw he was still asleep, still locked in his dream. When at last he sat up in the bed, hands covering his eyes, his body trembled. "Are you sick?" she asked.

"No, it's only a dream I have sometimes," he answered, his voice uneven. "It leaves me like this."

She reached out and touched his shoulder, but he drew away, shuddering. "It always begins the same way," he said; "the butterfly settles down on me and covers me and I feel warm and happy, the way I used to feel in church—when I first saw the saints and they were not plaster and the candles were light, not just wax. I believed. You know?"

"No, I don't know."

"But then the butterfly sucks out my breath and when it goes away tears my skin with it."

He was wonderfully touching, almost childlike as he spoke, and she felt more possessed by him than at any other time. For the first time she understood that for someone, someone else, loving him would be possible; until now she had thought him incapable of love, and that real tenderness and the absorption of another through it was beyond him. Through his dream she saw that what he searched for was not a symbol, but his own reality, just as she understood, of herself, that not until she had been utterly possessed and defeated could she accept the idea of being alone. For Tavio to have a woman, as he had had her, was not to fall in love but fall into fear of not forgetting Maria Anna.

"It's all like that," he gasped; "the colors of the butterfly pulling me out of sleep. I wake up feeling like ashes."

"Did you know that you spoke her name?"

He turned, questioning. "Whose name?"

"Maria Anna's; you said it over and over."

"Did I? I can't remember that. God!" he cried. "God!"

Miriam watched as he got up and prowled around the room, standing naked in the moonlight, staring out of the window into the white mist above the river. "You speak your name when you are awake the way you speak hers in sleep. You love her," Miriam said.

"No!" he protested. "I hate her—she's that one-way street named 'wife'—I told you about that."

"You told me. But you can't forget her."

"That's true." He got back into bed.

"What's she like?"

He sank back onto the pillows, hands at his sides, palms upward. "She's small and dark, not like you. Her legs are short, I don't like women with short legs." He turned and clasped her knees. "You— you're what I like."

"But you dream of Maria Anna."

He sighed. "Only to get her out of me. Hold me."

She put her arms around him; he felt soft and relaxed as he lay

358

beside her, the daytime hardness and tautness gone from him, his skin in the grayish-white glow yielding to her fingers. Then, galvanically, he stiffened, took her in his arms.

"Forget the dream," he said.

"It wasn't my dream to forget."

"But forget it," he commanded.

"It's for you to forget." His insistence, self-absorption, angered her.

He was silent a long time before he could speak again. Then he said, "If only it could be another butterfly I could fight it, but it's always the same one." He made a rough sound in his throat, ashamed to have revealed so much, and drew her closer. He no longer asked her consent but mounted her in the classic position, resting his elbows beyond her shoulders, thrusting, waiting, thrusting again, falling back exhausted. All encounters were one and the same to her now, except that now, with each one, time and hours were returning to her and she knew she was beginning to win over him through sheer passivity, hours passing, then hours in clusters becoming past, forgetfulness, a slow Nirvana, then an entire day, days. . . .

BOOK
SIX

C H A P T E R   1

The country freshness that, on most summer evenings, followed on a sweltering day had been lacking this night. From sunset to dawn the Corner and the entire valley lay beneath a blanket of humid heat that did not lift. The big, overloaded trucks, heaped high with crushed stone from the quarries, began rolling as early as four-thirty, as they did every morning except Sunday. They approached the Corner by way of the bridge from Subberton, air brakes squealing and hissing, black exhaust piped high above the driver's seat, then shifted gears at the stop signs and roared along the narrow road downriver. The noxious, black clouds drifted across walls and hedges and filtered into houses through windows that had been opened for air, such air as there was. Shouts could be heard as sleepers, roused by the trucks' clamors, rose and slammed the windows shut. The trucks rode the middle of the road's twin dividing lines, but even so, the many broken shoulders caused their metal superstructures to shudder and clatter and the sharp stone they were carrying to spill over the sides and spatter the roadside.

All during the night Miss Flora Bowyer's tremulous voice had been heard calling, "Spot? *Here,* Spot-Spot-Spot-Spot!" Sometime during the day, Spot had pushed his luck too far and wandered down the road, past the Fringes, where Miss Flora's calling could not be heard, toward Olympia. Late merrymakers saw him as he trotted back toward the quadrangular grass plot, supposing he was a night animal of a kind. When the first truck came toward him, he was trying to get past the railroad crossing, where drivers turned off for the quarries. But the driver didn't see him, and when the rounded, snubbed fender struck, it tossed Spot high in the air. He landed a good ten feet to the side of the road. For the space of time it took the next stone truck to appear, he lay stunned, then got up and, limping, started out again. This time the driver saw him and swerved, but too late. Spot lay in the middle of the road, a small, white, furry mound. For the next hour he looked like himself, white, with a single, dark marking. But before long the wheels that passed over him crushed him to a visceral bas-relief, bright as only blood and bones are bright; and then, as though being flattened for dissection, he became thinner and still more thin, and dun-colored. As he thinned, he was no longer a dog but anything that had got in the way—a squirrel, a groundhog, any small animal —and, at last, he did not look like anything at all, not even dead. Something that seemed a discoloration of the road was there, and when the road scrapers came by, they scooped up the something and Spot disappeared forever, one of the smallest, least important casualties of the summer. Miss Flora still could be heard, calling ever more hoarsely, "Spot? *Here*, Spot!" until, at last, her voice gave out.

What with party preparations beginning and the hasty, unscheduled trip he had to make to Long Island and back, to assure the client who had telephoned that her loggia was absolutely perfect, Teddy Hubbard didn't get back to the Corner until very late. But he was a daylight riser, and, knowing that Rafe Cadle opened early, and anxious about the Pierce, strolled up to the garage. Mae Cadle, he hoped, would not be around, because he had a score to settle; her fierce, nocturnal tirade had both soured and enraged him, and he intended speaking to Rafe about it. Not a dressing down, he couldn't afford that, because Rafe was the only mechanic within a radius of a hundred miles who understood the Pierce's perpetual and whimsical needs; a delicate allusion, nothing more. He found Rafe running a damp, finishing chamois over the Pierce's fenders.

"Good morning, Rafe."

"Morning, Mr. Hubbard." Rafe turned and touched his nonexistent forelock in respect. Despite being on the stuff still, he detected at once something different in Hubbard's mood and voice. "Yes, sir," he said, "got her all shined and ready to go. Bright as a new penny."

Teddy examined the fender repair and let his hands travel lovingly over the headlamps.

"Okay?" Rafe asked, worried.

"Seems fine," Teddy answered, but not looking directly at him. "About time I gave you a check, isn't it?"

"Don't you worry about that."

"I'll write it now, if you'll tell me what my bill is." Teddy unclipped his pen from his shirt pocket and waited.

Rafe's forehead corrugated. He habitually sent Hubbard a bill at the beginning of each month for servicing all three of his cars, and Hubbard, as habitually, dropped off a check next time he came by, thereby saving the nickel postage. "No hurry, Mr. Hubbard," Rafe said. "Anytime."

"I'll pay you now."

"If you insist." Rafe, whatever his faults, was a gentleman's tradesman; he never pressed for a bill, however due and unpaid. Still frowning, he went to the greasy old golden-oak desk, in which he kept his account book. He told Hubbard the amount and looked at the check Teddy wrote out and dropped silently onto the desk.

Teddy let the silence that developed extend to the breaking point. He saw how terrible Rafe looked, smelled how drunk he was; the whole place stank of whiskey; it obliterated even the usual acrid grease. Then Teddy said, "I came by before, thinking the Pierce might be ready."

Rafe looked at the floor. "Guess we were closed. Mr. Hubbard, you should pat yourself on the back. You're a lucky man, no goddam woman to drive you to drowning your sorrows."

If you knew, Teddy thought; but he said nothing.

"A little domestic trouble," said Rafe. "Christ, I must have been out cold. I didn't hear you when you came. Not that the Pierce was ready, I hadn't give her the grease guns."

"Your wife was here," Teddy said.

"She could have woke me."

"Oh, I wouldn't have let her do that, Rafe. I could have wished, though, that she'd been a little more courteous."

Rafe heard the fancy tense. "What do you mean?"

"I hope it was only that she was drowning her sorrows, too," Teddy answered, face impassive. Then he grimaced. "Because she went out of her way to be unpleasant."

"You mean, nasty?"

"Well, yes."

"What did she say? Tell me."

"I wouldn't care to repeat what she said. Best forgotten, I suppose; but I thought I'd mention it."

"Goddam right!" Rafe said. He was very upset. "Jesus Christ, Mr. Hubbard! You're one of my best customers, and you always treated me right—"

"And you've always treated me right, Rafe."

"Tried to. I *like* working on your cars, never none of that shit about estimates, how much will it cost, just go ahead. What in the name of smoking Jehoshaphat did Mae say?"

Teddy got into the Pierce and, after priming the tank, started the motor. "Open up the door for me, Rafe, will you?"

Muttering, Rafe hastened to throw the switch that caused the garage doors to rise, and Teddy Hubbard guided the Pierce to the gas pumps. He was silent as Rafe filled the tank.

"Mr. Hubbard?"

Teddy waited, putting the Pierce again into gear.

"You won't tell me what it was Mae said?"

"Maybe she'll tell you, if you ask her," answered Teddy, driving away.

Rafe, before he went upstairs, located his pint and put it into the pocket of his overalls. Mae was at the stove.

"You've really done it this time," Rafe said to her.

"Done what?"

"Wuddia mean talking to Teddy Hubbard anyway?"

"Could I help it? He was knocking the door down, wanting his old Pierce."

"And you pissed him off!"

"Don't you start that dirty talk with me again, I'm sick of it!" Mae fought back, cursing herself for having lost her temper with Hubbard.

"What did you say to him?"

"I called him a dirty old morphadite, that's what I called him,

366

and God knows it's the truth! He had it coming to him, beating on the door that time of night. Besides, he's never shown me proper respect!"

"Respect? *You?*" Rafe's laugh was a snarl.

"Yes, respect—not that you'd know what it is."

"You musta been drunk."

"I told you, I only took a few swallows."

"Pity they didn't do you more good," Rafe said. "Christ! Women! To think I ever got into bed with you!"

"You filthy pig—you should see yourself," Mae said. "Any woman that'd let you touch her'd be crazy. Besides, you were no good!"

"No good?"

"You hung me up, didn't you?"

"On purpose," Rafe said.

"Maybe, maybe not."

"You'll stay hung. You got no worries on that score—I wouldn't touch you with a ten-foot pole or my brother's prick!" He took the bottle from his pocket and raised it to his mouth, swallowed, put the bottle back.

"That's right! Talk dirty. Get drunker!"

"You ain't seen me drunk yet."

"At least Edie's not here!"

Rafe sobered momentarily. "Well, why isn't she here? I told you—"

"I don't care what you told me! *I* told her to get out and stay out till you sober up and come to your senses. I ought to call in the police, that's what I ought," Mae said, warming to it. "There's laws against men bothering their daughters in that way."

"Edie's not my daughter and you know it." Rafe's chin was wet where the shot of whiskey had run down from his mouth, and, wiping it with the back of his hand, he came lunging toward Mae.

"Don't you lay a hand on me! I'll scream, so help me God, I'll scream so loud Bentrup'll be here in no time!"

Rafe cuffed her across one cheek. "Now try screaming," he said. "But before you do, you're going to tell me the truth about a few things. The truth at last, Mae." He grabbed her by the front of her brunch coat, holding her. "Tell me where Edie is!"

"I don't know."

He cuffed her other cheek, harder. "You know. If you don't tell me, I'll break your head open!"

"I— There wasn't anybody— You ripped out the phone."

"*Where is she?*"

"I told you, I don't know. Honest!"

Rafe lifted his hand and struck her full across the face. Mae let out a howl of terror, but Rafe stopped it by slapping her across the mouth. Her lip cracked and started bleeding. "All right, you don't know. But you're going to level with me about Acie. She's his, I know it! Isn't she?"

"I've told you and told you a thousand times, I was never sure—"

Rafe let her have it on the jaw this time. "You're sure. Tell me one way or the other."

In a voice strained and hoarse, Mae pleaded, "Don't hit me any more, Rafe. Yes, I'm sure, now. Now you know. Now I've seen Acie again, I'm sure."

"You've seen him again?" Rafe's red eyes opened wide.

"I couldn't help it."

"When did you see him?"

"He—it was Wednesday or whenever." She was dazed, finding it hard to think. "The Gypsy night—"

"So that's where Edie is? With Acie?"

"I had to get her out, away from you—"

"Whore. Nigger lover!"

It was then that Rafe started forgetting what he did. He'd beaten Mae before, countless times, but this time was different. As he brought his fists down on her, a great exultation flooded through him, like an orgasm long delayed. And he could do it again and again—nothing to it, strike her and watch her fall, pick her up and hold her until he could hit her again and watch her fall. It was almost as if somebody else was doing it for him. He had her standing again now, and with one hand holding her by the neck, doubled the other and smashed her face. He could feel her cheekbone break beneath his knuckles, and when blood shot from her eye socket he felt a sharp, prickling pleasure, the greatest he had ever felt about her, sex, anything. It was like eating and drinking and screwing and paradise and he did it again, shifting his hold on her, this time striking the other eye. Magically the piercing

368

pleasure ran through him. He had broken her nose this time, as well, and was glad.

Mae was screaming like a whole sty of pigs, but Rafe didn't care. He went to work on her body next, punching with all the strength he had in him. He hit her in the breasts and belly until she howled even louder. She was all bent over now, trying to protect the next thing he would go for, but he straightened her up with a left and right to her jaw that sent her reeling against the sink. That knocked the breath out of her and her screams stopped for a matter of seconds, but he kept on, he couldn't make himself stop now. He made up his mind to beat her senseless, until she couldn't yell back at him. Then something happened that stopped him— Mae vomited and fell forward on her face. He stood looking down at her; it made him sick, the way she looked and smelled. Sweet Christ! he whispered, seeing what he had done to her. Her face and hair were covered with blood and her nose was a bloody pulp. Her eyes were beginning to swell shut. Taking her by the armpits, he dragged her to the bedroom and hoisted her onto the bed. She was limp as a sack of oats, all the weight going whichever way he moved her. He wondered if she was dead, but he could see the big vein in her throat pulsating. He'd really laid on, but he hadn't killed her. She had a heart that would never stop. She'd come to. He still had things to do.

There was someone standing in the doorway as he came downstairs to the workshop. Rafe had to look twice to see who it was against the light. Al—Al Hanter.

"God in heaven, man!" Al said. "What's going on up there? I've just come to work—I thought I heard Mae screaming for help."

"Yeah?" answered Rafe.

"Well—yeah." Al backed down a little; it was quiet now, not a sound. "Mae all right?"

"Mae's fine."

"Okay, then." Al waited for Rafe to pass the time of morning, say something, but when he didn't, turned and went back to the luncheonette.

Rafe found a fresh pint and opened it. It looked exactly like all the other pints, only full; he took a long swig. Then he went to the switch that controlled the doors and lowered them—people could honk outside all they wanted, he had his work. He started up the cars he was working on one by one, until he had all motors running. They sounded like music, took his mind off what he had done to Mae, which was so horrible he couldn't bear to think about it. But she had driven him to it with her talk about Acie, her ruining Teddy Hubbard's business for good and all.

In a state between thirst and retching he poured the whiskey into him. It helped him to figure things out better. He hadn't intended beating Mae that hard. He'd done it because she'd cut him down once too often, tried to cut his balls off, as she'd been doing for years by screwing every Tom, Dick and Harry that came by the place. If she hadn't said he was no good, he might have beaten her only a little. What the hell, he'd only given her what she deserved. She'd get it through her head now that he wasn't taking anything off her again, ever.

Ever. Ever was time. What time was it? What day? He got up and went around to all the cars, touching the accelerators, racing them and letting them slow back and idle. Sometimes he felt the sickness he had felt upstairs, yet he kept going, kept at the bottle until it was almost empty. A pint, like all other pints, the same.

Now he didn't care what time it was, felt calm and afraid of nothing. *At last he knew.* Everything was crystal-clear, now. He had a feeling that everything would fall into place, be the way it always should have been. He floundered among the cars, his mind full of mirrors that showed him what he was going to do. He seemed to hold inside him every memory he had ever had, and his mind worked feverishly now to remember them all, to do everything still to be done. Everything was quiet, right for remembering, only the motors tapped and putted. He dozed awhile, finding everything the same when he came awake. At the right minute, he lifted the bottle, drained it, threw it across the shop and into the waste barrel. He hit the bull's eye. It was funny, he couldn't hear it land.

From then on, things weren't so clear. It struck him that there was a sound different from the other motors running in the shop—a motor *outside*. He moved to the door and saw the pink Cadillac drawing away. Too late for something—for going after Acie. Too late. But Edie stood in the doorway and then, in slow, dragging motion, pushed the door to. It clicked shut, locking itself.

It became, then, a trick to keep her from going upstairs and find-ing Mae. It was easy—he blocked her at the stairway and got her past the doorway and into the shop. He laughed as he did this, feeling the excitement, the youth of her, well up inside him, the old, good excitement he knew so well but now didn't have to keep down. It was a feeling there was nothing wrong about; it had always been right and natural—he could never have felt it if she'd been his daughter. He could do anything he wanted now. Mae would never hear a sound above the motors. Nobody would hear. Nobody in the world.

He slipped off his belt and went toward Edie. She stared at him, eyes stretched in terror.

"No, Papa-Daddy!" she cried. "No! No!"

Rafe smiled. It didn't matter how long it took this time. Grasp-ing her arm, he turned her over his knee and raised her skirt. But when he saw the two round, plump spheres of her buttocks, he no longer wanted to beat her. Caressing them was what he wanted. It was better, too, when he tore her blouse off and at last got at her breasts, falling with her, kicking, to the floor.

"Papa-Daddy, please don't. Stop!" she begged.

He didn't hear it the way she said it; he heard it the way he had always wanted to hear it. "We're not going to stop this time," he promised. "You give it to all the others, now you can give it to me."

That far was clear to him. "You little nigger bitch—you're a nigger, did you know that?"

She fought him fiercely. It didn't matter. "Don't!"

"Did you let your nigger daddy have it? We'll soon find out, I can always tell—"

"Papa-Daddy!" She clawed at him with all her strength, tearing at his chest, his face, but nothing stopped him.

He had to be careful of his own strength. He remembered mounting her, and that the greasiness of the floor made it hard to hold her down. He remembered the sounds their bodies made to-gether and her trembling and her cries. But after that there was nothing he could get straight. There was the way his head felt, as though it had iron bands around it, and a sweetness that filled his mouth, like grapes. He could see. He reached out again for Edie— she wasn't there any more. Then he figured it out—the motors—

the closed doors. He tried to get to his feet to turn them off, one by one, as he had started them, and was sure he had done it, because he could see himself in those mirrors that were slowing him and everything he did. He didn't want the sweet taste and spat, breathing deeply afterward. There flashed into his biggest mirror, brighter and clearer than any memory, himself and Mae when young. He felt everything stop and his body relax and then the bright mirror went black.

Dr. Ingle had days when he wished he could junk Freud and Adler and find comfort in a belief like *Ahtman* (*There is no self, escape from life is possible*) and this was one of them. The heat wasn't helping, and his efforts to talk further with Bobby had met with no success; he was stubbornly remote and appeared tense and resentful. Ever since being unable to reach Edie Cadle he had kept to his room, coming out only to glower through meals and make attempt after attempt to reach Edie on the phone. Not only was there no answer from the Cadle place, but the last two times Ingle had driven by it, the CLOSED sign had been out. That the Cadles, Rafe and Mae, were there could hardly be doubted; outbursts of fighting and loud shouting alternated with no noise whatever. This seemed routine enough to Ingle; his extended period of observing them for his study had accustomed him to Rafe's rising, manic curves and alcoholic descents.

An emergency summons from Tuliptrees early in the morning brought him back to the polarized, psychotic worlds of Tulip One and Tulip Two—a repeater patient, a suicide case, awaited him, and, barely breakfasted and shaved, he hurried to his car.

The shortest and most direct route from the Corner to the clinic was by way of Olympia and, taking full advantage of his MD tag, he sped into the town, remembering only too late that it was Friday and the weekend of the Olympia Street Fair. Though early, he found himself caught in Busy Corner traffic, blocked before and behind by cars full of arriving tourists and trucks loaded with stone. He tried to relax and not grow impatient, for what he would have to try to straighten out at Tulip One would, he knew, require his best energies. Resolutely he let the motor idle and sat waiting for traffic to unsnarl.

Perhaps it was because he usually drove to and from Tuliptrees by the back roads, where he could pass through and enjoy the loveliest river scenery the county afforded, that now he saw Olympia as unusually repellent. A gaunt, artsy-craftsy woman in salad-bowl hat, Ubangi earrings and the inevitable wraparound-sunglasses disguise, squeezed herself between his front bumper and the truck ahead. She beamed at him a conspiratorial smile, which Ingle did not return.

He lighted a cigarette and watched the woman as she ran into one of the art galleries, where pastel portraits were done on commission. The come-on sample in the window was a typical local product, rather like a Breck shampoo ad with overbright highlights and too black around the nostrils. That true black did not occur in nature had never been observed by this artist. Olympia, he thought, was the lower bowel of exurban art, packaged as an aphrodisiacal sausage, one of those pockets that were springing up everywhere in America with the new leisure, fake reality, behind which was the pretense that existence was smoothly surfaced, with none of the edge cracks and laminations of real life.

In the hot sun the youngsters with arms entwined, oblivious of everything except each other, and the middle-aged and elderly moving in droves through the streets, searching for a Bohemia now as rare as the o-o bird and as legendary as the one-winged pihis of the Chinese, exclaiming, straining their necks, as usual depressed him. They seemed so many replicas of human beings, such as a conveyor belt on Mars, working from computer information radioed from Earth, might produce. But whatever might be said against the place, it did seem to offer potentialities for people of little importance or talent. Balding minor actors, instead of turning up on Mitch Miller, fled here, making the scene any way they could, and skipped the hairpiece. Those who did not or could not conform found it a haven, though it had open to them few employment loopholes—running a shop or restaurant (which implied outside income in nine cases out of ten, as well as the likelihood of bankruptcy in equal proportion), waiting table, washing dishes, baby-sitting or being kept in one of the socially acceptable or unacceptable ways. Ingle's colleagues, Dr. Gough and Dr. Braithwaite, alluded to Olympia as Failure Beach, saying it was a town of losers. Braithwaite often joked that the place needed panache and that, on retiring, he expected to open a Harry's Bar on Main Street, where you could find someone who spoke your language, as you did at Sank Roo Doe Noo in Paris, or the Calle Vallaresso in Venice. The poetry of moral failure and wasted lives was here, as Tuliptrees files bore witness, no matter how ardent the self-admiration campaign conducted "in depth" by local journals and the town fathers.

And I must hurry toward one wasted life and moral failure from this very conveyor belt, Ingle reminded himself impatiently, feeling his pulse rise, growing more and more nervous in the unmoving line. Against all his principles, he sounded his horn along with the others being held up. The din was deafening, but the traffic moved only imperceptibly. For another span of minutes, seeming like an hour, Ingle inched forward and sat staring at a canvas banner stretched above the Busy Corner intersection. TURN LEFT FOR HISTORICAL BARN AND GAY NINETIES GIRLS, it read. "GOOD GRACIOUS, GRACE!" TWICE NITELY 8 & 10. The GAY NINETIES lettering had been sewn over the ROARING TWENTIES of the previous year. Street Fair themes, no matter what fresh ideas were promised, alternated between the two; next year GAY NINETIES would be ripped off and it would again be ROARING TWENTIES. The local callipygian ladies invariably pulled on black net hose to the hip and showed all the bust allowed, if it was to be GAY NINETIES, or flattened their breasts, if a ROARING TWENTIES year. All were *récidivistes,* falling back on the cloche hat or the Merry Widow cartwheel. But *Good Gracious, Grace!,* so called or renamed and slightly rewritten, was perennial, heavily lifted from every Broadway success from *Good News* to *My Fair Lady.* . . .

The stone truck ahead slowly began to move. After another minute of shifting and stopping, Ingle was able to cut onto the highway and was at Tuliptrees in minutes. He went immediately to One, where a nurse met him with a thick folder. The woman was his particular patient and the clinic had a long history on her, furnished mostly by herself, but her tests had been thorough, too, everything from the Wechsler-Bellevue Scale to Pin-Man and the Minnesota Multiphasic. This attempt to take her life had been her third in as many years. Her first two efforts had involved overdoses of barbiturates, but this time the means had intensified—she had first swallowed a hundred grains of phenobarbital, then telephoned the clinic and slashed both her wrists. She was known privately to the staff as the Riemenschneider Altarpiece because of her delicate, Gothic appearance. Bringing her around this time had been hard work, the nurse told Ingle, who dreaded the confrontation; questioning the woman was like tangling with a clutch of wire coat hangers on the back of a door or stepping in gum.

"Well, Mrs. Mott," he said, entering the cheerful, yellow room.

"I'm so glad it's you, but please remember to call me by my maiden name," the woman answered. She was still very toxic, her speech slurred and unsteady.

"Very well, Miss Fuller." Ingle examined her wrists.

"They'll heal," she said. "But will I?"

"You'll soon be ambulatory," Ingle assured her.

"So I can go to the movies in the lounge and see all those ha-ha sea gulls flying off the cliffs? Who cares?" She made a sound very like a sea gull heard far away.

The etiology was unchanged. It was the same with her each time. She was in her late fifties and an hysteric, well-off financially, with no problems but herself. Though several times married and divorced, she clung desperately to her maiden image, as though by so doing she might rediscover the bright hope of her youth, which had been to become a sculptress. A sculptress she was, of bureau drawers pigeonholed and sprayed gold, of forest logs whittled and sprayed gold also. There was not much that could be done for her; she was ungifted, and beyond her desperate, self-invented therapy she could not go, ever. But she was defiant, following every change of fashion in art, swallowing whole the ideas of others. She had been reared, too, to believe that all men, if fallen in love with, could become the elusive father figure she sought. She was older than Ingle, but already he felt the tugs of transference.

"What are you going to do with me?" she asked, raising one hand and pulling awkwardly at the sleeve of his tunic.

"I think it's rather what you're going to do with yourself."

"I've tried to do as you said, meet everyday problems as they arise, live one day at a time, but I always come to this. I don't understand why."

"You always call help. That should suggest to you that there's hope."

"I'm just yellow," she said. "And sick."

"Yes, you are sick."

"Even so, I *am* an artist!" she cried out in her unsteady speech. "Though nobody besides me seems to think so."

"Don't think of that now. Think of what we can try to do—to get at the true reasons for your doing this thing over and over."

"You can't blame me for being what I am!"

"No one blames you."

"I blame myself!" Stretched out stiffly beneath the sheet, with once-golden hair now dyed and needing retouching at the roots, she seemed more than ever like an altarpiece figure. "What am I going to do?" she implored him agonizedly. "I want to be *big time!* I can't stand failure!"

"You're not entirely a failure, you've exhibited," Ingle began, but she interrupted.

"Yes, in vanity galleries, where you pay to show and pay to advertise and pay for the champagne for the critics—who never come! I've had no recognition." Tears formed in her eyes and rolled down her cheeks. "And I deserve it—even as a child I was the talented one, it was *I* who begged for Erector sets, but they were given to my brothers! *I* am the Edna St. Vincent Millay of the America that is vanishing. Why will no one see I have found the real poetry beneath the ordinary?" Her voice rose, haltingly, with the pace of a litany. "I scratch trees as the Indians did, to *communicate*, record the now! I'm at least as good as fifty or a hundred others."

"And do the fifty or hundred others do what you do?" Ingle gave the first challenge.

She evaded it, as always before. "You refuse to see it, too," she accused him through her tears. "Why won't you concede it's true, the plot? It is a plot. If you're not one of *them*, if you don't have those gallery connections and belong to the club, you might as well cut your wrists."

The rancor of the unsuccessful is with us always, Ingle thought. It could have been a tape playback of former sessions. "I am suffering for all who aren't in the club," she said.

376

"You are suffering because—"

The nurse opened the door a crack and beckoned, making a gesture of holding a telephone receiver to her ear. Ingle frowned at the interruption, excused himself and went into the corridor.

"Doctor, I know I'm not to disturb you when you're here at One," the nurse apologized, "but this time I thought I'd better. It's Mrs. Ingle on the phone and there seems to be trouble."

Ingle took the call at the floor nurse's desk. "Yes, Sue?"

"Dick," Susan's voice came tensely over the wire, "I had to have them put me through. It's about the Cadles."

"What about them?"

"Rafe Cadle seems to be dead and his wife may be too. It was Bobby who—" She broke off.

"What about Bobby?"

"It's all so confused and mixed up. I think—no, I know—" She was not making sense, but people under stress rarely do, Ingle knew.

"Are you and Bobby all right?"

"Dick, I'm out of my mind. The police are asking Bobby—"

"I'll come at once," Ingle said, and hung up. He didn't change from his tunic, stopped only long enough to find his bag and this time took the back roads to the Corner, though they were longer. From external indications of the past days, he realized that Cadle's death—murder or suicide, it could be either—would involve a crisis not only with Bobby and Susan, but also with himself. He was already involved in the Cadle situation, though empirically and clinically—but was it any longer empirical and clinical? In a single week—less—a balance had shifted, the shapes in the kaleidoscope had jarred, almost schematically reversing the pattern. It had not occurred to him when he began his study of the Cadles, when he had ambivalently justified to himself the use of Big Ear, that Big Ear might turn on him and blast back. As he maneuvered the narrow, curving lanes that took him first upward to the plateau above the river and then down to the Corner, he heard the blat of the Olympia "siren" and recognized the emergency ambulance signal. Tragedy was already cooling if the downriver squad had been sent for. He pressed his accelerator to the floor.

CHAPTER 2

When Edie first heard the sound penetrating through the other sounds and the thickness of air around her, she couldn't tell what it was. She was lying somewhere—on the floor of the garage, her arms flung ahead and her face cradled between them. The second time she heard it she thought of an animal whimpering. She was almost naked, except for where her torn blouse clung to one bruised shoulder, and when she tried to move she could feel the cold slick of oil on her stomach and legs and arms. It was on her hands, too, and it was when she held them up that she remembered. She had been tired, worn out, when she came in, from fighting off Acie and, finally, getting him to let her alone. Rafe would never have caught her if she hadn't been so exhausted. She had begged and begged him to stop, until she had no strength and no voice left, and when he finished with her she had crawled as far away from the horror of him as she could. The things he had said to her had been like a number on a door she had never quite been able to make out, but now she understood and knew everything, knew that she hated him and what he had done to her and could never forget. Before he let her go he had cursed himself and begged her to forgive him, and she had. But that had been because she had loved him once and now knew who Acie was. The light sleep that had closed her eyes had seemed a small forgetfulness, but now she was awake again and remembering and her head was throbbing with pain.

She heard the sound again, this time loud enough for her to tell what it was—her mother's voice, moaning, calling out her name. "Edie, Edie." She heard it faintly but unmistakably. She got to her knees and found her skirt, wiping off some of the oil and wrapping it around her nakedness. She felt light-headed and the floor was too far down and when she moved out of the shop toward the stairs it was a stagger. Her eyes were smarting from the air— no, not air, *there was no air*. She felt sick from the way Rafe had smelled and the oil and the fumes, and all she knew was that she must get away from what had happened, get to her mother upstairs. "Edie!" she heard the whimpering cry again, then felt dizzy and tripped and fell. She had hurt herself somewhere, but it was only part of the hurt she felt all over. She got up, facing the outside door, and tried to open it, but the knob was greasy in her hands. It took her what seemed a long time to realize that the door was locked. She knew where the key was, in one of Rafe's pockets, but she couldn't go back.

"*Edie!*" her mother's voice echoed down the stairwell. "Help me!"

Edie turned and struggled up the stairs. She got to the landing all right, but then fell again, and had to crawl the rest of the way. She raised herself to the banister and through the spokes saw into the bedroom. What she saw made her so weak she had to wait before she went on. The air was thicker here and, coughing and panting for breath, she half stumbled, half crawled, to where her mother was.

"Touch me," her mother begged, "so I'll know where you are. I can't see—"

Edie laid her hand on her mother's forehead.

"He tried to kill me, he almost did, and now he's trying to finish both of us—"

"M-mom!" Edie formed the word but no sound would come. Her throat felt gagged. "Oh, Mom, Mom!" She finally got it out. "Why? Why did he do it?" The moans her mother made were more terrible than the blood that was everywhere, on her face, her arms, her torn old brunch coat.

"If I die—"

"You won't die, Mom—I'll get you out."

"If I die—I want you to know—"

"I already know, Mom," Edie said. "Papa-Daddy—"

"He told you!"

"Mom, don't talk," Edie said, as her mother tried to get off the bed and stand. She collapsed in a heap.

Edie saw she would have to do everything. With a massive effort, she grasped her mother beneath the arms and raised her to her feet. "Hold on to me. Try to walk. If we can get to the stairs—"

It was like moving limp stone, but by heaving and pulling, Edie got them to the banister. Her mother rested against it, then dropped to the floor. There was nothing to do but drag her. Edie grasped the soft, white ankles and began to pull her down the stairs. There was a last, sharp cry as her mother's shoulders, then her head, struck the treads and she fainted. It made it a little easier because she could be quicker. Edie tugged, hearing the scrape and drag of their bodies as, a little at a time, they made it. It was no longer a stairway but a series of dropping ledges, each wide as a stone's throw, and the landing seemed a city block they could never cross. *Down, if I only keep going down,* Edie told herself. The fumes were beginning to choke her now, with every effort and breath she coughed. *But they were moving.* She saw the fissure of doorway beyond which was the shop and the cars running, running, running, all motors together, exhaust clouding beneath the ceiling. She could see Rafe, lying on his side, near the place from which she had crawled—it seemed days before. Then the cloud became darker and seemed to follow them down. Her mother's breathing was thick and loud and then, after she had moved her, it seemed to stop. But each time it came back, louder, like throttling in an echo chamber. The whole place was full of sound now, the engines like a roar that would burst the walls. There was another sound, too, from outside—someone was beating on the door and calling out her name. "Edie! Edie!" But she couldn't tell who it was. Her heart was beating blood into her eyes, and she could hear it like a drum above the motors. She coughed and this time blood came from her mouth. *If I only can get to the door—the door—to let them know we're inside.* . . . The door was everything. She let her mother's heaviness drop, pushing her forward, then with her last strength tore desperately at the greasy knob as blows from without fell on the thick, hard wood. Through the tears raining from her eyes she saw first a splinter of light; then the splinter became a widening, jagged hole through which air and daylight flooded.

"Get—get them out—" she managed to mouth as the door was kicked open, but she could go no farther because the place she leaned against dropped away from her. She felt herself fall and thought, *This is how it ends, soon I'll see everything, my whole life go by as I watch it.* . . . But she could see nothing and wanted only to breathe.

At least forty people swarmed around the Cadle place when Ingle arrived. Some were passersby, who had got out of their cars and hurried to see what was going on, the faceless pushers at any tragic happening. One of the Jersey Rescue Squad ambulances was already there, and the Olympia emergency crew pulled in as Ingle parked. Among the watchers he recognized Bentrup, trying to hold the crowd back, and a pair of state troopers waiting until the ambulance teams were finished before moving in to make their report. The Jersey boys had been doing everything they could. There were blankets and oxygen tanks near the gas pumps.

Ingle took in the situation at a glance, noting briefly that Susan was standing halfway between the yew hedge of their house and the crowd.

"Dick," she said.

Ingle, shaking his head, brushed past her. He saw that three stretchers lay in a row, far from the garage doors, near the road. A sickening layer of monoxide still hung in the air, though all doors and windows of the Cadle place had been opened wide. One of the Jersey boys, taller than the others, called out.

"Doc! Thank God you could make it! We tried everybody from Bensberg to Kidder and couldn't get anybody. Stand back, let him through," he commanded the pushing onlookers, and, seeing Ingle's tunic and black bag, they made a lane to the stretchers. Ingle recognized the tall boy from times he had brought emergency cases to the clinic.

Rafe Cadle lay on the first stretcher, Mae and Edie on those beyond. Rafe's face was flushed a cherry color and his hands, crossed on his chest, were even a darker red, almost black.

"It's too late for him, Doc," the Jersey boy briefed Ingle. "We gave them all oxygen right away and even used mouth-to-mouth on him, everything. He was a goner when we found him—"

"Get that oxygen going on him again," Ingle directed. "No matter how he looks to you, get it going and don't stop."

Ingle moved then to the next stretcher. Mae, again conscious, was crying out horribly in her pain. "I wish he'd killed me! Give me something to kill me! I can't stand the pain!"

"My God!" Ingle exclaimed involuntarily when he examined her.

"We gave her what we had, but it wasn't enough," the Jersey boy said.

Ingle opened his bag and administered an injection of a quarter

381

grain of morphine. Almost at once the quivering mass of pain became quiet and lay still. "Take her to Abingdon as fast as you can," he ordered the Olympia men standing by. "I'll phone ahead—"

"Phone's dead here, Doc. We had to use yours."

"I'll phone later. Get going!"

The Olympia squad lifted Mae into the ambulance and, siren going full blast, raced up Old Hessian. Ingle turned then to Edie, still with oxygen mask over her face, made sure she was all right and then went back to Rafe Cadle and knelt beside him. With his scalpel he made a quick, intercostal incision, inserted his hand and began manually to massage the heart. A woman in the group watching turned away, and at last the pushers and the curious, who had not been able to get enough of horror, began to disperse. Ingle worked steadily for five minutes, then withdrew his hand and stood up. He had done his best; it was hopeless.

"Towel," he said. "*Towel!*" Though he had been coldly efficient during the chest procedure, it was one he had forced himself to do and it took all the control he had to get to one of the rest rooms to wash up. When he returned, they had covered Rafe with a blanket and were about to move him into the remaining ambulance.

"No, he can wait," Ingle said. "The girl first."

The voices all talked together in Edie's clouded darkness. *Breathe, that's it, breathe deeply.* Her lungs filled deliciously with the sharp oxygen that was like flowers, and when she opened her eyes she saw quite clearly beyond the rubber mask. One of the voices took the mask away.

"Bobby!" she said.

Ingle had been so absorbed that it was only then that he saw his son. Bobby knelt beside the stretcher, taking Edie in his arms.

"You're going to be all right now," he said. "Isn't she, Dad?"

"She'll need rest and care. I'm going to send her to the hospital for at least a week."

"A week. That's nothing," Bobby said.

Edie was, Ingle saw, in the apathetic calm that precedes hysteria. "He couldn't help it, what he did to me," she said. She said it again and over and over, her voice rising, and she began to cry.

"Don't," Bobby tried to soothe her. "Don't cry."

"I want to cry!"

"Let her cry if she needs to and say what she wants," said Ingle.

"Why did it have to happen? Why?" Edie went on, torturing herself. "I hate—I hate everything. It's no use!"

"You'll be fine in a few days," Ingle assured her.

"What if I am? But Mom's dead. He killed her before he killed himself—"

"Your mother isn't dead. She'll be all right, too, though it will be a long pull."

Edie looked first at Ingle, then again at Bobby. "It was you at the door."

"Yes."

Edie closed her eyes halfway. Shock was beginning. The Ingles, the three of them, were the only ones left standing on the Cadle lot as Edie was lifted into the ambulance that had been waiting to take her to the hospital at Abingdon, where she could be near her mother—except for Rafe Cadle, lying beneath his blanket. Willie Bentrup and the two state troopers watched the ambulance draw away and then crossed the road.

"I guess the rest is up to us now, Dr. Ingle," one of the state men said.

"Yes, I suppose it is," Ingle answered.

Willie Bentrup stood looking down at the stretcher covered by the blanket. He leaned down and lifted one corner and looked at the face. "Poor bastard," he said. "You know, I can remember when he still had a chance, or thought he had." He shook his head. "I figured him for anything but this." He dropped the blanket back.

"Come on, Willie," the second state trooper said, embarrassed by Bentrup's words. "We've got work to do before the coroner comes."

Ingle recognized a familiar pressure on his arm—Susan. "Dick!" she said tremblingly. "Oh, Dick!" She was shaking and cold in the hot sun; it had been too much for her. He put an arm around her waist, leading her through the hedge and into their house, Bobby following.

"You'd both better tell me what there is to tell about this," Ingle said, when they had all sat down in the living room. "I have to follow the ambulance to Abingdon."

"But why should *you* go?" asked Susan.

"Because I must. And I want to."

It was a question whether Susan or Bobby was the more shaken by the experience. Bobby, his face drawn and white, said, "We kept smelling the fumes all morning, but they weren't worse than usual, at first. Then I kept hearing sounds—horrible sounds—and I couldn't wait any longer. I had to know about Edie and what was the matter. I'd seen her come in, and after that I knew I had to go over and break in." He swallowed. "You saw the rest."

"Not quite all the rest."

"Well, I broke down the door. I dragged Edie and her mother out and then Rafe Cadle. I think he was dead already."

Ingle nodded, waited.

"And I came back here and called the rescue squads. Mother called you then—or was it then?"

"After the police came," Susan said. Her hands were clasped firmly in her lap but still trembled. "It happened. It had to happen," she said hoarsely. "Dick, you knew it would—"

"I knew nothing of the kind. Your call was the first I—"

"Oh, no!" she interrupted. "You *knew*. The study you worked on so long—"

"No, I did *not* know," Ingle insisted. He looked tired. Life, about which he knew nothing, nothing, had finished the study for him; his own last few touches, to prepare the paper for publication, would be painful anticlimax.

Susan was bent forward, hugging her shoulders, eyes closed. "It's as I tried to tell Bobby," she sobbed. "It's all gray already, getting grayer. It'll soon be all black. I should have known, if you didn't—the noises told me and told me—"

"Susan!" Ingle said sharply.

"Don't try to stop me from saying what I'm trying to say! I've always tried to tell you there are voices underneath those quarry sounds—"

"Control yourself, Sue!"

"I know you won't admit it, Dick—I've known for a long time you think I'm making them up—"

"*Sue!*"

Susan sat up and looked at him, then at Bobby. She sighed. "Go on, now, go. That's what you both want to do, isn't it?"

Ingle went to her and, sitting beside her, took her trembling hands in his. "You're going to be all right."

"Yes," she said. "Yes." She wrenched her hands away, reached for a cigarette, let Ingle light it for her. She inhaled deeply and blew out the smoke. A brief, last struggle seemed to go on inside her. "Bobby," she said, holding out a hand to him. The catharsis had been painful, but she had acquired, Ingle saw, the resignation and acceptance that months of protest could not have brought about. "You want to go with your father, don't you? To Edie?"

"Yes, Mother."

"Then do." She let Bobby's hand slip from hers, found a handkerchief and dried her eyes. Then she reached for her pack of cards and riffled them. "They're not much, but they are *order* to me—you understand that? Dick?"

"We both understand, Sue. Come, if you're coming," he said to Bobby, who, after a last anxious look at his mother, followed to the car.

"Dad, is she going to be all right?"

"I wouldn't have left if I hadn't known she would be," Ingle answered, turning toward Old Hessian and the road to Abingdon. He glanced at Bobby, rigid beside him. "What worries me is, how are you?"

"Terrible! I can't believe it!" He shuddered. "God, Dad—that—what you did to Rafe Cadle! He was dead. How did you make yourself do it?"

"Such procedures are hard even for doctors. I did it because I thought there might be a chance for Cadle."

"You hated him, I know you did."

"Disliked. But that didn't mean I wouldn't do everything I could to try to bring him back."

"Does—what you did ever work?"

"Sometimes."

"I don't see how you did it."

"I've only done it twice before. Both times—and this time—I thought I couldn't make myself do it. To be truthful, this time I was afraid I'd break up. I just didn't. Almost but not quite."

" 'Not quite'—that seems to be it."

"The squeak between the professional and nonprofessional. A lot of life's a squeak, Bobby. You're learning that."

"God, am I learning!" Bobby stared straight ahead. "I learned something else, too, that you and Mother—I mean, what I said last night—I'm sorry I said it because it's not true."

"It's partly true," Ingle replied levelly. "Something goes—as you

385

heard through the door so long ago. That doesn't mean I've stopped loving your mother for a moment."

"It worked. When you took her hands."

"Yes."

They rode for some miles in silence.

"Will I be able to see Edie right away?" Bobby asked then.

"Not right away. She's still in shock. But then you can. You'll have to realize what she's been through."

"I realize it."

"Well, if you do, that's everything."

"Is it?"

"Isn't it? I saw your face when you knelt beside her."

"Yes. I've changed my mind about what I said last night. When I thought for those minutes she might be dead, I knew I loved her. I want to marry her."

"I thought love wasn't in your vocabulary."

"It wasn't, till today. All that time I didn't know where she was, when I heard what was happening—"

"You'd better tell her that, not me," Ingle said, as he drove into the hospital yard and parked. He got out. When Bobby did not move, he said, "I have to go on. I knew I'd have to leave you somewhere, sometime. I guess this is that time."

"Yes."

After a moment, Ingle heard the slam of the car door and Bobby's footsteps as he followed.

Bobby walked slowly into the hospital. It took him what seemed an endless time to find the wing where Edie was, and he waited still longer before he was allowed to see her, judging the hours as they dragged not by the clock on the wall, but by the changing light outside the tall hospital windows and the comings and goings of others—expectant fathers, people to whom death suddenly had become a reality, interns, doctors. He saw two attendants wheeling a figure beneath a sheet that he thought might be Edie, but he could not be sure. A Gray Lady brought him a sandwich and glass of milk, neither of which he wanted. At last, when it was almost dark, a nurse came toward him and touched his shoulder.

"You're Dr. Ingle's son, aren't you?" She waited for his answer, and when Bobby simply stared at her, smiled. "How like your father you are. Come with me." She led him into a small white room, at the end of which he saw Edie, sitting up in bed, her hands folded.

Bobby waited until the nurse had gone, then went to the bed. Though he had waited for this moment, he could find no words.

Edie found them. She said, "They tell me I'm going to be all right now. Thanks to you."

"Edie!"

"How did you know what was happening in the garage?" she asked, her eyes searching his face. "What made you come when I needed you most?"

"I'd been waiting and waiting to hear from you all Thursday and today. You said not to call you, but I did try to call you—and got nowhere."

Her lip trembled. "Nowhere. Yes, I know. I was nowhere. I mean, I was in a nowhere of my own."

"But where were you?"

Edie closed her eyes. She spoke with effort. "I'll have to tell you everything, sometime, but not now. Now I can only tell you part of it. The night the Gypsies came, he—my Papa-Daddy—he was so drunk, I knew I had to leave for Mom's sake. I got away the only way I could, with—with someone you don't know."

"A man?"

"Yes. But it wasn't what you think," she said quickly. "He—he's something else I'll have to tell you about later, now I know." She waited. "Oh, he tried everything to make me do what he wanted, but somehow I simply couldn't. I kept thinking of you. I got away from him, finally."

"That night? The Gypsy night?"

"Yes."

"But where were you the rest of that night, and the night after that?"

"I couldn't go home. I was afraid. I guess I just drifted. I don't remember much, except that I took a lot of buses and sat through a crazy movie in Trenton. I sat up all the second night in the railroad station. I slept some, until he—*him*—until he woke me. He'd looked for me until he found me and brought me home. If he hadn't, my Mom would be dead now."

"And your—"

She shook her head. "I can't talk about Papa-Daddy. Maybe sometime—"

"Sometime," he said.

She raised her eyes to his. "There'll be lots of time for us, won't there?"

"If you say there will be."

Her lips formed a crooked little smile. "Kiss me," she said. She sighed as their lips met. "Oh, Bobby, Bobby!"

"I love you, Edie."

"I love you too."

He held her in his arms a long moment, then felt the tiredness in her and let her sink against the pillows.

"I guess I'm still sleepy," she said.

"We won't talk any more now."

"Except to say one thing," she said, clinging to his hand. "Do you need me the way I need you?"

"Yes."

"We're not like our mothers and fathers. We have to be different —I don't know how to say it—"

"I wonder if we are."

"You think it's the same with us as it was with them? This, that we feel?"

"I don't know, but we'll find out." He gave her a last light kiss on the lips. "Goodby for now."

"You'll come back to me?"

"What do you think?" he said.

CHAPTER 3

Mrs. Hubbard's moods had shifted mercurially all day; one moment she would be talking about the advisability of a church wedding for Teddy, the next demanding to know what was playing on TV. Miss Hankins wondered if it could be some inauspicious crossing of medications—Mrs. Hubbard had had her usual, but two extra bladder pills, because of the party excitement, had been added, as well as an additional happy pill toward evening. Mrs.

Hubbard decided to wear the Grace Coolidge rose dress after all, rather than either of the blues; it would perhaps be a little warm, but as she remarked to Miss Hankins before asking her to press it, "Good heavens! When I think what I used to wear in summer— heavy linen petticoats, bloomers beneath, and buckram in both the skirt hem and the leg-o'-mutton sleeves!" The Coolidge rose was, admittedly, a comparative wisp. "And *she'll* like it better, I'm sure," Mrs. Hubbard added, alluding to Teddy's fiancée, now as firmly fixed in her mind as though she existed and was about to be met.

The many details of getting ready did not mean that Mrs. Hubbard would permit Miss Hankins to turn off the TV; during hair and nails, she kept one eye on one of the perennial afternoon *Tarzan* films. In this one Cheeta, the inevitable anthropoid of American film dramas, was involved in transporting a raftful of jungle virgins down a perilous river full of crocodiles. Jane was having a fit about the danger the virgins were in.

"Tarzan! Kimba, leave us!"

"No time for talk, boy in danger. Run, girls, Tarzan follow!"

"Even after Tarzan see leopard, he not fooled. If animal can act like man, maybe man can act like animal."

"Tarzan, please!"

"Tarzan have man's work to do."

"But what about these girls? They can't go to Uganda unaccompanied, Tarzan, they simply can't!" The Tarzanese dialogue droned on.

Miss Hankins knew all the Tarzan plots by heart, as well as most of the commercial segments accompanying the films, and hated them, finding the obsession with hair (getting it off in one place, but using miracle shampoos that insured its having *bounce and body* and *snapping back* in another) as tiresome as all the goings-on about not sweating under the arms. She used fuller's earth herself. *And* the children who hadn't brushed their teeth because they couldn't and ovens caked with burned-on lasagna, not to mention those gigantic grains of rice being shaped and smoothed for everybody's eating pleasure. There was a shutoff switch for the sound, which Mrs. Hubbard used during the commercials, but Miss Hankins could still remember them. On days as nervous as this, it was a habit of hers to supply the words mouthed by the many "spokesmen" and dreamlike girls using depilatories, hair-snap and God only knew what else.

". . . 'My dear, your hair! It's lovely! You haven't—?' 'Oh, no, darling, simply used THIS—brings out the hidden highlights!' "

"Miss Hankins, do stop that muttering!" Mrs. Hubbard complained. "You're getting positively odd!"

"If you knew how odd," Miss Hankins added to her mutterings. "Two more weeks and I'll be on my way to Egypt, I hope."

Mrs. Hubbard always found something to say about the film. Tonight, during the last segment, she observed, "I always thought Maureen O'Sullivan so much better a Jane than that Whoever-she-is."

"Brenda Joyce."

"Where are my bone hairpins?"

"Here, dear, let me finish you." Miss Hankins deftly gathered the wisps of white hair at the back of Mrs. Hubbard's neck, and the coiffure was complete.

"What's that?" Mrs. Hubbard said sharply, turning to the TV.

"Why, it's Mr. Bo!" Miss Hankins cried. "His new commercial! Isn't it exciting?" She found any image on television both brighter and more believable than life, especially if it was someone she had heard of. And Bo she knew, in the flesh! Though she disliked him, his appearance as Noodle Master brought on the realization that he was, *at this very moment,* downstairs and, no doubt, putting the finishing touches on the party preparations. "Oh, I do hope he's watching—should I run down and tell him he's on?"

"Cut him off!" Mrs. Hubbard commanded. "Stupid, grasping Swede! Teddy's marriage will fix his hash!"

"Dear, I wouldn't count on—"

"Let's have the news. Turn on Quincy Howe."

"It's Roger Mudd, now."

"Well, whoever."

Miss Hankins dutifully switched channels and a gourd-faced Chinese appeared. Whatever he was saying, to a great, milling crowd below him, was covered by the commentary, but the crowd raised its thousands of arms, as one man, in response.

"Oh, those Orientals! I never could understand why they stopped having *nice* news, as they once did in dear Mr. Hearst's newsreels," said Mrs. Hubbard. "You know, before everything became so political. The Holy Father used to be better than these idiots, whoever they are; you could always count on him. And Constance Bennett—they always showed her when she returned from Europe. She was a marquise, you know."

"Yes. The Marquise de la Falaise de la Coudraye," Miss Hankins intoned, not to be outdone; she was an authority on film stars of the past. "And Gloria Swanson was also the Marquise de la Falaise de la Coudraye."

"*What?*" barked Mrs. Hubbard. Her mood was shifting again.

"Never mind, it's time for us to go downstairs now."

"Ah, yes!" Mrs. Hubbard rose. "Miss Hankins, I can tell you, I've had a number of surprises in a long life, but none I've looked forward to as much as the one I'll have tonight. For once, it won't be all men and boys!"

Miss Hankins prudently said nothing to this, but led Mrs. Hubbard out to the hall, where the Inclinator waited on the stair landing to transport her down to the first floor. She looked, Miss Hankins thought, as sweet and nice an old lady as ever got mixed up.

The Hubbard household, curiously, was one of the last in the Corner to learn of the Cadle tragedy. Teddy had worked with Bo, getting rooms ready for the guests expected in late afternoon, and at 4:30 Bo left in the Mercedes to pick up those coming by way of Trenton. Since Hackersville, where the others would arrive, was not far from the Corner, Teddy did not leave the house until somewhat later. He was already in the Pierce and backing it down the drive when he saw Willie Bentrup, leaving his parked squad car and waving a hand to indicate he wanted to speak. Teddy knew that if Bentrup troubled to get out of his car, it was something of importance. Wondering if Bo had gotten into some scrape, he pulled to the side of the road.

Hubbard's relations with Bentrup were not unlike those of other city people who lived in the big Corner houses; they took little or no real part in local community life except as consumers, and existed independently, often as unknown to each other and the natives as though occupying separate pyramids at opposite ends of a desert. Bentrup knew who everybody was, however, and part of what he knew about Teddy Hubbard and Bo deWillig was that they sometimes gave a kind of noisy party at which men wore fancy dress, or, to give it its real name, drag; but unless some guest got fried and ventured off the lot in his costume and made trouble, Bentrup looked the other way. The Olympia area tolerated all kinds of odd behaviors, but drag was not among them, except, of course, at local street fairs and charity functions, where it was sanctioned as part of entertainment. Several years ago, two of Teddy's friends in full drag had wandered up to the Corner intersection and started cruising. Bentrup arrested them immediately; he had only been doing his duty, and money had changed hands before the matter was ironed out. Teddy and the local police had worked out a deal, never discussed, but nevertheless binding on both sides: he contributed liberally to the various fund drives, remembered Bentrup at Christmas, and as long as his guests behaved reasonably well, there would be no more trouble.

"Got a minute, Mr. Hubbard?" Bentrup asked, coming up and resting a hand against the Pierce, and, Teddy noticed, leaving a handprint.

"I'm on my way to Hackersville to meet the 5:40."

"I won't keep you but a second. I take it you've heard the news?"

"What news?"

"About Rafe Cadle. Suicide. Monoxide poisoning. This morning, in his garage."

Teddy's face grew taut. "Is this true?"

"Is it true? Hell, yes, it's true," Bentrup said. "The rescue squad worked on him for over an hour, but they got to him too late. His wife was taken over to Abingdon, beat to a bloody nub. Not to the Doylestown or one of the Trenton hospitals, but Abingdon. Christ, was she a job of fancy sewing! Rafe's daughter found her, and if she hadn't dragged her out, the two probably would've died the way Rafe did."

"Why, I saw Rafe only this morning," said Teddy.

"That's what I came to ask—we saw from his bills and your check that he'd done some work for you. Matter of formality. What time was it you saw him?"

"Early. Around eight. He'd been working on the Pierce and I walked up to get it."

"How did he seem?"

"Like himself. He was drunk."

"Yeah, he'd been drunk for days. But did he say anything to you that might give us a clue as to why he did it?"

Teddy gave the question consideration. "I gathered from what he said that he'd been having a little domestic trouble. In fact, that was the phrase he used, domestic trouble."

"The understatement of all time," said Bentrup, "from what the Hanters tell me. Seems Rafe and his wife had been fighting, but bad."

"That may be so," Teddy said. "I tried to pick up my car— Wednesday night, it was—but the place was closed. When I knocked, Mrs. Cadle told me Rafe was drunk. I think she was a little drunk herself at that time."

Bentrup shook his head. "Rafe must've been even drunker than usual this time, judging from that job he did on Mae. I saw her as the boys were putting her in the ambulance. Jesus! Were you in the war?"

Teddy shook his head.

"Then you wouldn't know. I was a medical orderly and saw just about everything. But for a dame still breathing, I never seen anything like the way Rafe left her."

"Is there anything I can do?" Teddy asked.

"Money? No. Rafe was well off, never spent a cent. As to the rest, everything that can be done's being done, or has been. Did you know the daughter? Edie?"

"No, only that there was a daughter."

"Well, she was in deep shock by the time we got around to questioning her. She's at Abingdon, too, and coming around nicely. Dr. Ingle wouldn't let us ask her more than so much. She kept screaming about her Papa-Daddy not doing it to her, and you know what I think? *I* think Rafe raped her."

Teddy said nothing to this, but he thought, Normies, always ready to put the finger on an old boy like me!

"Well, thanks, Mr. Hubbard; that was all I wanted to ask, when you'd seen him. Guess you must have been just about the last— people trying to get gas around ten-thirty found the garage shut up tight. The coroner figures it was shortly after that that Rafe did it."

"You don't think it could have been an accident?"

"Every car in the shop was running." Bentrup raised his shoulders in a shrug. "By the time I got there, the whole place was so thick with exhaust you couldn't breathe. Been real gas, it would've blown up. It was the Ingle kid—Bobby—who broke in the garage door so Edie and her mother could get out and called the rescue boys and me. Well, these things happen every day."

When Bentrup left him, Teddy drove slowly up to the intersection, past the Cadle place; it looked much as usual, except for two state troopers' cars parked near the gas pumps, and a small group of curious hanging around the grass plot. He steered the Pierce in the direction of Hackersville. He didn't know whether the deep depression that settled over him was because of the simple horror of suicide—anybody's, whether known or unknown—or because he felt guilt for having told Rafe about his wife's behavior. Actually, of course, he hadn't told Rafe anything; but perhaps that was worse. Whether worse or not, it was all over now. Mechanically, he tried to lift his spirits, transport himself from the world of horror into the *laissez-faire* good humor with which he customarily greeted his guests.

Those arriving for this weekend were old friends—Mikey and Allie (who would, once protected by walls, become Mary and Helen, to each other and everyone else present), Gordon and Herbert (Irene and Mavis), Louis and Monroe (The Pretty One and The Ugly One) and Otis—the oldest, hard on seventy (Maud). The train was already in the station, and regular Friday night commuters were getting off. Teddy saw at once that his group had fortified themselves in the coach where drinks were served. Mikey and Allie, each carrying a pug, were first to come down the platform. They were fortyish and prosperous, in the wholesale furniture business; had it not been for the way they moved and talked, they might have passed unnoticed, but both, when drinking, became giggly and gestured elaborately.

"I had no idea you were going to bring the dogs," Teddy greeted them peevishly; he was feeling less and less up to things every minute.

"We wish we *hadn't* brought them," Allie answered. "Duke and Duchess simply *hated* the train!"

" 'Es," confirmed Mikey, nuzzling Duchess, "it doesn't have to take nassy old train any more—Mikey-wikey'll get it a Carey Cad to go back in."

"It'll be Mikey-wikey who'll pay for it, too," said Allie, pouring cold water on it. Both pugs set up a yapping that was to continue all weekend.

Gordon and Herbie, unknown to the others until they met in the bar car, had in tow a small and slender dark boy—uninvited—and if Teddy's syrup had been pouring he would have found him appealing, since he was the embodiment of the type he liked, *le style pauvre* at its most poetic. But his mood being what it was, he said to Gordon, "Where did you pick *him* up?"

"Don't be rude, Teddy," Gordon answered, and then in a stage whisper, "He's Cuban or Puerto Rican. We found him in *Spanish* Harlem. My dear, he's a real artist! He's the *most* phenomenal thing in drag you'll ever see. Mei Lang Fang simply wasn't in it—Herbie and I were taken in completely. He does the simple young girl to perfection. His name is Raúl. Raúl? Come here! Teddy, this is Raúl."

Raúl's eyes were heavily ringed with dark lashes, as black as the clutch bag he carried. "At last I meet the great Teddy Hubbard." He smiled. Teddy saw that though still in his teens, he already knew how far he could go and the almost exact chances of getting away with it.

"Hello," Teddy said shortly, then to Gordon and Herbert, "You've got a nerve—you know we'll be full up this week. Heaven knows where he'll sleep."

"Oh, Raúl will find somewhere to sleep, don't worry," Gordon assured. "He doesn't look it, but he's a very ballsy little guy."

They stood waiting for Louis and Monroe, museum curators, who got off last. The "straight look," for which they had striven in their appearance, was almost a camp in itself—Yalie seersucker, crew cuts and slim-jim ties.

"I've often wondered which is Pretty One," mused Herbert. "They're both so terribly ugly. Which do you think, Teddy?"

"I wish you'd watch that talk," Teddy scolded. "We're in a public place."

"Get you, Ella," Mikey giggled. "Since when have *you* cared if it was public or not?"

Otis, the almost-septuagenarian, dignified as a Southern colonel, brought up the rear, and the boys flashed across the parking spaces to the Pierce, exclaiming over its antiquated grandeur. The passengers in the departing train regarded them with expressions of amused tolerance or distaste. Gordon and Herbert wedged Raúl between them in the tonneau, leaving Louis and Monroe the jump seats, with elderly but game Otis making do half on one lap, half on another. Mikey and Allie sat with Teddy in front, each holding a pug.

Teddy didn't like the way the weekend was beginning; if he had had the choice of calling it off, he would have, but now he was stuck with it. He was very upset by the Cadle tragedy, and Bentrup's question to him, casually put, and his own answer, as casually accepted, decided him on caution. There would be no Bacchanalian cutups this time, and all punches would be prudently pulled. He took a roundabout route returning to the Corner, making an excuse to stop in Olympia, so he would not have to pass the Cadle place again. Bo, he hoped, would approach the house the same way and, with luck, not hear of Cadle's suicide. Teddy would not speak of it, even to Bo and Miss Hankins, until he had to, and trusted to the isolation of the weekend to ensure their not finding out. Any distressing news was, of course, automatically withheld from his mother. When Bo arrived with Cliff and Ben (Dora and Trilla the Lampshade) and George Somebody—another uninvited one—Teddy could see the party would be unwieldy: eleven, and, with his mother and Miss Hankins and Bo and himself, they would be fifteen. While everyone was having drinks in the den, he gave orders.

"Look, dears," he said, "we've all got to be a little good this weekend. Your aging mother's not up to it."

"Why, you old killjoy!" Gordon cried. "What do you mean? I've been saving up all week!"

"I mean no drag," said Teddy explicitly. "My mother's birthday's tomorrow, though we're celebrating it tonight, and for once we're going to play it straight."

Allie laughed. "If you can imagine anything being straight around here!"

"Don't worry, we'll be very sweet with Mother Hubbard," Mikey said.

"What's with Teddy?" Herbie asked Gordon when, with Raúl, they went upstairs. Raúl was proving a sensation, being, except for George Somebody, the youngest, and had already had a very solid proposition from Otis the Old.

"Teddy's looking like the best that can be done," replied Gordon, "and, my dear, that's what he really is. Maybe he'll snap out of it."

The crescendo of bad behavior, which began almost the minute everybody reached their rooms, probably was due to determination not to let Teddy dampen the fun. The train journeys and drinks had put all in a mood for deviltry, it seemed, and Bo's openly falling for Raúl did nothing to offset the early changing of partners (supposed not to take place until after dinner at earliest), nor did the nips everybody had from upstairs bottles, to make Teddy's forbidding easier to forget. Mikey and Allie had a fuss about who should walk the pugs and give them their dinners; Mikey had forgotten to pack their Dash, and the upshot was that Mikey took off with Monroe for Olympia in the Ghia, to have a quick look around the art galleries, they said. This left Allie to forage for Duke's and Duchess's food in the kitchen with Louis, whom he couldn't bear the sight of. Louis, who liked snooping, soon figured out what dinner was going to be.

"My God, fairy pudding! Not again!"

"It wouldn't be a fairy party without fairy pudding, as you should know," Allie said over the pugs' yapping. "They always have it."

"Aha!" cried Louis. "What have we here?" He had discovered the copper molds filled with the blancmange. "My dear, I do believe they're supposed to be cocks!"

The news of the dessert spread, making Bo angry, because he had intended it as the *pièce de résistance* of the party. His mind was full of his defeat at the hands of Tavio, and every time he looked at the untanned bands on his wrist and fingers, where his watch and rings had been, he got the shivers. Raúl seemed just what the doctor ordered to get his mind off his troubles, and Bo was giving him all the eyelash work his blackened eye permitted, as well as his accent and "Phidias" poses.

Gordon and Herbie, out of loyalty to Teddy, were making it as hard for Bo as they could, but Raúl had his eye on the main chance and was sampling everything. They tried to explain to him that Teddy was the moneybags, and if he wanted to make an impression he couldn't do worse than pair off with Bo.

"I think Teddy could have allowed us a *bal de têtes*, at least," said Herbie. "What this wake needs is a bit of high-class drag, no matter what he told us."

"Do you think we should?" Gordon questioned.

"Not us, we'll abstain," Herbie decided, "but Raúl's too marvelous to let Teddy miss seeing. You start getting into your costume," he instructed the confused Raúl. "You'll be a sensation, dear, with none of the rest of us done up. Now, *do* do your shy girl bit, don't forget." Nodding, Raúl opened his black clutch bag, which contained his drag material, and did as he was told.

Up on the third floor, where Cliff and Ben had been detailed by Teddy to carry down a folding bed for George Somebody, things were equally nervous. The bed stuck in the angle of the stairs and no efforts would dislodge it.

"Oh, well," Cliff said, "it doesn't really matter, Teddy. How do you like George?"

"Yes, we thought he'd be just for you," Ben added. "He's from West Texas."

"With a face like his, he should open his shirt more," Teddy replied irritably.

George was either good-natured or dumb. He said, giving Teddy a calflike look, "Pappy, don't worry. Back home, I used to bunk in with my own pappy all the time."

With that, Teddy went downstairs to answer the telephone. It was Willie Bentrup, asking if he would mind coming down to the Olympia police station, to repeat to the state boys what he had told him earlier. There was nothing to do but go, and Teddy went. The state boys were less relaxed than Bentrup; they asked all kinds of questions it seemed to Teddy had nothing to do with Rafe's suicide.

"How old are you, Mr. Hubbard?"

"In my sixty-fifth year."

"Single?"

"Single."

Pause. Then, "Tell us, Mr. Hubbard, do you remember hearing anything, any noises from upstairs, at the Cadle place? Or seeing a young girl, Rafe's daughter?"

"I saw only Rafe. I heard no noises upstairs."

"Do you recall the last thing he said to you?"

"He asked what it was his wife had said to me that night when, as I've told Bentrup, I went to get my car and found the garage closed."

"What was it she said?"

"I didn't tell him."

"Why not?"

"It was offensive."

"Will you tell us what it was?"

"It has no bearing at all on the case."

The state boys exchanged looks. "You are under no obligation to tell us, of course—now. But should there be court proceedings—"

"Very well," Teddy said. "Mrs. Cadle shouted at me from the upstairs window. She called me a 'morphadite.'"

"Thank you, Mr. Hubbard, that will be all. We appreciate your coming down."

The interview further depressed Teddy; he was not accustomed to being summoned and dismissed. When he got back to the house, he found no one downstairs except George Somebody, and the kitchen dark. Some of the upstairs rooms were dark, too, and there was nothing to do but put on a tape, made from recordings of long ago, and let the hi-fi, piped into the room upstairs, move the party—or parties—down to the first floor.

"Pappy, what's that?" George asked, when the tapes began spinning.

"That's Gertrude Lawrence. You've never heard of her."

"You can say that again." George covered his ears. "How about a little Beatle bug?"

Teddy ignored this and went out to the kitchen. Old Otis, refreshed by his nap, was first to come down, followed by Cliff and Ben, who, since they were easy as old shoes in the house, took over keeping bar. Then came Allie and Louis, still sparring, though they called it off when Mikey and Monroe, looking not at all as though they had been doing art galleries, returned from Olympia. Teddy scolded them for having taken the Ghia without asking him. No one, he was aware, had noticed his own absence, and he later remembered that Gordon and Herbie had the look, when they appeared, of having swallowed a canary between them.

"Your mother's made her appearance, Teddy," Ben said, coming into the kitchen. "Shall I make her 'Mother Hubbard'?"

"No, I'll make it," Teddy answered. He prepared, in the electric mixer, the concoction his mother liked—dry and sloe gins, lime juice, thick cream and a dash of orange water, and asked Ben to take it in to her. Miss Hankins, he heard through a swing of the door, was asking for gin-and-it, her usual. Bo seemed to be nowhere, so Teddy, looking ahead, popped the fairy pudding into a low oven, so it would be ready to brown when serving time came. The blancmange had set stiffly and well, he noticed; but that would be Bo's *oeuvre*. What with getting out plates and napkins and setting up the Chemex for after-dinner coffee, he was tied to the kitchen and pantry for some time.

Mrs. Hubbard, seated in a comfortable chair not too far from the downstairs lavatory, should her bladder pills fail, accepted the birthday wishes of the boys with her usual courtesy, but tonight there could be detected in her attitude a slight reserve, as well as expectation. She looked around. Apart from herself and Miss Hankins, there was no other woman that she could see. It was therefore with relief and anticipation that she saw Raúl, done up to the nines and superbly wigged and made up, make his entrance down the big front staircase.

"I seem to have forgotten my lorgnon," Mrs. Hubbard said to Miss Hankins. "Please to fetch it for me."

Miss Hankins obeyed and Mrs. Hubbard beckoned from her chair. Raúl modestly advanced. His attitude suggested he'd got this dreadful old party's number right away, but was willing to play. The Coolidge rose was an utter camp and riot, like the house and everything in it, but Raúl was nothing if not obliging and, as instructed, was doing his *jeune fille* bit.

"Do come and sit by me, dear," Mrs. Hubbard invited, indicating a hassock. "I know this must be Teddy's way of breaking the news to me. You're lovely! I hadn't expected anyone so young!"

"I'm almost nineteen," Raúl confided, in a tiny voice.

"But no matter," said Mrs. Hubbard. "I've known many a marriage between May and September that's been very successful." Now this small, dark creature was seated at her feet, she saw somewhat better—the large black eyes, and the smile, though demure, white and dazzling. "You are Spanish?" she inquired.

"Hidalgos, on both sides," Raúl answered, with a downsweep of eyelashes.

"My late husband and I often traveled in Spain," Mrs. Hubbard went on reminiscently. "Seville in Easter Week, the Prado. Not that I much cared for the bulls—"

"I'm simply queer for bulls," said Raúl.

"You like them?" Odd way of talking. "I suppose that's only natural, though," she conceded after a moment. "Latin blood, after all." She nodded approval.

This old boy is almost as good in his way as I am in mine, Raúl thought. Everything from thrift shops, obviously; the entire ensemble, though, couldn't have cost too much—and he had the sagging figure to begin with. "You know," he confided, "in my work I have to do all types, but I've never been able to get the hairpins to stick out like that. Convincingly, I mean."

"Hairpins?" Mrs. Hubbard checked the wisps at the back of her neck; all were in place. "You are employed?" she asked.

"I work *and* play," answered Raúl roguishly. Who knew? The strangest old men got their kicks dressing up and playing—what? A mother part, obviously. Maybe he was loaded; the rings were genuine; nothing to be lost by indicating availability in case he liked them little and young.

"Well, no harm in playing," agreed Mrs. Hubbard. At this moment Miss Hankins returned with the lorgnon. "Thank you," Mrs. Hubbard said, taking it and raising it to make a closer inspection. Scrutiny only bore out her first impression. She placed a diamond-hung hand on Raúl's bare arm. "But I don't even know your name. We must be our own introducers."

All right, thought Raúl, one good line deserves another. "Doña Sol y Lucientes y Castador-Viejas." He tripped it off in his 110th Street Spanish but lisping the *c* in "Lucientes."

"Castilian!"

"*Sí, sí.*"

"Lovely, isn't she?" Mrs. Hubbard turned triumphantly to Miss Hankins, that doubter, that caster-on of cold water. Miss Hankins, who had smelled a rat from the beginning, pulled a long but straight face. "Well, what is it? Speak up!" Mrs. Hubbard demanded. "Don't you understand? It's Teddy's fiancée!"

"Dear, I think this young *person's* little joke has gone far enough," replied Miss Hankins, staring disapprovingly at Raúl, who stared back.

Why, there's hardly one here under sixty, Raúl was thinking, and perhaps even older. Who can this one be, dragging in that lorgnon business? "Listen," he said to Miss Hankins out of the side of his mouth, "what are you trying to be, some nurse or something?"

"I *am* a nurse!" Miss Hankins proclaimed.

"What? I didn't quite hear." Mrs. Hubbard turned. She had heard a little, however. "I suppose that's the new talk. Slang— lingo, I mean."

Raúl laughed, showing his white, even teeth. "You really are the one, Grandpa," he said to Mrs. Hubbard. "For a minute, when I came in, you almost fooled me. *Me!*"

"But I have no wish to fool anyone," Mrs. Hubbard answered, now confused. This lovely girl—a child still, really—seemed about to escape. Now things had gotten this far for Teddy, she wanted no hitch of any kind. "My dear Doña Sol," she said, "don't go. We've so much to talk about. Teddy will be here any minute, I'm sure, and then we can discuss everything—the linen, the silver, all that."

"Dear," said Miss Hankins to Mrs. Hubbard, in the slightly louder voice she used when her patient was obstinately contrary, "I think you shouldn't drink any more of your cocktail." Mrs. Hubbard's glass was almost empty.

"Go away, Miss Hankins!" commanded Mrs. Hubbard. "Have you no sense of delicacy?"

Miss Hankins threw her eyes upward and went to find Teddy.

"Now, then," Mrs. Hubbard resumed, drawing Raúl closer and herself leaning forward. "That silly Englishwoman—she watches me constantly—"

Ha-*ha!* thought Raúl. Nuts, too. *Loco.* "*Ya lo creo!*"

"Yes, the British. I daresay you know, dear."

"She's one of the butch ones, all right."

That lingo! "My dear," continued Mrs. Hubbard, determined, "I see that you're wearing several strands—they can't be genuine!"

Raúl bit his Teclas. "I took them out of the bank only this morning," he assured her, simpering.

"Oh, dear! Then it'll hardly do for me to offer you my single strand—"

Miss Hankins had found Teddy, who hurriedly came forward. "Mother!" he said.

But he got no further. Mrs. Hubbard seized his arm. "You're a devil and a tease—just as your father was," she reproached him. "Why didn't you tell me about Doña Sol?"

"Mother, this is your party, and—and this young man's dressed himself up so he can entertain later—"

"Young *man?* What? *Again?*" Mrs. Hubbard looked from Teddy to Raúl to Miss Hankins. "Miss Hankins, it's you who spoiled it—"

Nothing could have saved the situation. Raúl, who had gotten up from his hassock and lighted a cigarette, in a single dressing-room sweep removed his wig. Mrs. Hubbard stiffened, then gasped.

"Please go," Teddy said to Raúl, with restraint. "I thought I had explained—"

Raúl shrugged. "I only do what I'm told, dear," he said to Teddy. "How was *I* to know she was for real?" He moved away.

Mrs. Hubbard was in tears. "Dear, I told you you were making a mistake," Miss Hankins tried to soothe her.

"Mother, whatever in the world?" Teddy turned to Miss Hankins. "Miss Hankins, have you given her—"

"She's had everything she's supposed to have, Mr. Ted."

"Mother, I think you look a bit tired."

Mrs. Hubbard stared up at him. An expression he had never before seen came into her eyes. "Tired?" she repeated. "No, son, I'm not tired. After all the resting I've done and getting ready for my party, why would I be tired? And thinking—*hoping*—that you'd come to see the error of your ways at last! Why, *why* did you deceive me, Teddy? Why did you lead me to believe that you'd found a sweet young girl?"

"Where did she get such an idea as this?" Teddy asked Miss Hankins.

"From you!" Mrs. Hubbard cried. "You told me there would be a surprise for me. Well?" Teddy was silent. "I think it was a very shabby joke to play on an old lady. I can forgive your trying to fool me; what I can't forgive is—is—" She broke off.

"Your duty, Miss Hankins," Teddy said sternly, "is to see that she doesn't get ideas of this kind in her head. You could at least have told me."

"Mr. Ted," Miss Hankins replied defiantly, "if I told you of all the crazy things she thinks, you'd need a full-time secretary to transcribe them! I'm giving notice!"

"Please, Miss Hankins. If it's a question of money—"

"It's a question of sanity."

"I'll be going up now," Mrs. Hubbard said. "Miss Hankins, take me to my room." She got up from her chair and, leaning on Miss Hankins' arm, walked slowly to the Inclinator, settling tiredly into the seat. Miss Hankins moved the lever and then climbed the steps beside her. At the second-floor landing a door stood open, and from the darkness inside the room came two men's voices. One was sharp and rasping and the other pleading with an almost feminine cajolery, saying, "Now you stop, Bo. Stop, Bo! Don't, Bo, please! Please, Bo!"

Miss Hankins was glad the room had been dark and she had gotten Mrs. Hubbard past it without her seeming to notice. After what had happened, there was nothing but to give her the four red pills all at once. Just before Mrs. Hubbard went to sleep, she spoke.

"Miss Hankins?"

"Yes, dear?"

"Do you know what I really minded?"

"Don't fret yourself about it, any of it."

"It was that there didn't seem to be a cake. And it was my birthday, wasn't it?"

"Yes, dear, it was," answered Miss Hankins, turning out the light. Later, when she stole down to the library and found herself a book about Tutankhamen, she had to pass the dining room. Bo was carrying in the blancmanges to wild cries of appreciation. Miss Hankins averted her eyes from the monstrous pink erections. She was looking forward to her pulmonary case, but until the two weeks of her notice were up, Tutankhamen was the best she could do.

CHAPTER 4

Throughout Friday, despite his stubborn resolution not to be the first to speak and make up the quarrel with Nancy, Don MacFinden's thoughts had been all of her. A quarrel, especially a first quarrel, is an expanding cloud, darkening all other activities. Don's sleep the night before had been considerably less comfortable than he had pretended; though he had dropped off at once, he woke suddenly, shortly after three, and thought, "What is it? There's something wrong—" And then remembered he and Nancy were not speaking, except in the most perfunctory way, and that they had gone to bed with the cloud hanging over them. About the C.T.A. he had, he told himself, made up his mind: his love for Nancy, his memory of her lack of gratification, had decided him about taking all the risks of ways and means involved, whatever they might turn out to be. He longed to satisfy her, to have her relax after making love, as he did, spent and happy. He had heard her crying oftener than he cared to admit to himself. The C.T.A. decision had been, by comparison, an easy one. But to speak the first word that would dispel the cloud, when it was Nancy who was technically in the right, and he who had told the lie, white or gray or whatever color it was—impossible. What if he did reach out and search for her hand in the darkness? The question she had asked still would have to be answered; there was no explanation he could give her except the truth, and to give it, at this point, would be to negate the hopes he had that the C.T.A. would solve their problem.

Daylight had brought insight. Don came to the conclusion that the only way to get the quarrel out of the way would be to rush the fortress, pretend, for the necessary first strategic moments, that there had been no questions about Dr. Kidder and trust to proximity to do the rest.

On his way home, he stopped at a bar and package store in Jersey, to pick up a bottle of tequila. One thing he was sure of: if he could get a little tight—more important, if he could get Nancy tight—the whole thing would be easier. And, as a way of forgetting his thoughts of the day, he had a stiff double at the bar before going on.

Nancy was in the kitchen and spoke the first word, which was, for some reason he did not understand, of importance to him, but it wasn't the word he expected. "Did you hear about the Cadles?" she asked, not looking up from her stove.

Don looked blank and said nothing.

"You must remember them, I just did," Nancy said. "Mr. Cadle, whatever his first name was, I don't know what it was, well, he beat up his wife something terrible and then closed all the windows and doors in the place and turned on the car engines and killed himself. That gas—carbon monoxide. He almost killed the wife and the youngest daughter, too, but they got out in time."

Don's face sobered but he still said nothing. The MacFindens had never used the Cadle services, their cars being serviced along with the quarry trucks and gassed at Number Three, which had its own gas pump. "I knew old Rafe when I was a kid," he said after a pause. "He used to let us hang around." He had known the two older Cadle daughters, and well, but wasn't going to tell Nancy about them. "Gosh, how awful!"

"I used to know one of the daughters, not the youngest one, Edie, but the one in between," Nancy said. "She was ahead of me in school. She never finished, was suspended, I think, because she was too free with it with anybody who'd ask her."

"Yeah," Don said, remembering. "Poor old Rafe!"

"The township cop—Bentrup—came by here to ask if we could shed any light on why Cadle did it. I said neither of us knew the family."

"That's right, doll. My dad says keep to your own back yard." He set the tequila bottle on the sink. "Keep out of stuff like that. Nancy," he said.

She turned and ran into his arms. "Don, darling! Why didn't you phone me? I waited all day long, thinking you'd call. I didn't even go out of the house."

"If you knew how I've been waiting for this," Don said. "That was our first quarrel. I hope the others are easier."

"It wasn't a quarrel exactly," Nancy qualified. "Let's not talk any more about it, at least not now."

It was a truce. "What's for dinner?"

"Pot roast, potatoes and carrots baked in the gravy, Yorkshire pudding. Your mother's recipe, I hope I got it right. Hungry?"

"I'd like a shower and a few drinks first."

"Hard day?"

"Routine. But I worried about us."

"Go take your shower. I'll bring your drink to you."

Don was already halfway to the bedroom. "Rocks for me," he called. He quickly checked the medicine cabinet: the cakes of soap were still as he had left them, labels purposely upside down—all was okay and ready to go. He took a long swallow from the glass Nancy brought and shuddered; after all, it was tequila. When he had bathed and put on fresh shorts and shirt, he went into the living room, rattling the ice in his empty glass. "Front and center, doll! Make me another—you having one?"

"Haven't yet."

"Why wait?"

"Well, one." Nancy brought the drinks and sat on the sofa beside him. Don locked his elbow through hers and they drank a Dutch toast, switching glasses. "I love you, did you know?" he asked, kissing her.

"Yes, I knew. Did you know I love you too?" They sat, cheeks touching, finishing the drinks. "Shall I get the dinner on now?"

"Let's celebrate a little," Don said. "I can't bear to let you out of my sight. How's about my making the next round?"

She hesitated a fraction of a second. "All right," and from this she understood that what he wanted was bed first and dinner afterward. "Turn off the oven, will you, darling?" she called.

Don made the fresh drinks on the stiff side, and when he returned with them, perched a little apart from her, on the sofa's arm. They sipped the colorless liquid slowly.

"Glad I brought the tequila?"

"Mm-hm."

"I guess I wanted to hold on to the honeymoon a little longer— I can almost feel that sun, see those sunsets."

"Mm." She nodded, moving toward him. She wondered how she could have been so tiresome, held him away from her with her doubts. They had another and another, by which time both were a little more than tight. "Why don't we get into bed and be comfortable—if you're still not hungry?"

"I'm hungry for you."

She went ahead of him into the bedroom and he saw the omens were good—she drew the curtains with no suggestion from him; there was still a glow from the sunset. Then she undressed and got into bed. What a sweet, wonderful husband he was, she thought, as she waited for him to come out of his bath. If only—sometimes she was so worried about not pleasing him, she could hardly bear it. She knew he was unusually roused tonight, and some of his

407

excitement had overflowed into her: they had lain, during the last drink, locked together on the sofa, mouth to mouth, in the longest embrace she could remember. But he was as considerate as ever as he came and lay down beside her in the almost darkness, taking her hands in his and kissing them and then guiding them around his neck. It seemed as if it was the same long kiss they had begun in the living room. His tongue found hers and her breath quickened until she was almost gasping. He held her firmly, left hand pressing the small of her back, his right hand clutching hers behind his neck, as though he wanted their nearness never to end.

Then she felt the first, soft sensation and lay very still in his arms, waiting for the slow, beginning thrust that would gradually quicken and lengthen.

"Oh, darling! Sweetheart!" she whispered. "It's so wonderful! Let's not hurry tonight." It *was* wonderful—something new, incredible, was happening to her; it had never been like this before; she had dreamed of this so long she couldn't believe it.

Don felt he could relinquish his hold on her hands now, and they dropped, caressingly, to his buttocks, clasping them, guiding his movements. He had been right—the drinks without dinner had fired them both. He had still been anxious when he came out of his bath, the C.T.A. firmly secured, lubricated as Dr. Kidder had emphasized, with scrotum kept dry, holding his dressing gown in front of him, walking naturally. The moment he dreaded most had been when he stretched out beside her, but that had gone well; she had put her hands to his lips and, taking them in his, he had been doing the most natural thing in the world; guiding them into an embrace had been equally natural. The beginning had been pie in the sky. He had entered slowly, dreading lest he hurt her, but everything went naturally; the C.T.A. moved easily into her, until he could feel her pelvis firm and flush against his own. He had gone limp with worry at the moment of entry, but she had accepted everything, and he quickly came back to rigidity. God, if he had known it would be this easy! Because he had no more than gotten inside than she started crying out and clinging to him, telling him that he had never been like this before, that it was happening, she was sure it was, and that it was all glorious. He began to move slowly and regularly, in and out. It was his conventional rhythm, but Nancy's reactions were entirely different from other times; he had penetrated deeply enough, and her responses were even more ardent than he had hoped for—he was getting results. Like fire roaring through dry timber, it was rushing through her: a passion he had never dreamed she possessed started coming alive, a torrent of energy and desire. This was not like the nights at Uxmal or Mérida, or any night; it was vigorous, healthy, wave upon wave of wonder and delight. He felt her hands clutch his body frantically, guiding, slowing, begging. Her hips were grinding in a frenzy and he knew he was in command and control—but, as usual, he realized, a pang of anxiety returning, way ahead of her. Even with the tequila in him, he was fast, and the C.T.A. was like a small, pulsating, relentless vagina itself; each time he moved, he was closer to orgasm. He had feared, at first, among all his other fears, that the marvelously firm structure that was behaving so miraculously, as though part of him, would cut him down, kill his desire. But he could not conceal from himself that the smooth tube had brought with it a kind of perverse pleasure, young and almost stupefying in its excitement, like his very first, adolescent spasms of gratification.

Nancy's lips were parted and she moved, unexpectedly, spreading her thighs wide. Quickly Don adjusted. She seemed on the brink of gratification, but then tensed and waited, no matter how expert and intuitive his own pauses, for still deeper sensation. At last, he could hold off no longer and ejaculated. In the pause that followed, she did not relax her hold on his buttocks; she understood, from his quivering, that he had reached his climax, but she continued to move rhythmically. A brief revulsion suffused him— he knew this was the telling moment, when it would go either well or badly.

"Darling, I know it's me again," she said, the words wounding him as though she had, once more, found him finished and too fast. But the C.T.A. stood firm, and after a moment's rest, Don resumed the stroking rhythm. She quickly found the pace again and— though at first he could not believe it—he almost could feel her, deeply, up where the tip of the C.T.A. was. Going on was easy, and the friction within the tube again roused him to erection. She seemed to struggle a last, long moment, during which a second climax built itself in him anew, then her body suddenly arched, locked against him in a great constriction, and they experienced satisfaction simultaneously. Their flesh trembled as their breaths mingled, slowed, parted. Then they lay still.

"Oh, God!" Nancy said. "God! We've done it *together!* For once it wasn't my fault."

"Hush," he said. "Nothing's ever been your fault."

"But it has, it has! But not now. I was all right, wasn't I?"

"You were marvelous."

"And so were you." She sighed, happily. "Oh, why wasn't it ever like this before?"

For answer he kissed her. His second climax, following effort-fully so closely on the first, had tired him. She fell slightly away from him and worry returned—the C.T.A., though still moored securely to him, was beginning to withdraw of itself, and the elastic was constricting his testicles painfully. When he lowered his hand, to ease it, Nancy's hand quickly followed.

"Oh, no," she protested. "Stay, darling. Don't go."

He fumbled for her hand but was an instant too late. She drew away, as she had that very first night of the honeymoon, when, caressing him, she had seemed to find him small. Her hand, held now in his, was sticky from the semen and K-Y, and, at the very same moment, the C.T.A. emerged from her vagina. It was only a matter of seconds before the elastics, wet from his having tried to ease them, slipped away. The C.T.A. lay between them.

She broke the silence. "Don—it wasn't you."

He waited before he answered. "But you liked it—you were all right—for the first time it was as it should be. Doll—"

Nancy stiffened. "But what—I don't understand!" Her moist hand slipped from his and explored, stopped. "Oh!" she cried. "How could you!"

"Because I love you. Because—well, I wanted you to be satisfied, to feel everything."

"Ugh! It's a *thing!* What is it?"

Don contrived to seize the C.T.A. and drop it over the side of the bed and cover it with his dressing gown, crumpled on the floor. The tequila throbbed in his empty stomach. "Darling, try not to think of it that way," he begged. "What matters is that you liked it—you came. We came together."

Nancy said nothing; he felt her lying tense and rigid in the darkness. Her silence angered him, maddened him. "After all," he said, "I hated that pessary thing you insisted on using at first, too." If only, when giving instructions, Dr. Kidder had briefed him on what to say now!

She seemed to read his thoughts. "That's—*this* was why you were at Dutch Falls! To see that doctor!"

"Yes," Don confessed. "You hate me."

"Oh, you poor darling!"

This surprised him. He said, "Doll, I'm sorry if I—"

"No, I'm sorry for you," she said. "I don't hate you. It's only that—" She sought for words, seemed not to find them. "You— was it as wonderful for you, too?"

"God, yes! Couldn't you tell?"

"I thought— I wasn't sure."

He laid his hands on her shoulders. She still did not respond, though did not, this time, draw away from him. "Doll," he said to her after a long silence, "I can't be ashamed. I tried so hard. So did you."

"Don't be ashamed," she answered. "I know. You did it for me."

"For myself, too. I couldn't bear your not feeling anything, crying yourself to sleep."

"You heard me."

"I couldn't help it."

She sighed. "And I couldn't help it, either. I won't cry tonight."

Don's dreads were continuing—what would happen when they had to turn the light on? Darkness and the tequila had masked much. A smell of burning roast drifted into the room.

"The dinner!" Nancy cried. "You didn't cut off the oven!"

"I forgot."

In the confusion which followed of groping for the lamp switch and Nancy's running to the kitchen to turn off the stove, Don succeeded in getting the C.T.A. to his bath, washing it, and replacing it in its box. The pot roast was burned black and, after airing the house, they went out for dinner, to the Ferry Slip, in Olympia. Over the Gibson that seemed mandatory (after all, they still were in a buzz) and while waiting for their order, Don stood Nancy's silence as long as he could.

"Come on," he said. "Say it. You want to say something."

"I can't think how to say it."

"Try."

"Well, *I* don't care about it—*it,* whatever it is. I love you, and if it's easier and better for you that way, all right."

"And better for you, too."

"I suppose so," she conceded. "But sometimes I'll only want you, the way we were before. Just you." She paused. "Promise me only one thing."

"Of course."

"That I'll never have to *see* it. I'll know if you use it, and I'll try to get used to it or forget about it. But I don't want to know about it definitely."

"I promise," Don said.

That night Nancy made a decision without discussing it with Don—to stop taking the birth control pill, so that they could have their first child. Love, she had read somewhere, has many faces and, she began to suspect, as many moods—anxiety, frustration, anger, pain, as well as joy. As she had predicted, she did not cry that night. But she was unprepared for a shocking dream she had, which her censor quickly suppressed, but not quickly enough to keep her from remembering a part of it, in which she was wearing the thing Don had used, and was chasing him all over the house. She gave thanks she could remember no more.

CHAPTER 5

The tall French clock in Cort's studio, by which he had set his days of work, struck. The strike was halting and slow, and Miriam listened for the slight whirr, like a breath quickly drawn and let out, that heralded the next stroke. But it was a half hour—which? The clock needed winding; its striking slowed with the week always, and the little breath startled her, as had the peony petals dropping all at once to the floor. Absently she went to the clock, opened the case and seized the chain as she lifted the time weight, then raised the strike weight alongside it. At some moment, enclosed in the hour that followed, the pace of herself and her old

412

life returned to her—her world of order and belief, and she set it squarely against Tavio's chaos.

He was almost finished with the garden, and when he came up to the house for water, sought her out in the studio, reaching his hands toward her.

"No," she said, turning her head away. He smelled of some rank weed he had pulled. "No more."

He dropped his hands. "But you were crazy about me—only yesterday, two days ago, the things you said!"

"Don't remind me of them."

"You think I'm giving out? I'll give out, but not yet."

That was when she could laugh. He was not fooled; he was the captive now; there was a limit to the times he could make himself believe in himself. He took it out on her in anger and disparagement. "It's something you women all try, pretending you don't like it." He turned, indicating the house, the canvases in the studio. "This—it's all so much crud. Me—you: we're what count."

She held her tongue; he was his own answer anyway. She had crossed spaces of nowhere, had reached a plateau of indifference about him. The many times he had taken her had not blunted her excitement and pleasure, but now time had come back to her, and the minutes flowed one into another without any impact of feeling about him, either like or dislike. His vitality was ebbing despite his bravado, and in his eyes she saw he was content that it should; she supposed it was his way of revitalizing himself. He seemed older, gestured differently; his seamless movements were gone and his body moved angularly; his walk, too, was slower, less lithe. Surly and silent after his outburst, he flung out into the garden again, slamming the door after him.

The slamming door, the clatter of tools outside, told her it was almost over. She bathed, realizing, as she lay stretched out in the cool water, that not only was she no longer afraid of him, but that her relaxation and savoring of the bath was an acceptance in herself of what she had done, what she had permitted, even encouraged, Tavio to do. When she dried herself in front of the bath mirror, she marveled that her body showed no trace of what it had experienced. She was thirty-three—another five years and she would be no longer young; but now her slender flanks, her high, firm breasts, were still youth. This examination was for her-

413

self alone—it had not been the striking of the clock but the dream Tavio had the night before that had delivered the power of the situation into her hands. She felt new and clean, again in possession: her own woman. It had been an unwillingly learned lesson, and what she had learned from it she was not sure, except that it had been both tiring and renewing. With the flagging of day, she felt the need of a drink and, after putting on a fresh dress, went downstairs, mixed one, and carried it out to the terrace. Tavio had put the tools away and was showering in the bath below the beggar's room, but he no longer disturbed her, might already have gone.

It was night now and the black herons had dropped from the sky to the river's edge as the air slowly cooled. The sound of water stopped—he had finished scrubbing her from him, as she had washed him from herself. What would she say to him that she had not already said, or he to her? She knew that an experience so profound had to be paid out in time's recovery, just as she remembered what she had felt before Tavio came and knew with certainty what she would feel about him when he had gone, which was nothing. She rested on her knowledge that there would now be a man she would want and need and love as she had Cort. Where was he? Somewhere he was waiting for her, but how to find each other? In her mind's eye she could see this man, still unmet, still faceless: Tavio had been one writing erased to make way for another.

From the doorway she heard him speak and turned. His face had the restless, faraway look of the first time she saw him. He carried his newspaper bundle. "I'm going," he said.

She nodded.

"Do you find goodbys hard?"

"Not this one."

He smiled. "I do. I'll always remember you."

She was silent. His smile was the same; he seemed freshly careless, the next wanderer a passing motorist—a woman—would stop for. He stood before her chair.

"Kiss me goodby?"

"No," she said, and that was all she said. He stood a last moment, then turned and walked across the terrace and down the drive. Once she could have watched beyond that, but the rhododendrons, silhouetted darkly by the bridge lights beyond, cut off her view. A great relief flooded through her and the freshness of night air struck her lungs. Beyond the garden was a day—tomorrow. In the sky were the familiar constellations of her world. Not a cloud hung in their blue depths, auguring a beautiful day.

ABOUT THE AUTHOR

EDMUND SCHIDDEL, with *The Good and Bad Weather,* brings to completion his Bucks County trilogy. The first two volumes, *The Devil in Bucks County* and *Scandal's Child* (best sellers acquired by Warner Brothers and Columbia Pictures), established him as one of America's foremost satirists and commentators on the contemporary scene. His books have appeared also in England, France, Germany, Spain, Holland, Israel and Yugoslavia. He is now at work on a new novel, to appear in 1967, and a play.